Far

J. B. Priestley was born in 1894 at Bradford, the son of a schoolmaster. He went to school locally and served in the Army throughout the First World War, starting in the ranks and later becoming commissioned. After the war he went to Cambridge, where he read English Literature, modern history and political science. Having contributed articles to London and provincial papers since he was sixteen, he moved to London in 1922 and quickly established himself as a reviewer, critic, and essayist, publishing several books a year.

The Good Companions, published on the brink of the 1929 depression, was an immediate success, and has been filmed twice and dramatised for television. It was Priestley's third novel and made him famous almost overnight. His next novel, *Angel Pavement* was equally popular, as were later novels such as *Bright Day, Festival at Farbridge* and *Lost Empires*. In 1932 Priestley began a new career as a dramatist with *Dangerous Corner*, and went on to become very successful with plays such as *Time and the Conways, An Inspector Calls, Laburnum Grove* and *When We Are Married*. He also became involved in broadcasting, and regularly gave Sunday night radio talks, as well as wartime commentaries during the Second World War. He occasionally wrote for radio and television, but later in life devoted more time to public affairs, representing the UK at two UNESCO conferences. He died in 1984.

By J. B. Priestley

Fiction

Adam in Moonshine
Benighted
The Good Companions
Angel Pavement
Faraway
Wonder Hero
Laburnum Grove
They Walk in the City
The Doomsday Men
Let the People Sing
Blackout in Gretley
Daylight on Saturday
Three Men in New Suits
Bright Day

Jenny Villiers
Festival at Farbridge
The Other Place: short stories
The Magicians
Low Notes on a High Level
Saturn Over the Water
The Thirty-First of June
The Shapes of Sleep
Sir Michael and Sir George
Lost Empires
It's an Old Country
Out of Town (The Image Men I)
London End (The Image Men II)
Snoggle

Collected Plays

Volume I
  Dangerous Corner
  Time and the Conways
  Johnson over Jordan
  The Linden Tree

Eden End
I Have Been Here Before
Music at Night

Volume II
  Laburnum Grove
  When we are Married
  The Golden Fleece
  Ever Since Paradise

Bees on the Boat Deck
Good Night Children
How are they at Home?

Volume III
  Cornelius
  They Came to a City
  An Inspector Calls
  Summer Day's Dream

People at Sea
Desert Highway
Home is Tomorrow

Essays and Autobiography

Midnight on the Desert
Raid upon Godshill
Delight
All About Ourselves and other
  Essays (chosen by Eric Gillett)
Thoughts in the Wilderness

Margin Released
The Moments and other pieces
Essays of Five Decades
Over the Long High Wall
Outcries and Asides

Criticism and Miscellaneous

The English Comic Characters
English Journey
Journey Down a Rainbow (with
  Jacquetta Hawkes)
The Art of the Dramatist
Literature and Western Man
Victoria's Heyday

The World of J. B. Priestley (edited
  by Donald G. MacRae)
Trumpets over the Sea
The Prince of Pleasure and his
  Regency
The Edwardians
The English

J. B. PRIESTLEY

Faraway

Mandarin

A Mandarin Paperback
FARAWAY

First published in Great Britain 1932
by William Heinemann Ltd
This edition published 1996
by Mandarin Paperbacks
an imprint of Reed International Books Ltd
Michelin House, 81 Fulham Road, London SW3 6RB
and Auckland, Melbourne, Singapore and Toronto

Copyright © The Estate of J. B. Priestley

A CIP catalogue record for this title
is available from the British Library
ISBN 0 7493 2102 4

Phototypeset by Intype, London
Printed and bound in Great Britain
by Cox & Wyman Ltd, Reading, Berkshire

CONTENTS

CHAPTER I

UNCLE BALDWIN COMES AND GOES

1

IT WAS Tuesday evening and so William's friend, Greenlaw, from the Buntingham Grammar School, was there. When William dropped the stub of his cigarette into his coffee cup and said, 'Well, what about a game?' Greenlaw nodded and then replied solemnly: 'Let us play at the pieces.'

Greenlaw nearly always said this. Probably four Tuesday nights out of five found him at William's house, Ivy Lodge, saying, 'Let us play at the pieces.' Perhaps he said such things, with a kind of solemn facetiousness, because, after teaching mathematics all day, he found it a relief in the evening to be rather idiotic in his talk. He was capable of repeating faded jokes and dreary mis-quotations by the hour. Yet there was nothing idiotic about Greenlaw himself; he was a solid sensible school-master of fifty or so, one of those spectacled, bushy, smoky men who seemed destined to teach mathematics and to remain bachelors; and he and William were very good friends.

'There's a fire in the study,' said William, getting up. 'We'll go in there.'

'Lead on, Macduff,' said Greenlaw.

The study was a cosy higgledy-piggledy. It was a small high room, a muddle of oldish books, albums, letter files, and skewered receipts, cases of moths and butterflies, geological specimens, and other vaguely scientific odds and ends that proved that John Dursley, William's father, had once been a member of the Natural History Society of Suffolk. For forty years in this little room John Dursley had balanced his accounts, written out his cheques, played at science, and read the works of Rider Haggard; but the moths and the butterflies had outstayed him. The house belonged to William now, but he never thought of clearing out the study. It still seemed to him his father's room, and if he put a finger on the geological specimens and the other rubbish, he felt that his father, lying in wait round the corner, would suddenly pop out and cry: 'What are you doing, William? Put them down, boy, put them down.' So he left everything as it was. There was just sufficient space in front of the bright winking fire for the chess-board and table, another small table with whisky and tobacco on it, and the two old leather arm-chairs. It was very snug for chess, especially on a winter's night like this, with the gaslight and the yellow firelight meeting at the table's edge, and the wind and the rain troubling the ivy outside.

'To-night, William,' said Greenlaw, as he arranged his pieces, 'I propose to give you a tree-mendous beating. Let me see – who won last time?'

'You did. Don't you remember? You got me on the end game. It was one of your longest and dreariest.'

'I wore you down, I remember now. The end game beat you. No sticking power, William – that's your trouble.' Greenlaw lit his pipe, and then added, in his usual style: ' "'Tis not in mortals to command success, but we'll do more – deserve it." No sticking power at all, William.' He himself had any amount of sticking power, and his slow and stubborn game usually mastered William's more dashing and imaginative play.

'I'll admit,' William confessed, as he had done at least a score of times before, 'I get bored when the game lasts so long. That's how you beat me, Greenlaw. I like my chess to be a bit of an adventure.'

Greenlaw began shaking his head in the smoke, and contrived to look not unlike a friendly walrus in a mist. 'For a man of forty – but then, you're not a man of forty.'

'I am – worse luck!' cried William, who did not look it. He was slight and dark, and had a curiously youthful air about him, as if he had been put into cold storage at about his twenty-fifth birthday.

'If you're forty, William, then I'm a hundred. But what I wanted to say was – you can't have adventures at this game.'

'You can. I do. I believe that's why I like to play.'

'The game,' Greenlaw continued, just as if William had never spoken, 'doesn't allow adventures. You might as well talk about adventures in maths.'

'Not the same thing. This is more personal. Kings and queens and bishops and knights all having a shindy. That's what I like about it.'

'Mere symbols, that's all they are. So long as they had the same moves and the same power, you could call 'em anything. I believe they've got quite different names and shapes in some countries. And if you're having adventures while you're playing chess, William, that's why you generally manage to lose. I think of the game mathematically,' Greenlaw concluded, though actually he did nothing of the kind.

'I remember when I was at school,' said William dreamily, 'I used to think of the numbers as people. Five was a sharp, tricky little fellow. Seven was gentle and dreamy, rather religious. Eight was blustering, a bit of a bully. I can remember so much even now.'

His friend groaned at these fancies. 'There must be several boys I can think of in the Fourth now, who work on those lines. If you want *my* opinion, you can't really have adventures anywhere. It's a false view of life, William, and you ought to know better.'

'I don't see that. Why is it?'

'I'll tell you some other time. What we want now is a clean hearth and the rigour of the game.' His hand hovered over a pawn. 'I propose to begin with the famous Greenlaw gambit.'

'As usual,' replied William, smiling. And out came a knight, as it had done so many times before.

Everything was as usual. Here they were, the two of them, settling down to their Tuesday night chess. Mrs. Gurney, the housekeeper, was clearing away the dinner things, making a little clatter in the adjoining room. Outside, a north-west wind was hurrying through the streets of Buntingham and occasionally lashing them with rain. Those streets were now a wilderness of wet stone, gleaming puddles, and sodden and trodden dead leaves. The policeman on duty was standing in the shelter of the Market Hall front, talking to an acquaintance and glancing now and then at the deserted Market Square. There was hardly anybody to be seen anywhere, but that did not mean that the little town was asleep. It was only just after eight, and Buntingham was busy in its own way. One hundred and fifteen people were in the Olympic Picture Theatre, following the fortunes of a handsome youngster who had been unlucky enough to become the victim of a gang of New York crooks, ugly to a man. The choir of the Buntingham Baptist Chapel were wrestling with *How Lovely Are The Messengers*, the anthem for next Sunday morning. In the Parish Hall of St. Peter's Church, the vicar was introducing Mr. D. P. Kenworthy, M.A., who was about to give a talk on William Morris, the Poet and His Message, to twenty-seven of the parishioners, mostly female. In a little room behind the pork butcher's in High Street, nine men and three girls, representatives of the Buntingham Labour Party, were sternly passing resolutions. In an upstairs room at the *Suffolk Arms*, the treasurer of the Annual Flower and Vegetable Show Committee was submitting his report, and downstairs Mr. Jack Barwell, the auctioneer, was playing Ansdell, the landlord, a match of two hundred and fifty up at billiards, before a small but very appreciative audience of *Suffolk Arms* sportsmen. At the *Black Bull*, a humbler tavern, they were playing darts for half-pints of bitter; and at the *Falcon*, they were working up a tremendous argument, likely to last until closing time, about what Lloyd George promised or did not promise in 1918. Dr. Forester was leaving 27, East Street, where old Mrs. Cook had taken a decided turn for the worse, and was moving on to 8, Norfolk Road, where young Mrs. Murray was already in labour. Things were happening in Buntingham, even on this wet Tuesday night, but there was nothing unusual about them.

There was nothing unusual about the 8.10 from Ipswich (with connection from Liverpool Street), which arrived at the station, a good mile from the Market Square, prompt to time and with no hint that it might contrive to change anybody's life. The solitary porter on duty saw it deposit four passengers on the Buntingham platform. Three of them were fellow townsmen, regular travellers, who were obviously returning late from market at Ipswich; but the fourth was a stranger. He seemed to be an oldish fellow, and was short but immensely broad.

'Got a trunk and a box in the van,' he told the porter in a wheezy voice. 'Totten's the name.'

The porter found the trunk and the box, and by the

time he had wheeled them into the shelter of the platform roof, the 8.10 had gone chuff-chuffing away into the rainy dark.

'Got 'em?' said the new arrival. 'That's right.' Then he groaned.

'Eh?' cried the porter, startled.

'Cold, that's all. Perishing cold.' And as he said this, the stranger tried to disappear completely inside his heavy overcoat.

The porter rubbed his hands, perhaps to show that he was sympathetic. 'It's this cold rain that does it,' he announced.

'I don't know what it is that does it, but it's a blasted misery,' cried the other, in real anger. 'Gets in your bones. Freezes 'em. Rots 'em. Why did I ever come here?'

The porter shook his head, first from side to side to indicate that he did not know the answer, then up and down to show that he understood the position and was still sympathetic.

'Well, well, well, well, well!'

'And where d'you want this lot to go, sir?' asked the porter. '*Suffolk Arms?*'

'Not if I can help it,' the stranger replied. 'I want to go to Ivy Lodge. D'you know it?'

'Ivy Lodge?' The porter tapped his nose meditatively. 'Now wait a minute, sir. Ivy Lodge?'

Here the ticket-collector joined them. 'Ivy Lodge?' he said. 'That's Mr. Dursley's, isn't is, sir?'

'That the place I want,' the passenger wheezed. 'Mr. Dursley's. Ivy Lodge.'

'About a mile and a half from here,' the ticket-collecter continued. 'The other side of the town. Get these things taken on in the morning, easy enough, sir.'

'And what am I going to do till morning? If I tried to

walk a mile and a half through this stuff, you'd be holding an inquest on me by Thursday. I want to go there now. Can't I get a car?'

'George Jackson'll be coming down for the 9.20 to Ipswich,' said the porter. 'I know he's got some stuff for it. He'd run you there, sir, and your luggage as well for half a crown.'

'All right.' And the stranger walked forward to the entrance and looked out. The other two followed him. 'Is that a pub across there?'

They told him it was the *Railway Arms.*

'Well, that's where George What's-his-name'll find me at nine-twenty,' he declared. 'Tell him to call for me there. Totten's my name.' He gave the porter a shilling, the ticket-collector his ticket. 'Load him up with that stuff first. Oh, blasted misery!' He staggered out, a strange figure almost as broad as it was high, and they saw him slowly cross the dimly lighted square and then vanish into the *Railway Arms.*

'What d'you make of him?' asked the porter.

2

William had failed to make one of his dashing mates, with the result that the game dragged out and at half-past nine was by no means over, though the board was cleared of everything but two worried kings, one weary knight, two energetic bishops, three bloodstained rooks, and a few bewildered pawns. Greenlaw was now in his element, and William, as usual, was rather bored.

'Check,' said Greenlaw, moving one of his two rooks.

William did not sigh, but he drew a long breath in that laboured fashion which suggests a sigh. This was the third time he had been checked by this particular rook in this way. He put his king out of danger by giving him a little impatient push.

Greenlaw looked up, raising his thick brows high above the rim of his spectacles. 'The play's the thing, wherein I'll catch the conscience of the king,' he announced, and moved his other rook.

William had a sudden desire to tip up the board and scatter the pieces. Actually, he did the next best thing; he made a very silly move.

'What have we here?' said Greenlaw, pulling hard at his pipe, which made an irritating little gurgling noise. 'Do my eyes deceive me?' Determined not to be deceived and suspecting a trap, he spent several minutes considering his next move, leaving William, who could not be bothered to work out the consequences of his own absurd move, ample time to think about all manner of things. William thought about banks, jam, lorries, clergymen, coal, and Mrs. Gurney's son who worked at the G.P.O. in London.

'Check,' said Greenlaw, yet again.

All day William had been pleasantly conscious of the fact that Greenlaw and he would be playing chess after dinner, but now that they were playing, William was not enjoying it. This thought depressed him. He put out a languid hand to the harassed king.

'The way is barred,' Greenlaw warned him. 'You're putting yourself in check.'

At once bored and vaguely sad, William made a suicidal move with his remaining rook.

'Not a good move, William, not at all a good move.' And Greenlaw pounced upon the rook. 'Check again.'

Ah yes, check again. William felt sorry for himself, and, like many other more important and apparently wiser persons, pretended to be profoundly philosophical. All his life it had been check again, check after check after check. Why was he here, in this study, in this house, in Buntingham, playing this stupid and boring game? He went floating away on a tide of self-pity, while Greenlaw, imagining that he was considering every means of escape for his doomed king, waited patiently, but with a faint air of triumph. There came to them then, in that cosy little place, several noises, large confused sounds of a kind that Mrs. Gurney, the housekeeper, was not capable of making.

'Hello, what's that?' And William raised his head.

Greenlaw, who did not want to be robbed of his neat end game now, made a little movement of impatience. 'It's nothing. Your move.'

'Wait a minute, though.' And William had just time to get up from his chair and look towards the door. A second later, the door opened and Mrs. Gurney stood there, her eyes, which always stared at the world in babyish surprise above two vast swollen cheeks, nearly starting out of her head.

'Please, Mr. Dursley, it's a gentleman,' she gasped, 'and he says he's come to stay, luggage and all.'

'Who is it?'

'It's me,' cried another voice.

William gave a little jump and involuntarily turned his whole body round, to face the door, and as he did this, some part of him caught the chess-board and sent the remaining pieces flying.

The open doorway was now filled by a short elderly man, immensely broad in a thick ulster that glistened with rain-drops. He had an irregular thatch of white hair; his nose was a masterful beak; his heavy old face was a purply-red, but his eyes were as small and bright as diamonds. These eyes focused themselves on William, and were immediately alight with recognition. At the same time, his blue lips parted to make way for a roar: 'You're William Dursley, aren't you? Course you are. Knew you right away. You know me, don't you? Come on. Course you know me.'

He came forward a step or two, and brought with him a breath of cold night air, some scattering raindrops, and an unmistakable smell of brandy. The cosy little atmosphere of the room was shattered. It was as if the whole world had broken in, trampling and roaring.

William pushed back his chair, but kept his eyes fixed on the newcomer. 'Aren't you Uncle Baldwin?'

'That's right,' cried the other, in hoarse triumph. 'Your Uncle Baldwin. Baldwin Totten. Where's Lucy – I mean, your mother? Gone to bed?'

'Mother?' William was startled. For one mad second, it seemed as if everything had got out of control, as if time was running backward, as if events owed nothing to one another. Then it occurred to him that perhaps the old man was losing his memory. 'But you knew. Mother's dead,'

'What!'

'She died nearly a year ago.'

Uncle Baldwin clutched the chair that William had pushed away, and suddenly collapsed into it, breathing hard and looking more purple in the cheeks and blue about the lips than ever. Speech seemed to be impossible for him.

'I wrote and told you,' said William gently.

Uncle Baldwin fought desperately with some invisible enemy for a minute, then gasped: 'Never got it, never a word. What did she die of?'

'Heart,' William told him. 'It was quite sudden.'

This did not surprise Uncle Baldwin. 'In the family. Got

it myself . . . Heart like a rotten apple. That's what's the matter with me now. Have you any brandy?'

Mrs. Gurney, who had been standing all this time just outside the room, looking on and listening through the doorway, immediately went for some brandy.

'I think I'll get along, William,' said Greenlaw, who had contrived to efface himself somewhat by picking up the scattered chessmen. 'No, don't bother to see me out. Good night, William. Good night, sir.' And off he went.

Speech returned to Uncle Baldwin with the brandy. 'I never got any letter, but that's not surprising either. Couldn't find me, I suppose. But that's knocked me sideways, properly knocked me sideways. You come back,' he continued bitterly, not as if he were still talking to William, but as if he was putting a hard case to God or some beings responsible for the conduct of the universe, 'you come back to see your sister – haven't seen her for eighteen years – and they tell you she's dead, dead and buried. Younger than me too, your mother was – four years younger. She used to be very fond of me, Lucy did. I was the big brother. She thought the world of me when she was a girl, before she met your father. I knew *he* was dead. I got that letter. That's five years ago, isn't it?'

'Four. Nearly five, though.'

'He was getting on a bit when he died, wasn't he? Past my age, I fancy. I'm sixty-eight. A year ago I didn't feel fifty. Now I'm back in this country – oh, it's a blasted misery here in the winter – I feel a thousand, a million, anything you like, old Methuselah with a heart like a rotten apple. And another thing' – and here he began struggling with his heavy overcoat, so that William had to help him – 'another thing – the older you get, the more blasted misery there is all round you. The only news is bad news, damn me if it isn't. Everybody losing their money, taking to their beds, dying right and left.'

'Pull up to the fire, uncle,' said William, who had now recovered from his astonishment. 'I'll put your coat away. Have you had something to eat?'

'Plenty to eat, thank you, lad, plenty. I don't want much in that line. That's another thing – you don't take the interest in your food you used to do.' He produced a pipe and pouch. 'I'll smoke, though. Shouldn't be doing that, by rights, but – damn me – a man's got to do something. Can't spend all his time just sitting about, like a stuffed owl. I've got some traps out there.' He jerked a thumb at the door.

'Shall I—?' William began, looking enquiringly at him.

'They're all right. They're in the house. Leave 'em alone. Come and sit down.' He waited a moment until William had seated himself on the other side of the hearth, then he continued: 'You're the boss here then, now? Malting business – I suppose that's still on the go?'

William admitted that it was.

'House and everything?'

'What there is,' William replied.

'Well, it's more than I've got,' Uncle Baldwin wheezed over his pipe, 'and I've been hard at it most of my life. But I expect you're wondering what I'm doing here.'

William smiled vaguely, keeping his eyes fixed on his uncle's masterful beak, on which the firelight played as changing sunlight might play upon a bold mountain top.

'I've come for a visit, lad,' Uncle Baldwin announced. 'I didn't write, because I never write, got clean out of the habit. Where I've spent my life, there's no writing. Everybody's welcome. You needn't tell me that's not the way it's done here, because I know it isn't. But I knew your mother'd be glad to see her old brother again, after eighteen years.'

'She would have been,' said William. 'She often talked to me about you, uncle.'

'She did, did she?' This pleased Uncle Baldwin so much that he was compelled to run the stem of his pipe through his white hair. 'Well, she was the only one I ever cared a damn about – the only one. The rest of 'em could rot, for all I ever cared. Do you ever see your Uncle Edward?'

William admitted that he hadn't seen Uncle Edward for years.

'There's a long-nosed chapel-going human dummy, if you like. He's still on the go. I saw him in London, just had about an hour of him, and that was enough. He's got three shops now – making money as nice as you please. Making it, yes—' and here Uncle Baldwin gave a very hollow laugh – 'but not spending it – catch him spending it! He was just the same when he was a lad. The times I've kicked his behind, just to try and put a bit of life in him. And I'd liked to have done it again, the other day. I had my foot all ready. He never said a word about Lucy – your mother, I mean – not a word. Said nothing about anything, except his three shops. But that's not the point,' he concluded, in a very serious tone, 'that's not the point, not what I'm getting at at all.'

Here he stopped, so William looked at him questioningly. William did not feel at ease yet in the presence of this mysterious uncle of his from the other side of the globe, an uncle he had not seen since he was a very shy youth of twenty-two, years ago, before the war, in another world.

'The point is this. You're the boss here now, William. Here's your Uncle Baldwin, and though he *is* your uncle, you owe him nothing because he never did anything for you. Here he is, and here he wants to stay, for a week or a month or perhaps three months. Now say the word – and he goes. It's damned wet and it's damned cold, but never mind about that – you've only to say the word and he goes, straight out, back where he came from. He's got his traps here, but they can go just as easy as they came. That's the point.' Evidently he felt that the case had been very cleverly conducted, for he ended quite triumphantly.

'But of course you can stay if you want to, uncle,' said William warmly.

His uncle immediately shot out a hand, a very square hard hand, and William found himself shaking it. Then Uncle Baldwin thought of something. 'Half a minute. You're not married, are you?'

William replied shortly that he wasn't.

'That's good,' replied his uncle promptly. 'I don't mean it's good for you – it might be, and then again, it mightn't – but it's good for *me*. If you'd had a wife, she might have objected. They like to have a big say in these things. I know that much.'

'You've never married, have you, uncle?'

'Not what *you'd* call married, p'r'aps. But it's all the same out there. I'll tell you what, William, if you'd to search the Islands, you'd find some rummy cousins o' yours there – not at all the sort you'd want for the annual Christmas party. I'd like your Uncle Edward to see some of 'em. He'd learn something that would knock them three shops out of his head for an hour or two. I've been surprised myself, now and again, at what's turned up.' He gave a little obscene chuckle, which ended in a fit of coughing. When he had recovered from this, he enquired anxiously: 'You're not narrow-minded, are you, lad?'

'No,' William replied slowly, thinking it over, 'I don't think I am.'

'I didn't think you would be,' said Uncle Baldwin. 'But you never know how people turn out, do you? Eighteen years is a long time, and you might have turned into a sort o' parson, for all I knew. Having a good look at you, I don't think you've altered much.'

'I ought to have done,' William told him. 'I was twenty-two when you saw me last, and now I'm forty.'

Uncle Baldwin critically examined his nephew's thin, dark, clean-shaven face, with its high forehead, rather prominent cheek-bones, straight nose, pleasant eyes and mouth, and then passed his gaze over the slight figure in the dark blue serge suit. 'You still look a lad to me,' he announced. 'It must be living quiet here that does it – just doing your bit o' malting, or seeing somebody else does theirs, then coming back here all nice and quiet, playing your draughts and dominoes and suchlike, then getting to bed early; not much drink and no women. Keeps you young, I dare say.'

William flushed. 'It makes me feel old, especially when you put it like that.'

His uncle nodded and looked very wise. 'It might do that, too. I was going to say – it's a sort o' life that might keep you young, though what it's keeping you young for, what advantage there is in it, God only knows.'

'That's what I meant. Still – I was in the war, you know, and for a few years after that, I was glad of a quiet life.'

'I was forgetting that,' Uncle Baldwin admitted. 'And I must say, you don't look my idea of a soldier, William.'

'I wasn't anybody's idea of a soldier,' said William, remembering many things. 'But I had it to go through, all the same.'

'Now that's something you might say we missed – the war,' his uncle continued, in a voice rich with remi-niscence. 'Not that we didn't have our bits of excitements in the Islands, because we did, specially at the start. But most if it was a long way off. And quite right too. They knew what they was fighting about, I suppose, but damn me if I ever did, though all the same I was backing up the old country. I remember, months after it had started, going round to one of the Tongas and finding a German there, chap with a big ginger beard called Stenkel or Henkel – I'd met him years before on Rarotonga – and he didn't know the war was on, never heard of it, and I told him about it and argued the case with him, me talking about Kaiser Bill and Belgium and all that, and him talking about the Russians and the Boers and India, argued for hours and hours. I met that Stenkel or Henkel again, after the war was over, and in a very queer way, too. You mightn't believe what I'm going to tell you now, lad, but it's as true as I'm sitting here.' He paused, partly because he was out of breath and partly because he was an old and artful raconteur.

'Go on, uncle,' said William.

He went on, being now fairly launched on the wide and swelling waters of the Pacific. It was quarter to one when they went to bed, and as William climbed the stairs, schooners still flitted through his head, visiting magical islands, the vast albatross swept over the roaring South, flying fish skimmed along the Equator, strange voices chanted above the booming surf, brown faces smiled among the little rainbow fishes in the lagoons, and unfamiliar and fantastic constellations glittered in the sky. It was the most exciting night he had had for a long time. He felt dazed, vaguely happy, and rather drunk.

3

The excitement of that first night died down the next day, but though nothing much happened during the fortnight or so following Uncle Baldwin's arrival, that excitement did not vanish entirely. William felt it slightly all the time. It was as if a fuse was burning quietly along the ground. Now and again a whiff of it came to William's nostrils. His life was hardly changed at all, and yet he did not feel quite himself. Something very queer, he felt obscurely, was going to happen soon. He did what there was for him to do in the family malting business, which was really managed by his father's old foreman, George Kenfit; he listened to his uncle's stories, and so spent less time than usual reading the books he borrowed from the Buntingham Literary and Scientific Institute Library; on three afternoons, when a pale sun came through the clouds and the east wind dropped, he contrived to push on with his water-colour of the old mill just off the Ipswich Road (for William was an enthusiastic water-colourist and was considered one of the best amateurs in Suffolk); he played two games of chess with Greenlaw, to whom Uncle Baldwin had taken a strong and quite unreasonable dislike; he dined once at the Strouds' and there made a humble and faintly protesting fourth at bridge; and, in short, his life went on as usual. Yet it was not the same. He might have been falling in love again, though he knew he was not. The life that went on as usual was a little further away from his central core of self than it had ever been before. It was real, but there were other realities emerging from a cloud of dreams. Now uneasy, now happily expectant, he moved through the double routine of duties and accustomed pleasures, and waited.

All this, of course, was due to the presence of Uncle

Baldwin. So far as a retired Pacific trader, with a bad heart, a taste for liquor, and a shrinking horror of the East Anglian climate, can be said to settle down in a quiet little Suffolk town, Uncle Baldwin settled down. On fine days, he wandered about the place, stopping to chat with almost anybody who was free to waste half-an-hour with him. He was a great success at the *Suffolk Arms*, where he was soon on terms of roaring intimacy with everybody, from Ansdell, the landlord, to Doris, the junior barmaid. He would return, purple and panting, from that house of cheer and keep William up until the small hours. There were days, however, when he would never stir from Ivy Lodge, but would sit, dozing and moping, almost on top of the fire in the little study, and William soon learnt to leave him alone there. Twice he had Dr. Forester in, but William never knew what passed between them. Some bottles of a brown mixture made their appearance in the house, and Uncle Baldwin would occasionally take a contemptuous swig out of them, spitting and spluttering and cursing the whole medical profession, which at these times he seemed to hold responsible for his wretched condition. All that William knew for certain was that his uncle was clearly an unfit man.

Though Uncle Baldwin was quite ready to talk about himself, almost ready to drown William or anybody who would listen to him in a flood of reminiscence, yet like many such copious talkers he was really quite secretive and mysterious about his more intimate concerns. After the first few days, he began to write letters and, shortly afterwards, to receive them, but he never said a word about this correspondence to William. If he had any plans for the future, he never mentioned them. William knew that until the last two or three years, his uncle had been both an independent trader among the South Sea Islands and an agent there for a British firm and an American firm; but that is all he did know; the rest was like a wild travel film, a phantasmagoria of ships and islands, surf and lagoons, bungalows and palm trees, through which the broad figure of Baldwin Totten moved heroically and triumphantly. Obviously Uncle Baldwin was not without money; he had offered to pay William for his keep, and William had refused; and he spent a good deal down at the *Suffolk Arms*; but William could not tell whether his uncle was a rich man or a poor one, and Uncle Baldwin said nothing on the subject. Indeed, he liked to be rather mysterious, and had a trick, exciting at first, but afterwards rather irritating, of dropping hints that suggested he possessed the most wonderful secrets. These hints William almost ignored after the first week, though he enjoyed the romantic flavour of the talk they spiced.

It was not until he ran across Dr. Forester in the Market Square that William learned a little more about his uncle. Dr. Forester, as usual, was in a great hurry. He was the only person in Buntingham who was perpetually in a great hurry. During professional hours, which took up most of the day and half the night, Dr. Forester had long ago given up trying to talk like an ordinary human being; he simply barked like a fox-terrier; and William was so used to this barking that on the rare occasions when he met the doctor in an hour of social ease he was quite startled to hear him conversing naturally. On this particular morning, the doctor's car, which was also small, fussy, quick, a sort of mechanical extension of himself, caught sight of William as it crossed the Square, rushed across, and stopped beside him with a little screech. The doctor's pointed face shot out of the open window.

'Morning, Dursley,' it barked. 'That uncle of yours – he is your uncle, isn't he?'

'He is,' replied William, who always felt tempted to bark back. 'I've been wanting to see you about him. He won't tell me much. How is he?'

'Not good,' said the doctor, and muttered something about cardiac veins and the coronary sinus.

'Is it serious?'

'Of course it's serious. Very serious. Couldn't be more serious.'

'Is there anything I can do?' William asked, feeling quite helpless. Dr. Forester, who had attended both his father and his mother, always made him feel helpless. He was one of those doctors who give you the impression that they have been called in about five years too late, though they make it fairly clear that even if they had been called in at the proper time, things would have been almost hopeless.

'Not much,' came the answering back. 'Try to keep him quiet.'

William looked his dismay at this. What chance had he of keeping Uncle Baldwin quiet?

'Won't change his habits, of course,' the doctor continued. 'Never will, most of 'em. Expect you to work miracles. But keep him quiet. If there's any sign of trouble, let me know at once.'

'I will,' said William, wondering what exactly were the signs of trouble, for Uncle Baldwin seemed to offer so many signs.

'But I don't say I can do much. Too far gone for that. Interesting chap, I should think,' he added, in a slightly different bark. 'Quite a character.'

'Yes, isn't he?' said William, ready for a little chat about his uncle as a character.

'Morning,' and the face popped back; and the car, with an impatient rattle, shot away, leaving William bewildered, faced with an image of his relative that was not at all pleasant, changing rapidly from a character to a corpse.

Over the lunch-table, William kept glancing at his uncle, and every time he looked he saw the most terrible marks of mortality in that seamed and purple face. After hesitating for some time, he decided to say something about the doctor.

'I saw Dr. Forester this morning,' he began, trying to appear casual.

'What did he say about me?' Uncle Baldwin demanded.

'Well, he didn't say much—' William stopped.

'Now don't be silly, lad, don't be silly. I don't suppose he did say much, because from what I've seen of him, talking seems to hurt him. He yaps and scratches like an old phonograph record, that chap does. But he must have said something. What was it?'

'He told me you weren't very well—'

'Well, by heck, you knew that, William, didn't you? I could have told you that. Not very well!' Uncle Baldwin contorted his massive features into one vast purple sneer. 'Not very well! And then he thought he was telling you something, I expect. Half a guinea for that. Is that all?'

'He said something about your keeping quiet.'

'I'll bet he did. Did he ask you to keep me quiet?'

'As a matter of fact, he did,' said William, feeling very uncomfortable. Then he met his uncle's hard gaze and smiled slightly. 'But he didn't tell me how to do it.'

'Oh, he didn't. Nothing about getting the old man to bed early, eh?' Uncle Baldwin roared. 'It's too late anybody trying to keep me quiet. What do I want to be quiet for, anyhow? I'll be quiet enough soon, and quiet for a damned long time. But while the old hulk moves a bit, I'm going to see what life there is. Wouldn't you? Ah, but I dare say, you wouldn't.'

This annoyed William, who, in his own quiet fashion, was not without spirit. 'I don't know what I should do,' he retorted. 'Though I'll tell you candidly, uncle, I think it's idiotic going to a doctor and then objecting to every-thing he tells you to do.'

'Now, don't get your monkey up, lad,' said Uncle Bald-win, neither angry nor abashed. 'I oughtn't to have said that about you, I'll admit, because I don't know enough about you. I can see there might be a bit more in you, William, than meets the eye. But it's no good telling me it's idiotic. Of course, it's idiotic. Either I ought to leave the doctors alone or do what they say. But I can't do either, that's all, and when you're my age and you've got this leaking old pump inside you and they tell you you might go popping off any minute, you'll be the same. I can't lie in bed, drinking gruel. It'ud kill me in a week. If I have to die anyhow, let me die in my own way, like a man and not like a damned old washer-woman. And for that matter,' he added, with the glorious inconsistency of a man determined to defend himself at all costs, 'I'm quiet enough, never was quieter. If Dr. Thingumtybob thinks the life I'm leading now is a razzle, he's a lot to learn. Never been quieter in my life.' He ended triumph-antly.

'All right, uncle, let's leave it at that,' said William, getting up from the table.

'You're not wanting to get rid of me, are you, lad?'

'No, of course I'm not.'

'And I don't believe you are, either, though I know I'm a rough old devil about the place. There's one here'll be glad to see the last of me.' He lowered his voice and jerked a thumb towards the door leading into the kitchen. 'Mrs. Gurney's had enough o' me here. Oh, yes, she has. And that reminds me, William.' He searched his pockets, no easy task for a man of his girth, and finally brought out a letter, at which he peered for a moment. 'I'm having some visitors on Thursday.'

'Visitors!' William was surprised. He thought of his uncle as a solitary.

'Yes, visitors. And why not?' Uncle Baldwin looked quite reproachful. 'Did you think I didn't know anybody? Let me tell you, lad, there's nobody in this town knows more people – and more different kinds o' people, by gosh! – than I do. A lot of 'em's ten thousand miles from here, I admit, but a lot of 'em isn't, too. These two, for instance. They're coming down to see me from London on Thursday, and they're coming about lunchtime, so I thought I'd start off by giving 'em a bit of lunch. Well, the point is, shall it be here or shall it be the *Suffolk Arms*? Just say the word, lad, and it's the *Suffolk Arms*.'

'Why should it be?' cried William. 'We can give them lunch here. Thursday? Let me see. I'm going to London on Thursday. I have to see Pantocks, the brewers, and I shall stay the night, and come back here Friday night or Saturday morning.'

Uncle Baldwin looked interested. He also looked slightly relieved.

'But I needn't go until after lunch on Thursday. Bring them here for lunch. Who are they?'

'Well, old acquaintances o' mine, you might say,' replied Uncle Baldwin, turning himself at once into a mystery man, to William's amusement. 'He's a bit of a mixed breed – South American and what not – and his name's Garsuvin. I won't say he's exactly a friend o' mine, because he's not. But he's an old acquaintance. I've had business dealings with him. That's why he's coming here. He'd like to do a bit more business.'

'I thought you'd retired.'

'Not altogether,' said Uncle Baldwin cautiously. 'In a way, I've retired, but then in another way, I haven't.'

Evidently the mystery man was still there; so William changed the subject. 'Who's the other one?'

'What, with Garsuvin? Ah!—' and Uncle Baldwin now looked waggish and his tone of voice was quite different —'that's Mer-dam.'

'Mer-dam?' William was puzzled.

'Mer-dam,' repeated his uncle firmly.

William saw light. 'Oh, madame. Madame Who?'

'Mer-dam anybody you like. Mer-dam Garsuvin, Mer-dam Johnson, Mer-dam Tom-tiddly-om-pom – take your choice. There's another mixed breed – French, Spanish, Kanaka, and God knows what, proper League of Nations with a few cannibals thrown in, that's what she is. And what a piece!'

William laughed.

'Oh, you can laugh, lad, but you've not seen what I've seen. She's not as young as she was – I've known her a good few years – but she's young enough yet to make all the mischief she wants to make. The first time I ever set eyes on her, she was sixteen – and what a piece, what a picture! That wasn't yesterday either.'

'She was a beauty, was she?' said William, a frieze of flashing dark-eyed beauties flickering rapidly across his mind.

'She was. She was a peach. And she's not so bad now either. Better than a drowned policeman, as we used to say. Oh, but what a character!' Uncle Baldwin struggled with a metaphor. 'Champagne and dynamite.'

They sounded a rum pair, and William, as he went off to tell Mrs. Gurney about Thursday's lunch, admitted to himself that he was curious to see them, even though he was certain that his uncle had the old traveller's romantic trick of making everything seem twice as strange and exciting as it would actually turn out to be. William was so curious about these two visitors that he forgot the beginning of the talk he had just had with his uncle. He saw Uncle Baldwin as an acquaintance of the mixed breeds, Garsuvin and his Mer-dam, and not as Dr. Forester's doomed man.

4

Uncle Baldwin, for once, had spoken the truth. His visitors *were* a rum pair. William discovered them already at their ease in the house when he returned from business at one o'clock on Thursday. Mr. Garsuvin was quite unlike anybody William had ever known before. He looked like a melancholy intellectual clown with a queer touch of decayed and unscrupulous aristocracy about him. He was middle-aged and quite bald in front, and this baldness made his head seem fantastically long, for he had a very high and narrow forehead and it went up and up until his head was almost pointed at the crown. He had hardly any eyebrows, but his dark eyes glinted in the shadow of vast lids. His nostrils were cut sharply upwards; his mouth was very wide and thin-lipped; and his clean-shaven face was covered with an enormous number of tiny lines and creases. He wore a suit of bright checks, very loud in a foreign fashion. As a patch of colour, however, he was dim compared to his companion. Mer-dam took William's breath away, for she was a blaze of scarlet and emerald green, like a great bird of paradise in the room. It was some time before William could see her as a person. Even then he never formed a very clear idea of what she was really like, for her clothes were so brilliant, the cheap but flashing jewellery she wore so dazzled him, she was so thickly bedaubed with rouge, lipstick, powder, so over-poweringly perfumed, that he saw her only as a prettyish exotic woman who might be twenty-five or thirty-five and possessed extraordinarily bright brown eyes, beautiful feminine eyes. She was indeed so tremendously feminine that she frightened William. It was like listening to the ordinary tinkling feminine music being played by ten brass bands. He felt that it would require the combined masculinity of a regiment or a battleship's company to answer the challenge of Mer-dam.

When they sat down to lunch, which they did almost immediately after William had entered and had been introduced, Mer-dam, who was sitting next to him, leaned forward and stared at him with those gigantic brown eyes, making him feel very uncomfortable. A moment later, she made him feel more uncomfortable still. 'Aw, but he has a vairy nice face,' she announced in her queer soft foreign voice. 'Baldy,' she went on, grabbing Uncle Baldwin's arm to attract his attention, 'your nevew – Mistair Villiam – he has a vairy, vairy nice face.'

'What, nicer than mine?' said Uncle Baldwin.

'Moch nicer,' she cried. Then she turned again to William and flashed a smile that nearly stunned him. 'Moch, moch nicer. Quite deef'rent.'

'They y'are, William,' his uncle wheezed. 'Compliment from Mer-dam, and worth having, too. What d'you say, Garsuvin?'

'That is so,' said Garsuvin, whose voice had a queer tone of its own, at once harsh and sibilant. He never spoke loudly, but he contrived to command your attention the moment he began talking. Now he gave William a little bow. He had an unusual formal politeness, of a rather theatrical quality. 'Madame is a fine judge of faces. You must accept it as a great compliment, Mr. Durss-ley.'

'Thank you, I will,' said William, feeling a fool.

'You're making him feel shy, Mer-dam,' said Uncle Bald-win. 'He's not like me, y'know. He's had a quiet life.'

'That I can see,' cried Mer-dam, nodding and smiling and jangling and glittering, and sending great waves of perfume in the direction of William's small shrinking nose. 'Tell me,' she continued, staring at William again, 'where 'ave you been?'

'Where have I been?' William tried to carry it off lightly. 'Well, you know, I haven't always been here. It's not quite as bad as that. I went to France during the war, and I've been to Germany two or three times – partly on business—'

'On business, eh?' said Mr. Garsuvin, with grave politeness. 'You have a business here, of course. This business—' he lifted two large fingers, as if they would make the sign of a question-mark, 'it is—'

'Malting,' William told him. 'I'm what they call here a maltster – like my father, and my grandfather before him.'

'Malting?' And Mr. Garsuvin shook his head regretfully, not because he disapproved of malting, but to show how sorry he was that his own ignorance of it must now hold up the conversation.

'That's for brewing,' cried Uncle Baldwin, coming to the rescue. 'You want malt to make beer.'

'Yes, yes, yes,' Mer-dam put in, enthusiastically, 'for Eng-lish and Germans – always beer.'

'Of course,' said Mr. Garsuvin, nodding respectfully at William. 'Malt for beer. A very good business, eh?'

'Plenty, plenty, *plain-ty* of money!' cried Mer-dam.

William shook his head. 'Not now there isn't. Not for a little independent malting house like ours. All the big brewers do their own. Still, I don't suppose you want to know about that, do you?'

What Mer-dam wished to know now was what other thing he did besides malting.

Before William could reply, Uncle Baldwin had begun to answer for him. 'Paints pictures, to begin with, don't you, William? Good uns too, if you want *my* opinion.'

'Artist,' cried Mer-dam. 'Like Gauguin.'

William, who knew enough about Gauguin to know that there could not have been a wilder comparison, smiled and shook his head. He was shaking his head a good deal at this lunch, probably because he felt that foreigners needed something more than plain negatives and affirmatives. 'Not a bit like Gauguin. I paint water-colours – you know, paint and water, not paint mixed with oil—'

'Very interesting,' said Mr. Garsuvin in an unusually deep voice. He seemed to say it quite sincerely.

'And I just do it to amuse myself,' William continued. 'Sometimes I send one or two to exhibitions, and now and again I sell one. Just local landscapes, you know.'

'I didn't know,' said Mr. Garsuvin gravely, 'but I am glad you have told me.' William gave him a sharp glance. He looked serious and concerned, and more than ever like a French or Italian clown who was off duty but a little worried about a new act.

Mer-dam appeared to be determined to keep the talk to William. 'You are too – too – too—' she moved her fingers rapidly, as if to conjure the missing word out of the air – 'too – you know—'

'Old,' said Uncle Baldwin, hopefully.

'No, no, no, no, no.'

'Young then,' said Uncle Baldwin.

'No, no, no, no, no,' Mer-dam cried again, with despair in her great eyes.

'Mr. Durss-ley is too modest,' said Mr. Garsuvin.

Mer-dam crowed in triumph. 'That is it. Too, too modest. You should not be modest – not in this world. Go to many, many places, and say to them, "See, 'ow big I am." Like your oncle Baldy.' Having said this, she screamed with laughter, then took a formidable pull at her whisky. All three guests were drinking whisky, and were drinking it at a rate that William had never known before at a lunch-table. It looked as if a bottle would not see them to the end of the meal.

'You must come to the South Seas,' said Mer-dam.

'I'd like to, some day,' William told her.

'Not some day. Some day is no day. You should follow your oncle.'

'His uncle never made a fat lot out of it,' Uncle Baldwin pointed out, 'though I admit I've had my fun. And I've escaped about thirty years of this blasted misery they call weather here. But I've never made a lot – you can't say that.'

'Aw, but Baldy – you see – perhaps you have not finished yet, eh?'

As she said this, Mer-dam flashed a glance at Mr. Garsuvin, and William was quick enough to see the glance she got from him in return. It was most expressive; the heavy lids withdrew a little from those two dark eyes, and the eyes said quite plainly and peremptorily: 'That's enough of that. Shut up.'

'I may have finished, and then again, I may not,' said Uncle Baldwin ponderously. This was one of his favourite mystery-man expressions, and William took no notice of it. They began talking about other things, the damp cold in London, the superior attractions of Paris, the French mail-boats from Marseilles, one Richardson who had turned up in London, San Francisco and Sydney and other places, food and drink and clothes and weather. It was pleasant, interesting talk, but it did not amount to much.

Looking back on the little lunch-party, as he did to amuse himself on the early afternoon train to Liverpool Street, William felt compelled to admit that it had been rather disappointing. It had begun well, for in appearance Mr. Garsuvin and his woman were fantastic enough for the wildest of Uncle Baldwin's yarns. Seated round the familiar table in the dining-room, they composed a picture that captured the imagination at once: Uncle Baldwin, with his heavy old purple face, his great beak of a nose, his white ruffled thatch of hair; Garsuvin, with his long pointed head, his myriad lines and creases, his hard eyes; Mer-dam, with her rouged brown skin, her opulence of colour, glitter, and perfume, her magical eyes that still stared out of her lost enchanted youth; these figures were to William both strange and picturesque, creatures of romance. When he had first sat down with them, it had seemed as if the dining-room had been quietly conjured out of ordinary reality into a film of exotic adventure, in which he, William Dursley, was both player and spectator. But after that, the shrewd air of East Anglia, the humdrum sense of Buntingham, had asserted themselves, and the dining-room, after wavering a little, had returned to Ivy Lodge, winter daylight, and the world of malting, chess, water-colours, and trains to Liverpool Street. Only one really interesting thing had happened, and that was the glance that had so effectively silenced Mer-dam. It suggested, that glance, that there were things to be talked about at the proper time, and that the proper time was not when he, William was there. The thought of that glance did not annoy William; it pleased him. He remembered it so well – for there was no forgetting Garsuvin's face and it had reached its highest pitch of expressiveness when it produced that look – that he was able to recall it exactly several times; and he amused himself, as he stared out of the carriage window at the darkening fields, by turning little flying bits of East Anglia into Garsuvin's heavy lifting lids and angry eyes. Nevertheless, he concluded that it meant little or nothing, like his uncle's elaborate mystery-man stuff. It seemed that these people were all alike. Perhaps they felt they had to live up to a tradition, once they were back in Europe. When he had left them, they were talking hard, and having emptied a bottle of whisky between them (another part of the tradition), they were a trifle flushed and rather noisier than they had been, but it was more than likely that they would spend the rest of the day simply talking trivialities that happened to have a tremendously romantic geographical background. Perhaps to somebody from their part of the world, a chat between a few Buntingham people would seem equally picturesque in its names and details.

Life, William decided, was much the same everywhere. He had told himself this before, a good many times. He had, indeed, worked up a little consolatory philosophy on the subject, for there had been a time, a year or two after the war, when he had wanted to leave Buntingham and the malting business, when he had wanted to put the few hundred pounds he possessed into his pocket and to see what he could do in some remote and exciting part of the world; but first there had been his father, ageing and ailing; then his mother; and he had stayed at home. He did not despise Buntingham; he liked the old place, and felt that he would never want to settle down anywhere

else; but then, he had not really wanted to settle down at
all. Thus, he had got into the habit of consoling himself
with the theory that life was much the same everywhere,
that what he had come to know so well in Buntingham
he would find, in its essentials, wherever he might go.
He felt obscurely that his uncle and the two visitors,
so captivating to the imagination at first sight and so
commonplace after further acquaintance, only confirmed
this theory. He ought to have been pleased to have had
his theory so neatly confirmed, but actually he felt a
certain resentment. Somehow, it made his own life seem
duller than ever. It might be bad to hear the doors of
escape banging to on every side; but it was still worse
to discover that they were wide open and did not lead
anywhere. Cheerlessly, he watched the heavy Essex fields
roll past. Then at last, pretending a brisk business-like
manner, he opened his case with a smart snap, pulled out
some papers, and examined a few figures that he had to
put before Pantocks, the brewers. He caught a glimpse
now and then of the middle-aged humble woman sitting
opposite, who was giving these mysteries of high finance
a respectful glance or two. He felt that he would have to
make the best of something like that.

5

William was still the smart business gentleman when he
returned home on the following afternoon. He was rather
tired of the part – for his little trip to London had been
very dreary – but he could see no other for himself and
so kept on with it. Neat, almost dapper, in his dark grey
overcoat and hat, he marched through the winter dusk
back to Ivy Lodge, swinging his little case as he went.

When he reached the house, he was surprised to find it in complete darkness. Not even a flicker of firelight showed anywhere on its ivied front. The place looked so desolate, it might have been empty for a month.

The hall was dark. There was neither light nor sound coming from the kitchen at the end. Obviously, Mrs. Gurney, who usually came out to welcome him back and to tell him that a meal was waiting for him, was not in. He went into the dining-room, and a lighted match showed him nothing but ashes in the fireplace and a dreary confusion of dirty plates and dishes on the table. Astonished and rather perturbed, he returned to the hall, and it was then that he heard a curious sound. It seemed to come from the study, and it suggested an animal in vague distress. For a moment, William remained still, his heart thumping away in the dark. Then he struck a match, went into the study and there fell over something, so that he had to strike another match before he could light the gas.

It was his uncle who was making the noise. He was lying, grotesquely constricted, in an arm-chair, and somehow looked as if he had been there for hours and hours. He was in his stockinged feet; he was without his collar and tie; but otherwise was fully clothed. He had not washed or shaved that day. The little room was foul with the stale smell of brandy and cigar smoke, like a room in some riotous pot-house. There were two empty bottles on the table, and one of them was lying on its side, near a great stain of spilled liquor; there were several dirty glasses, two of them broken; one of the cases of butterflies was lying on the floor, smashed; a chair was upturned; the geological specimens were all over the place; somebody had knocked down a row of files; the fireplace was a litter of white ash; and everywhere there seemed to be a filthy scattering of cigar and cigarette ends, tobacco ash, torn paper, crumbs, and dregs of brandy. In the middle of this beastly mess, Uncle Baldwin, purply-white, with huge hands grasping at nothing, his thick blue lips wide apart and stinking of brandy, was lying huddled, making queer and shocking little noises. The Garsuvin pair seemed to have passed through the house like a combined carnival, tornado, and plague.

William touched his uncle on the shoulder. 'What is it?' he cried. 'What's the matter, uncle?'

Uncle Baldwin opened one eye very slowly. 'Hello, lad,' he wheezed.

'Tell me. What's happened?'

'Rotten,' said Uncle Baldwin.

'Do you mean you're ill? I can see that.'

'Hellishly rotten,' his uncle groaned, changing his position with considerable difficulty.

'You ought to go to bed,' William told him.

Uncle Baldwin's only reply to this was to nod in a melancholy fashion.

'I'll get you to bed,' William continued, 'and then I'll send for the doctor.'

Uncle Baldwin kept on nodding, and closed the eye that had been open.

William felt desperate. 'Where's Mrs. Gurney?'

His uncle thought about this for a moment, then replied, in a very sad husky tone: 'Gone.'

'When did she go?'

'Can't remember now. She just went.'

Fortunately, William knew where Mrs. Gurney would be. She had a sister living in the town, and would almost certainly be staying with her. He could attend to that afterwards. 'Do you think you can get back upstairs?' he asked.

Uncle Baldwin thought this over, then muttered that he could, with some help. As a matter of fact, he needed a great deal of help, and by the time William had got him into his room, undressed him, and settled him in bed, the best part of an hour had gone. He telephoned to Dr. Forester's house, asking him to call as soon as possible. His uncle was dozing now, and William did not want to disturb him until the doctor came. The next thing to do was to get hold of Mrs. Gurney, but he could not leave the house until the doctor had been, so he spent the next hour and a half prowling about downstairs, giving himself a cup of tea and some food and then doing what he could to clean up the sad mess in the study, where he managed to light a rather untidy fire. But when the doctor did come, Mrs. Gurney was with him.

'It was the goings on,' she explained. 'I've been used to quiet respectable homes, same as you always keep yourself, Mr. Dursley, and it's too late in the day for anybody to think I'm going to wait on people who sit up all night drinking and throwing things about. Not with you out of the house too, Mr. Dursley. "Late as it is," I said to myself, "and inconvenient as it may be tomorrow, I go and I don't come back till Mr. Dursley comes back." And that word,' she concluded, solemnly and dramatically, 'I kept.'

'But what happened?' William enquired, rather irritably.

'They stops in till after tea, then they all goes to the *Suffolk Arms*, and then – lo and behold! – at half-past ten at night, back they are again, still at it, drinking like fishes – the woman as bad as the men. I told your uncle, Mr. Dursley, right then and there, I wouldn't take the responsibility, and what was more I wouldn't stay five minutes longer in the house, unprotected as I was, with such goings on. So I went to my sister's, and lucky for me she'd just been to the second turn of the pictures and hadn't gone to bed. And a rare mess they've left it in here, I'll be bound.' And off she marched into the study.

William joined Dr. Forester at his uncle's bedside. Uncle Baldwin stared at him for a minute in the most melancholy fashion, and then said, in a slow husky whisper: 'Made a bit of a mess o' the place, didn't we? Sorry about that, lad.'

William told him that it was all right.

Uncle Baldwin would not have this. 'No, no, not all right – not good enough. But I'll make up for it. You've been kind to me, William. I'll make up for it, lad.'

'No more talking,' Dr. Forester barked, bending over his bag.

'And there's another thing, while I remember,' said Uncle Baldwin.

William looked questioningly at the doctor, who replied with a little nod, as much as to say, 'Let him get it off his mind, then.'

'What's that, uncle?' asked William.

'Have no truck with Garsuvin,' said Uncle Baldwin earnestly. 'Remember, I'm telling you now. Never mind what he says. Have no truck with him.'

'All right, I won't,' said William, who felt that the old man must be humoured. 'But I don't suppose I should, anyhow.'

'You might. You might – easily.'

'But he's gone, hasn't he?'

'He's gone,' Uncle Baldwin admitted. 'But he'll turn up again, sooner or later. You'll see. And remember – I'm telling you now, plain as I can. Have nothing to do with him, whatever he says. And I'm not saying that now, just because we've had a dust up. I'd have said it any time, any time.' His voice sank to a mutter; he closed his eyes, then turned his face away, a face that looked now like that of a very old man, monstrous in its nose, but sunken everywhere else; and within a few minutes, he appeared to have dozed off again.

'I said he had to keep quiet,' Dr. Forester barked at William in the hall, 'and of course he hasn't kept quiet.'

William told him briefly what had happened.

'Well, he was a sick man before, and now of course he's more of a sick man than ever. In fact, Dursley, your uncle's in a very bad way, a thoroughly bad way. There isn't a lot I can do for him.'

'Ought he to have nurses or anything?'

Dr. Forester pursed up his lips and made his features more pointed than ever. 'Can if you like. Not a lot to be done. Might have a night nurse. I'll send one along if I can lay my hands on her. I'll look in again in the morning. He's got to be quieter than ever now. Any more gala nights with his old pals and he's a dead man.'

All Saturday and Sunday, Uncle Baldwin was a bed patient and as quiet as Dr. Forester could desire. William saw him frequently, but did not exchange twenty words with him. Sometimes Uncle Baldwin looked at him, and there was a sort of irony in his pale stare that William found very disturbing. It was an unpleasant week-end, and William spent most of it restlessly tiptoeing from one futile occupation to another.

On Monday, however, Uncle Baldwin seemed to return to life. He had more colour, more energy, and seemed disposed to talk. When William came back from the malting-house in the evening, he found Uncle Baldwin sitting up in bed, quite excited. 'I must have a talk to you, lad,' he said.

William smiled at him. 'Go on, then, uncle.'

'It'll take time. The doctor'll be here soon, won't he?'

'He ought to be,' William replied. 'Some time during the next half-hour.'

'We'll leave it then till after dinner,' said Uncle Baldwin. 'Come up then, will you, lad? Mind you, it's important.'

'I'll be here,' said William, trying to look as if he, too, thought it important. It was quite pathetic to see the old man still keeping up his pretences to the very end. Even on Friday night, when he was very bad indeed, he had insisted on warning him solemnly against Garsuvin; and now it looked as if there was to be some more of this vague mystery-man stuff. Poor Uncle Baldwin, if he only knew it, he needed no melodramatic hints and nudges to be mysterious and impressive now, for throughout the week-end he had stared at William out of the hollow eyes of death.

When William returned to the bedroom after dinner, he found his uncle in a new and curious mood. His excitement had gone, and in its place was a dignity tinged with melancholy that William had never discovered in his uncle before, nor ever expected. It was as if he belonged already to the sober aristocracy of the dead.

'Now sit down there, lad,' he began, 'and let me do the talking.' He looked at William steadily for a moment or two, then continued: 'If you ask me – my passage is booked. I came here for a short visit, but I look like being here for a damned long one. Now, say nothing; let it go at that. This is the point. You've been very kind to me, lad.'

William made the usual vague noises made by most modest men in this situation.

'You needn't have been – except that you're your mother's son – but you have been. Most people would have had a lot to say about that kick-up we had when you was out of the way, but you've never said a word, though you may have thought a lot. I told you then I'd make up for it. Well, that's why you've got to listen to me for a few minutes.' Having said this, he looked at William hard, and William, feeling embarrassed, glanced here and there, and said nothing.

'Now don't get it into your head I'm going to leave you a lot of money, like an uncle in a story-book,' Uncle Baldwin continued, 'because I'm not. I haven't got it to leave. You're getting what I have got, but when that's paid for my board and lodging and the doctor and the rest of it, there won't be much left, only about enough to pay your fare to the South Pacific and back.'

'But I'm not going to the South Pacific,' said William lightly, more from want of anything better to say than from necessity.

'Well, we'll see about that,' said his uncle quickly. 'I hope you are, else I wouldn't be telling you what I'm going to tell you now. And – by gosh! – why shouldn't you go, eh? It won't kill you to get out of sight o' the Market Square here and your chess-board, will it? At your age, too! Go and see something. Go and see something before it's too late.'

William flushed at this, and the slightly contemptuous suggestion that he lacked the spirit to leave Suffolk for the wide world stung him at once. He was about to make a retort when his uncle, holding up a hand, went on talking, and with a marked change of tone.

'Apart from that bit o' money, not worth talking about, all I can do for you, lad, is to let you into a secret. Now I'm not going to make a long tale out of it, but you've got to understand one or two things. Nine years ago, I took a passage in another man's ship – I'm not going to tell you where, and you'll understand why, later on; I'll just say it was the South Pacific, which isn't saying much

– and we got blown a long way out of our course. She'd an auxiliary motor, but we'd used up all the juice for it. I've never known a ship get further away from her course than we did that time. Well, we sighted an island, and it wasn't an island you'll find marked on any of the charts. And don't let that surprise you. They can talk as they like, but it's not all charted yet. And this isn't one o' them volcano islands, here today and gone to-morrow, either. It's solid rock, and a few thousand feet out of the water in parts, too. But it's rock and hardly anything else. A few trees and a drop o' water, and then you've finished, and hard to land at into the bargain – sort of island that isn't any good to anybody, you'd think. Well, there it was, a few miles of it, sticking well up out of the water, large as life, and not a sign of it on the charts. We landed there – chiefly on chance of getting some fresh water – and I called it Faraway – one word, d'you see, lad. I think it's a good name.'

'It's a fine name,' cried William, who was really interested. 'And wasn't there anybody there at all? Was it a genuine desert island?'

'It was,' said Uncle Baldwin grimly. 'And none o' your Robinson Crusoe, everything-to-be-had-for-the-asking islands either. Mostly rock and birds, and not so many birds – a real God-forsaken place, miles from anywhere, and more like a dam' great heap of coal sticking out o' the sea than anything else. And that's Faraway.'

'You're not going to tell me there's pirates' treasure buried there, are you?' asked William.

'No, I'm not. I'm not so silly. I wouldn't be doing you a good turn if I handed over one of those pirates' treasure yarns. I've known some good men go soft in the head with that buried treasure stuff. All my eye, most of it. But this is different. This is sensible. I don't suppose there was ever a pirate within a thousand miles or more of this island.'

'I'm glad about that,' said William. 'I've always been suspicious about pirates' buried treasure. I was reading an article about it only the other day in one of the magazines. But go on, uncle, about Faraway. It's a fine exciting name, anyhow.'

'And it'll be a fine exciting place for somebody,' said Uncle Baldwin. 'I wish to God I'd gone through with it earlier. The chances I've missed! That's what gets you when you're lying like a stuck pig – the chances you've missed.' He could not speak for a minute or two, and when he did, it was to ask for some of the medicine that Dr. Forester had given him. When he had taken this, and cursed it, he continued his tale in a much quieter tone. 'When we landed on this island, I did a bit of exploring, though it was as hot as hell with all that rock about and no more shade than you'd get on a billiard-ball. What took my eye, once I'd climbed from the beach, was a lot of black stuff sticking out all over the place. I thought it was coal at first, but when I got a bit nearer, I saw it wasn't, and fancied it was a sort o' pitch. Now, lad, just put your hand down to the bottom o' that trunk there and you'll find a hard lump o' stuff about as big as your fist. Bring it here.'

William did as he was told, and came back from the trunk carrying a heavyish piece of dull black stuff that reminded him of the lumps of solid tar he had seen on roads that were being repaired. It seemed a singularly uninteresting substance.

'This is it,' said Uncle Baldwin, taking it in his hand and holding it up. 'This piece came back with me from Faraway Island. It's travelled, this stuff has. And there's tons and tons and tons of it there, and as easy as pie to get at. I brought this bit away just out of curiosity, and then I showed it to a fellow once, a fellow who knew a bit about these things, and he said something that put me on the track. Then – like a blasted fool – I didn't bother for a few years. But the first thing I did when I got to London was to have that stuff tested, this piece here, and then I knew for certain.' He paused dramatically.

'Why, what is it?' cried William, not regarding the lump of black stuff with any great confidence.

'It's pitchblende,' said Uncle Baldwin.

'Pitchblende.' William frowned over this. 'I've heard of that somewhere, but I can't remember what it is.'

In his excitement, Uncle Baldwin leaned forward and was about to speak when William saw his eyes dilate and his mouth twist round in the most grotesque fashion. Instead of talking, Uncle Baldwin gave a horrible gasp. He made a gesture towards the medicine bottle. William, with a shaking hand, poured out another dose for him, and anxiously watched him swallow it and gradually revive.

'Pitchblende,' said Uncle Baldwin, half an hour after he had last spoken. 'That's it. It's a uranium ore, or if it isn't, it's got uranium ore in it. And out of uranium ore, they get radium. Now d'you see?'

'That's where I'd heard it before,' cried William. 'I remember now. I was reading something about Madame Curie, and pitchblende came into it.'

'It did, lad. I've read about it myself. They gave her some from Austria or Bohemia or one o' them places, and she and her husband got radium out of it, first we ever had. Well, this is the stuff, here. Best stuff there is for making radium. The radium's somewhere in it now, in this lump here – so the chap told me at the museum in London. You can test it, even this bit, for radium.'

'But it takes an awful lot of this stuff to make the tiniest bit of radium, doesn't it?'

'It does, but the market price o' radium's about quarter of a million pounds for an ounce. A quarter of a million.' Uncle Baldwin gloated over this tremendous figure. 'And let me tell you, lad, they've scoured the world for this stuff I'm holding in my hand. The Belgians have got most of it, down in the Congo, and they tell me that's why one Belgian company's got almost a monopoly of radium. Can't get the ore, y'see, the other people. And here's this island with tons and tons and tons of it, waiting to be picked up. Takes your breath away, doesn't it?' he concluded, with a noticeable absence of breath himself.

'It's completely staggering,' said William, staring at the purple face above the sheets.

'You see, William, I've figured it out this way. Nearly all these small Pacific islands is either coral or volcano, and that's why they've never been any good for anything in this line. But Faraway's diff'rent. It's a lump of good old rock, millions and millions of years old rock, that's somehow got stuck up there. Mind you, this island's a long way from anywhere, not easy to get at, and it's going to take money to get the stuff away. I don't say it'll take a lot o' money, but more than I've ever had to play with. That's nothing, though. We can leave that.'

'And you had a secret all the time,' said William musingly. Then, after thinking for a moment, he added: 'Does Garsuvin come into this?'

'He does and he doesn't,' replied Uncle Baldwin, with great care. 'He knows something and he's been trying to ferret out the rest. I've finished with him, though. But there's two chaps I owe something to, because they both did me good turns once, real good turns, things you don't forget – or at least I don't. And the only thing I can do for 'em is to let 'em share in this island. That's fair enough, isn't it?'

'Of course it is,' said William heartily.

'My idea at first was to let 'em share it together, if I couldn't do anything myself, but after I'd been here a week or so and I'd taken a fancy to you, William, I thought o' something diff'rent.' He stopped to take breath.

William opened his mouth to say something, but then thought better of it. He might easily side-track his uncle, who did not find it easy to talk, though it would be cruel now to try and stop him talking.

'Now, I've told you, William lad, all about this island and what there is on it, and you're the only man in the world beside myself that does know. That means, y'see, that half the secret's yours already. But I haven't told you where this island is, exact bearings, you understand, and I'm not going to. And I'll tell you why. I want these other two chaps, who did me a good turn, to have a share in it, too. Well, so I got an idea – I won't say it's exactly my own idea 'cos I got it from a book I read once, one o' these buried treasure yarns – but it's a rattling good idea and I take the credit for having the sense to remember it. Working on this idea, I wrote a letter to each of these two chaps, saying who I was and all that, and I gave one the longitude and the other the latitude. Do you get the idea?' he asked proudly.

'Of course I do,' said William. 'I've read those tales, too. It's an old device.'

'And none the worse for that. You see, I've fixed it so none of you can get on without the other two. Mind you, you can bring in who you like once you've all three arranged about your own shares. You might have to do that to raise the money. That's diff'rent. But none of you can walk off with the whole thing.'

'No, I see that,' said William. This was all absurd, like suddenly being plunged into a boys' magazine serial story. And even Uncle Baldwin, fantastically falling upon him almost out of the skies, could not turn life into a boys' magazine serial story. He must have looked bewildered.

'Now take it easy, lad,' his uncle continued, with benevolent patronage. 'You've got to think about it a bit first. Get it all clear. Y'see, you know about the island and what there is there, and these two, between 'em, know where it is. I give you their names, and if you're going on with it, you go to 'em, explain it all and go shares. And if you don't do anything within a year, you've got to promise me you'll write to both of 'em and explain all about it, and leave it to them. That's fair enough, isn't it? And, mind you, lad, this is more complicated than it was in the book. This has taken some ingeniousness working this out, I give you my word it has. But it's a fair deal, isn't it?'

William admitted that it was. 'But suppose they don't get your letter? Suppose one of them's dead? Or both of them? What then, uncle?'

'I've thought o' that, too. There's a lawyer in London by the name of Grantley – brother of a chap I used to know very well in the Islands – and he's done one or two bits o' business for me. Well, he's got a sealed envelope with this latitude and longitude inside, it, and if you can prove to him that one or other o' these two chaps is dead or missing or hasn't got a son or daughter who'll do as well, then, so as not to put a stopper on the whole thing, he'll let you have that envelope. So there it is, lad. Now you get a bit of paper and a pencil, you write down these two names.'

'You know, uncle,' said William, feeling in his pockets for a pencil and his diary, 'if you don't mind my saying so – and I'm very grateful to you for what you're doing, tremendously grateful – but if you don't mind my saying so, if you'd told me the whole thing and then told me I had to give equal shares to these two men, it would have worked just as well. I'd have kept my promise, you know.'

Uncle Baldwin shook his head, very slowly, deliberately. 'Not the same thing, lad. No doubt, you might have kept your promise, but I wouldn't like to put you nor anybody else under the temptation. You don't know what it's like yet knowing you've got a big fortune under your hand. You've not had time to know, not had time to think it over properly yet. But I *do* know. Wouldn't be fair on you. Now, are you ready for these names?' Uncle Baldwin waited until William's pencil was poised exactly above the blank page in his diary. 'The first one is Commander Ivybridge, Royal Navy, retired, and one o' the finest gentlemen you ever set your eyes on. He did me a good turn while he was still in the Navy. I'll tell you about it later on, if you'll remind me.'

'Where does he live?' asked William.

'I wrote to him care o' the Admiralty. I've had no reply yet, but they'll find him all right. Must know where he is, because of his pension. Well, he's got the longitude of the island, and that's all he has got. The chap that's got the latitude is an American, and another o' the best. He's P. T. Riley, and "care of Brown, Woburn and Brothers, San Francisco," will find him all right. He's been with them over thirty years. Have you got him? P. T. Riley—'

'Care of Brown, Woburn and Brothers, San Francisco,' William read out. 'And the other one is Commander Ivybridge. That's right, isn't it?'

'That's right. Now you've got all the necessary partic'lars, but of course we've got to talk a lot more about it yet.'

'Yes, but not to-night, uncle,' said William gently. 'You're tired out. You've talked too much already. If Dr. Forester knew—'

'That yapper,' said Uncle Baldwin, with a most contemptuous wheeze. 'But you're right, lad, for all that. You go downstairs and think it over.'

But William found it very difficult to think over. If this extraordinary conversation had taken place a fortnight before, it would have left him wildly excited; but at the moment he could not persuade himself to accept the remote island, the tons and tons of pitchblende, Commander Ivybridge and P. T. Riley, the whole fantastic thing. It was not that he actively disbelieved in it. It was simply that it did not enter as yet into the category of things that must be either believed or disbelieved. His uncle might have been reading a boy's storybook to him for an hour. What was real and urgent in that room upstairs was not this island stuff, but his uncle's condition, a fact so solid that it seemed to reduce those other facts, if they were facts, to the thin and shifting texture of a dream.

6

When William looked in on his uncle the next morning, the old man seemed much better. He was sitting up and asking about newspapers and his pipe. He promised to give William further details about Faraway Island, about Commander Ivybridge and P. T. Riley, that very night. William left for the malting-house, convinced that Uncle

Baldwin, like the tough old fellow he was, would live to weather a few more tornadoes of reminiscence, argument and brandy; and the thought warmed him, for he had an affection for the old man and during these last few days that affection had grown. But Uncle Baldwin never lived to see the day out. In the middle of the afternoon, Mrs. Gurney, hearing the sound of a fall, hurried upstairs and found that he had struggled out of bed, out of the room on to the landing, and was lying there, cold, stiffening. William, summoned from the malting-house, arrived only in time to hear Dr. Forester explain briefly and pungently what exactly had happened to stop the worn machinery of heart and nerves.

For the third time within a short period of years, William spent the next three days in that chilly and creeping twilight which is not so much the atmosphere of death, the swift, clean, inevitable stroke, as the atmosphere of the mortuary, the coffin, the wormy grave. At the funeral there was only a handful of people, one or two friends of William and a few acquaintances that Uncle Baldwin had made at the *Suffolk Arms*, but among them was one surprising figure, that of a dejected, bearded fellow, whom William dimly recognised as a man who sold fish and fruit in a village four miles away. When they were all coming out, William found himself next to this man and hinted at his astonishment in seeing him there. 'I'd no idea you knew my uncle,' he said. 'He didn't know many people round here.'

'You're his nephew, are you?' said the gloomy bearded one. 'Oh, I knew him all right.'

'Did you meet him here?' William asked.

'Only once set eyes on him here,' was the reply. 'Knew him twenty years ago in Rarotonga.' And not another word did he add to that, but nodded and stumped away to his fish and fruit.

William could not have told anybody why this little encounter made such a deep and curiously melancholy impression upon him. It was certainly not the familiar nonsense about the world being a small place. He was not left with the feeling that it was a small place, but rather, a huge place, desolatingly wide and weary, a place of lonely trudging epics, where you found yourself in Rarotonga and then years, bleak echoing years, afterwards, you looked into a grave in Suffolk and then drearily dragged your feet down some wet road in the gathering dusk. And nobody could know it all, not more than a poor particle of it. William, his mind hollowly busy with lonely little figures stumping away across this spinning ball that is all they know of the universe and that yet is never quite their home, told himself again that he wished he believed in God.

He returned to an Ivy Lodge that seemed to have shrunk and faded a little. That night he sat in the study alone, sometimes hearing the rain in the garden outside, sometimes hearing the seas break and thunder ten thousand miles away. On the table, in front of him, was a piece of dull black stuff about as big as his fist, a thing that Mrs. Gurney, who was more short-sighted than she would admit, might easily toss into the coal scuttle. His diary was open on that page which bore the names of Commander Ivybridge and P. T. Riley of San Francisco. An atlas was there too, a good atlas even if a trifle out-of-date; but William was not consulting it. He was chasing a grey mountainous shape that trembled above a foaming desolation. Now his mind held it; now it was gone. Faraway.

CHAPTER II

THE TWO COMMANDERS

1

A FORTNIGHT after his uncle's funeral, William walked into the Radium Institute in Riding House Street, just behind the Queen's Hall. He carried with him a small suitcase and in that case was the piece of black rock from Faraway Island. Uncle Baldwin had said that it had been already tested and proved to be pitchblende, but William felt that he must make sure. He had mentioned the stuff to Greenlaw of the Grammar School, and Greenlaw, it seemed, knew a man who knew a man at the Radium Institute. So William found himself standing in the blue-green tiled hall of the institute. The two uniformed commissionaires appeared to regard him with some suspicion. He began to wonder if he had the look of an expert radium thief. Finally, however, one commissionaire went away to deliver William's message, and the other showed him into a waiting-room, not unlike that of a doctor or a dentist. Here he was left, with the usual assortment of illustrated papers, for some twenty minutes, during which time he had ample opportunity to feel rather foolish and unreal. When you have travelled for years from Buntingham to London only on malting business, to see the managers and foremen of breweries, there is some excuse for you if you do not quite feel at ease when you are there with a bit of rock from an unknown island. Moreover, the attitude of the commissionaires had not been reassuring. Everything depended now on Greenlaw's man's man, the radiologist or whatever he was, for if he seemed surprised and contemptuous, William saw himself picking up his suitcase, rushing out, and finding the nearest taxi for Liverpool Street. Even when we are possessed of great secrets, when we have been left an island and a potential fortune, our movements may still hang upon the turn of a stranger's eyebrow.

The radiologist, however, did nothing that made William want to bolt. William stammered something about a geological collection, brought out his lump of Faraway stuff, and asked if he might have it tested.

'Looks like pitchblende,' the expert remarked, as he took charge of it. He spoke in a high, rather tired voice; and he had a manner that William had noticed before in hard-working scientists, a detached, somewhat weary, faintly quizzical manner. 'But we'll soon see. Come up and see for yourself.'

'Thank you. It's very good of you.'

'Not at all. We're always doing that sort of thing here. This way.'

They went up in a lift, then hurried along corridors, climbed a flight or two of steps, and arrived at last in a small bare room at the very top of the building. 'Have to be here,' the host explained, 'to get as far away as possible from the radiation downstairs.'

'Of course,' said William politely.

The radiologist brought out a small piece of apparatus from its wooden case and rapidly assembled it on the table. William was reminded of the swift delicate precision one finds in the movements of a good conjurer. The apparatus was surprisingly simple. A little telescope looked into the interior of a white metal cylinder, behind which there was a powerful light.

'This is how we do it,' the radiologist explained. 'Look in there. Do you see that bit of gold leaf?' William looked, and saw a tiny fragile ribbon of gold leaf suspended before an illuminated scale inside the cylinder. Apparently, that bit of gold leaf, which a breath could have blown away and the movement of a finger could have crushed to powder, was about to decide whether Faraway Island was merely one dull lump of rock out of many or an Arabian Nights discovery, better than Ali Baba's cave. Wizardry was in the air.

'We'll now proceed to charge it,' said the scientist, in the manner of a slightly bored but indulgent uncle. He jabbed the cylinder once or twice with a noisy little instrument. Instantly, the ribbon of gold leaf stiffened. 'Now if we put a bit of ordinary rock – quartz, if you like – in this tray or on top,' he continued, 'that gold leaf will hardly move at all. But if we bring radium near it, or if we put any ore containing radium, such as pitchblende or carnotite, on the cylinder, you'll see that gold leaf make a really decided movement. We can't get this piece of yours inside, on the tray, so we'll put it on top. Now let's see what happens.'

'Well?' William gasped. His heart had suddenly become far too big for his body. He had not felt so excited for years.

The radiologist, who had been bending down to squint through the telescope, now stood upright. 'See for yourself.'

William did. The wisp of gold had decided. 'Yes, it must be pitchblende, mustn't it?' he cried, rather wildly.

'It's pitchblende all right,' said the radiologist, smiling at what he imagined to be William's innocent amateurish enthusiasm and excitement. He handed over the speci-men, and began dismantling the apparatus. 'Very good little electroscopes these,' he announced.

'That's an electroscope, is it?' said William. 'I suppose you could – er – use that anywhere, couldn't you? I mean, carry it about with you?'

'Yes, rather. I take this one all over the place. Hospitals are always losing their radium – that sounds careless, but as a matter of fact it's a pretty easy thing to do – and then they send for me and find it with this thing – among the sheets in the laundry basket sometimes. Like Hunt the Thimble.'

'Can you' – William hesitated a moment – 'buy those things?'

The radiologist laughed. 'Of course you can. But you're not thinking of buying one, are you, on the strength of possessing a bit of pitchblende? You're not going pros-pecting for uranium ores, I hope?'

'Not exactly,' replied William, who felt that he was rather a deep fellow. 'But I just wondered. I suppose there are lots of people looking for this pitchblende stuff, aren't there?'

'There are. All over the world. And can't find any – worse luck! If somebody could only find another big deposit of pitchblende – like that the Belgians found in the Congo – it would make a wonderful difference, bring the price of radium down with a rush. And that's what we want. Radium's far too expensive. The price is holding up everything. This way.'

They were going down the stairs. In William's overcoat pocket was a genuine piece of pitchblende from Faraway Island. In William's mind a sort of fair, with any number of steam organs and glittering roundabouts, seemed to be in progress, making him feel rather dizzy.

'Where did you get that piece of pitchblende from?' the radiologist enquired casually.

'Oh – from an uncle of mine,' replied William, as casually as he could.

'Probably from the Bohemian mine originally. You go down here.' The radiologist indicated the lift. 'Now if you'd told me you'd found a whole heap of it somewhere, I should be excited,' he added, and laughed. 'Well – glad we could help you. Good day.'

Returning to the waiting-room for his suitcase, William had to pass the two commissionaires. They still seemed to regard him with suspicion, but this time William almost swaggered past. He knew something that the Radium Institute did not know. He had made no definite plans before coming up to have the piece of ore tested, except that if it had failed to test, he had made up his mind that he would return to Buntingham at once and dismiss Faraway for ever. Nevertheless, he had brought with him a suitcase; and now his plan was formed. The first step was to find Commander Ivybridge, who had the longitude of the island. P. T. Riley of San Francisco, and the latitude, could wait. He went from Riding House Street straight to the hotel he usually stayed at, booked a room there, and then went in search of *Who's Who* and any other necessary works of reference.

2

'I wonder if I could see Commander Ivybridge?' said William.

'On business, sir?' asked the man at the door.

'Yes, it's – er – on business, yes.'

'Have you an appointment, sir?' the man demanded.

'No, I'm afraid I haven't,' William told him.

'Then you see the secretary first,' said the man, opening the door a little wider and stepping aside to let William in. 'This way, sir.' And he showed William into a small room on the first floor. It seemed to be filled almost entirely with press-cuttings. The table was thick with them; they foamed and surged about the typewriter and the telephone; there were scores of them in wire baskets on the floor; and there appeared to be several hundred lying neglected on the carpet. Seated in the very midst of this orgy of print was a tall slender girl, with a pale triangular face, shining black hair, and enormous swimming violet eyes. She was smoking a cigarette in a very long scarlet holder.

'Gentleman to see the Commander on business, miss,' said the man, and then promptly closed the door behind William.

The girl uncoiled herself from her chair like a black snake, until she looked down upon William. 'How *do* you *do?*' she said, and smiled sweetly.

'Er – good-afternoon,' said William. He felt this was very inadequate, but it was all he could do.

'Won't you sit down?' she said, still smiling sweetly. '*Do* sit down.'

William sat down, then looked up at those enormous violet eyes. 'My name's Dursley,' he began, timidly. 'I'm afraid Commander Ivybridge doesn't know me—'

The girl flicked some ash off her cigarette, coiled again round her chair, and broke in with: 'That's quite all right. The Commander can't know *every*body, can he, even though *every*body knows him or knows about him?'

'No, I suppose not,' said William, trying to imagine why everybody should know the Commander.

The girl now put her head slightly on one side and

looked at William as if he was a puppy attempting his first trick. 'I know,' she said enthusiastically. 'You needn't tell me. It's about the Imperial Unity League, isn't it? You spoke to me this morning on the telephone. I recognise your voice.'

She was so pleased at this and so impressive that William had to summon all his courage to tell her that his visit had nothing to do with the Imperial Unity League.

'But wait,' she cried, interrupting. 'How stupid! How *ter*ribly stupid of me! It wasn't the Imperial Unity League at all, was it? You're the man from the Malay States who wants to see the Commander about his scheme for developing the fishing. Is it the fishing,' she enquired, with a ravishing smile, 'or it is planting something?'

'I don't know. I'm not that man at all. It's something quite different. You see, it's rather complicated—'

This time, after removing the cigarette holder, she did not uncoil but shot straight up, very dramatically, and in the eyes she fixed on William was doomsday in violet and black. 'You're from the Commander's constituency,' she cried accusingly. 'And the Commander has given instructions – I sent out a notice myself to the *Hempton Chronicle* – that he can't see anybody from his constituency. He can't be worried now. He's promised to go down to Hempton on Saturday week and explain *every*thing. So you *see*.' And now she gave him a little tragic smile.

'It's not that at all,' William protested, determined this time to have his say. 'It's a private matter entirely, nothing to do with politics or anything of that kind.'

'Oh, *so* sorry.' She produced the sweet smile again as she drooped into the chair.

'You see, my uncle – who has just died – knew Commander Ivybridge, and – well, it's something to do with that,' he concluded lamely.

'Is it *really* important?' she asked, leaning forward about a yard and nearly drowning him in swimming eyes. 'You know – the Commander's *fright*fully busy just now. Of course he always is – I mean, what with his work as a member, and then the Imperial Unity League, and the Malay fishing or planting scheme, and the Australian Domestic Service thing, and his directorship of the There-By-Air business, and *all* the other things – well, I mean, at *any* time, we're simply *deluged* – but just *now* – I *ask* you!'

'He sounds a tremendous sort of chap,' said William, rather dubiously. This was not at all the man he had imagined.

'But of *course*,' cried the secretary, bringing up fresh reserves of enthusiasm. Clearly, she adored the Commander.

William decided that it was time this girl had a healthy shock. 'It's funny,' he said, with an air of quiet musing. 'I've never heard of him before – except from my uncle.'

The girl did not actually get up from her chair, but she shot up at least a foot and a half, staring wildly at William. 'You've never heard of Commander Ivybridge?' And she came near to shrieking.

'Not a word,' said William sturdily.

'But *every*body's heard about him. Where can you have been?'

'Just down in Suffolk. That's where I live.'

'But I mean – you can't possibly read the papers or *any*thing. Why, the Commander's *the* coming man – might be future prime minister or a millionaire or *any*thing – there's no *possible* doubt about that. Oh, you're *too* absurd.'

'Very sorry,' said William, who felt much better now.

The girl slowly rose. 'I'll see if the Commander can see

you now,' she announced, speaking as if from a height of several miles. 'What did you say your name was?'

He gave her a card. 'And tell him, please, that he knew my uncle, Mr. Baldwin Totten.'

The girl rippled out, then rippled in again, to say that the Commander would see Mr. Dursley for a few minutes. 'And *please*,' she added, bringing out a smile of colossal sweetness and making her eyes larger and more swimmy than ever, 'please don't stay too long, because if you do, *every*thing will get into a most *fright*ful mess. Straight through there, to the library. Gerd-afternoon.'

By this time, William had said good-bye to any image he had previously entertained of Commander Ivybridge, whom he had seen as a very quiet, shy, retired naval officer and not as a coming man, a committee in himself, with a room full of press cuttings and about two undulating yards of adoring secretary. Therefore he was not greatly surprised by the man he found in the library. There was still a slight suggestion of the naval officer about the Commander, but only enough to hint that he had once been an actor who had played naval officers for a year or two. All the rest was Coming Man and Imperial Unity and Malay Fishing and Australian Domestic Service and There-By-Air and press cuttings by the van load. Commander Ivybridge was tall enough to play Adam to his secretary's Eve; he looked about forty-five; he had black hair brushed back and varnished, a pink clean-shaven face, a noble brow, a Roman nose, and a very large jutting chin; and altogether he was a grand senatorial figure. If William had seen him on a public platform, he would have been impressed. At close quarters, he was not impressed; and he had not been in the room half a minute before he was convinced that it would be quite impossible for him to go looking for Faraway Island in the company of this personage. It simply could not be done.

'How do you do, sir? Let me see, I don't know you, do I?' The Commander's voice was so rich, so strong, that he sounded as if he was beginning an impassioned baritone solo.

William explained briefly about his uncle and the letter.

'I remember something,' the Commander intoned, 'but I'm rather vague, in fact distinctly vague.' He rang a bell, and then when his secretary answered it, instantly became more imposing and noble than ever. 'Miss Porstead, could I trouble you for the incoming T file? We're looking for a letter addressed to me from a Mr. Baldwin Totten. That was the name, wasn't it?' He turned to William for confirmation, then added: 'You might put your finger on that letter, Miss Porstead, and bring it in.' When the letter arrived, it had been detached from the file, and he held it up and examined it gravely for a few minutes. 'I remember this letter now,' he told William. 'It puzzled me at the time, but then a great many of my letters puzzle me and would puzzle anybody, eh? Ha-ha-ha-ha. One of the penalties of being in the public eye, eh? Now, you know, I don't remember meeting this Mr. Totten, your uncle, either. I may have done. He says it was when I was still serving.'

'Somewhere in the South Pacific, I imagine, wasn't it?' said William.

'Some time ago, eh?'

'I fancy so. Quite a long time ago.'

'That settles it,' the Commander boomed. 'I'm not the man.'

'Not the man?'

'Not the man,' the Commander repeated in full diapason. 'There are two of us, you know. There's another Commander Ivybridge.'

William stared at him, with mounting excitement and hope. 'Do you mean,' he said quickly, 'that my uncle may have sent this letter to you instead of to the other one, who's the right one?'

'It's happened before. This other Commander Ivybridge is much senior to me, though he only retired a few years before I did. Did you say your uncle was a trader in the South Seas? Then you can take it from me that this letter was sent to the wrong man. I never knew him. I might have done him a good turn, you know, if I'd known him – ha-ha-ha-ha-ha—'

'Ha-ha-ha-ha,' William echoed feebly.

'But I didn't know him. Obviously the other Ivybridge did. That's the man you want.'

'I found you in *Who's Who*,' said William. 'But there wasn't any other Commander Ivybridge there.'

'Oh, no, he wouldn't be in *Who's Who*. Very quiet man, and never done much, though he had a good name in the service, I believe. Typical specimen of the older type, you know. Not like me – ha-ha-ha-ha.'

'Could you possibly give me his address?'

'I could.' He fished out an address book, and read out: 'Fourteen, Bombay Terrace, Lugmouth. That's where you'll find him. Do you know Lugmouth? Messy little place, I always think. But I believe he comes from that part of the world.'

'Thank you,' said William, after jotting down the address. Then he hesitated a moment and glanced at his uncle's letter, which was on the blotter in front of the Commander. 'I shall have to take the letter, of course.'

The Commander picked it up. 'Of course you will.' He glanced at it again. 'No use to me even if it *was* mine. I don't think I want any more longitude bearings. Curious idea this – if you don't mind my saying so. Looks like one of these treasure stunts.' As he said this, he gave William a sharp glance that surprised an affirmative in the mere expression of his face. 'Ha-ha-ha-ha-ha, you needn't reply. Well, it's no business of mine, evidently' – and it wasn't, but, nevertheless, William, to his annoyance, saw him look at the figure in the letter and then write something quickly on his blotting pad – 'but if it's any more of this buried treasure, Spanish galleon, pirates' hoard, doubloons and pieces of eight, nonsense, if you'll take my advice, you won't bother your head about it. Simply a waste of time.' He handed over the letter.

His patronising air hurried William into what he felt afterwards to be an indiscretion. 'I agree with you,' he said sharply, as if he knew a great deal about these subjects, far more than his listener. 'But it isn't the ordinary buried treasure business at all. Something much more real and important.'

The telephone buzzed at the Commander's elbow. 'Who?' he asked it. Then, after a pause: 'I don't know him, do I? I see. Very well, I'll see him a minute. You might find out what it is exactly, though, Miss Porstead.' He stood up now, a very massive figure of a public man, and looked down upon William smilingly. 'Something much more important, eh? And am I allowed to ask what that something is?'

'I'm afraid you're not,' said William hurriedly. 'It's – er – well, it's a secret yet.'

And William made way for the next visitor. As he closed the library door after him, the door across the way, that of the secretary's little room, opened a few inches, and as he walked towards the stairs he heard her voice and another voice answering her. And all the way down the stairs, he thought about this other voice, for it sounded exactly like the voice of somebody he had met and it had a curious timbre of its own. It was not until he reached the front door that he suddenly remembered his uncle's visitor, Mr. Garsuvin, of the pointed head, the thousand little creases, the loud check suit, the suggestion of the melancholy intellectual clown. Yes, Mr. Garsuvin had a voice like that. For a moment or two, William was not in Holland Park and chill winter twilight, but in the heated atmosphere of sensational fiction, of plots and plotters and sinister coincidences. Then he smiled at himself, and found a bus that took him towards his hotel. He was warmed by the feeling of relief that invaded him when he discovered that there was another Commander Ivybridge, possibly not so important, oratorical, and insufferable. The right Commander, he had been told, was a quiet man living in a small seaport, and that description, meagre as it was, did at least chime with his thought of the man. He could not have become the partner in adventure of a combined committee and Albert Hall Mass Meeting.

As soon as he reached his hotel, he did a fantastic thing. He took out the folded letter, gave one glance at the signature to make sure that it was his Uncle Baldwin's, then, without reading it, without a sight of the longitude bearing, he put it into an envelope, addressed the envelope to Commander Ivybridge, 14, Bombay Terrace, Lugmouth, stamped and posted it. The old man had wanted it to happen that way, and that was the way it should happen. That letter would go down to Lugmouth on the night express. And next morning, on the famous 10.30, William would follow it.

3

Lugmouth is one of those small towns on the South-Western coast that have never been able to come to terms with Time. It is a port that is always about to turn into a resort, and a resort that is always about to turn into a port. A hundred years ago, Lugmouth was probably considered to be a town with a fine future; and now it is regarded as a town with a great past. It has never had a real present. It exists in a perpetual state of rapid development and decay. On the hill, near the railway station, it is a resort, thanks to the two deceptive arts of photography and poster-drawing, which can conjure the sight of a few hard little palms into a semi-tropical paradise. Up there, you will find the new *Lugmouth Hotel*, the *Riviera Hydro*, the *Palms Private Hotel*, the *West Lugmouth Tennis Club*, the *Doris Tea Rooms*, and the usual little eruption of arts and crafts. Once it has descended the hill, Lugmouth turns itself into a typical small country town, with one long Market Street containing an astonishing number of chemists' shops, gaily bedecked with photographic materials and bottles of liquid paraffin, and circulating libraries where you may order your own private Christmas cards. The brave Woolworth, in his crimson and gold, is there too. Beyond Market Street, Lugmouth tumbles ungracefully into the harbour and estuary, leaving a sad litter of rotten piles, old iron, rusty cables, sodden heaps of rope, backs of little public houses, clothes out to dry, squawking gulls, and groups of men who sit and spit and stand and sit and spit again. Near the water front, floating among all the bits of paper, empty tins, odd lengths of rope, and masses of seaweed, are a few rowing boats; and beyond them are several forlorn little yachts, a larger sailing vessel or two, and an ancient three-master occupied mysteriously by crowds of small boys with shaven heads; and further out still there are always a few old and careless steamers who seem to have waddled in to have a week's quiet smoke. The only energetic creature in the whole estuary, apart from the every restless gulls, is the very small steamboat that puffs to and fro between Lugmouth and the villages on the other side, in order that numerous red-faced retired gentlemen may change their circulating library books. This steamboat lands its passengers and their literature (*Twenty Years in Burma*, by R. E. Higglethwaite, C.B.E.) at a tiny pier that leads forward to an open space, in which there are four automatic machines, a company of accomplished spitters, a public lavatory in red corrugated iron, a fountain that has long ceased to play, two taxicabs that have a faintly nautical air, and an uncompromisingly Early Victorian hotel, both family and commercial – the *Lugmouth Packet*. It was to this hotel that William, brooding on the romance of the sea, allowed himself to be driven, at the end of his six-hour journey from Paddington.

He had chosen this hotel because he had liked its name, which seemed to him to have an adventurous nautical ring about it; but no sooner had he signed the register and visited his bedroom than he began to wish he had tried some other place. The *Lugmouth Packet* frowned upon his enterprise. It raised again all those doubts that he had been able to ignore on the way down. He had been able to ignore them because journeys to places he had visited before, and especially journeys by express train, were still an excitement and a pleasure to him. Once you had brought your ticket, swift travel did not seem to demand any solid reasons; it outdistanced common sense; it was almost its own excuse, an end in itself. But now that he had arrived in this strange town, had unpacked his tooth-brush and razor and pyjamas in this unfriendly bedroom, in the gloomy shade of its lace curtains, doubt returned to him in full measure.

The hotel itself was the spokesman of doubt. Every inch of faded gilt lettering it had, every yard of lace curtaining and pickled-cabbage-pattern stair carpet, every dark and roast-mutton-haunted corner, told him not to be silly. 'Have you a good reason, family or commercial, for staying here?' it asked him. There were lights already on the water, but it was only a few minutes past five, so he ordered tea from an uncommonly small waiter, who looked like a pale Pekinese. The tea was served to him in the lounge, a large room overlooking the sea and containing two splendid fires, a jaded conference of elderly leather chairs, reading matter that consisted of a hundred copies of *The Autocar, Who's Who* for 1911, the *Schools of England,* and a row of bound volumes of the *Stock and Market Record,* and, in addition, perhaps in order to show that the last trump had not yet sounded, it also contained an idle fat man with a wife and a busy fat man with a notebook. The latter was soon joined by two blue-suited solid men, who ate and drank and smoked and talked very heartily. They had the look of men who had left the sea to take some shore job with the same shipping companies, and evidently they had come down from London. William kept an ear open for their talk; but it offered him no magic casements or faerie lands forlorn. Most of it was about one Mac at the office. 'Of course, since Mac's been in the office,' one of them would begin. 'Mind you, another thing about Mac being there in the office,' the other would say. None of this gave William any confidence. Though at no time large or expansive, he now tried to make himself smaller than usual, almost pretending that he was not there at all. He could hear another Commander Ivybridge, even larger and louder than the first, roaring with laughter at him. Faraway Island appeared simply fabulous. William felt himself to be a sort of travelling impostor. He nibbled at his bread-and-butter like a mouse.

After tea, he thought of a dozen different excuses for not calling on the Commander until morning. Thus, he did not know where Bombay Terrace was and it might be hard to find in the dusk; he was rather tired after the journey down; if he waited, it would give the Commander more time to think over the letter; probably the Commander would be out at this hour: in short, William was for once thoroughly dishonest with himself. So instead of visiting Bombay Terrace, he merely went for a stroll round the town; looked idly at all the chemists' shops and circulating libraries; stared at the twinkling lights in the harbour; wondered at the number of men simply standing at the pavement edge, as if watching some procession invisible to other eyes; and inspected the Customs House, the Town Hall, the Post Office, and Woolworth's, where he bought a sixpenny detective story. With this he might be able to defy the hotel.

He forgot, however, that the next move was the hotel's – dinner. The meal itself, which began with soup out of a tin and then passed by way of watery turbot and tough beef to a particularly liverish, and therefore ultimately depressing, helping of apple tart and clotted cream, was obviously designed to sink the spirit of man to a very low, damp, dark, Victorian family and commercial level. Then there were no less than six solid men taking dinner, and their talk was mostly in that Clyde accent which dismisses nearly all consonants and might be described as the low swamp in human speech. There was nothing in their talk to restore William's confidence.

The hotel did not invite him to stay in it after dinner

and read his detective story. He returned to the long Market Street, which was now filled with giggling girls and jostling staring hobbledehoys, all busy with the preliminary tactics of courtship and mating. Feeling rather small, old, and melancholy, William pushed his way through the drab Venusberg, and arrived in front of a picture theatre. At eight-thirty he was admitted into this outpost of American civilisation, and, rather to his surprise, contrived to enjoy himself inside it. The chief film was a talking picture of the adventures in New York of an ambitious young boxer, and it presented some reasonably good scenes of low life and high life in American pugilistic circles. Compared with the hotel, this film was the Renaissance itself, crowded with roaring strong men, passionate women, threatening mobs, glare and smoke and drink and dancing feet, and these shouting shadows touched some little strings of fear and hope in the spectator and sounded vague chords in the smoky darkness. William returned to the hotel feeling somewhat heartened. He said good-night to the pale Pekinese waiter, who was still on duty and looked as if he would never find his way off it, went up to bed whistling softly, stood at his window for a minute looking at the harbour lights, determined to see the Commander as soon after breakfast as was decently possible, turned in, made the acquaintance of the corpse in his detective story, then quickly succumbed to the sleepy salt air.

4

It promised to be a glorious morning. Winter seemed to have gone, and so did everything else that belonged to yesterday. There was no water, no harbour, no hills and sky, nothing but a hollow of pale gold in which hung certain smoky shapes of steamers and sailing boats. With his chin half lathered, William cast a delighted water-colourist's eye on this enchantment. It would not be long before the sun came bounding out. If this could happen on a December morning, William decided, then Lug-mouth had a right to its palm trees. Suffolk, sullen and damp, seemed ten thousand miles away. He regarded the gold and the blue of the morning as a good omen. March-ing down the stairs to breakfast, he felt twice the man he had been the evening before. He nodded to one or two of the solid men, now feeding themselves so quickly and thoroughly with porridge, haddock, sole, bacon and eggs, toast and marmalade that they looked as if they were troops suddenly ordered to evacuate the town. William actually felt sorry for them because they had nothing better to talk about than Mac at the office, had no Faraway Island in their heads, no magical lattitudes and longitudes to discover. He ate heartily, smoked a pipe in the lounge, and stared through the great bow window at the twinkling water, then set out calmly to find Bombay Terrace and the real Commander Ivybridge.

Bombay Terrace was not so foolishly named as most streets are, for it actually stood upon a terrace, high above Market Street, and boldly fronting the estuary. And no doubt at one time you had only to look out of your bedroom window there to catch a last glimpse of the men and ships bound for Bombay. It consisted of a single row of small square houses, pleasantly designed in the fashion of a hundred years ago, and still trim in their new coats of brown or dark green paint. To William, whose mind was busy with nautical matters, though he knew nothing about them, these houses had a neat quarter-deck appearance that pleased him. He had a vision of captains and mates of clipper ships coming home to this terrace, filling every house in it with Chinese silks, porcelain and ivories. Just before he arrived at Number 14, he saw a little old man with a bushy beard come blinking out into the mild sunshine, carrying a tripod and a telescope, with which he took his stand in front of the terrace and began carefully examining the estuary. William was so pleased with this little old man, so much at home in the atmosphere of the place that he might have been put there by an artful theatrical producer, that he wanted to rush across and shake him by the hand. Bombay Terrace was splendid. If Commander Ivybridge lived up to his address and surroundings, all would be well.

The door of Number 14 opened about six inches. But that space was quite enough, it appeared, for the woman who opened it. She was the narrowest woman William had ever seen: her head, features, neck, shoulders, all looked as if they had been compressed, ceaselessly, ruthlessly, since childhood; she was like an image in a distorted mirror. She looked at William so narrowly that she only appeared to be examining a section of him, but at that section she stared so hard and suspiciously that William almost felt as if he was being bored into by a couple of gimlets.

'Yes?' she enquired, after William had waited for the door to open at least another two inches.

'Does Commander Ivybridge live here, please?'

'No,' she replied, to William's dismay, 'Commander Ivybridge does *not* live here.'

'Oh,' he stammered. 'I'm sorry. I – er – thought—'

'Commander Ivybridge,' she continued, severely, 'does *not* live here. But he lodges here. Did you want to see him?'

'I did – I mean, I do,' said William, greatly relieved. 'Is he in? I want to see him on rather important business.'

'If it's insurance, you're wasting your time. They've tried before. No use. He won't insure.'

'No, it's nothing to do with insurance or anything like that,' William told her.

'And he won't buy anything neither. No use you trying to sell him anything. He hasn't got the money.'

'I don't want to sell him anything. It's purely private business, and it's important. He's had a letter about it already.'

'Came yesterday morning,' said the woman promptly. 'I saw it myself. He doesn't often get a letter now, so I noticed it. You'd better come in.' She led the way into a small sitting-room, crowded with photographs, huge shells, and inferior oriental vases. 'You can wait for him here,' she continued. 'He's only gone to get his paper. He always gets his paper himself now. It gives him some-thing to do, and it's cheaper than having it delivered. He might take it into head to have a walk, but I don't think he will. You can wait here for him.'

'Thank you,' said William, with a tiny flick of irony.

'As a matter of fact, this used to be his sitting-room, but now he's given it up and only has the bedroom upstairs. He couldn't afford to keep this on, but I let him use it now and again, if he has anybody to see him.' And now she lowered her voice, and her eyes, which sat so close to her long thin nose that they were like two berries on a stalk, gleamed with secret satisfaction. 'The Com-mander's had a come-down.'

'A what?' cried William, staring at her.

'A come-down, a nasty come-down. Very different now, the Commander is, to what he was when he first came here. Did you know him before?'

'No, I didn't,' replied William shortly. He did not like these revelations, and he did not like this monstrously narrow woman, who seemed to him to resemble a large confiding insect. Already, his sympathies were with the Commander, who had had to give up his sitting-room and to fetch his own paper after his 'come-down.' Why couldn't the woman keep these facts to herself?

'If you've just arrived and you've come here on business, you might be wanting rooms yourself for a while,' the woman went on, looking at him like a speculative mosquito. 'If so, there's accommodation here, and Thrine's the name – Mrs. Thrine.'

William nodded, but said nothing.

Mrs. Thrine waited a moment, then said: 'I didn't catch the name.'

'You didn't catch it,' said William solemnly, 'because I didn't give it to you. But if you want to know my name – it's Dursley – D-u-r-s-l-e-y. William Dursley. And I live at Buntingham, Suffolk. And I came down yesterday afternoon from London. And I'm staying at the *Lugmouth Packet*.'

Mrs. Thrine accepted the ironical recital of these details quite coolly. 'If you'll wait here, Mr. Dursley,' she said, putting her hands together in front of her body, so that it seemed as if she was about to compress herself to a mere crack in the door, 'you ought to see him in a minute or two.' And then the crack was no longer there.

A few minutes later the Commander arrived. William heard him talking to Mrs. Thrine outside, then in he came. 'Mr. Dursley, isn't it?' he said, fixing two remarkably clear blue eyes on William's face. 'Yes, I'm Commander Ivybridge. I understand you've come to see me about that letter I got yesterday.'

'I have,' said William. 'My uncle wrote that letter just

before he died, a few weeks ago. But it was sent to the wrong Commander Ivybridge.'

'Ah, that explains it,' said the Commander, smiling rather shyly.

'I called to see him the day before yesterday. He gave me back the letter and gave me your address too. That's how I found my way here.'

'It's happened once or twice before,' the Commander remarked. He had a pleasant voice, but he spoke rather jerkily and with a certain effort, like a man who found it difficult to talk. 'He's a much more important person than I am, these days, so when there's a doubt about it, things go to him.'

'I gathered that,' said William, who only spoke to fill in a break, for the Commander had suddenly stopped.

There was another silence now, however, and the Commander only broke it with an effort. He was half shy, half rusty, and obviously did not talk easily to strangers. But he pulled out a pipe and a pouch, and they seemed to help him. 'Will you smoke? I'm afraid I haven't any cigarettes here. A pipe? Have some of this stuff? It's good, though you may find it rather strong.'

'Then I'd better stick to my own, thank you,' said William, smiling. The atmosphere was now lighter and friendlier. Both men filled and lit their pipes, and took stock of one another across the haze of smoke.

This Commander Ivybridge was not so imposing, not so large and lusty, as the other in London. He was older; perhaps sixty. He was only two or three inches taller than William, and though he seemed strongly built, he carried himself rather stiffly, as if afraid of relaxing under the pressure of the years. His hair was grey but still thick and crisp. The icy blue of his eyes was almost startling in that red-brown cleanly-shaved face, though round those eyes there seemed to be dozens of tiny wrinkles. It was a strong self-reliant face, with wind and weather in its cheeks, yet there was about it a queer suggestion of innocence and even childlike simplicity. It was not the kind of face you often see in the malting business in Suffolk, or in any other sort of business, and William, who had an eye for faces, found himself examining it with unusual interest. The Commander's clothes were very neat, very carefully brushed, but they were old and soon they would be shabby, which only confirmed Mrs. Thrine's remarks about him. Undoubtedly, Commander Ivybridge had had 'a come-down.' But if he resented it, if he felt bitter, there had not been time for this resentment to leave a mark upon him. Here was a man whose whole life, from boyhood onwards, had passed like a dream, leaving the boy still there, staring and wondering. Such was William's conclusion, and it gave him so much pleasure that he regarded the Commander with a new friendly feeling. Faraway Island would meet with no roar of laughter here.

'I couldn't remember anything about your uncle at first,' said the Commander. 'But after a time I did. I can't think why he remembered me. I did do some little thing for him, but it was nothing much, the sort of thing you'd do for any decent fellow-countryman.'

'Well, it must have impressed him,' said William. 'I'd better tell you all about it.' He told the story of his uncle's visit and illness, of the island and its pitchblende, of the latitude and longitude and P. T. Riley of San Francisco, to all of which the Commander listened in silence. When William had done, the Commander rose abruptly out of his chair.

'It's a fine morning,' he said, glancing at the window. 'Let's go out. I can talk better outside. Do you mind?'

'I'd prefer it,' said William. 'Let's walk round and then

end up at my hotel, the *Lugmouth Packet*, and then we could have lunch there.'

The Commander thanked him gravely. They walked slowly along the terrace, and it was very pleasant in the mild sunlight, with the whole estuary shining mistily before them. To be strolling like this on a morning in December was in itself something of an adventure to William, who was now gathering confidence every hour.

'This pitchblende stuff,' said the Commander slowly, 'is it all right? I know what it is, of course. I've read about radium.'

'I've got the actual piece in my bag at the hotel,' William told him. 'I'll show it to you. It's real enough. The first thing I did, of course, before I tried to get into touch with you, was to have it tested.'

'Quite right,' the Commander murmured.

'I went to the Radium Institute and had it tested there. They were very curious about it, but I didn't tell them anything. There's no doubt about it being the genuine stuff. And my uncle swore there was any amount of it, tons and tons and tons, just waiting to be picked up and carted away.'

The Commander gave a long soft whistle. 'It's an astonishing yarn,' he began.

'You believe it, don't you?' cried William anxiously.

'Yes, I do. It's reasonable there should be such an island. I know myself the charts haven't got every island yet. But other people may have found this particular island, since your uncle was there.'

'I've thought of that,' replied William. 'It's quite likely that lots of people have seen it or even landed on it, since my uncle was there. But I don't think that matters very much. What isn't likely is that they've noticed the pitchblende. To begin with, the pitchblende is some way inland, my uncle told me, and there's nothing about the island to tempt people to explore it. Then again, even if somebody did come across the pitchblende, it's very unlikely they would know what it was or even be curious about it. It looks very dull stuff.'

The Commander considered this carefully. He had the slow brooding habit of a man who has lived much alone. 'I certainly think you might risk that,' he announced, speaking very deliberately. 'If anybody had actually removed the ore, we should probably have heard about it now. I think that's fairly certain.'

'What if—' cried William, nearly running into a perambulator, of which there were many abroad that morning. 'Sorry! I was going to say – what if somebody's on Faraway Island this minute, looking at all that black stuff, and saying, "Yes, that's pitchblende all right. Get the men up to-morrow and we'll start clearing it away"! That's a horrible thought.'

'Not having second sight, I can't help you there. That's a risk you have to take.'

William corrected him. 'You mean, a risk *we* have to take. Don't forget, you're in this, just as much as I am.'

The Commander stopped and looked thoughtful. 'What – because your uncle gave me the longitude? But you must know what it is, because it was you who sent on the letter to me.'

'I don't know what it is. I sent on the letter without looking at it. I thought it was the only fair way of doing it.'

The Commander gave him a quick friendly glance. 'So it was, but not everybody nowadays would see it in that light.' He fixed those clear blue eyes of his on William's face. They were now standing at the corner of the terrace. 'It's my turn now, then. The longitude of your island is one hundred and twelve degrees thirty-six minutes West. Don't forget. One hundred and twelve degrees thirty-six minutes West.'

'But you mustn't give it to me like that,' cried William. 'Not before we've come to some agreement. Don't you see, I might go away now, knowing the longitude, and you might never hear of me again?'

'No, you won't do that,' said the Commander, smiling. 'You're not that kind of man. If you had been, you wouldn't have sent me the letter. I told you the longitude in return for your having sent me the letter without looking at it. We don't need all these complications.'

Here they were interrupted by an elderly man with a mahogany face, a very large nose, and a very fierce manner. He pounced upon the Commander as if he was about to arrest him. 'Morning,' he snapped, still grasping the Commander's arm. 'Is it next Tuesday or Wednesday we're going up there?'

'Morning, Cap'n,' said the Commander, not at all disturbed. 'I said we'd go up on Tuesday. That's all right, isn't it?'

'Scrumdoolious!' replied the fierce Captain, to William's delight and astonishment. 'I wanted to know because if we're going there on Tuesday, I'll go to Plymouth on Wednesday. And when I do go, I'll tell those brainless apes something.' He now became fiercer and fiercer. 'And – by God – would you believe it? – I've had a letter this morning from some gutless ninny of a clerk attached to the Liverpool Chamber of Commerce, and he says I don't know what I'm talking about – or if he doesn't say it, he means it. And that's all the satisfaction I shall get there. Then people wonder why this country's going to pot! Who's your friend?'

'Sorry! Mr. Dursley – Cap'n Stapledon,' the Commander muttered, in the usual manner.

'Glad to know you,' said Captain Stapledon, grabbing hold of William's hand and then shaking it violently. 'Staying here?'

'I may be here a few days,' said William.

'Come and see me. Number thirty-two, along there. Cap'n Stapledon. Glad to talk to a sensible man any time. I'm spending two-thirds of my time, these days, writing and talking to the biggest nincompoops that God or the devil ever cursed this island with. I tell you, they're enough to make a man lie down on his head and die – out o' sheer misery at the thought of 'em. Members of Parliament? I've talked to dozens. They've never done any thinking and if they had to start now, it 'ud hurt 'em like hell. Chambers of Commerce? D'you think a man can get any satisfaction out o' them? Don't make me laugh,' the Captain roared, to the whole terrace. 'I say, don't make me laugh. If I've written to one, I've written to twenty. Chairmen of banks, what about them?' He stopped now, and looked at William so hard that William felt embarrassed.

'Chairmen of banks, eh?' said the Commander, encouragingly.

'Now I don't say *they're* damned silly. They're not. What I say about them is – they're damned artful. I write to 'em. Do they answer? *Do they answer?*' Here the Captain produced the most sardonic and hollow laugh William ever remembered hearing. 'They don't answer. I challenge 'em, I challenge in a style to make a man's blood boil – I insult 'em. They sit tight and say nothing. They know when they're all right. "Damn you, Jack, I'm all right," that's what *they* say. You and me and the Commander here and that chap going down the road there –

we can all turn our pockets out and scratch our heads and wonder where the next bob's coming from, and the country can go to pot – but they're all right, or they think they are – *they think they are*. That's so, isn't it?'

William nodded, and hoped this would pacify the fierce old man, who appeared to be conducting some mysterious campaign.

'You come round and see me,' he continued, in a quieter tone. 'Number thirty-two. And I'll give you something to think about until you do come. It's this – what'ud happen in this country if we adopted the silver crown, the old five-shilling piece, as the basis of our currency? Don't say anything now. Just think that over. Glad to know you. Morning. Morning, Commander. See you on Wednesday. No, Tuesday. That's right – Tuesday. See you then, if not before.' And off he went, walking at a tremendous pace.

'I think we'll go across the beach and then round,' said the Commander, moving off. 'We'll just get back in time for lunch. What did you think of Stapledon?'

'He's a very queer old chap, isn't he?'

'Very. He's an old retired merchant skipper – great sailor in his time, I believe – and lots of them get eccentric like that. They've had to spend so much time alone. Poor old Stapledon's a bit cracked now. But there's no harm in him. He's a splendid old chap.'

'Is this campaign of his connected with the five-shilling piece?'

The Commander laughed. 'That's it. He believes that if we make the five-shilling piece the basis of our money, we can pay our debts in no time and increase our trade and work wonders all round. He's explained it all to me dozens of times, but I must say, I can't make head or tail of it. Neither can anyone else, but he goes on writing to people explaining it. He and I go fishing together sometimes. That's what he meant about Tuesday. I don't mind him. In fact, I like him. If you keep off five-shilling pieces and chambers of commerce and banking, you couldn't want a better fellow.'

'Probably we're all a bit mad really,' said William cheerfully. 'Lots of people would think I was crazy if they knew I was leaving a decent business to look for this island.'

'But you're not giving up your business, are you?'

'No, actually I'm not. In fact, I know very well that it can get on without me, if necessary for a year or two.'

'That's all right then,' said the Commander. 'But you talk about *looking* for this island?'

'Of course I'm going to look for it,' cried William. 'I hope we're all going to look for it. Even if we made some money out of it, there wouldn't be much fun just telling some company that there was pitchblende on a certain island in a certain latitude and longitude. And we shouldn't make anything like the amount of money out of it that way as we should if we did it all ourselves.'

'But where do I come into this?' the Commander asked, looking puzzled. 'I've no claim.'

'Of course you have. You've as much as I have. Don't you see there are three of us who've got equal claims? You and I and this P. T. Riley of San Francisco. We're the three that my uncle wanted to share in this thing. He made that perfectly plain. We have equal shares. And the only way to do it is to go and find the island first, to make sure that the pitchblende is really there. After that, we can arrange to have it removed, and then sell it to some company ready to manufacture radium, or to form some new company.'

'I see,' said the Commander slowly. By the time he spoke again, they had crossed the little headland, leaving

the harbour and estuary behind, and had arrived at the
edge of the open sea. They walked down to the pebbled
beach, which was strewn with great clumps of seaweed,
twisted roots and enormous rubbery ribbons of it lying
there in the sun, filling the air with its peculiarly salty
fishy savour. William sniffed appreciatively, and his gaze
swept the horizon, a pale mystery of foam and sunlight,
where the moving ships were only tiny fading shadows.
Only a few hundred yards away, just beyond the glistening
rocks, the tide poured itself smoothly over a rusty thing
on which the gulls rested between their short screaming
flights. On that piece of battered iron, William's glance
remained, turning itself into a speculative stare.

'U-boat,' the Commander explained. 'There are two
more just down there.' He pointed to the right.

William nodded and moved a few yards nearer the
water. For a few minutes he lost himself in a huge dim
reverie, through which he saw, like a man in a dream,
the changing sheen and glitter of the sea, and heard the
melancholy music of the shore, the long hiss of the
spreading wave and the roll of the pebbles. When he
turned at last, to meet the enquiring glance of the Commander, it was as if he had come back from a long, long
journey. He did not feel quite the same man. He was not
so eager, perhaps not so hopeful, as he had been before,
yet he was far more confident. He felt he was ready to
go anywhere and to do anything. Somehow, during that
reverie, he had enlisted and had volunteered for the
front. The sea, old and careless, spawning lives by the
million million, had apparently contrived to challenge
that other life, that life of the impulsive and militant
spirit, that life in which the soul of man knew itself, that
glorious lost cause in the universe. William had taken up
the challenge. Perhaps the draughts of strong salt air were

too much for him: he felt almost drunk. He turned to his companion, poised by his side in this grey gleaming bubble of earth, sea and sky, and held out a hand.

'Commander Ivybridge,' he cried earnestly, 'you and I must go ourselves and find that island. We *must*. Let's shake hands on it.'

They shook hands on it. But the Commander seemed troubled, and he frowned a little and bit his lip.

William felt rather foolish now. 'He's probably thinking I'm a terrible ass,' he told himself. 'These naval men have very fixed ideas. Good form and all that. He may have decided that he couldn't go ten miles with a man like me. He looked surprised when I insisted upon shaking hands. Why the devil did I want to shake hands? I must be cool and business-like now.' He looked at his watch. 'Hadn't we better be getting back?' he enquired.

'I don't see that you can make any definite plan,' said the Commander, as they turned away from the beach, 'until you've heard something from the fellow who has the latitude – the San Francisco man.'

'P. T. Riley,' said William. 'That's true. I keep forgetting him. I think he might be the snag. The name annoys me somehow. P. T. Riley. He's probably a typical retired American business man, who'll want to sell out the whole thing at once to some company, if he can find a company to listen to him. I must confess I've never bothered much about his part in it.'

'How did he come to have a part in it?'

'I told you all I knew about him,' William replied. 'He comes into it just as you do. He did my uncle a good turn once. He was an agent for some American firm in the South Seas.'

'He might easily be a very good chap,' said the Commander. 'If he was doing that sort of job, he'd hardly be a typical American business man. You wouldn't call your uncle a typical English business man, would you?'

William laughed. 'Hardly. My uncle wasn't a typical anything. He was a character. Perhaps his friend P. T. Riley's a character, too.'

'Like Captain Stapledon,' the Commander suggested.

'Now he'd be a man to go looking for an island with,' cried William. 'Even if he is a bit cracked, I'd go with him like a shot.'

'So would I,' said the Commander. 'And so would he. I mean, he'd go anywhere and join in anything.'

'It's simply P. T. Riley's name and address that put me off,' said William reflectively. 'But I shall have to be doing something about him soon. Obviously, I can't leave him out of it.'

'No, you can't do that. Even if you knew the latitude, you couldn't do that. It wouldn't be fair.'

'I agree. And without the latitude, I don't see that we can even begin making any plans. The island might be anywhere along that longitude.'

'No, it's not so bad as that,' said the Commander slowly. 'Evidently you haven't looked it up on the map.'

'How could I,' cried William, breaking in, 'when I've only just learned the longitude this morning?'

'Of course. Sorry.' The Commander walked on in silence for a few moments, then continued, in a more zestful tone than William had noticed in his voice before: 'Yesterday, I looked it up. Couldn't resist it, you know. Well, if you look up longitude one hundred and twelve degrees thirty-six minutes West, you'll find it runs down from Lower California – that long narrow peninsula on the West Coast of Mexico – to the Antarctic. If you're looking for an island on that longitude, you haven't the whole western hemisphere to choose from, not a bit of it.'

'Well, my uncle admitted that the island was in the South Pacific,' said William.

'I didn't know that yesterday,' said the Commander, smiling. 'But if you look at the map, you'll see that with that longitude the chances are that it would be in the South Pacific, assuming that your uncle wasn't an Antarctic explorer. If he said it was in the South Pacific, we can take it that the island lies between the equator and forty degrees south. It could be further south than that, but it isn't likely, because your uncle wouldn't have been going that way, unless he was sailing right round the Horn. You've heard of Easter Island, haven't you?'

'I should think I have,' cried William. 'You mean the island that has all the huge mysterious statues on it. I've been fascinated for years by that island. There's one of the statues just outside the entrance to the British Museum, brooding away there in Bloomsbury. He gives you a look every time you go in or out of the Museum. But don't tell me that Easter Island comes into this!'

The Commander laughed. 'I've always been an Easter Island enthusiast, too. It's a place I've always wanted to visit. But I mentioned Easter Island because it has nearly the same longitude. Easter Island is one hundred and nine degrees something West, and your island is one hundred and twelve degrees thirty-six minutes West. The latitude, of course, may be twenty degrees different.'

This information excited William. 'You mean, Faraway is somewhere near Easter Island?'

'It depends what you mean by "near",' replied the Commander, somewhat dryly. 'We can't tell until we know the latitude, but I imagine that your island is probably within a thousand miles of Easter Island.'

'Oh!' William's voice went sliding down the scale. A thousand miles seemed to him an enormous distance. They were now out of sight of the open sea, back in Market Street among the chemists' shops and circulating libraries; and Market Street made a thousand miles seem a colossal distance.

'You sound disappointed,' said the Commander, smiling. 'But I assure you, a thousand miles is quite a neighbourly distance in that part of the world. We can't talk here, though. I'll explain later what I'm getting at.' They were threading their way through the shoppers and idlers whose presence crowded the narrow pavement. They said no more until they reached the hotel.

'Would you like to come upstairs and have a wash,' said William, 'and see that piece of pitchblende, a genuine bit of Faraway Island?'

Which seemed to him, on reflection, the most astonishing invitation he had ever issued to anybody in all his life. Together they climbed the dreary stairs of the *Lugmouth Packet.* Family and Commercial indeed!

5

It was not until they reached the lounge, after lunch, that they began talking seriously again. William had discovered an old atlas among the bound volumes of the *Stock and Market Record,* and they looked at it together in the big bay window.

'You see what I mean?' said the Commander, pointing a long brown finger at the faded ocean and the tiny blurred islands. 'If you're going to find the island yourself, your best plan is to get as near to it as possible in the

ordinary way, and then to charter a trading schooner to
take you to it.'

William nodded, though he could no more imagine
himself chartering a trading schooner than he could see
himself leading an expedition across central Greenland.

'Unless the latitude is wildly different from anything
we expect,' the Commander continued, still with his
finger on the map, 'the place you'll have to make for first
is Tahiti.'

'Tahiti?' cried William, his mind crowded at once with
highly coloured South Sea Island stuff.

'Yes. Papeete – that's the town – must be the place of
any size nearest to your island.'

'Good!' cried William. 'Very good!' These geographical
details were going to his head.

'In Papeete, you ought to be able to pick up a schooner
that will take you to the island. You'll have to charter it
specially. That will cost a certain amount of money, of
course, and afterwards, if you find the pitchblende there
and begin removing it, you will find that a very expensive
business, even with Kanaka labour. But you've thought
about all that, of course.'

'Some of it,' replied William cheerfully. 'But wait a
minute. There's something that's worrying me all the time
– you know, like a fly buzzing about at the back of my
head. I know what it is.' He looked gravely at the Commander. 'Why do you keep saying *your* island and *you*
ought to do this and that? You talk as if you had nothing
to do with it. It's your island as much as it's mine, and
you're in the thing just as much as I am. You should say
– Tahiti's the best place for *us*, and *we* are going to charter
a schooner there.'

The Commander smiled, then shook his head. 'Sorry.
Not me.'

William stared at him. 'Do you mean to say you're not going to help me to find it?'

''Fraid so.'

'Why? Don't you believe in the island or the pitch-blende or anything?'

The Commander looked straight at him. 'Yes, I do. I believe it's just possible someone else may have got there first, but when one considers what there is at stake, that seems to me a very small risk.'

'That's a relief,' cried William. 'But I don't understand. Why don't you want to join in? Don't you – er' – he hesitated a moment, then rushed to his destruction – 'feel up to it?'

'What the devil do you mean?' cried the Commander, snorting. 'Feel up to it? I feel up to anything. You talk as if I were an old man.' The Commander was really annoyed, and the single eye visible to William was glacial.

William, alarmed and contrite, floundered into vague but sincere apology. 'I thought perhaps you weren't keen on leaving England,' he concluded. 'After all, you're not like me. I've been stuck in England most of my life, but you must have spent years and years away, and I thought perhaps you'd had enough of it.'

The Commander took several deep pulls at his pipe, blew out a lot of smoke, and recovered his temper. 'That's true enough. I've spent years and years out of England, and there's no place like England – not for an English-man. It's the best country in the world to live in, even now it is, when everything's changing and going wrong. But I don't mind leaving England for a time. Why should I?' He took out his pipe, then turned sharply. 'Do you know what it's like being retired, with nothing to do and with very little money? I'll tell you. It's damnable. You feel yourself rusting away. Never try it.' Having shot out these sudden confidences, he immediately stiffened, looked away, and almost gave the impression that he had never spoken to William in his life.

William saw that if there was to be any more talk between them, the subject would have to be changed at once. Fortunately, there was an important one to hand. P. T. Riley. 'If I can send a cable from here to Riley, I'm going to do so,' William declared. 'I'll do it this afternoon, and ask him to cable back here at once.'

'What are you going to say to him? You can't explain everything in a cable.'

'I hadn't thought of that,' William admitted. He thought hard for a moment or two. 'I can tell him it's really important, a sort of treasure island – he knows that much, because my uncle must have told him in the letter – worth a fortune, and then I can ask him to let me know how he feels about joining in and letting us have the latitude. Something like that.'

The Commander stared out of the window at the harbour and kept up a regular puff-puff-puff with his pipe. Finally, he said abruptly: 'Was your idea that the three of us, you and I and this Riley, should have equal shares—'

'But of course,' William interrupted.

'Yes, yes, but I haven't finished yet. Was it your idea that the three of us should share equally with the expense too?'

'More or less,' I suppose,' said William vaguely. 'I thought we could each stand our own expenses for the first trip to the island—'

'Which would probably cost more than you imagine,' the Commander pointed out. 'You have to get to the South Seas, find your schooner or whatever it is, and then perhaps sail three thousand miles in it, there and back.'

'Well, I thought we'd manage that all right between

us,' William continued. 'And then afterwards, when it came to removing the stuff, I thought we'd have to try and work out what it would cost, and if we couldn't raise the money between us, we'd then have to borrow some capital or bring a rich partner into the concern. But there's plenty of time to bother about that.'

The Commander stood up, moved stiffly forward a pace or two to the window, then turned round to face his companion. 'You see,' he began abruptly, 'I can't do it. That's what I meant. I doubt if I could raise my passage to Tahiti. I certainly couldn't do my share in the charter. I've been rather unlucky lately.'

'Oh, but we could arrange about that,' cried William hastily. 'There wouldn't be any difficulty about that.'

'Thanks. I know what you mean. But it wouldn't work.' The Commander shut his mouth, tightened his lips, and focused his wintry blue eyes on some part of the opposite wall. Now, apparently, it was his turn to think hard. It was some time before he spoke. When he did speak, his eyes looked straight into William's, and William's eyes, faced with this Arctic glare, began to water a little. 'There's a man here,' the Commander began, 'a visitor, and I've seen a good deal of him. He's a queer chap, and I didn't take to him at first. I like him now, though. He's a business man, and quite straight. D'you mind if I tell him some of this?'

William hesitated.

'All right, if you don't want me to, I won't,' said the Commander.

'No, no,' cried William. 'You do. Only I was thinking that you'd better leave the pitchblende part out of it.'

'I intended to do that. But I have an idea. There may be nothing in it. I'm seeing this man to-night, and I'd

like to say something to him about this business. You're
sure you don't mind?'

'Quite sure. I'll begin thinking about that cable now.'

'Thanks for the excellent lunch,' said the Commander,
with a slight smile. 'You're staying on here for a day or
two, of course?'

William nodded. He gave a quick glance round the
room. There was nobody in it but the two of them, standing there in the window, with a vague treasure island
floating somewhere over their heads. 'I hope I may be
able to see you again in the morning,' he said. Then he
added, with more earnestness than he had shown before:
'But tell me this before you go, Commander. Do you want
to join in this business? Do you want to go and find this
island?'

Instantly, all traces of winter vanished from the other's
face. The boy who had lived on in the Commander leaped
up and set fire to the man. 'I'll tell you,' he cried, with a
little hoarseness in his voice. 'There's nothing in the
world I'd like better. It's like – ah, well – you wouldn't
understand. You haven't been stuck on a shelf yet.'

'We're going,' William announced.

CHAPTER III

THE PARTNERS

1

'HERE YOU are,' said the Commander. 'You got my chit?'

'Yes,' replied William.

'But that's a silly question, isn't it, because you wouldn't be here if you hadn't got my chit,' the Commander observed, smiling.

'That's true,' said William, also smiling.

'He'll be along in a minute,' the Commander continued. 'He had to run away.'

The Commander referred to his friend, the visitor whose acquaintance he had made in his walks along the sea-front. This man, whose name was still unknown to William, had invited them both to dinner at his hotel, the *Lugmouth Hotel*, the big place near the station, so new, so white, so brittle, that it looked not unlike a colossal wedding cake. William and the Commander were standing in the entrance lounge, which was filled with palms in tubs, fat chairs, tables covered with beaten copper, and the other appointments that accompany an American Bar, Ballroom, and Permanent Resident Orchestra.

'I hope you didn't mind being asked up here,' the Commander said, after a little hesitation. 'I saw him last night, and I said something about this business of ours – though I couldn't tell him much, of course – and he was very curious, and insisted on our both coming here to dine with him to-night. He's rather a queer chap – I think I told you that yesterday, though—'

'Yes, you did. But you said you liked him, I remember, so that's all right. But do you think I can tell him – well, all about it?'

The Commander looked thoughtful. 'You'll see. He's very keen to know, and I'm sure he's a straight fellow. He's a business man, too, and I know he has money to invest in anything that amuses him. He told me so, last night. It would make all the difference to me if he could come in. But we can talk about that later. No time to explain now. He's coming now.'

William saw a stout man of about fifty approaching them. He was very broad and heavy, but nevertheless he seemed to bounce along. As he drew nearer, he beamed upon them. His rimless spectacles glittered with a jovial recognition. His clean-shaven face, almost as wide and flat as a dinner-plate, shone with his appreciation of this happy moment. Introduced as Mr. Ramsbottom, he shook William's hand with enthusiasm.

'Very pleased to meet you,' he cried, stepping back and looking at William with the greatest interest, as if William's whole appearance was both remarkable and beautiful. 'It's good of you to come. It is. It's good of you. And don't mind me, Mr. Dursley. Ah'm Lancasheer, you see – a Lanc'sher lad, if you like – and Ah say what Ah think and it all comes out, like emptying a chest o' drawers – and you mustn't mind me. That's right, isn't it, Commander? Well, we're all here.' Then suddenly his enormous smile vanished, and he looked earnestly from one to the other. 'Mr. Dursley, Commander, you'll both take a drop o' something before we start? What's it to be? Cocktail or drop o' sherry or what?'

'I don't think I want anything, thanks,' said William.

'Nay, you must have something,' cried Mr. Ramsbottom reproachfully. 'So must you, Commander. 'Ere, Albert—' and he called a waiter, to whom they were compelled to give an order.

'Do you know that waiter, too?' asked the Commander.

'Who, him? Yes, Ah know him. Albert, his name is. Only been 'ere a week. He used to be at the Metro. at Blackpool, Albert did. Ah knew him well there. You ask him. He's got a little girl that's won five prizes with the concertina, and she's going on the stage with it. He was telling all about her yesterday. Ah'll tell you her name in a minute.' Mr. Ramsbottom tried to think of her name, but catching sight of the Commander's smile, he laughed and then turned to William. 'He laughs at me 'cos Ah know all about everybody, but Ah say – damn it all, if you're stopping at a place you might as well know the other folk and Ah don't care a brass button whether they're waiters or barmaids or what they are so long as they've got a civil tongue in their heads. And if it hadn't been for the staff 'ere, Ah'd have gone days and days dumb and speechless.'

'Have you been here long?' asked William.

'Nearly two months,' replied Mr. Ramsbottom, looking solemn. 'Ah came for my 'ealth. Doctor told me to come 'ere. Ah'd two doctors and a specialist.' At this moment, the waiter arrived with the drinks, and Mr. Ramsbottom immediately sat up and became bustling and genial again. 'Well, 'ere we are, gentlemen. That's yours, Mr. Dursley. That's yours, Commander. Well, 'ere's the best. That's good stoof.' He smacked his thick lips appreciatively, nodded his head, and beamed at them through his glasses. 'Now what was Ah talking about?'

'You were talking about your health,' William prompted.

'So Ah was.' And instantly Mr. Ramsbottom began to

droop and dwindle; the light faded from his eyes; his cheeks fell in; his whole figure sagged; he was a sick man. 'Well, Ah'd two doctors and a specialist. Ah couldn't eat and Ah couldn't sleep. Dizziness, too – oh dear, awful dizziness! And Ah'd a pain in my back – just round there – no, a bit lower down – there – oh, dear, dear, dear, Ah didn't know what to do with myself half the time. Chaps I knew in business or at club said to me, "Nay, Johnny Ramsbottom, you're looking bad." And Ah told 'em. Ah said: "Ay, an' Ah'm feeling bad." Couldn't eat, couldn't sleep, couldn't attend to my business properly. Ah'd got a buzzing in my 'ead like a circular saw. And trouble with my bladder, too – on the run every ten minutes. Ah said to myself, "If this goes on, Ah might as well hand my checks in. Life's not worth living." Mind you, Ah'd always had a bit o' bother with my inside. Anyhow, Ah went to one doctor, and he says, "It's your kidneys. That's what's wrong with you – your kidneys." Wait a minute. Dinner's up. We might as well go and peck a bit.'

On their way to the dining-room, Mr. Ramsbottom continued his recital, and without troubling to lower his voice. 'Well, Ah went to another doctor, and he said, "Ah'm sorry to say, Mr. Ramsbottom, it's your heart that's at fault." Ah wasn't surprised either, 'cos Ah'd always had an idea my heart wasn't all it should be. Ah'd noticed it knocking a bit for years, you might say. However, Ah saw a specialist too, best man in Manchester, and he pretended to make light of it, and he sent me to Harrogate first, and then when Ah went back, he told me to get some medicine to take, put me on a diet, and said if Ah could afford it Ah'd to knock off business for a year or so and get out o' Manchester and find some fresh air. Then Ah went back to my own doctor, and he said come down 'ere. So Ah did.'

'I hope you're feeling better now,' said William politely.

Mr. Ramsbottom halted at the dining-room door to give this question his full attention. 'Well, am Ah? It's a question, that. In a way Ah am, Ah dare say. Ah've lost that buzziness and dizziness and Ah eat and sleep better, but Ah'm not right, you know – oh dear no! Ah'm not right, and Ah never will be. Ah'll have to look after my inside. An' Ah still get that pain i' my back. Just a sharp twinge, you know, Mr. Dursley, a right sharp twinge now and again, like as if somebody might be running a red-hot knitting-needle into me. Excuse me a minute.' He turned aside, in the dining-room, to greet three melancholy girls in black, who evidently constituted the Permanent Resident Orchestra. They smiled at him wanly above their instruments. The pianist was arranging some music, and the violinist and the 'cellist were tuning up. It was the 'cellist, the most melancholy of the melancholy trio, whom Mr. Ramsbottom addressed.

'Have you heard from your mother, Miss Grierson?' he enquired.

'I had a letter to-day, thank you, Mr. Ramsbottom,' replied the sad musician. 'She's a bit better, but she'll have to spend another fortnight in bed.'

'That's nothing so long as she's better,' cried Mr. Ramsbottom. 'Is it now? A fair answer to a fair question. No, of course it isn't. You tell her from me to sit up and get some good stoof into her, Miss Grierson. And play us a few nice pieces to-night. Do your best.'

After this short exchange, he led the way down the room, which was large and nearly empty, to a table set for three near the fire.

'Didn't know you knew the orchestra too, Ramsbottom,' said the Commander, as they sat down.

'Oh yes, know 'em well by this time. Ah know all the

pieces they play too, which is a pity. Ah'm getting a bit
sick of most of 'em. That's Miss Grierson Ah was talking
to, and her mother's poorly. She's been upset about it.
She comes from just outside Birmingham, and she's a
nice quiet girl, though she can't play that 'cello for toffy.
You listen when they start. She gets so far off the note
sometimes it brings tears to your eyes, like eating little
green gooseberries. She's got no more ear than this table.
What d'you think of the table? Done it nicely for us,
haven't they? Ah told 'em Ah wanted it special tonight.
And they're cooking a special dinner, too. They're careful
what they give me now, Ah can tell you, Mr. Dursley.
Commander knows all about that, don't you?'

'I do,' said the Commander, suddenly producing fifty
more fine little wrinkles round his eyes. 'Ramsbottom
here is a great authority on food. He's an epicure, a
gourmet.'

'Nay, Ah don't say that. But Ah do like good stoof.
Ah've always been used to good stoof, and Ah know it
when Ah see it and taste it, which is more than most
people do. And Ah'm partly in the business, you
know – 'cos Ah'm a wholesale grocer – and Ah take an
interest in what Ah eat and drink. First two days Ah was
'ere, Ah just tasted what they gave me and said nothing.
Then Ah went to see the manager. "Ah'm stopping 'ere
some time," Ah told him. "Ah know you are, Mr. Ramsbottom," he said. "But Ah'm not stopping another day if you
don't give me better stoof to eat," Ah told him. "Why,
what d'you mean?" he said. "We only use the best provisions, and our kitchen has a very good name." This
made me laugh. "If you believe that," Ah told him, "then
somebody's cheating you." He stared at me. "What's
wrong with it?" he said. "Oh, Ah'll tell you," Ah said. And
Ah did. Ah told him, to start with, the bread was poor

quality, too much alum and potato in the flour, and they'd been putting a lot of margarine in his butter, and selling him the cheapest coffee on the market. Ah told him if they were going to get their soup out of tins, they'd better get some better brands, and Ah said they'd been using some bad fat in the kitchen and didn't seem over-particular about cleaning the pans, and that bits o' rock salmon shouldn't be called sole, and that their prime English beef must have been kidnapped and sent round the world because it had just been frozen. "And that cake you serve with afternoon tea," Ah told him. "If you're paying more than sevenpence a pound for that, you're being swindled." "Ridiculous," he said. "Ah'd like to see you buy cake like that at sevenpence a pound." "Oh you would, would you?" Ah said. "Well, Ah can let you have as much as you like of cake that quality at sixpence a pound, and Ah'll book the order now – much as you like. Only don't offer it to me at teatime, 'cos Ah don't eat stoof like that – it's muck. Ah like good stoof," Ah told him. "And you can't diddle me, Ah know too much about it." And Ah've not done badly since. They look after me. The dinner you're going to have now mightn't look as good on paper as the one they're offering everybody. But don't you believe it. It'll be plain and simple, but it'll be all good stoof, something to nourish you.'

William, staring at Mr. Ramsbottom's great flat face and bursting shoulders, thought that nourishment was the last thing his host needed. He said nothing, being busy wondering, not without awe, what would happen if Mr. Ramsbottom suddenly found himself grappling with the food at the *Lugmouth Packet*. Dare he ask him to a meal there? The idea fascinated him. He had a vision of Mr. Ramsbottom, a knight-errant of 'good stoof,' bearding the gloomy manageress in her cabbage-haunted cave.

Meanwhile, the dinner they were eating proved that Mr. Ramsbottom was not merely boasting. It was plain, but it was undeniably good stuff.

'That's the trouble nowadays,' Mr. Ramsbottom observed, with the curious self-satisfaction that always accompanies this sort of statement; as if the speaker had been personally responsible for the Past, but had not been allowed to have any hand in shaping the Present. 'You can't get good stoof. There's many an old working chap up in Lancashire or Yorkshire who's getting better stoof to eat than your millionaires. And why? Because he's got a wife who does everything herself and sees that he still gets some good stoof. Money won't buy it, unless you're taking trouble as well. Ah know. You'd be surprised. You know the Colossal Luxurious Hotel in the West End? All right. Well, you get good stoof there, don't you?'

'Yes, I suppose so,' said William, who had never been in the Colossal Luxurious.

'Well, you don't then. It's all fancy and lah-di-dah, and maybe it looks well, but there isn't any good stoof in it. Ah wouldn't be paid to go and eat there – Ah wouldn't, Ah wouldn't be paid. Give me two tea-cakes – not the bits o' things you get down 'ere, but two proper big home-made tea-cakes – and some fresh butter, and a pot of tea that's mashed in the right way, with water just come to the boil and in a clean fresh teapot – give me that, and you've given me a meal Ah'd rather sit down to than anything they do at the Colossal Luxurious. And why? Because it'ud be all good stoof.'

William would have liked to have asked this enthusiast for pure wholesome food how he came to be so elaborately wrong in his inside, but he had not the courage. Mr. Ramsbottom's large face, which at this moment was beaming and glistening, was certainly not that of a healthy man: it was too pasty and oily and sweaty. In truth, he was not a very prepossessing personage; and William was not sure that he liked the man's rather dominating manner and loud flat voice. Yet there *was* something likable about him, William decided. His immense gusto had an infectious quality, and though there might be a glimmer of folly in everything he did or said, yet he was obviously no fool. He prided himself on knowing a great many facts about this world, and he did not do this without reason. Thus, later in the dinner, he learned that William was in the malting business, and immediately he began talking about malting in a very knowing fashion, so that William could not fail to be impressed. What was more important, however, was the stout man's enormous fund, or rather his flood or volcanic eruption, of good humour, which was not something negative, a mere absence of bad temper or intolerance, but a positive force, a huge drive of well-wishing. The eyes behind the rimless spectacles shone and flashed with kindness. William, like many shy, reserved, and scrupulously sincere persons, was apt to feel a certain resentment against these large, affable, easily dominating personalities, and he was quick to tell himself that one can soon have too much of these shining eyes, these beaming faces, these great warm baths of kindness; yet in spite of this, and in spite of his instinctive distaste for Mr. Ramsbottom's person and manner, William could not help liking him. And he was a friend, or at least a very friendly acquaintance, of the Commander. A very queer pair they made, too; the Commander so taut and trim, if shabby, so quiet, so frosty-eyed, a figure from long years of discipline and keen weather; and Mr. Ramsbottom, so large and loose, sedentary, so loud-tongued, impudent, and genial. It was difficult to believe that they were willing to go adventuring together. But were they?

And was William himself ready to agree that they should? He asked himself these questions, but allowed the dinner to end before he tried to find any answers to them.

2

'We'll 'ave our coffee in the Smoke-Room,' Mr. Ramsbottom announced. 'Though why Ah go to a smoke-room, Ah don't know, 'cos Ah don't smoke. No, Ah don't smoke – never got into it somehow, and Ah don't want to start now. Spoils your taste, you know, Mr. Dursley – oh yes, spoils your taste all right, smoking. 'Owever, that's about only vice Ah haven't got, so you needn't worry. But let's go in. You chaps'll want to smoke, and Ah've got a cigar or two that won't bite you.'

As William followed the other two into the Smoke-Room and settled himself with them in a corner there, he felt as if he had known them both for years. Their faces, their figures, their speech, took on the semblance of an inevitable familiarity. It was very odd. He had made the acquaintance of one of them only yesterday morning, and of the other only an hour and a half ago, and he had to confess to himself that he knew little or nothing about them; yet there it was, they had quietly stepped into some place that appeared to have been prepared for them years ago. So strong was this feeling that William wondered if he had dreamt about them. Some people thought you caught glimpses of the future in the ghostly confusion of dreams. Perhaps he had talked to the Commander and listened to Mr. Ramsbottom many a time before. And the island itself, was that really new? Had there not been an island before, nothing solidly geographical, of course, not a place you could recognise perhaps, only a shadow on a veil and seas breaking in an inland night, yet an island? Had they all three been there already? Was this only a slower and chunkier repetition of an adventure through which he had floated before, between dull days in the malting-house? Absurd. He stared at his two companions and told himself again that it was absurd. But then something occurred that turned his backbone into a fiddle-string and brought a huge spectral hand to pluck it. *The three of them sitting on a rock, very hard, hot, jagged, talking earnestly.* It had happened somewhere, and now he remembered it. That was why it seemed so inevitable to be talking to these two, and why all strangeness departed from them so swiftly. And the rock was there, he could swear to the rock. The hand plucked the fiddle-string again; his bones melted; his flesh crept; and he stood for a moment in a world of ghosts, in which Time merely juggled with diaphanous curtains and dissolving views.

'What did you say?' he cried apologetically. 'I'm sorry – I was day-dreaming for a minute.' But he was back again now in a corner of the Smoke-Room of the *Lugmouth Hotel.*

'Ah was just saying,' said Mr. Ramsbottom, 'we'd better 'ave a bit of a talk about this business of yours, if you've no objection.'

'No, of course not,' said William, though he hesitated a moment.

Mr. Ramsbottom noticed the hesitation. 'Well, it's bit ticklish, Ah dare say. It always is in these circumstances, 'cos you see, Ah can't say anything till Ah know what it's all about, and you don't want to say much till you know it's safe. That's it, isn't it? Oh, it's happened to me before.'

The Commander suddenly got up. 'Look here, you fellows,' he said abruptly, 'I'm going to leave you alone for an hour, or the rest of the evening, just as you please. I've got a letter I want to get off.'

'What is it now?' said Mr. Ramsbottom. 'Quarter-past nine. All right, Commander, you go and look after your letter, but come back again in an hour. There's plenty of time.'

The Commander nodded, gave William a quick glance, then turned away stiffly and went out.

'You might think he was going up on the bridge on a rough night, mightn't you?' said Mr. Ramsbottom, chuckling a little. 'England expects every man to do his duty, and that sort o' stoof, eh? Ay, but he's a grand chap, the Commander is. You mightn't think he was my sort at all, but Ah've taken a right fancy to him. You like him, don't you – what you've seen of him, Ah mean?'

'Very much,' replied William, without hesitation. 'I think I've been lucky. I struck another Commander Ivybridge first – he was the wrong one – and I couldn't have done anything with him.'

'Ah heard something about that. Well, Ah'm glad he's gone 'cos it does make it easier to talk. Now Ah'll tell you how it stands with him. He's dying to go on with you, but he feels he can't because he hasn't the money.'

'But I told him—' William began.

'Ah know, Ah know, but that doesn't make any difference. You see, it's not a matter of not being able to put up any capital. It's worse than that. He's not enough to make a start. He had a bit of money and he had his pension, but as far as Ah can gather – and he doesn't say much; he's like a man out o' wood when you try to get anything out of him – he had a sister that was always ailing and he paid out for her, and then he put a bit o' money into some daft thing and lost that, and now he hasn't even got all his pension, only part of it. Result is, he's only just enough to live on, and he's got to be careful then. Ah don't rightly know what he has got, but if it's more than three pounds a week, Ah'll be surprised. Oh, it's a damned shame, but there it is. He's come down in the world, the Commander has, no getting away from it.'

'Yes, I know that,' said William, troubled.

'All right. Well, this is the idea. Suppose he's got an equal share with you—'

'He has. I told him so, yesterday.'

'Good enough. Well, he splits his share with me, and Ah put money up, whatever's needed, just like you do. You can think of it this way. Split it into four shares. You've two shares, 'cos you pay your own expenses and put half money up; and me and the Commander's a share apiece, and Ah pay both our expenses and put up same amount you do. You follow that?'

'Yes, I follow that. But there's another person in this, too. It's a chap in San Francisco, and I'm expecting a cable from him any minute.'

'That's all right. If he can put his share of money up, like you and me, then we divide into six and he gets two shares, like you. If he can't, we divide it into five, and he gets one share. Of course, we might have to take in outside capital – if it's a big job – then we'd have to divide it again. That's simple enough, isn't it?'

'That would suit me all right,' said William. 'It's a business-like arrangement.'

'Mind you,' said Mr. Ramsbottom, bringing his huge face nearer to William's, 'Ah'm a business man and Ah wasn't born yesterday and you don't catch me buying a pig in a poke. Ah want to know what Ah'm in for before Ah start. Ah don't suppose the Commander would have said anything, only Ah'd been saying to him Ah wouldn't mind having a bit of a flutter in something new, specially if it involved travelling.'

'This does. Very extensive travelling, as a matter of fact.'

'Ah gathered that,' Mr. Ramsbottom continued. 'Now that suits me down to the ground. Ah've got my business in Manchester going on nicely – Ah can leave that, been told to leave it – and anything that took me a long way off, so long as there's no North Poles or steaming jungles of Africa and Asia in it, would be just what the doctor ordered. Matter of fact, he told me to go round the world, but if Ah'm going that far, Ah'd like to have something to go for and not just be gaping about. At same time, Ah don't fancy any wild-goose chases, you know, Mr. Dursley. Ah can afford it, but Ah've got the reputation of being a knowing sort o' chap where Ah come from and Ah'd like to keep that reputation and not do anything that'ud make me look silly. And it gets round, you know, it gets round. You can hide nothing nowadays. Make a fool o' yourself this week in Timbuctoo, and next week they're calling you names for it in the smoke-room of the Midland Hotel, Manchester. So Ah don't want to look soft. But then, for that matter,' he added, with the air of a man making a considerable concession, 'Ah don't suppose you do either.'

William admitted that he didn't. Then they looked at one another for half a minute and said nothing. The moment had arrived. Could Mr. Ramsbottom be told? After this last flicker of hesitation, William made up his mind.

'Do you know what pitchblende is?' he asked quietly.

'Ah should think Ah do,' cried Mr. Ramsbottom. 'It's stuff you make radium out of. Ah was only reading all about it the other day, in one o' these fortnightly parts Ah've been taking – *Science For Every Man*, they call it, and very good too, plenty for your money. But you're not going to tell me, Mr. Dursley, that pitchblende comes into this?'

'It does. This place we're going to find is supposed to have tons and tons and tons of pitchblende in it. My uncle brought a piece away with him, and I've had it tested and I know it's pitchblende all right.'

'Oh Ah say!' cried Mr. Ramsbottom, staring at him. 'Oh Ah say! 'Ere, hold on a minute, we must have a drop o' something before we talk about this. What's it to be? Whisky? All right, well you try my blend. Ah've made 'em stock it here.' He walked over to the bar in the corner of the room, and returned shortly with the drinks. 'We don't want any waiter nosing round here,' he explained. 'They've got long ears, some of these chaps, and they're not so silly as they look. You never know where you are with waiters. You'd be surprised. Well, taste this. *Loch Tay* – Ah never drink any other sort now, that is, if Ah can get this. Once when Ah was in Scotland, Ah put it straight to a chap there who was in the business. Ah said, "Now tell me, honestly, what's the best whisky you know." And he told me – *Loch Tay.* And he was right. He knew.'

'It's very good,' said William.

'Now you've told me so much,' Mr. Ramsbottom continued, 'you might as well tell me the lot. If you don't tell me where the place is, Ah couldn't do you down, if Ah wanted to, and Ah don't. Let me share in with the Commander, and Ah'm too well off to try and do any diddling. Ah'm saying this, because, if what you say is right – my word, you're going to have to be careful. There's folk looking for this stuff all over the world, and you let 'em get a smell of it and – good-bye. But you know that as well as Ah do.'

William recognised the truth of this, and promptly got

a dramatic thrill out of it. He remembered the mysterious Garsuvin, who, at this distance, made a fine sinister melo-dramatic figure. But he felt now that he could talk openly to Mr. Ramsbottom, and he did, repeating the story he had told the Commander the day before. And Mr. Ramsbottom, for once, listened and said nothing.

'And so you see,' William concluded, 'all that I'm wait-ing for now is some word from this P. T. Riley in San Francisco. When we get the latitude of the island from him, we can start out to find it.'

'And you've cabled?'

'And I've cabled and hope to get a reply any time now.'

'Well,' said Mr. Ramsbottom slowly, looking at William with eyes that were magnified by his spectacles into solemn dark orbs, 'if you'll have me, Mr. Dursley, Ah'll come in. And the terms are – Ah share with the Com-mander, and Ah pay both our expenses looking for the island, and then after that, Ah put up the same amount you do.'

William nodded his agreement.

'And this Riley,' Mr. Ramsbottom continued, 'he comes in on the same terms. If he puts up the money equally with us, he gets two shares, like you, and if he doesn't, he gets one share, like me and the Commander. Now say the word. Is that all right to you?'

'It is, Mr. Ramsbottom.'

'That's grand. We must shake hands on that. We make a sort o' syndicate job of it now, don't we? And you just notice the Commander when we tell him. If it couldn't have been worked this way, Ah don't know how it could have been worked, and he'd have been that disappointed he'd have been sick and tired o' life. And, mind you, he's had a bellyful already, the Commander has. He's dead set on this. Not the money, y'know – though Ah expect he'd

like to get his hand on a bit as well as the next man –
but just the chance of something to do and getting on
the move again. Now just notice him.'

They had not long to wait. The Commander returned
prompt to the minute, when his hour was up: he might
have been reporting for duty. Mr. Ramsbottom did not
give him time to ask a question.

'Commander,' he cried, beaming fatly upon him, 'Ah'll
get you a whisky. Then you can drink the 'ealth of the
new syndicate—'

'Syndicate?'

'Syndicate—' and Mr. Ramsbottom's voice sank to a
hoarse but fruity whisper – 'now about to be formed
for the purpose of re-discovering and exploiting Faraway
Island, somewhere in the Pacific Ocean.'

The Northern Lights could be observed, for a second or
so, in the Commander's face. But all he said was 'Good!'

3

The next morning began very gloomily for William. The
surprising sunshine of the last two days had vanished, and
now wild gusts from the Atlantic brought slashing rain.
All the colour was drained away from the estuary. There
was nothing worth seeing through the streaming bay windows of the lounge, in which William, anxious now for a
reply to his cable, spent most of the morning. He was
tired of the *Lugmouth Packet*, of its dark corners and smells,
its funereal manageress, its Pekinese waiter, its solid blue-
suited guests. Not having any more news, he felt he could
not look up his partners so early in the day, so he stayed
in the hotel, read a newspaper or two, and mooned about
the lounge, occasionally going down to the ground floor

to see if any message had arrived for him and to glance through the open doorway at the little wet square. It was a foolish tedious morning, so much good time drearily wasted. He began to dislike P. T. Riley of San Francisco.

The answering cable came, however, and it arrived a few minutes before lunch, so that he was able to telephone immediately to Mr. Ramsbottom at the *Lugmouth Hotel* and catch him in. 'I've had a reply from San Francisco,' he announced.

'That's good,' said the voice at the other end. 'What does he say?'

'He says that he's got the latitude, but won't let me have it unless I go there and explain it all to him.'

'Well, that's not so bad,' Mr. Ramsbottom told him. 'Ah think that's reasonable. What d'you feel about it?'

William thought for a moment. 'I suppose it's all right. Anyhow, we'd better talk it over and make some plans.'

'That's the idea. Let's get started, soon as we can. Look 'ere, Ah'll get hold of the Commander, and you come up this afternoon, soon as you like. Ah'll send a message round to him now. No good wasting time. Ah say, let's get on with the job.'

This suggestion of energy and determination pleased William, and the slight depression he had been feeling all the morning now left him. He yearned for bold plans and rapid movement. 'All right,' he cried. 'I'll come up after lunch and we'll talk it over.'

An hour and a half later the syndicate marched up to Mr. Ramsbottom's bedroom, a fairly large room with bay windows looking out to sea. There was a cheerful fire to vanquish the watery grey desolation of the day. On a little table in the middle of the floor there was a grand atlas, and by its side some sheets of paper and Cook's *Continental Time Table*. Mr. Ramsbottom had not been idle, and, after noticing these preparations, William regarded him with a new respect. Clearly he was about to prove himself a very useful partner.

'Well, gentlemen,' Mr. Ramsbottom began, in the manner of a chairman, 'let's get to business. First thing to be decided is this San Francisco job. This Riley says he won't part with the latitude unless somebody goes and tells him all about the business. And he's quite right. Ah wouldn't, neither. You can't blame him. Well, the point is – who's going?'

'I am,' said William. 'I'm the obvious person to go. Don't you agree?'

They did agree.

'Now the next point is this,' Mr. Ramsbottom continued. 'If you go by yourself out there, what are we to do in the meantime? Are we to wait till you've done your job or are we to get on with something ourselves? And just let me put a word in 'ere. What Ah say is this – we've got to get a move on, else we'll find somebody else a bit smarter has gone and nobbled that island. There's no time to waste.'

'That's true, Ramsbottom,' said the Commander. 'The sooner we get there, the better.'

'I see that,' said William. 'But that means that the only thing for you to do is to come to San Francisco with me. We can't start for anywhere before we have the latitude of the island, can we?'

'I'm not sure about that,' said the Commander. 'Don't you remember what I told you, the other day, when I lunched with you? If we have to charter a schooner to visit the island, then the obvious place is Tahiti. I worked it out for you, but if you've forgotten—'

'No, I remember,' cried William. 'We know the longitude and we know it's somewhere in the South Pacific, and so Tahiti's obviously the best place for our – eh – what d'you call it?—'

'Our base,' said the Commander, smiling. He was enjoying all this, and already he seemed a far brisker and more determined person than the retired and somewhat faded naval officer William had first met.

'Yes, our base,' William continued. 'So whatever the latitude may be, Tahiti's the place, is it?'

'I'm positive it is. We shall have to pick up a schooner there.'

'Well, then, how does one get to Tahiti?'

'There are two routes,' replied the Commander. 'One is from San Francisco, by the monthly New Zealand boat—'

'There you are then,' cried William triumphantly. 'It works out beautifully. San Francisco is on the way, so we all go there.'

'What about that, Commander?' enquired Mr. Ramsbottom, turning to the Commander, who had hesitated.

The Commander picked up the *Continental Time Table*, but did not open it. 'The other route is direct by sea from Marseilles, by the *Messageries Maritimes*. That's slower – it takes about six weeks – but it's much cheaper, and as I don't see why we should incur unnecessary expense, that's the route I should prefer. Much less fuss, too. You're in one ship from Marseilles to Papeete – across the Atlantic, through the Panama Canal, then from Panama to Papeete. It's much simpler, costs about half as much, and may not take any longer – that depends on the dates.'

'We'll have to have a good look at that time table in a minute,' said Mr. Ramsbottom.

'What you propose is this, then,' said William, speaking very deliberately, 'that I go to San Francisco, see P. T. Riley and get the latitude, and you make for Tahiti from

Marseilles, and then I join you in Tahiti from San Francisco?'

The Commander gave him an apologetic smile. 'That's it,' he admitted. 'Though I must say it does look as if we're simply piling all the extra expense and fuss on you—'

'Oh, I don't mind about that. We've got to have the latitude, and obviously I'm the person to see Riley.'

'My word, we're going to do a bit o' travelling, aren't we?' cried Mr. Ramsbottom, flashing his spectacles at one and then the other of them. 'Ah'm feeling dizzy already with your Marsailses and Panamas and San Franciscos and Tahitis and Pappy-what's-its. You're talking about meeting at Tahiti as if it was just down the road. You're frightening me, you are. Ah used to think Ah was throwing myself about a bit when Ah used to nip across to Paris and Hamburg. Yes, an' Ah've seen the time when Ah thought Ah wasn't doing so bad when Ah got as far as Llandudno. 'Owever, Ah'm game. They're all nice places, aren't they?'

'Tahiti's supposed to be a sort of human paradise, isn't it?' said William.

'Pretty good show,' replied the Commander. 'Or, at least, it was. It may be spoiled now. Most places are.'

'Oh well, that'll do then,' said Mr. Ramsbottom. 'Let's have a look at this atlas and see what we're in for.'

'But have you thought of this?' William asked them both. 'Suppose I can't get the latitude from this chap Riley? Suppose he won't give it to me, or demands impossible conditions? Suppose he dies before I get there and my uncle's letter is destroyed? You'll be stuck there in Tahiti, and I might arrive without the latitude.'

'Well, that'll be that,' said Mr. Ramsbottom. 'It's one o'

the risks you've got to take. Anyhow, we'll have had a good trip and seen something for our money.'

'Yes,' said the Commander reflectively, 'we've got to risk that. Though even without the latitude, all chances of finding the island aren't completely lost. I admit it would be a terribly tall order to sail along a longitude looking for a small island, but it's not impossible. I think I could narrow it down considerably if I went to work with a good chart and then made a few discreet enquiries among the skippers in the islands.'

'I'm willing to risk it,' said William. 'I'd risk it for something far less important than this. Why – hang it all! – look what this discovery means. We're taking it terribly coolly.' As he spoke, his excitement grew, and he lost all shyness. 'It will be one of the great discoveries of the age. It's much more important than diamonds or gold—'

'Ah'm not so sure about that,' Mr. Ramsbottom put in. 'We're badly in need o' gold. 'Owever, go on.'

'It's more important to me,' William declared, quite aggressive for once. 'I'm sure it means more to humanity. It would bring the price of radium down with a rush. Doctors would be able to use radium more and make more experiments with it. Thousand and thousands of people might be cured who haven't a chance now, and are dying in misery. Risk! Why, we're not really taking any risks yet. We ought to be ready to risk everything – yes, *everything*—'

The Commander looked at him steadily. 'We may have to risk a lot yet, you know. Looking for an island in the Pacific, five hundred or a thousand miles from anywhere, isn't a picnic. There may be risk enough before we've finished. Not that I don't agree with you. It's worth it a hundred times over.'

'Ay' – and Mr. Ramsbottom rubbed one of his chins –

'well, Ah suppose Ah'm ready too, though Ah must say –
and mind you, chaps, Ah'm not grumbling – Ah'd had
an idea up to now it was a bit of a picnic. Seemingly it
isn't. Never mind, in for a penny, in for a pound. What's
the next thing to settle?'

The Commander had been turning the pages of the
Continental Time Table. 'The French boat leaves Marseilles
for Tahiti a week to-morrow.'

'Whoa, horse, whoa!' cried Mr. Ramsbottom. 'Steady
on a bit, steady on a bit. When's the next?'

'They sail every six weeks, so that one boat is dropping
Anchor at Papeete when the next is leaving Marseilles.'

'That means you wouldn't get to Tahiti until next
spring,' said William. 'It would take you over three
months. That is, if you wait for the next.'

'Not good enough,' said Mr. Ramsbottom, sticking out
an enormous underlip. 'Too long to wait, an' Ah hate
waiting – oh! – it bothers me, waiting. No, we've got to
get this one, and we've a week to do it in. Can you manage
it, Commander?'

'I can. But what about you? It's a rush, y'know.'

'Oh, it's a rush all right. But Ah can just do it, at a
pinch. An' Ah like a bit of a rush – stops you thinking
and Ah hate thinking. But before we settle this, what
about Mr. Dursley here? When does he go?'

'What? To Tahiti?' The Commander, who was obviously
a time-table man, began turning the pages again. 'Union
Royal Mail, San Francisco to Papeete,' he announced,
with the happily proud air of all time-table men who have
found the right page, 'the next boat sails on the 24th of
this month, Christmas Eve, in fact. That's no good, I'm
afraid.' He looked enquiringly at William.

'No, surely not,' replied William, who was beginning to
feel bewildered by all these great wheels and churning

pistons that he seemed to have set in motion. 'Look here, I've got to clear things up here, then cross the Atlantic, then cross America, then have it out with Riley in San Francisco all before the 14th. I can't do it.'

'Try again,' said Mr. Ramsbottom.

'The next boat leaves San Francisco on the 21st of January. That's better Dursley,' said the Commander. 'If you leave here about Christmas, you can do it comfortably and have plenty of time in 'Frisco to argue with Riley.'

'There y'are then,' cried Mr. Ramsbottom.

'There I am,' said William. 'I'll do that. And you two are going to catch this next boat.'

'If we can do it, we are.' And Mr. Ramsbottom brought his fat hands together with a tremendous clap and then rubbed them vigorously. 'Hell for leather, lads. And the sooner we get busy, the better.'

'We'd better make sure we can get berths in the boat, first, Ramsbottom,' said the Commander.

'They'll have an office in London. Ah'll telephone 'em to-day. Then Ah'll take first train to Manchester in the morning – might get one to-night, for that matter. Settle up there, and then – wollop! Passports, money, clothes, everything's got to be thought of. Put on your thinking cap, Commander. You're the chap Ah'm depending on i' this business. Make a list. And now, before we go any further, Ah think we'd better put our names to a bit o' writing – y'know, business-like. Ah drafted out a thing this morning – Ah don't say it's legal an' all that, but it'll do.' He produced a rough document that plainly set out the terms they had already agreed upon, with suitable provision for Mr. P. T. Riley of San Francisco, who could come in simply as a fellow adventurer, with one share, or as both an adventurer and a backer, with two shares. After signing it, they looked at one another rather solemnly.

The other two began talking again, but William drifted over to the window. The rain had stopped, but the day was as grey as ever and the light was rapidly draining out of the sea and sky. Idly he stared out at the vast restlessness of water, and finally his eye was caught by a small steamer, the only ship to be seen, which was plunging westward, now dipping almost out of view, now riding royally on the crest of some invisible wave. She was like nothing but a mad toy at first, but gradually she took on a purposeful aspect for him, until at last he could even read determination, a governed energy and the knowledge of a goal in the fading black pennon of her smoke. In that huge hollow sphere of wind and foam, she alone had meaning, and when she had gone, there was no sense left in it, only an endless shifting and curdling and blustering. Half frightened, half elated, he turned away, to discover what further plans had to be made.

4

The next day, William returned to Buntingham, taking with him a number of travel notes and a mind like a mad atlas. The journey down to Lugmouth had seemed quite an adventure; now the journey back seemed a mere step or two, for already he was beginning to think in terms of thousands of miles. Buntingham looked very grey, very dull, and he was astonished to think that he could ever have consented to spend his life in such a place. Only one important item of news awaited him at Ivy Lodge. Mr. Garsuvin had called (to Mrs. Gurney's horror and disgust), and not finding William at home had left a note. This note, in a very foreign spidery handwriting, William examined with great curiosity.

Dear Mr. Dursley, it said, Forgive me for troubling you at such a time, but I go abroad again very soon. This is what I wish to say. Since some years, because of financial help I gave to him, your uncle entered into agreement and partnership with me, as I can prove to you. We had each a signed document, and I have mine yet, but your uncle may have destroyed his. I make no claim to money or little possessions he may have left, but I have the legal and moral right to half share in any new enterprise, such as discovery of hidden treasure. As I am certain you are a man of moral integrity, you will wish to investigate this, and I am at your disposal. For one week more I am at the Burlington Hotel. With many apologies for troubling you and regret at not renewing the charming acquaintance, I remain, Yours very sincerely, Louis Alphonso Garsuvin.

William did not like the look of this note. He did not believe for a moment that Garsuvin, against whom his uncle had warned him so earnestly, had any real claim, but it was very queer that he should have chosen this time to point out that he had a claim. The only possible inference was that Garsuvin knew something about Faraway Island. What had happened that day when he and his woman had come to lunch and had stayed on drinking, and, apparently, quarrelling far into the night? Had something been said about the island then? Why had Garsuvin called upon the other Commander Ivybridge? These questions, to which he could find no satisfactory answers, were very disturbing. As he put them to himself, there rose unbidden the image of that curious face, with its high peak of forehead, its myriad tiny lines, its searching dark eyes, its air of melancholy intellectual clownship, mingled with an odd suggestion of decayed aristocracy. Those eyes seemed to stare at him out of the Burlington Hotel, sixty miles away. He suddenly saw himself, a little figure bustling about ineffectually, in the light of those melancholy staring eyes. It was unpleasant, vaguely humiliating. Damn Garsuvin!

The very next night, however, he removed all the odd papers that had been lying at the bottom of his uncle's largest trunk, and took them down to the study. He had not examined them properly before, because they had not seemed to be of any importance, but merely a collection of old receipts, advice notes, menu cards, and snapshots. Now he gave them a thorough examination. It turned out to be a queer, rather moving business. His uncle came alive again, and together they journeyed among islands ten thousand miles away, trading and feasting and making love. Out of these curling and yellowing bits of paper and pieces of stained cardboard, there came a whole rich life. It was like looking at the South Pacific through a series of little windows. You bought and sold copra and pearls; you despatched cases of tinned meat, hardware, and tobacco by schooners to remote islands; you ordered gin and whisky and French rum; you paid for dinner for six, with five courses and three different wines, at the *Tiare*, Papeete; you got roaring tight with old Robson or quarrelled for good and all with old Fourain; you were sulky with meddling officials; you packed off Tetuanui, who was making herself a nuisance – the little bitch! – and installed Vaite in her place; you staggered from the bank, where there was at least one decent Chink, to the doctor, whom you still owed one hundred and thirty-five francs – and let him whistle for it! Even ghosts were not lacking, for there was one snapshot of a very thin elderly man, dressed in nothing but a large straw hat and a pair of white trousers, and on the back was written, in Uncle Baldwin's schoolboy hand: *Cap. Staveling up in the Manihikis just after hearing his big-headed Tupapau knock on the roof. Last time too. Never saw poor Cap. again.* William had heard a sufficient number of his uncle's stories of the islands to know that *Tupapau* means a ghost. So poor old Captain Staveling – who looked spectral enough himself in this photograph – had heard, and apparently had been in the habit of hearing, a ghost knocking on the roof of his bungalow; and now Staveling himself was a ghost, and so was Uncle Baldwin – all ghosts, ghosts, ghosts. William stared at the miserable snapshot, with its wraith-like figure and dim background, as if some precious secret might be wrested from it. Was it possible that life, once caught in these islands at the other side of the world, these specks in that huge smiling sea, would reveal things not even to be guessed at here in Buntingham? Or was it all an idle dream? He remembered a sentence from some prophetic book – was it the Talmud? – that ran: *The things above are as the things below.* Did that apply to this ball? If he walked head-down in space among the palms and breadfruit trees, would he be still William Dursley of Buntingham, Suffolk, a little apprehensive, a little bored, but bewildered and a trifle angry at the very heart of him because year after year cheated and cheated and then went slinking away? He asked the ghosts – and big-headed *Tupapau*, Cap. Staveling, and the purple image of Uncle Baldwin – but they made no reply. He returned to his task with the papers.

There it was. Garsuvin had not lied. It was dated Papeete, 7th of May, 1924, a somewhat fantastic document that a solicitor might snap his fingers at, but an agreement, for all that. It stated that in return for certain assistance, not specified, Louis Alphonso Garsuvin was entitled to a half share in any enterprise of Baldwin Totten connected with the uncharted island known as Faraway. It was typed, in a rather sketchy fashion, and bore the signatures of both men. There was no mention of pitchblende in it, and William guessed that Garsuvin had not been told why the island might be a valuable property. It was not difficult to imagine what had happened. His uncle had returned from the island, met Garsuvin and probably borrowed money from him, and then, probably in liquor, had boasted vaguely about his island, with the result that Garsuvin had persuaded him to sign this agreement. And yet there was nothing to prove that this had happened. His uncle had solemnly warned him against Garsuvin, and obviously the two men had had a quarrel on that fatal Thursday. What was to be done now?

Still holding the paper in his hand, William looked into the fire and thought about the Commander and Ramsbottom and the P. T. Riley who awaited him in San Francisco. He felt he could not go to them with this monstrous document. The thought of admitting Garsuvin into their secret and giving him a partnership was extraordinarily unpleasant. It was not a question of money, for William had hardly begun to think of this affair in terms of money; it was a question of keeping alive the comradeship and adventure and romantic glamour of the quest. No, no, he would rather stay at home than bring Garsuvin into this. But to stay at home now was unthinkable. William jumped to his feet, crumpled the paper into a ball, and threw it into the fire. So much for Garsuvin! And now he did what was for him a very unusual thing, when he was alone: he mixed himself a large whisky and soda, and took a great gulp of its pale gold and mellowed fire. The whisky joined him in condemning Garsuvin as a sinister fellow, a crook and a meddler. All was well.

He spent odd moments of the following day hoping that Garsuvin had taken himself and his glittering brown female out of the country. On the afternoon of the next day, however, while he was still at the malting house, he

was told there was a personal trunk call for him. A Mr.
Garsuvin, had already got through to the house, wished
to speak to him on urgent business. William stood looking
at the boy who had brought the message. For a moment
he was the victim of a feeling that he had not known for
a long time; he felt a spasm of guilty fear. He might have
been a man wanted by the police who had just caught
sight of a blue uniform at his doorstep. He dwindled and
mentally cowered, for a dark melancholy gaze penetrated
all those brick walls. 'Mr. Garsuvin?' he repeated, pretending to be at ease. 'Oh, I can't be bothered with him.
You've not told him I'm here?'

'It's not him, Mr Dursley,' said the boy. 'It's the telephone people. They wait till they've got you, and then
they put him through.'

'Yes, yes, of course,' said William hastily. 'Well, just say
that I'm not here.'

If the boy had so much as raised an eyebrow at this,
William felt that he could have cursed and beaten him;
but happily the boy showed not the slightest sign of surprise. This must be Garsuvin's last attempt to get into
touch with him, William concluded; and probably the
fellow was on the eve of sailing. And thank God for that!
What a nuisance the man had contrived to make of himself! The upper levels of William's mind were flooded
warmly with righteous indignation, but somewhere below
there was an uneasy stirring, like that of a soft hunted
beast, all ears and apprehension. It was not long, however,
before that beast went to sleep again, for by the next
morning William was convinced that Garsuvin had left
the country. He was free of that grave fantastic pest, free
to plan and to dream, to question the ghosts again, to
follow the fading island into the darkness of sleep.

5

After that first day's respite from the haunting Garsuvin, the adventure began. For William it only meant a journey up to London to bid God-speed to the Commander and Mr. Ramsbottom, who were leaving to catch the French boat at Marseilles. But it was the first real step, and at once it conjured the search for the island out of the easy realm of fancy and talk and tobacco smoke. It was a grim morning of sodden fields, wet pavements and chilled thick air. William hastened across a London already decked out for Christmas, though it was only the beginning of December, and made his way into Victoria Station, where he found Mr. Ramsbottom, wrapped in the very largest overcoat he had ever seen, waiting for him under the clock.

'Commander's 'ere,' said Mr. Ramsbottom, whose vast moon-face seemed bigger than ever, 'but he's busy with the luggage. Ah never knew a chap that liked organising more than he does. And – my word! – he can't grumble, 'cos he's had a bellyful these last few days. You wouldn't believe the palaver there is to get to this Tahiti place. They wont let you land there unless they know for certain if your grandmother was spoken well of by the neighbours. It's a marvel to me anybody goes anywhere nowadays, fuss there is. 'Ere he is.'

'Hello, Dursley. Glad to see you.' The Commander was very trim, very brisk, and already looked younger than he had done down at Lugworth. 'Everything's in. We'd better get along too.'

They marched towards the boat train, Mr. Ramsbottom mountainously leading the way.

'You must have had a rush,' said William to the Commander.

'We did.' The Commander grinned. 'Haven't had such a rush for years, and haven't enjoyed myself so much. You made your plans?'

'More or less. I shall book my passage to-day, I think. To America, I mean. The *Gargantua* sails on the 30th of this month, and that will give me plenty of time to catch the Tahiti boat from San Francisco on the 21st of January.' William brought out these travel details with a certain shy eagerness.

'And then we meet in Papeete about the end of January or the beginning of February,' the Commander observed.

'Yes; queer, isn't it?'

'Queer?' The Commander looked at him questioningly. 'Why, that's all right, isn't it? There's no difficulty about our meeting there, is there?' He was frankly puzzled.

'No, of course not,' replied William, telling himself not to be a fool. They had now arrived at the entrance to the compartment. 'I only meant it was all rather odd our arranging to meet at the other side of the world.'

'Odd!' cried Mr. Ramsbottom, turning round. 'It's daftest piece o' business Ah've ever been mixed up in. Ah was just thinking about that. 'Ere we are, setting off to go Ah don't know how far, to find something we've only heard tell of and that mightn't be there when we do get to the other end. If some o' my Manchester pals knew about this, they'd say Ah'd gone loony. 'Ere, you go round by Australia and Ah'll go round by Klondyke, and we'll meet in Hootsy-Tootsy, under the palm trees, seven weeks o' Tuesday. That's how we talk, isn't it?'

'Well, I don't see anything very strange about that,' said the Commander, a trifle stiffly. 'After all, we have to get there.'

'Course we have,' cried Mr. Ramsbottom. 'Ah'm not grumbling. But it's nothing out o' the common to you,

Commander, 'cos all your life you've been packing up and off somewhere, at a minute's notice. Report off the coast of China, six weeks o' Wednesday. Proceed to Malta at once, and await orders. That's been it, hasn't it?'

'Something like it.' And the Commander gave a short but companionable laugh.

'All right then. But to me and Mr. Dursley 'ere – a couple o' stop-at-home civilians, business men – it's a rum go. But we're not grumbling, are we? All aboard then!'

Their seats were next to the platform, and they opened the window to have a last word or two with the waiting William.

'As soon as we get there,' said the Commander quietly, 'I'll begin making enquiries, very discreetly. And good luck, Dursley. You'll enjoy the trip to San Francisco.'

'And don't forget to mind what you're drinking in America,' said Mr. Ramsbottom, pushing his huge face into the window space. 'And if this P. T. Riley's a decent chap, get him to join the party. He'll be a bit o' company, and we'll have four for a game o' cards. Well, look after yourself. And Ah'll keep the Commander out o' mischief.' And Mr. Ramsbottom produced a wink so prodigious that the train was able to move on with it. A farewell wave, and they were gone.

As usual, the station seemed to have shrunk and grown duller as William retraced his steps through it. There was only one thing worth doing now, and that was to go at once and book his passage on the *Gargantua*. London could be nothing but the chill foggy old cannon that would shoot him out soon into the blue, into which the Commander and Ramsbottom seemed to have already disappeared.

CHAPTER IV

P. T. RILEY

1

ON THE morning of December 30th, somewhere in Southampton, perhaps at the top of the long gangway leading to R.M.S. *Gargantua*, reality broke down for William. He walked through an invisible crack into another world. No sooner had he been conducted into the interior of the *Gargantua* than he said good-bye to sense; and the safe little world, with its fixed boundaries, fell away from him. The interior of the *Gargantua* was crazy; as if a monstrous hotel had been cut in half, one of the halves compressed and then wildly mixed with parts of a seaside promenade, a fancy fair, and a factory. After visiting his cabin, that iron box in the Louis XIV style, and unpacking some astonished clothing there, William set out on a tour of exploration, and stepped, bewildered, from a gymnasium into a half-timbered Tudor smoking-room and from there straight into a barber's shop, and, moreover, a barber's shop that appeared to be filled with large dolls and false noses. Then everything that happened had an incalculable and lunatic aspect. Uniformed personages made a fuss; there were huge vague noises; much waving of handkerchiefs by tiny figures far below at the dock side; and then Southampton gently disengaged itself from the *Gargantua* and went sliding away into the cold mistiness, taking with it the world that could reasonably contain

Buntingham and its malting business, Greenlaw of the Grammar School, water-colours and chess. The *Gargantua* was glad to be rid of such last vestiges of sanity, and immediately abandoned all pretence. It sounded bugles, played waltzes, and conjured forth cocktails and salted almonds and toasted cheese in the smoking-room, and whisky and bottles of beer and Scotch broth and Lancashire hot-pot below in the dining-saloon. After that, everybody but William seemed to disappear, and he went for long lonely walks along glass-enclosed promenades and through empty drawing-rooms in red and gold and writing-rooms in blue and silver. The outside world grew dark and sleety; it took to whistling hard; and finally the *Gargantua* halted near some noises and a few flickering lights that called themselves Cherbourg. Some cold wet people came aboard, stared about them for a moment with great disdain, then disappeared for days.

The year expired in a vast heaving idiocy. All night the *Gargantua* laboured and protested and groaned, with much dragging and clanking of chains, like an industrious spectre. William's bath water retreated from him and tried to form a wall; his dressing-gown stretched itself and stood out stiff; something in the pit of his stomach turned over from time to time; and he treated the huge menu card, which broke into Old Year-New Year gaieties, with a certain ascetic scorn. Only a few red-faced hearty men kept his company during those first days, though on one of the decks, securely swaddled in chairs, were four young American Jewesses, whose faces, painted with bright orange cheeks and purple lips, suggested the most glowing health, but whose anxious eyes seemed to be staring out of another life. With enormous lengths of heaving promenades and rooms in five different styles practically to himself, William felt very lonely and not quite right in his head. Suddenly, however, on a morning when a little pale sunshine could be seen and the *Gargantua* did not protest and groan quite so much, the place swarmed with people, and people apparently on the easiest, friendliest terms with one another. They ate and drank down in the dining-saloon and up in the restaurant and the smoke-room; they played games, went in for competitions, flirted, danced, wore funny hats and threw paper about; they stayed up half the night having rounds and rounds of drinks and sandwiches and shouting the most intimate confidences to one another. William was nearly one of these people, but not quite: he felt rather like a neglected older inhabitant. But he found that he had a companion, almost an old friend, in the man who sat next to him at table. This was Mr. Julius Thedalberg, of the Gard Burrastein Products Inc. of New York; a pale and sad-faced man of indeterminate middle age, who spoke in the slowest and most despairing tones that William ever remembered hearing, but who yet contrived to enjoy himself enormously and to eat and drink and smoke more cigars than anybody else there. Within half an hour of his first appearance at table, Mr. Thedalberg had adopted William, who really began to feel that somehow he must be one of Mr. Thedalberg's old friends. Mr. Thedalberg marched him round and round the decks and in and out of the smoke-room, and talked firmly to him about business conditions and the Gard Burrastein Products Inc. (of which he was a proud executive) and prohibition and home life and divorce and ward politicians and Paris and his daughter in college and his son at school. The sunshine was blotted out by alternating visitations of fog and sleet, but nobody cared any more about that, for they were all busy eating more and more caviare and sardines and olives and salted almonds and drinking more and more dry Martinis and double Side-cars and staying up later and later every night to reveal their last secrets. William sometime felt he had been pitchforked, with baggage and bed, into an endless birthday party given by a stranger. By this time, there was nothing about Mr. Thedalberg that William did not know; but, on the other hand, Mr. Thedalberg knew nothing about Faraway Island, the pitchblende and P. T. Riley, for when William discovered a certain golden haze in the smoke-room, a haze through which Mr. Thedalberg loomed as his oldest and dearest friend, and found himself wanting to talk about such matters, something always told him it was time to go to bed.

Then one morning the *Gargantua* suddenly stopped groaning, and the mists outside were wiped away to reveal an incredible place of grey gleaming towers. Mr. Thedalberg took William by the arm, pointed to this and that, and was proud and sentimental. He was also surprisingly helpful. In his ignorance of America and the Americans, that land and race of born hosts, William had imagined that once they were within sight of New York, Mr. Thedalberg's ancient friendship would suddenly melt away; but there he was wrong, for Mr. Thedalberg was on hand both before and after they passed through the customs, gave William the address of a good hotel, and insisted that they should spend the evening together. William was only too glad to accept these kind offices. So far as it is possible to like a person who is not quite real, William liked Mr. Thedalberg; and Mr. Thedalberg at least was more real than anybody or anything else, for now the unreality of the *Gargantua* was replaced by the still wilder unreality of this city, into which William plunged as if he had suddenly jumped up from his seat in the Buntingham picture theatre and had dived into the life

shown on the screen there. He spent the day being whirl-
ed up and down elevator shafts, walking along streets
that were roaring canyons, and staring up at cliffs and
mountain sides of reinforced concrete and shining brick
façades. Prompt to time Mr. Thedalberg arrived in the
evening, complete with programme of hospitality, all of
which was carefully announced in that sad and despairing
voice, and so began William's first and last night in New
York City.

They went first to a speak-easy that was nothing but a
dim back room, and there they swallowed two fiery cocktails each. Then they moved on to an Italian restaurant
speak-easy that appeared to have been constructed out of
a hastily covered backyard, and there they dined, heatedly,
heavily and indigestibly. The next item on the programme
was a cheap burlesque show down town, at which they
finally arrived, to William's astonishment, in an elevator;
and this show consisted of three battered Hebrew com-
edians who exchanged grim and smutty jests, and of a
chorus of tired and bored girls, who proceeded, time
after time, to remove what scanty clothes they wore and
to reveal their rather chalky pulpy charms for the benefit
of rows of glassy-eyed and teeth-sucking clerks and warehouse men. Struggling with the wild weather inside him,
in which indigestion provided the thunder and raw alco-
hol the lightning, William sat dazed before this powerfully
and aphrodisiac spectacle, which Mr. Thedalberg, for his
part, regarded with neither approval nor disapproval, but
with a sort of vague scientific interest. After an hour or
so of it, they left for a German speak-easy, a place of
Gothic gloom, sham armour and imitation carved wood,
where a roaring crowd of patrons sweated over seidels of
synthetic beer, waltz choruses, and vast limp sausages.
Here, flushed girls would suddenly jump up, wriggle viol-

ently to the music, then scream with laughter, and to one of the noisiest of these William, to his embarrassment, was introduced by the solemnly waggish Mr. Thedalberg as a fellow citizen of Knoxville, Iowa. It was late when they left this underground bedlamite Nuremberg for the keen air and hard glitter of the street, but Mr. Thedalberg had not yet completed his schedule, and so William, who by this time was desperately tired and rather depressed, could not suggest that he would like to go to bed. Thus they arrived, sometime between one and two in the morning, at the colossal arena of the Madison Square Garden, in time for the beginning of the fifth day of the Six-Day Cycle Race. A few thousand spectators, a mere handful in that vast interior, were staring and blinking and yawning and chewing, their faces cruelly etched in the glare of the arc lights. A band blared brassily from some distant ærie. Ghosts in white jackets hawked peanuts and hot dogs and ice cream. Loud speakers made announcements, but they did it in such tones that it seemed as if metallic giants were roaring in agony and proclaiming the eve of Doomsday. Stringy little cyclists were busy coming on or going off duty, some sleeping beside the track, others stretching their legs towards the masseurs, and the rest of them silently and gravely circling around the course. William felt he was looking on at some fantastic ritual. There was something hypnotising about these circling figures. Time perished: it was neither late last night nor early this morning; it was no hour that could ordinarily be found among the twenty-four. William stared as a drowned man might stare at the antics of the deepsea creatures in some green gulf. His head was too large, too heavy; his eyeballs were bound in brass; his legs ached; his mouth was a desert of cactus and old bones; but he knew these discomforts only vaguely. He was not happy;

he was not unhappy; he was fathoms deep in some ugly trance. How long the wheeling figures went round and round without any sort of break he could not have told, but at last, after many years, the band and the voices broke into a note of new urgency, the spectators sat up, the ghosts turned to stare, and suddenly all the cyclists shot forward and went racing like mad, as if one last effort would enable them to escape from the circling hell of the track. Instantly, Mr. Thedalberg, like the other spectators, was insanely resurrected: 'Attababy!' he yelled, springing to his feet and waving his hat. 'Come on, come on. Attababy!' A wild fear swept through William's bewilderment. At any moment, now, it seemed, this city might go mad. Reason was rocking beneath these lunatic towers. But the pot of wheels and legs and pedals, which had threatened to boil over, now simmered down again, and Mr. Thedalberg, as quiet and sad as ever, said that they might as well go. In the entrance was one of those dwarfs who occasionally find their way on to the stage, a manikin with a large unhappy face, the body of a small child, and the legs of a baby. William nearly fell over him, for he suddenly came reeling out of the shadow, to wave a doll's hand at one of the attendants there and to greet him in a high cracked voice. For once the melancholy face of this dwarf wore a smile, or rather a wide idiotic grin: he was very drunk. William stared at him for a moment, then turned to Mr. Thedalberg, thanked him for the evening, and said that he felt tired. Mr. Thedalberg, announcing the fact that it was now three-thirty, said that he thought they could call it day, shook William's hand, and made a short, solemn speech proclaiming the solidity and worth of their friendship. William felt that if Mr. Thedalberg had been slightly more real, he could have grasped Mr.

Thedalberg's hand and wept over it. Never had he felt
more lost and homeless.

Twelve hours later, he was on the train to Chicago, still
tired, and rather hot and short of breath. A large and
untidy landscape, powdered with snow, went jolting past;
he sat and stared and tried to read jumping print among
a strange people, mostly with loud confident voices, dried
cheeks, and anxious eyes; black men, easy and jovial fellows who seemed to have retained some secret of a rich
luscious life that their masters had lost, set before him
unfamiliar dishes, admirable to the eye but queerly disappointing to the palate and digestive system; he
undressed and slept behind green curtains, and brushed
his teeth and shaved himself in a lavatory-cum-smoke-
room in which too many travellers had been sweating and
smoking cheap cigars for far too long a time; and Chicago
came, roared and rattled at him, showed him a bright
glimpse of an icy lake, darkened above him, then finally
sped away, before the windows of another train, into the
double shadow of night and fading illusion. It was not
long before the landscape became larger and untidier
than ever, and gradually men began to disappear from it.
Dusty plains followed the cultivated fields, only to be
followed in their turn by sheer desert, leagues of fantastic
rock, and hills as uncompromisingly barren and as
wrinkled in the sun as an old man's brown gums. The
train stopped at stations with names that seemed the very
syllables of outlandish romance, but the places themselves
were rarely more than a dull huddle of boxes along the
track. Somehow, little or nothing came to light up his
sense of wonder. The landscape, the look of the skies,
and the very climate, these changed as the miles,
hundreds and hundreds and hundreds of them, were run
off; but there was something alternately maddening and

depressing about the way in which the lives of these people refused to change, as if God had ordained that they should carry with them into these wildernesses an Ark of the Covenant containing specimens of Chesterfield and Lucky Strike cigarettes, the universal Lifesavers, chewing gum, and Coca Cola, and a model of a Ford car. But William was only maddened or depressed in a sort of huge dim dream. He found it all more and more difficult to believe. His mind, removed from its base of custom and accepted fact, drifted like the tumbleweeds he stared at through the window, the tumbleweeds that blew across the desert plains. What wonder there was sprang from the simple act of constant journeying. It was incredible that this now familiar interior of hot dry, air, magazines and dollar novels, ice water and steak and apple pie, had just shaken him out of Cheyenne, Wyoming, and was even now climbing towards Ogden, Utah. On a Sunday morning of crisp sunshine, he stood among a group of his fellow travellers, all busy photographing, in the observation car at the back of the train, and gaped at the Great Salt Lake, a vast sheet of blue glass, across which the train went rattling for more than an hour. He told himself firmly that now he was actually crossing, on a cut-off that retreated into a knife edge, the famous Great Salt Lake, round whose incrusted shores, where the salt seemed to sparkle ready for the cruet, were spread those legendary and sinister creatures, the Mormons. But nothing happened inside him. It was all too unreal. Utah went, and Nevada arrived, a place of extraordinary desolation, merely so much geology. Among mountains as bare and remote from life as a relief map, he retired yet once more behind his green curtains, performed the familiar acrobatic trick with his pyjamas, listened to the train hooting through these chasms of the moon, and fell into a vague melancholy reverie. The Commander and Ramsbottom – where were these shadows now? Faraway Island, with its black treasure of pitchblende – was it a dream? He thought of his life in Buntingham, the familiar round of the malting house and of his water-colours and books and chess and bridge, friends like Greenlaw, and the few women he knew well and the other women he always thought he would like to know better and yet could never really trouble himself about; and all this life and these people retreated into something very small, dull, faded. Yet that was all that was really his, that small, dull, faded patch of life. Beyond it was nothing but changing shadows. Reality was not here for him. At the moment it was nowhere for him, and he felt curiously sick at heart. It was as if for years and years he had been the victim of a spell that prevented him from breaking through into some infinitely richer life, a glamorous world of colour and passion and careless laughter. He knew that world existed: sometimes the wizard veils were cruelly twitched aside for a second, and there was a sudden flame of colour, a glimpse of a profile, or the sound of voices raised round some enchanted supper table. The spell had been lifted for a moment when Uncle Baldwin had first spoken to him of Faraway; and it had been lifted again when he had stared into the bubble of sea and sky at Lugmouth; but now that he had actually begun the quest, had let himself be carried half the globe away from his old life, the sinister magic had descended upon him again, spreading a grey film over this whole continent. Very tired, nervously exhausted by the long rattling journey, he stretched and turned in his berth, as if some new posture might release him from his depression. There was nothing heroic about William that night: he was a miserable little man.

Yet in the morning it was all different. It ought not to have been, but it was. He had had a poor night's sleep, and was compelled to cut it short, for everybody had to be up early. They were due into Oakland, the railway terminus for San Francisco, at about eight that morning. William and his fellow green-curtainers had to leave their berths at a much earlier hour than usual, and there was the usual unpleasant congested bustle of washing and dressing and packing in a small space. Nevertheless, William felt that it was all different. The train seemed to be descending rapidly now, as if anxious to plunge them all into the waiting Pacific. This place had no likeness to the barren world he had quitted last night; there was dew in it, and sap and blossom; it was green and luscious, beginning to sparkle already with the clear sunlight; a man could be happy among these vestiges of noble forests, these orchards hanging on the hills; and William found himself with another and sweeter taste in his mouth. He was tired no longer, and all depression fled. He was eager again, and he noticed a similar eagerness in most of his fellow travellers. They might have all come to this California looking for gold. Perhaps they had, and were already finding it. Here, on these rich hillsides and in these fragrant gulfs, was gold enough, the last witness, it might be, to that golden world where lovers and philosophers fleeted the time carelessly, as they were reported to do in Arden. William stared out in a mounting excitement, and when the train arrived at Oakland, he was among the first to leave it for the San Francisco ferry. It seemed to him, as he walked down the long platform, that the air was like a fine dry sherry; and he found it whetting his appetite for life.

2

Reality returned to him on that ferry between Oakland and San Francisco. It came on a curious tide of emotion. As he stepped on to the big ferry boat, among a crowd of business men and stenographers making for their offices in the city across the water, there came to him a sudden sense of release. He was the happy traveller, and everything he saw gave him pleasure. He stared ahead at the blue water, broken here and there by the churning of the ferry boats, and thought with delight that already this was the Pacific. The morning was now as clean as a new coin, and its crisp salted air revived him like some magical draught. He could have clapped his hands at the gulls, whose lovely evolutions made a sort of music for his eye. He felt a quick friendliness for all the people round him, sharing this happy little voyage. These people were as strange as those on the train had been; but he realised now that Americans were foreigners and not, as he had thought at home, a kind of obstinate Colonial English, who persisted in speaking and behaving in a queer and rather objectionable fashion. He perceived that they really were inhabitants of a different continent. Their very faces were foreign: most of the men near him had broad, flattish, clean-shaven faces, evenly tinted a pale brown; and the girls – and there were rows and rows of them, bending over books and magazines or chattering in rather hard shrill voices, and all as pretty as you please – had something curiously piquant and exotic about them, not entirely to be accounted for by their smart clothes or their determined orange-and-crimson make-up. Here, William told himself, was a race new to the world, genuine brand-new kinds of men and women, the product of unimaginable adventures in pioneering

and gold-rushing, lust and love, of the strangest encoun-
ters of odds and ends of humanity from the older peoples.
The very thought was exciting. His heart went out to these
fellow travellers, and though he was a very shy man, he
would have instantly responded to a word or a smile from
any one of them. If they had not all been so busy reading
or talking to one another, he might have risked speaking
to one or two of them, which suggests, for William, a state
of mind bordering on inebriation. In truth, he had not
felt so expansive, so exalted, for a long, long time.

The white water-front of San Francisco rose enchantingly above the blue bay. It reminded William a little of
New York, for there was the same piling up of sky-scrapers,
but the differences seemed more significant than the
likeness. This skyline was not so huge, grim and impressive; it was far more friendly and gay; and above the bright
towers you could see the rest of the city, shining on its
hills. William felt at once that here was a place in which
life could be enjoyed, and enjoyed without any crazy or
sinister twist being given to it. He knew that he was going
to like San Francisco, and that the city would live up to
its superbly romantic reputation. It sat there by the water
like some grandly heroic tenor, some golden-haired Wal-
ther or Siegfried, about to burst into song. As the boat
drew nearer the great clock-tower of the Ferry Building,
William's happy excitement burst all reasonable bounds.
For the time being, all doubt left him, and he said good-
bye to his Buntingham self. That he should come across
the world to this city, to see a man he did not know, to
discover the latitude of an island that was not marked on
any chart, all this now seemed a good and proper thing
to do. It would have been a shame to approach this city
on any baser errand. What was working in him he did
not know: it may have been something in the salt blue

air, the cool bright sunlight, or the adventurous look of the place, or its richly romantic associations; he did not know and did not care; all that he knew and cared was that some load had mysteriously dropped from him, that what had seemed a mad dream in Suffolk now seemed in this atmosphere the solidest reality, and that for once he was happy.

The mood survived his passage through the Ferry Building and his drive to the hotel. The city fulfilled as much of its promise from the water-front as it is possible for any city to do. It was like no other that William had ever seen, though it could be vaguely reminiscent of other cities all over the world. It was America, China and the Mediterranean all mixed up, but its incredible hills, its clear cool sunlight and sharp shadows, its side-walks piled high with gigantic blooms, were all its own. William's excitement remained with him. A vista of Peking, with dragons and lanterns and all, flashed past his taxi window, and then the taxi itself, a magnificent affair in purple and black-and-white check, did a little more switchbacking, seemed to spin madly round a few times, but finally landed him safely at a most dignified entrance. 'This is it, chief,' said the driver genially.

The Clift Hotel received him with equal geniality. There was something unusually soothing about its interior, which was cool, spacious, half American and half mysteriously foreign, like a place in one of those imaginary countries of romance and decorative revolutions. William's room was very high up, so that when he looked out of the window, which he did almost at once, he could see a great chunk of the city sloping away from him, all as sharp as new print. The room was very pleasantly furnished. On the little table in the centre was an astonishing basket of fruit – 'with the compliments of the manager.' Never had

William seen such oranges, apples and pears. He touched them gingerly, as if they might easily crumble to pieces. They were incredible; fruit out of Eden. There was also an enormous metal flask containing ice water, and before he began unpacking, William solemnly poured out a gloriously chilled glass of this water and toasted the city. He needed that water, for his mouth had been dry all the morning. He was excited. For once his unpacking was not methodical. He would take out a shirt and a collar or two, then wander round the room, glancing out of the window, reading the hotel notices, or examining yet once more that glorious basket of fruit, which now proved to have tangerines, figs and nuts in it as well as oranges, apples and pears. However, he did all the unpacking that was necessary before beginning the real work of the day, which was, of course, to get into touch with Mr. P. T. Riley.

There is always something adventurous about telephoning from an hotel bedroom in a strange city. It is almost incredible that the telephone should work at all. William found it a panicky business. He was still excited and, moreover, this was no ordinary telephone call, but the last link in a chain that might swing him into Faraway Island and a fortune. When he had found the number of Brown, Woburn and Brothers and had given it to the hotel exchange, he was quite ready for another drink of the ice water.

'Yeh, this is Brown Woburn,' sang a little voice.

'Is Mr. P. T. Riley there, please?' And what if he were dead or had disappeared or had been sent to a lunatic asylum? What indeed!

The little voice wanted the name repeated.

'Riley,' he told her. 'P. T. Riley.' And he was greatly relieved when he was asked to hold on, for at first the telephone girl had sounded a trifle mystified. He was a minute or two holding on, and had ample time in which to tell himself that all manner of things might have happened to P. T. Riley.

'Who's that?' This was not the same girl. This girl spoke in a lower and less sing-song voice. But why another girl?

'This is William Dursley, of Buntingham, England, and I want to speak to Mr. P. T. Riley.'

'Pardon me, but would you mind saying that again?'

William swallowed hard, then very firmly repeated: 'This is William Dursley, of Buntingham, England, and I want to speak to Mr. P. T. Riley.'

There were little sounds, suggesting intense enjoyment and appreciation, coming along the wire. 'Oh, isn't that cunning!' said the voice, in girlish ecstasy.

'What!' roared William.

The voice was penitent. 'Listen,' it continued, serious now, 'I've got a message for you. P. T. Riley says will you come for supper at his apartment to-night at eight o'clock?'

William instantly said he would.

'All right then. You put this address down and don't forget it. But I'll tell you where it is, first. Do you know the Marina? No, of course you don't. Well, it's right down by the water edge, next to the Presidio – that's the military reservation. I'll bet you don't know where that is, do you? Oh well, you just put this address down and then tell your taxi-driver it's down on the Marina.'

'And I'm to be there for supper at eight o'clock to-night,' said William carefully, after writing down the address. 'Please thank Mr. Riley, will you?'

'I'll think about that,' was the astonishing reply, and before William could remonstrate with the girl, she had rung off.

Undoubtedly an odd way of doing things, but then this

was the far west of America. Probably girls in offices here were hopelessly spoilt, perhaps even encouraged to be bright and impudent. William saw P. T. Riley as an indulgent elderly business man with a pretty pert secretary, who was allowed to tell his acquaintances that they were cunning. Cunning? Obviously not used in the English sense. He saw what she meant. 'Oh, isn't that sweet!' an English girl would have cried. An impudent chit. However, it did not matter. His business was with P. T. Riley, and to-night at eight he was to eat and drink with P. T. Riley, and before bedtime he ought to be a good step nearer Faraway. He went over to the window again and looked down upon the enchanting city. He took a pear from the basket, the largest and most luscious-looking pear he ever remembered holding in his hand, a pear of the most perfect shape and colouring, and then returned to the window. Here he was, William Dursley, in San Francisco, holding an emperor of rich Californian pears, the gift of the manager. To-night he would see P. T. Riley, and Faraway Island would be as good as charted. In a fortnight's time, he would be in the South Seas. Why, he was alive now. He had broken through into the real world. This very pear belonged to that real world, and may have been hanging on its Tree of Knowledge.

Happy and a boy out of school again, he bit hugely into the pear. He chewed; he swallowed; and then he stared speculatively. The pear had hardly any more flavour than so much wet cottonwool. It was a pear to to be looked at and dreamed over, and not to be eaten. After a few more disappointing bites, he pushed the thing aside, then glanced at the basket and the remaining fruit. Their contours were delicately illuminated by the morning sun, and nothing could have been more irresistible than their

bloom and sheen. A trifle bewildered, he took another
drink of ice water.

                              3

In the taxi that evening, on his way to P. T. Riley's, William
thought a good deal about San Francisco. After visiting
the offices of the Union Steam Ship Company, to make
the final arrangements for his passage to Tahiti, he had
spent the rest of the day exploring the city. Quite early
in his explorations, he had come by accident upon a
funny little square, filled with idlers, where there was
a monument to Robert Louis Stevenson, a short column
crowned by a galleon under full sail. Stevenson was an
old favourite of William's, and after that sight of the
monument, the whole city took on a Stevensonian quality.
It became a metropolis out of the newest Arabian Night.
This was not at all the San Francisco that Stevenson had
known, for that city had perished in the earthquake and
fire, but nevertheless it was obvious that the San Francis-
can atmosphere, gay, lavish, and adventurous, had persisted. William explored Chinatown, gazing at its antique
and inscrutable faces and its displays of porcelain and
jade, lacquer and embroidered silks; he wandered down
streets that looked as if they were going to drop him
into the Mediterranean; he was duly impressed by the
municipal magnificence of the Civic Centre; he caught a
glimpse of the big boats from China and South America,
the tramp steamers and yachts and schooners, and the
Italian fishing fleet; and he admired the golden poppies,
the golden girls, and the hearty brown men, who no
doubt had hearts of gold. He lunched, somewhat idiotically, off sea food in a restaurant designed to look like a

ship. There was something characteristic in that absurd restaurant, which was half an inspiration and half a piece of tomfoolery. Here there was none of that anxiety, that constant sense of strain, he had noticed among the people in the Eastern and Middle-Western states. These San Franciscans openly and heartily enjoyed themselves. There was still a suggestion of gold-mining lavishness and devil-may-care attitudes about them. They were like advance specimens of a new tall pagan race. They were also rather like large children. William found himself feeling slightly resentful, perhaps rather envious. He told himself it was all too good to be true. Even the weather seemed to be too good to be true, for there was something unreal, almost uncannily disturbing, about this clear sunlight, crisp as a biscuit and oddly lacking in warmth. At any moment, he felt, the magic would be turned off and real January weather would be let loose upon them. But in spite of his doubts and his touches of envy, he had enjoyed his day.

It was dark now in the outer spaces, but not in the city itself, which was glittering magnificently, with an opulence of hard clear electric light that surpassed anything he had ever seen, with the small exception of New York's Broadway. Every electric bulb seemed about twenty times as brilliant as it would have done in England. You felt that the place was celebrating something. It was not long, however, before the taxi carried him out of all this rich bedazzlement into something that faintly resembled night time in ordinary cities. They were now near the residential quarter at the bay's edge, where P. T. Riley had his apartment. William caught a glimpse or two of the bay itself, so much dark blue velvet spangled with lights. The Marina seemed to be very rich and strange, something between the suburb of some impossibly Spanish Spanish city and a number of lavish stage sets. Clearly it was a very charming picturesque quarter, but it was so determinedly charming and picturesque that it looked astonishingly theatrical to William, who could not believe that real people lived there. The lighting, which fell so cunningly on white walls, quaint windows and doorways, fantastic steps overhung with baskets of flowers, paved courtyards artfully complete with evergreens and wrought-iron lanthorns, was downright impudently theatrical. The taxi finally stopped outside a set that was ready, from its topmost pantile to its last bit of crazy-paving, for the first act of a romantic comedy, preferably with music. It was a building in a sort of tropical Spanish style, and quite large. William regarded it dubiously. If Riley lived there, then Riley was not the man to throw in his lot with William and the others. But the taxi-driver, who knew his way about this neighbourhood, explained that the apartment William wanted must be at the top of this building. Then William saw that a flight of steps led up to the first floor, which was very spacious and had a balcony good enough for a musical comedy, and that a further flight of steps, so quaint as to be almost maddening, went up from the first floor to the flat roof, and that on this flat roof was perched a Spanish-Mexican-South-American-comic-opera doll's house. And that was where P. T. Riley lived. Riley's window, behind which was William's supper, was up there, a stab of crimson in the purple night. William slowly ascended the two flights of steps, and tried, entirely in vain, to imagine what sort of man Riley could be. Incredible to think of a man travelling to and from an exporter's office and warehouse to this wildly theatrical eyrie. Riley ought to be sitting up there wearing false moustachios and playing a guitar.

And indeed, Riley, or somebody in Riley's apartment,

was playing a guitar, or if not a guitar, then some romantic stringed instrument. When William arrived on the roof and at Riley's front door, he waited a minute.

> 'They told me I was crazy;
> They said I was ma-ad . . .'

A girl was singing in there. The song seemed to be one of the conventional crooning jazz things, and the girl, whoever she was, was no vaudeville genius, but nevertheless William kept his hand away from the ornamental door-knocker and stood listening.

> 'They told me I was crazy;
> They said I was ma-ad.
> So now I go without you
> And pretend to be gla-ad.
> But honey, I know,
> And honey, you know . . .'

the husky voice chanted softly, to one of those plaintive little cheap tunes that are unbearable after a month's acquaintance, but yet can achieve a tiny, momentary but real poignancy, as if they expressed the heartbreak of a favourite puppet. This tune achieved that poignancy now. For a moment or two, William stopped worrying about P. T. Riley and Faraway Island and the latitude, and abandoned himself to the easy theatrical emotion of the time, the place, and the atmosphere. There was a genuine loveliness in the night, the white walls and the dark evergreens and the glitter of distant lights, and William, standing there, perfectly still, found himself oddly moved at heart. He felt luxuriously sorry for himself. He was not in love; he was not even desperately out of love; and for years he had not really lived, but had merely gone through a routine of living, a dried little stick of a fellow. He pretended to be a boy still halting on the edge of life, but he was forty, already treading the downward slope. What if he was embarking on a quest for a treasure island? One supremely desirable and enchanting woman was worth more to a man's imagination than fifty such islands. He was trying to dope himself with geography.

> 'But honey, I know,
> And honey, you know. . . .'

Oh bosh! If such tripe could make him feel sentimental, he must be getting half-witted. He grasped the ridiculous door-knocker and gave a very sharp *rat-tat*, at one silencing the husky honey nonsense.

'You Mr. Dursley?' said the girl in the doorway. 'Glad to meet you. Come right in.'

In the tiny sitting-room, bright with Indian rugs, was a supper-table laid for two. The girl, who was not at all embarrassed, looked at him quizzically. 'Mr. Dursley,' she announced, to his further bewilderment. 'I'm going to take a chance. I'm going to tell you I'm disappointed.'

William could only gape at her.

'Yes, I'm disappointed,' she continued, smiling at him. 'When I heard you on the phone, I made sure you were one of those tall Englishmen with a bored look, an eye-glass and a little moustache. And spats. I think I was counting on those spats. And now you're all different, I'm disappointed. And I'm nervous.'

This seemed to William the most astonishing impudence. The girl was as bold as brass. And who was she, anyhow? Why should he, here to meet Mr. Riley, have to listen to this rubbish? 'I'm sorry,' he said stiffly, not looking at her. 'But I don't quite understand. You see, I came here to meet Mr. Riley.'

'P. T. Riley.'

'Yes, of course. We arranged it on the telephone, this morning. It was you I spoke to, wasn't it?'

'Yes. But – you see – I'm P. T. Riley.'

'What!' He stared at her, open-mouthed.

She gave a short laugh. 'Well, I thought I'd surprise you, and this time I'm not disappointed. You registered surprise all right.'

Now that he had recovered from his first shock of surprise, William felt annoyed. This girl seemed bent on making a fool of him. She did not seem to realise that this was a serious business.

'But I don't understand,' he said sharply. 'There must be some mistake. The P. T. Riley I came here to see is a man – and an elderly man too, I imagine.'

'Sit down,' she commanded. 'It's no use saying "Let's eat" just yet, before I explain. And anyhow, you don't look as if you wanted to take supper with me. You look as if you've just been put into a room with a loony. I don't think it's as bad as all that, Mr. Dursley. But just you listen – and see.'

He sat down, and for the first time really looked at her. He was quite ready to dislike her, but had to admit to himself that there was something singularly, perhaps alarmingly attractive about her appearance. She was a girl in her twenties, his own height or perhaps a shade taller, and very shapely. She had thick straight hair of the very darkest hue, the real blue-black; a rather square face; a generous mouth; and heavily fringed eyes of midnight depth and indigo. There was nothing dark about her skin, however; she was an extraordinarily vivid person, and there was about her cream and blue-black beauty a curious sheen that was almost metallic. Her voice was pitched low, and was rather rough and choky; not at all a good voice, but oddly attractive. Obviously this was an unusual girl, and William could well believe that she fascinated all manner of men; but he did not feel prepared to like her.

'The P. T. Riley you came to see,' she explained, and now she was perfectly serious, 'was my father, Patrick Terence Riley. He passed on three years ago. For a long time he represented Brown, Woburn and Brothers down in the South Seas, and that's where he met your uncle, Mr. Dursley. I know he did because I've heard him talk about him. He used to tell me all his adventures. That's partly why I'm just crazy to go there – but wait, we'll come to that later on. Now I'm the only one of the family left. But I'm P. T. Riley, too. Yes, I'm Patricia Teresa Riley, and that's what I have to put down when I sign on the dotted line. But you can bet I keep it pretty dark. Everybody calls me Terry – at least everybody that gets further than Miss Riley with me. And I must say, Mr. Dursley—' and she laughed – 'right now you don't look as if you wanted to get even that far. You look as if all you wanted was to get your hat and go. Is that right?'

'But the letter – with the latitude – and my cable – and everything?' William stammered.

'Oh, don't you worry about them. That's all right. I've got the latitude, and you can do business with me just as you could have done with my father. Though you might have known there was a woman and not a man at the other end when I told you you would have to come and tell me all about it. I think that's where I'd have made a good guess. Let's eat now, shall we? Do you like fruit cocktails and crab salad?'

Still a trifle bewildered though also considerably relieved, William drew his chair forward and faced her

across the little table, which had so much gaily coloured
food on it that it was as bright as one of the Indian rugs.
No sooner had they begun eating than she commanded
him to tell her the whole story of the island. This he did
quite frankly, feeling that his only sound policy was to let
her see that he trusted her, and went on afterwards to
explain exactly his relations with the Commander and
Mr. Ramsbottom and what their plans were. To all of
which she listened with most eager and flattering interest.
She was just as much excited about it all as he had been,
and here, it was plain, was another romantic soul. William
found it strange and not entirely unpleasant to repeat
these now familiar but still exciting details, and to see
across the lighted table this eager vivid face.

'Mr. Dursley, it's the swellest romantic thing I ever
heard of,' she cried when he had done. 'And if I'd have
heard of this and not been in it, I'd have died.'

This enthusiasm ought to have pleased William, but
somehow it vaguely annoyed him. 'You understand about
the sharing terms?' he enquired coolly.

She nodded. 'But I've a special condition of my own.
And unless you agree, you can't have that latitude.'

William raised his eyebrows.

'And don't look so sore about it, Mr. Dursley,' she
continued. 'It's not going to hurt you any – at least it
shouldn't. It's this. I've got to come along, too.'

'What do you mean? To look for the island?'

'To do just what you're going to do. That's why I insisted
on you coming here from England and telling me about
it, and that's why I didn't let on that father was dead and
this P. T. Riley just a girl. I've been wanting to go down
there to the South Seas for years and years, and this is a
swell chance.'

'But—' and William hesitated, for he could think of so

many objections. He chose one of the most harmless –
'Can you leave everything here?'

'All I've got to leave here is this place and a job I don't
want at Brown Woburn's. And I've got nearly a thousand
dollars, and that ought to pay my expenses there and
back – if I want to come back – oughtn't it? Then that's
settled.'

'Is it?' said William dubiously. His tone was so uncomplimentary that she laughed, and he had to laugh, and then
they both laughed together a little.

'But I doubt if you'll be able to get as far as the island
itself,' said William.

'We can see about that. If I can't, then I can stay in
Tahiti. I've always wanted to go there. Any more objections, Mr. Dursley? You mightn't believe it, but there are
some men in this city who'd have jumped right out of
their chairs for joy if they'd been in your place a minute
back. They'd think they were in luck. But you looked as
if you wondered what I was trying to put over on you.
Listen! – I won't speak to you on the boat going down, if
you like. How's that?'

William tried to begin an elaborately gallant apology,
but she quickly cut him short. 'All right. You're awfully
sorry, and I'm awfully glad you're awfully sorry, and so
everything's fine. Well, when does that Tahiti boat go? I
ought to know, I'm in the business. A week Wednesday,
isn't it?'

'No. Next Wednesday.'

'*Next* Wednesday?' she shrieked, jumping to her feet.
'Doesn't that just serve me right for not paying more
attention to the business I'm in? I've got to be on that
boat, and so from to-morrow breakfast on, I've not just
got to hurry, I've got to go mad. But I can make it easily
enough. Don't worry, Mr. Dursley, I'm not going to start

this minute. Come and sit down here. And have a ciga-rette. Have you seen anything of our city yet?'

He made himself comfortable, then told her what he had seen of the place.

'And you like it?' she enquired eagerly.

'Very much,' he told her. 'It's one of the most interest-ing cities I've ever seen. I want to see some more of it.'

'Of course you do. You've seen nothing yet. Folks from outside laugh at us here. They say we're all dippy about San Francisco, but so they would be if they'd lived in it as long as I have. Yes, I was born here. The Great Fire and I arrived at the same time, and that's telling you exactly how old I am. My father wasn't born here. He came from Ireland.'

'Are you Irish?' William asked, and not out of mere politeness, for he was curious to know – especially after his recent meditations on the subject of the new race here – how so brilliant and unusual a physical type came to be bred.

'No, I'm American,' she replied promptly. 'Otherwise, I'm mixed enough. My father was Irish – all Irish. My mother was a mixture, and a pretty cute mixture, too. *Her* father was New England, came out here in the good old days. And *her* mother – my grannie – was a Spanish Jewess. So you see before you a Spanish-Jewish-New England-Irish American girl.'

'That's interesting,' said William, staring at her specu-latively. 'I thought it must be something like that. I believe it's the odd mixture that does it.'

'Does what?'

'Produces such an unusual and beautiful physical type,' said William simply, speaking his thought aloud, without considering his listener.

Miss Riley sat up, and looked hard at him. 'Are you telling me I'm an unusual and beautiful physical type?'

'Well, yes, I am,' said William shyly. 'Most unusual and very beautiful. If you don't mind my saying so.'

'If I don't mind you saying so! The way you got that in! And I thought you were dumb!'

'Dumb?'

'Never mind. Well, it's very nice of you to pay me such a compliment. And I don't mind you saying so. That is, so long as you don't look at me as if I was a biological specimen or something.'

'Sorry,' said William, more at ease now. 'But we're all biological specimens, you know.'

'Yes, I guess we are – to God or the Life Force or whatever there is,' she retorted, with unexpected swiftness, 'but not to one another. I'm Terry Riley, of San Francisco, and you're Mr. William – it is William, isn't it? – Dursley of Buntingham, Suffolk, England. And the way you say that name and address is cunning – if you don't mind my saying so,' she concluded, parodying him.

He rapidly began revising his opinion of this girl, who was clearly something a great deal more than an exquisitely decorated façade. He saw, too, that it would be folly to jump to any quick conclusions about her, conclusions all based on his experience of English girls. This girl might speak almost the same language, but the fact remained that she was a foreigner. She interested him, and though he could not decide at once that he liked her or that her intrusion into the Faraway syndicate would be anything but a nuisance, he had to admit that he had stopped disliking her.

'What's the boat?' she asked.

'The *Marukai*.'

'I know her. She's one of their best. Nothing very grand

or super-de-luxe about her, but she'll do. And I'm to be allowed to travel in her, am I, as an executive of the Faraway Island Corporation?'

'If you really think you'd like to go,' said William gravely. 'You mustn't imagine that I objected in any way to your coming – and anyhow you've as much right to come as the rest of us – but I wanted you to realise, I still want you to realise, what you're in for.' And having said this, he felt he had been talking like a silly old fogey, and hated himself. What must the girl think of him?

'I've done enough thinking about that. That's settled then. I sign on, and the latitude's yours whenever you want it. And if it isn't all the craziest thing!' she cried, giving him a dazzling smile. 'And you look so quiet and thoughtful and sad. I'd never have thought you'd have come all this way to see me, to begin with. And then going after that island! Solemnly marching out of Buntingham, Suffolk – without a word to anybody, I bet – just like that! If you'd been an American, you'd have had ten brass bands and the Mayor and aldermen and five avenues full of Lions and Kiwanis all seeing you off to the station, and you'd have been on the movies now. There's nothing we can't do here – especially in California – but I guess we've got to make a noise about it all the time. That's where you're different. Well, I never pretended to understand Englishmen.'

'And I,' said William promptly, 'never pretended to understand American girls.'

'Californian girls, you mean. Even if you knew all about them in New York and Chicago, you'd have to start all over again out here. Well,' she added, and gave William a thrill he was rather at a loss to account for, 'if we're going to be partners, we'll have to do something about it, eh? Now listen – I'll be flying around to-morrow, fixing things, but to-morrow night, you must come here at seven and meet some friends of mine, and we'll show you San Francisco.'

'Thank you. But I was wondering if you wouldn't come and dine with me.'

'No, no. You must come here, and we'll all go out somewhere to dine. That's the way we do it in California, and you mustn't start objecting. I'll dine with you when I come to Buntingham, Suffolk.'

They chatted for a few more minutes, then he thanked her and made a move towards the door. She followed him, and on her way idly picked up the instrument she had been playing when he arrived.

'What a marvellous night!' cried William, as they stood together outside her fantastic front door.

'We get nights like this all the time, unless there happens to be fog. Out there is the Golden Gate. We'll be going through it next Wednesday, to find your island.' She plucked a string.

'I stood out here a minute and listened to you singing,' William confessed.

She laughed. 'When your heard that noise, you must have thought P. T. Riley was in a bad way. Did you stop and wonder whether to turn back? What was I murdering? I forget.'

'Something about being crazy and mad and glad,' said William vaguely.

'They're all like that, but I think I know the one you mean. I've been crazy about it the last few days – I heard it at the Fox Theatre last week – and by next week I guess I'll be dead sick of it. This is the one, isn't it? But wait a minute. How you going to get back to your hotel? You want a taxi, don't you? I'll phone for one.' She soon returned, to lean against the white wall, near the open

doorway. 'It'll be round in a minute. Like to be entertained by my well-known moonlit balcony act? All right.
This is what you heard, isn't it?' She played a few melancholy chords, then began to croon in a husky whisper:

> 'They told me I was crazy;
> They said I was ma-ad.
> So now I go without you
> And pretend to be gla-ad . . .'

Most of the light there was came from behind her,
through the open doorway, but there was a sort of blue
gleam in her hair, and her face and neck and arms were
faintly luminous. William could not have said how much
of her face he actually saw and how much he imagined
there, from his vivid memory of it. But what he stared at
was something so beautiful that it made him catch his
breath.

> 'But honey, I know,
> And honey, you know . . .'

He remembered himself standing there not three hours
before, and it seemed as if that had been a self standing
in another world. Yet nothing had happened to him, he
told himself, crying above a rising tide of excitement.
Hastily he shook her hand and hurried down the steps
to the waiting taxi.

Once in the taxi, the excitement immediately dwindled
to a muffled pulsing beat somewhere in the dark of his
mind. The clever conscious William took no notice of
that tiny beat. He made appropriate comments on the
evening, and with a certain pompous emphasis, as if he
were in committee. The girl was not as awful as she had

seemed at first, but it was a nuisance that she should insist on coming out herself. The real P. T. Riley, her father, might have been a help to them, with his knowledge of the South Pacific, but this girl could at best be only a passenger, and might easily be a positive hindrance. Spoilt, of course. They were all spoilt, these American girls, and thought they could do just what they pleased. He would have to be a little cooler with her to-morrow night. He had begun well to-night, but had thawed far too soon. Well, that could be soon remedied. Well, well, well, well, well.. ...

4

As the next day wore on, William found, to his disgust, that he was looking forward quite eagerly to the engagement at seven o'clock with Miss Riley and her friends. He was finally able to come to terms with himself by attributing this eagerness to the fact that he was solitary all day. He appeared to be the only solitary person in San Francisco and its environs, whose citizens, all large, brown, gregarious animals, worked and played in crowds. He moved among them like a shrinking but faintly sardonic gnome. Armed with the Official Map of the City and County of San Francisco, he continued his explorations, this time further out, along the coast. From the Cliff House, round which hung an atmosphere of faded bean-feasting, he dutifully stared out and saw the seals upon the Seal Rocks. He had a glimpse of the Fleishhacker Municipal Pool (world's largest; 6,000,000 gallons warmed sea water), and thought it very fine, very fine indeed, and obviously the world's largest. He observed a great many large brown Californians of both sexes playing tennis both fiercely and accurately, and understood dimly why a European victory at this game must seem out here like a violation of a natural law. It seemed odd that these people should ever lose at anything. He had an astonishingly long and rather exhausting walk through Golden Gate Park, where he had a very Japanese tea in a Japanese Tea Garden that seemed to him really quite as Japanese as a Japanese colour print. (Incidentally, there was a genuine thrill in standing on that fantastically curved wooden bridge and looking down into the Oriental mirror of the water, bright with reflected blossom. It was as if he had alighted, a tiny two-dimensional figure, on a colour print. And he felt more at home in it than he did in this large brown boisterous California – no place for a small shy man with a taste in water-colours.) Golden Gate Park had to be admired, for it contained everything that a park should contain, except peace of mind. And all the time the queer unreal sunlight, with its brilliance and odd lack of warmth, poured down upon him, and every now and then he would think about it, this sunlight, and wonder if somebody, perhaps Fleishhacker, was not manufacturing it and turning it on for twelve hours a day on State contract basis. But he had nobody with whom to exchange such fancies; he was alone in a community in which no man seemed to walk by himself; and so he found a serviceable excuse for the mounting eagerness in him towards the evening's engagement. He admitted quite freely to himself, however, that he was curious to see if Miss Riley really was as good-looking as he had thought she was, for though he could remember her voice quite well, he could not recall anything like an exact image of her face. A sort of dark but luminous girl, that is all she remained in his memory.

But when he came face to face with her again, in the

little apartment on the roof, a few minutes after seven, it was as if he had never lost sight of her. Incredible that he could have forgotten that blue-black hair, the indigo glance of her remarkable eyes, the set of her mouth, the poise of her head on her firm, delicately bronzed neck. It was all – what it had no right to be – quite bewitchingly familiar, and this fact annoyed him. Fortunately it is possible to take pleasure in a girl's appearance without liking the girl herself. He greeted her warily, while she, on her side, without the smallest blink of shyness, hailed him as if he were one of her oldest friends. At least, so he imagined, until her friends actually arrived, and then he noticed the difference.

These friends were a young married pair called Stensen, and they made William feel more gnome-like than ever, for they were both enormous tawny bouncing creatures, the girl being coy and arch on a gigantic scale, like a kitten suddenly turned into a lioness, and the man being a kind of loud, affable and nasal Viking. When they arrived, it was as if fifty people had come into the room for a college reunion. It was quite impossible for William to play up to their huge stentorian friendliness; he could do little but grin and mutter; but he had the grace to be ashamed of this reserve, for their friendliness was so obviously quite genuine. They all drank a mysterious cocktail that Miss Riley had prepared, a greenish cocktail that tasted like an explosive ammoniated tincture of quinine.

'Well, Terry,' roared the Viking, slapping her on the shoulder, 'what's this I hear about you going down to the South Seas?'

'I'm going native,' said Miss Riley lightly. 'And I shall learn to dance the what's-it – you know – the *hula-hula*.'

'I know,' screamed the Lioness. 'Like this.' And forthwith, to William's embarrassment, she extended her arms and began violently waggling her considerable behind, all to the accompaniment of screams of laughter.

'You certainly got a hot number there, Clarry,' said the Viking approvingly. 'But next time you do it in a bigger apartment.'

Clarry, the Lioness, sat on the table and finished her cocktail. 'It's Mr. Dursley who's taking Terry away. Isn't that so, Mr. Dursley? He comes right out from England and the next minute Terry says she's going to the South Seas with him.'

'How d'you do it, Mr. Dursley?' enquired the Viking, with immense waggish solemnity. 'I been trying for years – haven't I, Terry? – and could never get her even across the Bay to Mill Valley. I'll say this for you, Mr. Dursley – you know how to pick 'em.'

'If you think Mr. Dursley's taking me away, you're wrong,' said Miss Riley. 'You ought to have seen his face when I said I was coming, too. It dropped a mile.'

'Sorry!' And William grinned sheepishly.

'Hell! – why be sorry?' the Viking bellowed. 'I don't know what the idea is – what is the idea, anyhow? – but if it's anything short of a Queen of the South Pacific Beauty Competition, I know darned well Terry's going to be in the way. Look at her, Mr. Dursley. What you going to do with anybody like that? She oughta be under lock and key in Hollywood, and if I'd my way, she'd be there now. You blood-sucking man-eating Spanish vamp – you!' And he gave Miss Riley a vast fraternal hug.

'Now can you wonder I'm jealous?' enquired the Lioness archly of William, who failed miserably to think of an adequate reply.

'But say – listen!' cried the Viking. 'What is this South Seas idea anyway, Terry?'

William flashed a warning glance at her, but apparently

it was not necessary. 'Oh, it's just some business connected with my father,' she replied easily. 'And I thought I'd like the trip. Shall we go and eat?'

'All right,' said the Viking. 'This is where I take charge o' the party. To-night we're going to show you San Francisco, Mr. Dursley, and if you don't like it, there's no hope for you – you'll have to live in Los Angeles. Well, I thought we'd go down and eat at Jewzeppy's. They know me there, and we oughta be able to get a bottle or two of red wine. Come on.'

Going down the steps outside, William was able to detain Miss Riley a moment. 'You do understand, don't you,' he whispered, 'there mustn't be a word to anybody about Faraway and the pitchblende. It's terribly important.'

'I haven't said a thing so far,' she told him.

'Well, please don't. There are people looking all over the world for this stuff, and we've got to keep our discovery a dead secret.'

'A dead secret?'

'Yes.'

'Isn't that great?' she cried, in a delighted soft voice. 'All a *de-ead* secret. Well, I promise faithfully. And I'll tell you what, Mr. Dursley – I think you're the sweetest thing.' And off she went down the steps.

They arrived at Giuseppe's in an incredibly short space of time in the Viking's car, sat down to eat a rather fatty dinner, and, after what seemed to William a somewhat embarrassing argument between the Viking and the waiter, succeeded in obtaining two flasks of a red wine of extraordinary rawness and potency. Following as it did the explosive ammoniated tincture of quinine that Miss Riley had served, this strange red wine had a marked effect upon William, who began to feel very muzzy indeed.

He did not feel intoxicated – for this suggests some degree of exhilaration – but simply muzzy, so that all the edges of things were blurred, and time and space were more illusory than ever. It was as if he had just been given gas at the dentist's and could not quite come round from it. The Viking and his mate were now larger and louder than ever, and William himself was merely a stupefied mouse. At the end of the meal there was nothing outwardly wrong with him; he spoke and moved easily and correctly; but inside there was a sad hot chaos.

He was not surprised to find himself in the Viking's car again, with the intensely brilliant lights of San Francisco once more whirling about him. He was not surprised, seeing that there had already been some talk of 'taking in a show,' to find himself in a dark interior, pushing his way with the others to a seat. But what was taking place there was very surprising indeed. On the stage was an Oriental young woman who, to a fiendish accompaniment of tortured strings, gongs, wood banged on wood, and a sound like that of a gigantic cork being pulled out of a bottle, proceeded to mew and gibber for what seemed to be hours. Finally, she was joined by a very old Chinese gentleman, who howled at her like a stricken dog. A second man, rather younger, arrived to put in a howl or two, only to be most ferociously mewed at by the girl. William sank lower and lower in his seat, though it was a most uncomfortable wooden seat, and tried to force his mind away from this inferno. But it was no use. He had to attend to it, and yet there was nothing really to attend to, except this constant barrage of sinister sounds. It went on and on. The Chinese girl, like a demoniacal doll, faced the two men; she mewed to their howling; and strings were plucked devilishly, gongs were struck, more wood was banged on more wood, and relentlessly the gigantic cork was pulled out of the bottle: it was a grim cycle of Cathay. William felt that he got lost in some nightmare of China.

'Well,' said the Viking, loudly and cheerfully, 'what about moving on? A little of this Chink theatre goes a long, long way with me.'

They were all for moving on. Once outside, Miss Riley cast a curious glance or two at William. 'I thought once, in there, you'd passed out, Mr. Dursley.'

'Perhaps I had,' he groaned.

'Oh, don't worry. We're used to that here. And if we can't always hold the stuff, with our asbestos insides, what chance has a poor visitor from England? Matter of fact, you only looked a bit sleepy.'

'I didn't feel exactly sleepy,' said William carefully. He was busy telling himself that this P. T. Riley was a really nice girl. 'Muzzy's the word, I think. I still feel it. Everything's rather unreal.'

'I know, I know,' cried Miss Riley heartily, as if she had been the oldest of topers.

'Well,' said the Viking, with a grin, 'I thought you'd like to see some of our hills at night.'

Miss Riley and William sat in the back. It was a large fast car, and the Viking proved to be a large fast driver. For a time he amused himself switchbacking about the town at the greatest possible speed. The hills of San Francisco are intimidating enough by day, but at night in a large fast car they are infinitely worse. William began to feel he was rocketing round on some endless scenic railway in a mad fairground. He did not know whether to shout and sing or to be sick: sometimes he was near one extreme, sometimes near the other; but, on the whole, vertigo had it. Brilliantly lighted doorways and windows flashed past at an angle of forty-five degrees. Streets shot up before the car as if somebody had suddenly jerked them up like ribbons, and other streets would fall away like cataracts of illuminated cobblestones. The Viking, upon whom the raw red wine had had a definitely exhilarating effect, shouted and sang and urged his car to wilder and wilder feats, while his great leonine spouse by his side shrieked her encouragement, as if she, too, were bent on sudden death. Patricia Teresa Riley, across whose lovely face the lights made fantastic play, was not so noisy, but obviously this was her idea of pleasure too, and the wide eyes she turned on William, when she wanted to give him some information, as she frequently did, were bright with a childish joy in this lunatic careering. As for William, now dizzy as well as muzzy, he would not have been surprised to have caught sight of San Francisco upside down, with a myriad skysigns beneath their wheels and the crowns of a thousand hats bobbing above them.

'Some hills!' roared the Viking.

'Some hills!' cried Miss Riley appreciatively, rather as if she and the Stensens had made them. 'Eh, Mr. Dursley?'

'Some hills!' repeated William carefully, in a small but firm voice. His back – but alas, only metaphorically – was against the wall, and he was upholding the honour of England.

The Viking now set his monster's nose to the upward trail, and they seemed to go roaring up and up in a great spiral, until at last most of the city lay blazing beneath them. Market Street was a river of molten gold, the tower of the Ferry Building a bright index finger, jewelled on top, and Oakland glittered across the water. They drew up at last, on a summit high above the constellated city.

'Well, Mr. Dursley,' said the Viking, when they had all got out, 'that's San Francisco. How d'you like it? We think it's pretty good.'

Shaky, still rather muzzy, but genuinely thrilled, William said that it was more than pretty good. Then he struggled with a thought. It was not a very profound one, but then any thought had to be wrestled with to be expressed at all at such a moment. When he began, he spoke more confidentially than he had yet spoken to any of them, even to P. T. Riley. There was something in their situation, high in the night, poised between the stars and the urban radiance below, that made for confidences. 'You know, San Francisco's a fine place. You could have a jolly life there. I can see that—'

'I'll say you can.'

'You be quiet, Clarry. I want to hear this. Go on.'

'Well, I was only going to say – I know you can have a grand time down there, where we're looking now, but all the same, you can't have – and I don't care who you are – you can't have as good a life as you imagine, when you're standing up here. I mean to say, if you took an absolute stranger, a man from another age altogether and a man with some imagination, and put him here and said "Look there – that's where you're going to live," he'd think he was in for something wonderful. And after a day or two down there, he'd be bitterly disappointed, wouldn't he?'

Mrs. Stensen, who clearly considered this a reflection on her native city, replied rather tartly: 'Well, I must say, Mr. Dursley, seeing you've only just come to San Francisco, I don't see what right you've got to say that. You can have as good a time right here—'

'Aw shucks! That's not the point, Clarry,' said her husband. 'You've got him wrong. I know what he means. He means it may be a swell place, but it's not so good as it looks from here – not by a thundering long chalk. And he's right. I see your point, Mr. Dursley, but for all that, I don't see what you're getting at.'

'I think I do,' said Miss Riley reflectively.

William found himself shrinking a little, for it looked as if the other three were about to turn themselves into an audience, and he had no lecture to deliver. 'Only this. It's not so good as it looks. It's rather like that pear I ate yesterday morning.' He explained in a few words about that pear. 'Now I'm not criticising America. I'm criticising life. Why – if you've got any imagination at all – is nothing as good as it looks at first? Why isn't there a life in San Francisco as good as what you can imagine it to be, looking at the place all glittering in the night? Now I'm going to the South Seas—'

'So am I,' Miss Riley put in, hastily. 'And I'm going to be thrilled to death with them, and I don't care what you say.'

'I hope you are,' he continued. 'I hope I am, but I've got a notion – simply based on previous experience – I shan't be, that I've got a South Seas in my head that beats the real South Seas hollow. And why should I? Would it be better if I'd nothing in my head, if I expected nothing?'

'You couldn't do it,' said the Viking, who had suddenly turned himself into a pessimistic philosopher. 'Here, let's sit down. There's a seat over there, and we've got coats, haven't we? Well, what I say is, you couldn't do it and keep on living. Wouldn't be worth the bother.'

'What a thing to say!' his wife cried. Possibly she saw in this statement a reflection on herself and their relationship, or again, as a woman she may have thought it her duty to defend the solid reality of life.

'All right, all right,' continued the Viking, with a large tolerance. 'But you don't get my meaning, Clarry. Mr.

Dursley's saying nothing's as good as it looks at first, and he's worried about it. Well, I'm not worried about it, because I know darned well it isn't. All the same, I guess you've got to keep on thinking it's going to be – if you get my meaning – otherwise you wouldn't keep on.'

'I would,' the Lioness declared stoutly. 'And if you ask me, a lot of things turn out a lot better than they look, though I don't say you're one of them, you big knocker. Look at that time we had to go to Del Monte.'

The Viking made a noise expressive of philosophical disgust at such an instance.

'Well, I agree with Clarry,' said Miss Riley thoughtfully. 'It's sort of – mixed. Sometimes you expect a lot and you're disappointed. Other times, you don't expect much and you're surprised at what's handed out to you. You expect too much, Mr. Dursley.'

'Don't bother answering them, Mr. Dursley,' said the Viking, with calm staggering effrontery. 'They don't get you. They think you're talking about having a picnic one day. Women! They've got no real imaginations. That's what makes 'em so tough, and why they don't take to sousing or go dippy or blow their brains out, same as men are always doing. No real imagination.'

After the two girls had made their inevitable shrill protest against this view of themselves, William, staring at the lights across the water, continued: 'I don't think it's just a question of expecting too much. Though it may be, and I may be making a fuss about nothing. What you feel is more than ordinary disappointment. It hurts more, takes more of the life out of you. But what I wonder is – whether it would be better to live entirely inside one's head, so to speak, or whether it would be better to have nothing inside one's head, imagine nothing, expect nothing, and then enjoy whatever comes along. It's the half-and-half arrangement that doesn't work and leaves one miserable. It's funny you should tell me not to expect too much. I ought to be telling you people that, for I'm easily the oldest person here. I'm forty, you know.'

'Well, you don't look it,' said the Viking quickly.

'Forty!' cried Miss Riley playfully. 'You're not really forty. You only think you are, Mr. William Dursley, of Buntingham, Suffolk, England. Forty must be different in England. I'm going to tell you something, whether you like it or not – you're only a boy, and you've just been talking like one.'

William retorted good-humouredly, and then the four of them, with the Viking in the van, wrangled amiably on. A certain cosy friendliness descended upon them, four pygmies huddled together in that little darkness between the two star-brimmed spaces, and William, as he pursued this thought or returned again to that, found himself holding the hand of Miss Patricia Teresa Riley. It was a firm well-shaped hand, hardly smaller than his own, and it frankly returned his grasp. No amorous pressure, no electric thrills, were there; and when they all rose to return to the car, the two hands parted without embarrassment, just as their owners, sleepy now, parted without embarrassment less than an hour later. But as William went back to his hotel, with a thousand distant lights still glittering in his memory, he carried with him a tiny patch of happiness, a small glowing spot that could not be exactly located, but that was unmistakably there, a sort of friendly Will-o'-the-Wisp that would not move too far out of bounds. He attributed its existence to the romantic charm of San Francisco, most romantic of New World cities, and did not suspect he was wrong until very late that night, when he ought to have been asleep.

CHAPTER V

ON THE PACIFIC

1

THE UNION Steam Ship Company's R.M.S. *Marukai*, conveying passengers, mails and cargo from San Francisco to Papeete, Rarotonga, Wellington and Sydney, was a middle-aged vessel of some 8,000 tons. It bore only the most fleeting resemblance to William's old acquaintance, the *Gargantua*. But though the *Marukai* was so much smaller, less spacious and luxurious, she had at least the advantage of seeming much saner. Once aboard her, you felt you were in a ship and were not wandering about in an hotel out of a nightmare. William went aboard early, and it did not take him more than ten minutes to explore all the first-class quarters and to see all that there was to see: his own cabin, and the bathroom opposite; the dining-saloon, aft; a shrouded and virginal drawing-room-cum-writing-room just above the dining-saloon; the general lounge, on the top deck, where there was space for a few games; and, at the other end of this deck, amidships, the bar and smoke-room. Nothing that he saw excited him, but most of it pleased him; and he acquired at once what he had never been able to acquire in the *Gargantua*, a faintly nautical air. He felt now he was really in a ship. After his preliminary tour of inspection, he settled down happily, not far from the head of the steep gangway, to watch the dockside bustle and the arrival of his fellow-passengers.

The most impressive arrival, beyond a shadow of doubt, was that of Miss P. T. Riley – now, at her own request, known to him as Terry – who came aboard like a princess, dazzling in white and apple-green, and escorted by a troop of friends, including the Viking and his Lioness. When she caught sight of William and waved a hand at him as she mounted the gangway, he swelled with pride and happiness. Within an hour or so, this ship, very trim, very snug, would take them out into the wide Pacific; and somewhere in that blue, pacing between coral and palm, were the Commander and Ramsbottom; and somewhere even further in the blue was Faraway, waiting with its treasure; and here, so radiant that she made all the other people look faded, was Terry, ready to sail the Pacific with him. This was to be alive at last. He would not have been elsewhere for a fortune.

'Hello, Bill,' cried Terry. 'Here we are. Excited?'

'Yes. Are you?'

'All lit up and sizzling. D'you know everybody here? This is Mrs. Littlebrun. And this is Charlie Drazin. Aren't you going to smile, Charlie? Clarry you know. Oh well, never mind. It's too late to start introductions, anyhow.'

Mr. Drazin and two other young men appeared to regard William with the gloomiest suspicion, as a mysterious alien who had suddenly and unaccountably decided to rob San Francisco of its brightest ornament. William returned their dark glances blithely, and the more depressed these enamoured young men seemed to be – and two of them were good-looking youngsters – the higher they raised his spirits. This was a new and heady sensation for him. He really began to feel that he was carrying off this lovely creature, and he did not stop to reflect how far his mind had travelled these last few days, since the time when she had made a nuisance of herself by insisting upon coming. There was now an orgy of facetious advice, hand-shaking, and photographing, in all of which William had his share.

This was a very different sort of departure from that of the *Gargantua* from Southampton. Perhaps the bright sun made all the difference: it ripened this leave-taking into something very demonstrative, colourful, exotic. Although the *Marukai* had not stirred an inch yet from her prosaic berth among the sheds piled high with tinned fruit, she already had about her a flavour of the South Seas. Among the second- and third-class passengers and their friends were some people of a fine dusky hue, with a soft midnight in their eyes, and William suddenly realised with a thrill that these were natives of the South Seas, genuine Polynesians, members of that strange dying race which had existed these last hundred years in a dimming twilight of the gods: the coral waxes, the palm grows, and man departs. There they were, large as life, chattering and hugging one another and hurling strange syllables to the dockside below, where others of their race were staring up and laughing and crying. They varied a good deal, these people; there were one or two men like shining brown bulls, and there were one or two syphilitic-looking scoundrels; there were one or two young girls, like lovely shy animals, and there were quite a few yellow fat middle-aged women. Among those to be left behind, standing below, was a terrible figure, a woman, possibly a half-caste, who might have been only middle-aged or might have been elderly, but who seemed to stare up, and sometimes grin in the ghastliest fashion, out of the very grave, for her face was eaten away to a death's head. Had this creature remained immobile and silent, it would not have been so bad, but as the time of departure drew nearer she began to nod and grin, and out of her skeleton's throat came hoarse shouts and farewell speeches in some Polynesian tongue, and the way in which these were received, with screams of laughter from the dark passengers, suggested to William that some of them were native obscenities. For a minute or two, William forgot Terry and her friends waving from below, and lost himself in fearful contemplation of this figure and voice of corruption. He could not see her, as he might easily have done, as a poor wasted creature trying to be cheerful with her friends and compatriots to the very last, a not unheroic being. He did not really see her as a person at all, only as a dread symbol. The *Marukai* moved off. He leaned over the rail with Terry and waved to her friends below. The other passengers waved and shouted. The Polynesians shouted and laughed with tears streaming down their cheeks. As the green strip of water broadened, William caught a last glimpse of that upturned face, and it seemed then as if the last shreds of rotting flesh had vanished from it, leaving it white bone in the sunlight.

'I'm going to do my unpacking afterwards, when we get out,' said Terry, as they steamed down the Bay. 'I want to see the last of good old S.F. Don't you?'

William said he did. They walked slowly down the deck together. 'I may never see it again,' he added, staring at the shore. And at that moment he had a sudden conviction that he never would.

'Now for the Golden Gate,' said Terry. 'I've been through it before, of course – many a time, but only just for little trips. I once went down to Los Angeles by water, and that's as far as I have been, this way. But this is different, isn't it, Bill? First stop – Tahiti. Over three thousand six hundred miles away. Ten days of the Pacific. Isn't that grand?' And she gave his arm a little squeeze.

'You know, I think I'm going to like this ship,' he observed solemnly.

She laughed. 'You know, Bill, you make me laugh. No, you mustn't get sore about it. If I didn't like you a whole lot, I wouldn't laugh at you – not that way, anyhow. It's because I think you're so cunning. You knaow,' mimicking him, 'Ai think Ai'm going to laike this ship. No, I can't do it.'

'Well, don't try then,' he remarked, a trifly stiffly.

'Sore? On your dignity?' And she cocked a bright eye at him.

He had to smile. 'Not a bit, Terry. It's just my silly English stiffness and shyness. It'll wear off. It's wearing off now.'

'Then I'm doing you good.'

'Yes, you are,' he declared, perhaps more fervently than the occasion demanded. 'Look at the gulls. I don't know how it is, but those birds have a most curious effect upon me. It's just as if they're writing poetry all the time – flashing about like that. Sea poetry – you know, beautiful but rather melancholy. There's a mist out there.'

'One of our afternoon fogs,' she told him. 'We shall hardly see the Golden Gate.'

'I hope that isn't a bad omen. I mean – about the island and everything.'

'You're not superstitious, are you, Bill? I shouldn't have thought you would be.'

'I wasn't. But I think I am now – a bit. Are you?'

'I should say I am. If you ask me, all girls are. I believe *everything* – cards, palmistry, crystal, astrology, tea leaves, *everything*. I had my fortune told last night.'

For the life of him William could not pretend to be superior about it. 'What did they say?'

'It was a swell fortune, I can tell you. You were in it too,

Bill – a short dark man from over the water. But I'm not going to tell you what she said about you. All kinds of exciting things were going to happen to me. Never a dull minute for Terry. But the island didn't come out strong.'

'I'm sorry about that. Do you mean, you weren't going to make anything out of Faraway?'

'Something like that. Never mind, whatever happens, Bill, I shan't blame you. I'm going to like all this, and I've been wanting some excuse for a long time to hop out of Brown Woburns and San Francisco, and have a few adventures. A man I know wanted me to go down to Hollywood and have a screen test, but I didn't like the look in his eye, and he said he'd have to take me himself, else I wouldn't have a chance. California's just full of men who'd have to take you themselves, else you wouldn't have a chance. Not like you, Bill. You didn't even want me to come along, did you?'

'I didn't – for about five minutes, that's all. I'm quite sure now, you know.' They stopped and leaned against the rail. They could feel a little more movement in the ship now.

'Wouldn't it be hell if we were sick most of the way?' said Terry dreamily.

'That's not likely. The Pacific's usually calm, isn't it?'

'They say so. Though when we went down to Los Angeles the ship nearly rolled the inside out of me. But that's down the coast all the way. This Tahiti run's supposed to be one of the easiest going. We'll be able to lie about and just get browner and browner. And I'll tell you the story of my life, Bill, and you shall tell me all about Buntingham, Suffolk, England. How's that?'

'It's a bargain, though I'll get the best of it. Hello, what's that?'

Terry looked. 'Pilot boat. We'll be dropping him soon.

We're in the open sea now. Nothing over there between us and China, and nothing this way – except a little coral island or two – between us and Tahiti. I'm going to unpack now, Bill. See you later.'

'Yes, at tea.'

'Gosh! – yes. I'd forgotten this was a British boat. I suppose there'll be tea every five minutes. All right, I'll meet you for tea.'

William lingered for a few minutes, saw the pilot climb into his boat, and watched the pilot boat herself vanish from sight. The wind freshened, the waves rose with it, and now the *Marukai* settled into a steady humming drive through air and water. Barring accidents, that rhythm, William knew, would not be broken until she had taken them over the rim of the world, had floated them into another life, far away, under strange stars. And he was happy, younger than he had felt for years, very much alive.

2

The next few days, under a sun that climbed higher every morning, grew fiercer, and sent most of them into thin white clothes, the *Marukai* steadily cut her way through an element that had lost all resemblance to water and looked like purple-black marble, across which a few rapidly fading lines of foam went arrowing from her bows. Nothing was to be seen but this enveloping saucer of shifting marble and a haze of sky; there were no passing ships, no birds, no leaping fish; it was as if the *Marukai* had sailed away from everything for ever. Only the crackle of wireless linked them with the outer world of markets and murders. The *Marukai* was now their world, and they slipped without effort into her idle, almost piggy routine.

By nine they were at breakfast, and generally eating a little more than they intended. During the morning they spent their time on the upper deck, reading, chatting, or playing deck quoits, a game at which the captain, a rosy New Zealand Scot, and the first officer, a long narrow Australian, were cunning and triumphant with the male passengers and immensely and tediously chivalrous with the ladies. They lunched, to the brassy strains of a panatrope, at one. After lunch, they would gather for coffee in the lounge, exchange little jokes for half an hour or so, and then retire for a siesta. Teatime found them in the lounge again, sometimes accompanied by the same little jokes. As dinner came early and most of them dressed for it, there was not much time between tea and dinner. The panatrope played steadily throughout dinner. Afterwards, there was coffee again in the lounge, games of bridge and rummy, occasional dancing on the deck (chiefly for the benefit of the ship's officers), and drinking in the smoke-room, where a long thin elderly steward attended to your wants, and did it in a very melancholy disillusioned fashion, like a man pressed into service by a suicide club. The best times of day were the early mornings, which had a lovely salt blue freshness, and the velvety nights, when you could sit about anywhere outside in complete comfort and let the soul expand. The hours between these two happy extremes were apt to be rather heavy and sticky, and were increasingly so as the ship moved further south.

There were only about thirty first-class passengers all told, and as they could hardly avoid one another, they quickly emerged into definite personalities. There were, first, the two people who shared a table in the dining-saloon with Terry and William. Mrs. da Silva was a little elderly Californian widow, with a heavily powdered face, *pince-nez* a trifle on one side, and a passion for gossip and sweet cocktails. Her favourite word was 'pretty,' which she pronounced as 'pruddy.' 'My!' she cried with genuine enthusiasm to Terry, on the very first night, 'but ain't you pruddy!' She considered the whole Pacific 'pruddy,' but not as 'pruddy' as California, of which she was never tired of boasting. She was a great traveller, and was now on her way to Australia, where she had relatives. Mrs. da Silva, however, was not so great a traveller as their other table companion, Mr. Cantock, a rather mysterious little man in his late fifties, of British nationality. Mr. Cantock appeared to have been on the move for years and years, for no particular reason. His talk, which he conducted in a queer squeaky voice, seemed to William unique, for it was at once dull and fantastic. It was fantastic because, before you knew how you had got there, Mr. Cantock had taken you into China or Central Africa or Siberia, and you found yourself accompanying him into some mysterious night-club in Shanghai or on a dubious train that ran from Harbin; and it was also dull because once he had got you to these outlandish places, nothing much happened, and, so far as you could gather, all the fuss was about the price of a cup of coffee or a courier's fees. At first, William had thought that there must be something wrong with him, when he could find no exact point in Mr. Cantock's stories, but on exchanging notes with Terry – a very delightful occupation, this, in which they thoroughly indulged themselves – he discovered that she could make even less out of them and was giving Mr. Cantock the most brilliant attentive smiles when she had not the least idea what he was drivelling about. William was more patient, and even found a certain fascination in

Mr. Cantock's reminiscences, a sort of cross-word puzzle fascination. 'Yes,' Mr. Cantock would be squeaking, in the middle of lunch, 'you had to be careful about the monkeys. "Don't go that way," they say, "or you may have trouble with the monkeys." So I told Mrs. Carruthers, and she said she didn't want to risk it. So I asked them if there was any other way, because we wanted to avoid the monkeys. They told me we could go by boat, but Mrs. Carruthers didn't want to do that. "Very well then," I said' – and here Mr. Cantock's voice would rise to a triumphant squeak, and he would look at them all triumphantly, and Terry and Mrs. da Silva, who had no idea what he was talking about, would reward him with smiles – ' "we'll have to risk the monkeys." Mrs. Carruthers agreed, and we got two natives to go with us. Oh yes – we saw the monkeys. And they saw us. . . .' And William, scooping away at his avocado pear, would wonder where they were supposed to have been, and who Mrs. Carruthers was, and why the monkeys were such a menace. For the rest, Mr. Cantock was very attentive to the ladies, and, though tremendously chivalrous in true ship's passenger style, there was a certain look in his eye that suggested that Mr. Cantock had hopes that in some ship somewhere, if only the voyage were long and dull enough and the cocktails held out, there would be a grand amorous adventure for him. Meanwhile, he plunged resolutely into his strange bogs of reminiscence.

Among the English passengers, there was Miss Settle, a brisk spinster about sixty, who would not miss anything and went from person to person, group to group, picking up scraps of information and gossip as a fowl picks up seed. She was on her way to New Zealand, like any of the other passengers. Then there was Mr. Boothroyd, a large stout North-countryman, who reminded William of Mr.

Ramsbottom, though he was not so huge a lump of character as Ramsbottom. Mr. Boothroyd's favourite pastime was staring, in a mild humorous fashion, at other people's activities, and several times at least during any one day, you would turn to see his large plain face, not unlike a vast potato, anchored near you. There was also another middle-aged English business man, whose name, if he ever really knew it, William could never succeed in remembering. All that William could remember about this man was that he lived, when at home, in South Norwood. He was a somewhat featureless, amiable fellow, so amiable indeed that it was very difficult, as William discovered several times, to conduct a conversation with him, for he instantly agreed with every remark you made and so kept you at pains to furnish an endless supply of such remarks. But he was in great demand for making a fourth at games. Then there were several pleasant mild New Zealanders, who gave nobody any trouble. This could not be said of their neighbours, the Australians. These included the fellow passenger whom William disliked most. This was one Rogers, an engineer from Sydney, a tall, sun-burned, spruce fellow in his thirties, not ill-looking, though somewhat foxy and narrow-eyed. He had a muscular brown body and being, like most citizens of Sydney, an excellent swimmer, he was very fond of displaying his prowess in the ship's swimming pool. There was nothing retiring about Mr. Rogers, and he loved to talk at the top of his voice in a vile Sydney accent. William could not bear him, and set him down from the first as an insufferable bounder; but there was more than this in his dislike. Rogers, clearly a ladies' man, had been very attentive to Terry from the beginning, and she was not as quick to see what a bounder he was as William would have wished. In short, William was jealous. The other

Australians were Mrs. Matherson, a massive woman with a trained Christian Science smile but a hard eye, and her young friend, Miss Stroud, who had a very long nose and a very small mouth and an Austrylian accent even more pronounced than Rogers': both these two were arrant gossipers and had something mean about them, and William, who was rapidly developing a hearty prejudice against Australia, disliked the pair of them. The only other noticeable Colonial was a mysterious sad Canadian called Forest, who seemed to spend nearly all his time in the smoke-room, silently sipping gins, though occasionally, late at night, he would suddenly start shouting in the most dramatic and terrifying manner. There was, in spite of his long silences, something vaguely theatrical about Forest: it was as if he had once seen one of those strong plays of tropical life and had become fascinated by the part of the gin-sodden waster.

The only other people who spent as much time in the smoke-room as Forest were the Burleckers and the Stocks, two youngish married couples from the Middle-West. The two men were like brothers, and both were big, bouncing, loud and brassily genial; while their respective wives were small, compact, hard, looking as if they were made of much tougher stuff than ordinary people and had been thoroughly enamelled and varnished. At times these four descended into the dining-saloon to eat, and now and then they would throw a deck quoit, but for the rest, they stayed in the smoke-room and passed their days, in a happy enchantment of alcoholic freedom, ordering and consuming all manner of drinks, to the increasing despair of the long thin elderly steward, who seemed to see the grave yawning for them. There was nothing exclusive about the Burleckers and the Stocks; they liked nothing better than to gather as many people as possible into their loud bibulous circle; but of course if they had any preference it was for Americans; and it was this that earned for them William's dislike, for they were always insisting upon Terry joining them, and when she did, as she sometimes liked to do, then William was faced with the unpleasant alternative of staying outside or joining a noisy silly gang of people who did not know how to drink properly. They were sometimes joined by a Mrs. Kinderfield, a vaguely literary woman, also from the Middle-West, who was on her way to settle for a time in Tahiti, where she had been before. She was a tall droopy creature, with eyeglasses and an uncertain profile, and she was capable of being instantly and devastatingly soulful with all comers, though she was also capable of sitting half the day and half the night with the Burleckers and the Stocks, keeping pace with them round after round, and of going off into horrible screams of laughter. Another American who would occasionally join them, though he always remained detached, was a grim little man called Jubb, who had something to do with films, steadily wore one shabby suit, and gave the impression of being more thoroughly disillusioned than any other human being on earth. He could outdrink all the others, and then quietly retire, merely a little grimmer than ever.

There was of course an outer ring of vaguer people, many of whom never achieved names and personalities, but remained mere appearances. Among these were a big American woman who always sat in a deck chair away from everybody, was said to be rich, and was known to be for ever complaining to the officers; and an invalidish little man, who appeared and disappeared like a ghost; and several French people, bound for Tahiti, the most noticeable of whom was an elderly one who wore a black béret and marched indefatigably round and round the deck, and was known to Mr. Burlecker as 'M'soo.' It is not on record what the elderly Frenchman thought of Mr. Burlecker.

And then there was Mr. William Ernest Tiefman, of Cincinnati, Ohio. He did not belong to any outer ring of vague people. Mr. Tiefman was the strangest character on the passenger list, and during the first half of the voyage he proved to be a treasure and a joy, for he broke the ice for everybody, and everywhere he went he left behind him a rising tide of conversation. It was only later in the voyage, when everybody knew everything about him, that he became such an intolerable nuisance and people fled at his approach. Terry discovered him first – for he had an eye for a pretty face – and promptly shared him with William on the very first evening, and soon they were all gloating over him. He was nothing much to look at, being a short stoutish fellow of fifty, who beamed at the world through thick horn-rimmed spectacles. Nor was there anything remarkable about his history; he was born in the Middle-West, of poor parents from somewhere in Central Europe, and after a long struggle had finally established himself in business, in the wholesale meat trade. It was as a traveller that Mr. Tiefman was unique. Never having seen anything in his life, he had suddenly determined, five years before, that he would see everything worth seeing, and to this end he had begun to collect time tables, tourist guide books, and travel brochures, until at last he had an astounding collection of these things, referring to every part of the world that a tourist would wish to visit. 'Yes, sir,' he would declare proudly, 'I reckon I got the most complete collection in the States.' This was only the beginning. After making a thorough study of his collection, he started to compile an itinerary that would take him round the world and enable him to see everything of note in the shortest possible time. He determined to create an itinerary that would put all the tourist agencies to shame, and he did. It took him four years, but at the end of that time he was triumphantly in possession of the *Great Itinerary*, in which all his movements for nearly a year were carefully set down, and, except for those periods, like this, when he was compelled to idle at sea, every waking hour of every day had its programme. This itinerary was a fair-sized volume, which he carried round with him and proudly exhibited, calling it his 'skedool' or, more often, his 'sked book.' His only reading was in this 'sked book' and you never saw him parted from it. 'Yeh,' he told everybody, on first acquaintance, 'this is my sked book. I got my itinerary in this. What's yours?' And he was constantly amazed – half proud and half disgusted – to find himself in a world of travellers who had only the vaguest notion of what an itinerary could be, who journeyed dreamily with the merest ghost of a 'sked.' Very soon it became one of the recognised ship's diversions to make Mr. Tiefman delve into his itinerary, out of which the most astonishing details of touristry were forthcoming. 'But what about Java, Mr. Tiefman?' some solemn wag would enquire. 'Surely you're not going to miss Java?'

'No, sir,' Mr. Tiefman would reply, promptly and proudly, whipping open his 'sked book.' 'I got a wonderful skedool for Java, right here. Here it is. May 19th. Get up at 5 a.m. to see the scenery. 9 a.m. arrive at Sourabaya. Clear baggage through the customs and take an automobile to the Oranji Hotel (reservations made by letter dated November 23rd). See bank, photographers, and collect reservations on touring car to Batavia (reservations made by letter dated November 23rd). If time, visit bazaar before lunch. Have a rice taffle for lunch—'

But the enquirer, having had enough of it by this time, would clap him on the back and say: 'You've certainly got a wonderful itinerary there, Mr. Tiefman.'

Another method was to ask him what he would be doing on a certain date. 'Now, Mr. Tiefman, you talk a lot about that itinerary of yours, but I bet you don't know what you'll be doing on June 11th.'

At this, the innocent creature, beaming through his thick glasses, would instantly turn to the 'sked book,' and begin reading the entry under that date. 'June 11th. Singapore. Get up at 5.45 a.m. Take an automobile to the Seaview Hotel and watch the sun rise, have a swim, and back to hotel. 9 a.m. breakfast. 9.30 a.m. visit the silk and curio shops in High Street. 10.15 a.m. visit Raffles Museum. 11.15 a.m. go to John Littles for a gin-sling—'

'Wait a minute, Mr. Tiefman. Sure that's all right – I mean, about going to John Littles for a gin-sling?'

And Mr. Tiefman would explain that it was the habit of residents of Singapore to go to that particular place at that particular hour for that particular drink. His itinerary made a special point of these details, and its accuracy could not be questioned. Wherever he went, it made sure that he did the correct thing at the correct time.

The more malicious wags, among whom his fellow Middle-Westerners Burlecker and Stock were prominent, used to torture him by gravely discussing, in his presence, the chances of various boats being two and three days late. 'That's so,' Mr. Burlecker would say to Mr. Stock. 'That's the trouble, I guess, with these Eastern boats. Can't keep to time. Must be the typhoons. They think nothing of getting you in three days late.' For this, of course, was Mr. Tiefman's nightmare. One delay would throw his whole itinerary out of gear, and from that time onwards he would be a lost man. The very thought of it made him look piteous.

But this was not all. Mr. Tiefman had ideas of his own on the question of the amount of baggage to be carried by the really efficient world traveller. 'Yes, *sir*,' he told them all, 'if you ask me, baggage is the bunk. And why? Cuts down the efficiency of travel. You got to plan it, that's all. You don't catch me with these big wardrobe trunks. No, *sir*. Don't need 'em. I travel with two little suitcases, and I say it's enough for any man.' And then he would explain, at any length his listeners allowed him, his economical system. His raincoat, which was silk-rubber-lined, served as dressing-gown, rug, and overcoat. He had a wonderful combination of walking-stick, umbrella and sword-stick. He had only one hat, one pair of shoes, and one peculiarly repulsive tie. He carried only two suits, both very ugly; one a dark chocolate, for evening wear, and the other a light striped yachting suit. And he had a special socks system, which was the joy of the ship. He had only three socks, not three pairs but three individual socks, all of course of the same pattern. Every night, before going to bed, he washed the sock he had been wearing on the left foot, and the next morning he put the spare clean sock on his right foot and transferred yesterday's right-foot sock to his left foot, thus wearing one clean sock every day and more or less achieving a clean pair every two days. All this he explained quite seriously to anybody who cared to listen to him, and for the first few days out, he did not want for listeners, having established himself as the ship's butt. His fellow Americans, including Terry, were especially assiduous and adroit in drawing him out and making him exhibit at full length his innocent folly, and to William, who became bored with the man as quickly as anybody, but to the last found something rather pathetic in his beaming idiocy, there was a disquietening touch of cruelty in the way in which they exploited and enjoyed his folly and then relentlessly flung him aside. Undoubtedly, Mr. Tiefman, once you were thoroughly acquainted with his various systems, was a most outrageous bore. There were moments, however, when William envied him his cast-iron cheerfulness, his untroubled self-absorption. Others he bored, himself he could not bore. Such was Mr. William Ernest Tiefman, of Cincinnati, Ohio, a man of ruthless efficiency, no doubt, but yet a man not without wonder and poetry in his composition, for through years of the wholesale meat trade in Ohio he had carried with him a vision of arriving at Sourabaya at 9 a.m. on May 19th, of going at 11.15 a.m. on June 11th for a gin-sling to John Littles in Singapore. A dream had come through the multitude of business. This was a fact that William could now appreciate, for he too was travelling in a dream.

3

Every morning, William awoke to find by his bedside, next to the glass of chilled orange juice, a copy of that day's *Wireless News*, which gave typewritten extracts from the world's news, mostly in terms of Australia, and in addition, presented its readers with various items of information about Polynesia. *Birds in the air, and seaweeds in the water,* it would observe, *indicated the nearness or absence of land; and there is actual record of one voyager aiming at Rarotonga from the north know he had missed it by the coldness of the sea; without delay he about ship, and soon made the island.* Or it might be: *Pearl fish-hooks, though of ancient fashion, are still used and highly esteemed in the Marquesas and other isles of the South Seas. A strip, some five or six inches long and nearly one wide, is cut from a pearl shell, and carefully shaped and polished to resemble a small fish, the natural curve of the shell aiding the likeness* . . . Or again it might be: *I shall never forget the landing of the first horse on the island of Lifu in 1862. We cast anchor in Wide Bay, on a Saturday afternoon, as near shore as was prudent. The horse had been brought from Sydney, and had been on board about a fortnight* . . . It was like catching a glimpse of a little signpost or two each morning. Here he was, with every hour bringing him nearer these fabled South Seas. That unchanging blue vacuum, in which they seemed to be poised for ever, would soon give place to coral, coloured fish, black sand, rows of nodding palms, and sunsets behind dark jagged peaks. Just as if, one morning soon, a curtain would go up.

That, however, was only one journey he was making. There were others, even more adventurous, here in this ship. He was living so much more intensely now than he had done for many years, that it was as if he had just been born. Nevertheless, he was more William Dursley than he had ever been before. The other had been a mere shadow of this self. Somehow he contrived now to look more himself than he had ever done before, and these days he was frequently to be found glancing at himself in the mirror. Already he was deeply tanned, and this suited his natural dark complexion. His face had filled out a little too, and his eyes seemed brighter. There was something even boyish about his appearance, in these easy white clothes. It was a boy who frowned back at him out of that glass in his cabin. Why – hang it! – most of the time now, he felt a boy again.

But not always, of course. There were times when he fell into a sudden panic. The worst of them came in the middle of the night, when something – perhaps the heat, perhaps a touch of liver – worried him and would not let him have unbroken sleep. Then, staring into the shrouded half-light of his cabin, listening to the *whirr* of his fan and the long-drawn sibilants of the moving ship, he would ask himself in quick alarm what he was doing there. The whole business of the island would then appear lunatic in its unreality. He saw himself in the middle of the Pacific on a crazy errand. Even Terry herself, at these times, would seem an unreal, rather frightening figure, as if she were a spectre he had somehow raised. Once or twice, when he awoke to find himself trapped in this black gulf between two days, his feeling of panic dropped almost immediately into one of complete despair, and he would be nothing but a tiny quivering point of consciousness in a vast dark negation. He had had innumerable bad moments at home, but none to equal these descents into the pit. Looking back on them, when he was calmer, he would ask himself if he were merely paying for this new intensity of life, or was simply the victim of a tormented liver. Always, however, the morning sun, his orange juice and the *Wireless News* issued him into a golden world again, and he would begin thinking about these approaching South Sea islands. He would also – and perhaps far more often – begin thinking again about Terry.

He knew now, only too well, that with this girl he was falling fathoms deep in love. He had not felt like this about anyone for years, perhaps never before, and he had an obscure conviction that he would never feel like this about anyone again. Such reason as he could still command told him that this sudden infatuation was absurd, that he hardly knew the girl, that she was years and years younger than he was, that her whole background was different from his, that no good could possibly come of it. But not a word of this went home. It was the strangest thing, as if a bomb, charged with colour and sweetness, had suddenly burst inside him. He was a boy again, staring and raving. Certainly it had been all very sudden, yet now it seemed inevitable. That he should have gone to San Francisco expecting to meet an elderly trader called P. T. Riley seemed both droll and pitiful, and made him see that other little self as a pathetic manikin, scarcely out of the womb. He could not tell when Terry had first captured his imagination, but now she queened it securely there. She was at once the most real and the most unreal person in the world. The moment she was out of sight, she became strangely unreal, and he would try to piece her together in the dark of his mind, to make some image that would correspond to the haunting essence of her that was always there. When he saw her again, her reality was overwhelming, as if he was looking at a human being for the first time. She might have been there for ever. This was what a woman's face and a woman's body should be. All the legends gathered here, and shone in truth. And already he was past the point at which she simply appeared mistily lovely and desirable. It was the little things, the sudden intimacies of appearance he discovered in her, that would give him a quick pang of heartache: the down along her arms would catch the sunlight; there was a magical mole on her left cheek; and when she was tired, two faint blue shadows would appear beneath her eyes, and at the very sight of them he could have cried out with tenderness.

She was harder, more openly cynical, than other girls he had known in England, and there were moments when he winced, as if some throbbing nerve of sentiment had felt the probe; but nevertheless nearly everything she told him about herself seemed to him exquisitely pitiful, enchanting. He looked back on San Francisco as on a

city in a fairy-tale. Her father and mother, her friends at
school and college, even the Viking and his wife and the
others who came down to the boat, all were touched with
glamour. He caught glimpses of different Terrys through
the years, from the fat little girl up to the clear-cut shining
creature by his side, and that magical growth, that epic
of stored sweetness, seemed to him the most marvellous
thing in the world. She was amused by his interest in
these details of her past life, but she was also moved by
it, for though she had had many admirers and one or
two definite lovers, it seemed, they had never displayed
that kind of interest in her. Moonstruck as he was, he did
not imagine that she was wonderfully witty or wise or even
unusually sensitive; but then she had for him some quality
that transcended wit and wisdom, and made an undue
sensitiveness look foolish. Her high spirits, which seemed
to him to burst out of a youth far more splendid and self-
confident than that of any English girls he had known,
were adorable, even though at times they might frighten
him a little, by making him feel rather old, timid, faded.
When he did feel this, he was immediately disgusted and
angry with himself, passing nothing on to her. He was
convinced that to deny, out of a sudden fit of timidity,
the radiance that she cast on the life about her would be
to sin against the light; and that if fear or pride or both
caused him to turn aside from her, then the best in him,
the last spring of youth, would be lost for ever, and
nothing would be left to him but to wither. All the rich
islands in the world could not compensate him then.
This, even more than Faraway, was a test. He was now
embarked on more than one voyage.

He did not know yet, after five days out, what she
thought about him. He did not even know if she realised
he was in love with her. Accustomed to being openly

admired at once, she had obviously been a little piqued by his cool treatment of her at their very first interview, when he had not hidden his dismay at the idea of her coming with him to Tahiti. It had been a challenge that she had accepted at once, and so she had taken some pains to win him over. His initial attitude towards her, he could see now, had given her a certain respect for him; she had known too many easily admiring and amorous males. The Californian, if she was to be believed, seemed to be an unusually predatory male animal. Then their common interest in Faraway Island, their common enthusiasm for the South Seas, had very quickly given them a solid footing together, and not for a moment did he doubt her friendliness. She was always glad to see him, never seemed bored. There had been times – chiefly when they had joined the Burleckers and the Stocks and the other Americans in the smoke-room – when William had suddenly felt that he had completely dropped out of her attention, when he had been visited by that maddening baffled sense of not being able to do or say anything that would ever arrest her attention again, as if he had suddenly dwindled into a creature not six inches high, piping into vacancy. He had to admit, however, that this did not often happen. It was understood vaguely in the ship that Terry and he had some business to transact together in Tahiti, and some of the other passengers were under the impression that their respective fathers had once been partners. But of course there seemed something very odd about this very attractive American girl and this rather quiet Englishman being associated in this way, especially as the nature of their business was never revealed, with the result that there was a certain amount of gossip about them, as Terry had said from the first there would be. Mrs. Matherson and her friend, Miss

Stroud, those desiccated Australians, looked somewhat sourly upon this pretty Miss Riley. Neither were they very cordial to William, who, for his part, detested the pair of them. But even they, so far, had not been able to collect any new evidence. William's cabin was on the opposite side of the ship from Terry's, and they took good care not to call upon one another.

It was not to be expected that a girl like Terry could be aboard ship and not be surrounded by attentive males. Of these, Rogers, the tall brown engineer from Sydney, was the most persistent and easily gave William most annoyance. Mr. Cantock, their table companion, was frequently on hand to proffer a cocktail and be immensely chivalrous; but William did not mind him much. Burlecker too, when he could escape from the hard gaze of his wife, was very attentive. And one of the vague Frenchmen, young and not bad-looking, was daily becoming less vague, so far as Terry was concerned. Thus William discovered, to his horror, that he could be wildly jealous. It was impossible to do anything about it. He had opened a wide window, the better to enjoy the moonshine and starshine and tangled scents of his love, and so this panther had come bounding in. Hateful, hateful, but there it was. He could hardly bring himself to be decently civil to Rogers, a loud, patronising, ignorant fellow, but unfortunately just the sort of bounder who might easily capture a girl's fancy for the length of a voyage. He was a good dancer, a fine swimmer, played an excellent game of deck tennis and quoits, and always had a fund of silly rattling talk. And Terry, William would point out to himself, very carefully, was not to know that the man was a cheap bounder: it would take an Englishman or a fellow Australian to see that. But William dropped hints to her, rather mean little hints; and sometimes he said similar things about the other men he found her laughing and talking with; and then he would feel rather sick with himself about it. So it was not all a happy enchantment. After being on the heights for an hour or so, he would suddenly find himself in one of these nettlebeds of jealousy and suspicion, and then, after the first soreness had worn off, he would creep away feeling empty, forlorn. But then a smile, a word, or a sudden sharp recognition of the adorable quality of her, whether she was with him or not, would set him on the heights again, smiling and dreamy in full sunlight. Every day had its own bitter-sweet flavour.

At the end of the fifth day out, on a marvellous night of stars, he was compelled to say and do something. They had been dancing on the chalked space of the upper deck, just outside the smoke-room. The ship went gliding along like an old slipper over a Persian rug. The Pacific was purring, velvety. From the amplifier, connected with the panatrope below, came those impudent little dance tunes that gradually took on a mellow and somewhat melancholy quality as the night grew vaster round them. William had danced, not too successfully, for he was woefully inexpert, with Terry; had then been seized by the sprightly old Miss Settle; had had a caricature of a waltz with the tall droopy Mrs. Kinderfield; and had then sought rest and decency on a neighbouring seat, where Mr. Boothroyd, the stout North-countryman, had joined him and had talked at length on a variety of subjects, from rabbit skins to tunny fishing. People gradually drifted away from the music, some to the smoke-room for a last drink and a sandwich, others to their cabins. William had exchanged languid remarks with half-a-dozen people, and, finally, seeing that Terry was going on dancing, alternately with Rogers and the second officer, a tall fair youngster from New Zealand and a great dancing man, he had wandered into the smoke-room, with the dance tunes still making a faint wistful melancholy in his head, to have a large whisky-and-soda. He did not stay long there. The Burleckers and the Stocks, with Mrs. Kinderfield and the grim Jubb, were being very noisy, and Forest, the drunk Canadian, showed signs of bursting into one of his idiotic shouting fits. Mr. Cantock, in a corner, was being very gallant over sandwiches and long drinks, to little Mrs. da Silva. William did not want to join any of them, and so finished his drink fairly quickly, and then went out, to stroll about the deck. Terry was still dancing, and she and Miss Stroud were the only women there. Rogers looked delighted with himself. William walked slowly past the little lighted space, and, pursued and oddly taunted by the music, moved forward down the deserted deck. That last drink had been just enough to make him feel sorry for himself. He smoked meditatively, watched the glimmer of reflected lights in the water, in which a ghostly foam went racing, and then stared rather sadly out into the distance where dark water met the starless edge of sky. He was troubled by a feeling of confused dumb pathos. The dance music went on and on, maddening now in its monotony. Damn them! – why couldn't they be quiet for an hour? There was a hateful little peevish voice crying in his head.

He moved nearer the dancers, then leaned against the rail again and looked out to sea. There came a silence, which instantly made the night completely solid. He did not turn round, but continued to look far out, sullenly.

'Hello, Bill! Thought you'd gone for a drink.'

She was coming up to him, with Rogers hanging about, rather uncertainly, a few yards in the rear. To-night she was wearing an evening dress he had not seen before, of palest blue and with a curious shimmer to it, and it made her look very vivid and lovely. He looked at her, then turned his head. He knew he was being stupid, but for the life of him he could not help it.

'I did go for a drink,' he said, in a rather muffled voice. 'That was some time ago.'

'Well,' she said cheerfully, 'what about another? There's just time.'

'I'm not keen. Unless you want one particularly.'

'Why, what's the matter?'

'Oh!' – and he hunched up his shoulders – 'they're too noisy in there. That crowd bores me. I want to be quiet for once.'

She joined him on the rail. 'Bill, are you telling me to go away?'

'No' – he paused – 'of course not.'

'You sound like it. I think I'd better go. Mr. Rogers wants to stand me a large drink, he says.'

'So he ought,' said William bitterly. Oh! – it was idiotic. He was forty and talking like a snubbed schoolboy. But there was no help for it. 'You've earned it.'

'Oh!' And for a second she drew back, and it looked as if she was going to turn away from him. But then she gave a short laugh, took him firmly by the arm and marched him down the deck. 'What's the matter with you to-night, Bill?'

'Nothing.'

'I believe – I do believe – you're jealous of Mr. Rogers.' William did not reply.

'Let's stop here.' They were in a corner, in shadow, and there they remained, leaning against the rail. The night was so wonderfully soft that William could hardly believe in it. There was still a fine glitter of stars. Some of the familiar constellations were now behaving very queerly, moving over to different parts of the sky and standing on their heads. Within the next two days, they would be crossing the Equator. All very odd.

'If you're jealous of Mr. Rogers, Bill, you must be crazy.'

'I think I am crazy.'

'You? What, Mr. William Dursley, of Buntingham, Suffolk, England! Never. Bill,' she added, more seriously, 'nothing's really upset you, has it? If you're not used to it, this hot weather can be pretty grim.'

'I don't mind it,' he told her. 'Except I rarely get a whole night's sleep. I wake up at odd times in the middle of the night, and sometimes when I just lie awake in the dark, and it isn't to-day and it isn't to-morrow, it's just nothing, you know – I get frightfully depressed. About everything. Do you ever feel like that, Terry?'

'I should say I do.'

'I shouldn't have thought you would.'

'Shows what *you* know about me, Mr. Dursley. Sometimes I get the most God-awful blues you could imagine. That's when I began thinking about life. I say, a girl shouldn't think about life. It won't stand it.'

William was taken aback by this. It was the sort of thing he might have said himself, but he did not expect Terry to say it. And if it had been anyone else, he would have felt an instant slight contempt, for there is always something rather childish about other people's pessimism. It is absurd that they should luxuriate in such moods.

'Now this' – and with a vague gesture she indicated the night – 'is different. I could stand here for hours and hours – yes, by myself – just staring and thinking in a fuzzy sort of way, seeing it all very big and me very little, and feeling bee-yutifully sad, Bill. That's grand. I like to pretend I'm hard-boiled all right, but really I'm just as sentimental as a greeting card. I guess you are too – aren't you, Bill?'

Bill believed he was.

'The nicest folks are,' she continued, slowly. 'But you've got to put up a show of being tough nowadays, especially if you're a girl, or else they'd all be walking over you with nailed boots. They do that anyhow, in the long run, if you're a woman.'

'Why do you say that?' William was curious rather than argumentative. 'You seem to me to have a very good time. As a matter of fact – and I'm not whining – you have a much better time than I've ever had. Until just lately, I don't seem ever to have had a chance of doing what I wanted to do. There was the war, then my father and mother – and the business to be kept going. And you put off doing things you want to do, just for a year or two, and then another year or two – and then suddenly you find half your life's gone, and the better half. And it takes the heart out of you. It shouldn't, I suppose, but it does. It was only the accident of my uncle coming along when he did, I believe, that shook me out of it. But you know all about that.'

'Yes, Bill. I haven't forgotten any of it. Though when you begin the old-man stuff, you make me rather tired. That must be a bad English habit. You wouldn't catch a Californian talking like that, especially to a girl on a night like this. You ought to have seen some of the "boys" – as they called themselves – who've said things to me – fifty-five and sixty, some of them, and sagging all over – ugh!'

This ought to have been consoling, but that 'boys' made William wince. He said nothing.

'What do you mean, though, saying I seem to have such a good time?'

'Well,' replied William, trying to achieve a detached, judicial air, 'you've obviously lots of friends – and admirers. Everybody seems to like you. You're young and strong and healthy—'

'Go on, Bill,' she laughed. 'And clean – and fairly honest.'

'And you're lovely to look at,' he continued, soberly.

'Now when you say it like that,' she broke in, eagerly, 'you know – just quietly – well, it sounds the nicest thing anybody has ever said to me. If you thought that out, Bill, then you're very clever, you're deep.'

'I didn't think it out. It doesn't need thinking out. I'm merely trying to tell you, Terry, why I think you have a good time. You're lovely – and you know it – and that ought to make you happy. You've got grand high spirits – I've seen that already – so that you can always have fun, if you want it. And it seems to me you go and do what you want to do. For instance, you wanted to visit the South Seas – and here you are. I don't suppose you thought about it, beforehand, a tenth of the time I did. Of course that may be because you're an American. It seems to me there's always one nation that just does what it wants in the world. A hundred years ago, it was the English. They just went anywhere, and didn't give a damn. Now it's the Americans. Perhaps in twenty or thirty years time, it'll be the Russians – or the Chinese. But there you are.'

'Well, when you put it like that, I must say it all sounds fine – and I feel I ought to be ashamed of myself if I'm not having the swellest time. I suppose I was thinking – about different things. What goes on inside your head. Perhaps that's more important to a girl than it is to a man.'

'I doubt it,' said William.

She put her arm through his, and after a moment their fingers interlaced. William kept very still. The huge soft breath of the night was all about them, faintly salt. His eye rested on the dim curve of her cheek as she continued to look out to sea. 'I've just come through a bad time, Bill,' she said quietly, without turning her head. 'Not the first either, but the worst. I fell in love with a man, and he fell in love with me – and he was married. I don't say there's anything startling in that, but this was different. It wouldn't work, and yet we couldn't stop it. Three times we went away together – not for good, but just to see what happened. And it happened all right, and worse every time. I'd see him tearing himself in two. He'd look at me, and I'd know he was hating me. And then I'd hate him, or sometimes I'd hate myself. And we'd say bitter things. We'd run off and just keep on hurting ourselves. Why have we always to be hurting ourselves, Bill? Well, it had to finish. You can't keep tearing yourself in two for ever, can you? I said I wouldn't see him again. He got transferred East – to Philadelphia, I think – and moved out. I didn't know that at first, and it wasn't till I broke down, felt I had to see him again, that I found he'd gone. I hated myself for that too. It's bad enough to be as weak as that, and it's worse when you're weak for nothing, if you see what I mean. I had to get over it. Talk about high spirits – my God! – if you'd seen me then. I was all raw, felt all empty inside. Sometimes my heart seemed to stop. That's what I meant – about women. It can't be as bad as that for a man.' She stopped abruptly.

'I'm sorry,' said William, as quietly as he could. 'Have you – got over it now?' He had never felt so queer a pang. There was jealousy in it, no doubt; there was certainly pity; but indeed there were so many things in it that he felt strongly without knowing what it was he felt. But he had time to notice that their interlaced fingers were hurting.

Now she loosened them. 'Yes, I'm through. Just about out of convalescence, except perhaps on bad nights. It's a rotten shame we're not more sensible in our dreams, isn't it? The old unconscious won't keep up with you, and will let you down. Give me a cigarette, Bill. No, don't bother. I don't want one.' She faced him, and even in that shadow her eyes were very bright. It was queer how different they looked from all the eyes he had ever known, just because they were set a trifle obliquely and rather more widely part than most people's. And really she herself was not so very different from a thousand other girls; she talked and felt and thought as they all did; probably in San Francisco there were scores of girls who behaved in almost identically the same way; and so it was queer that her eyes should be so different. But then her eyes were part of her, like that rather rough choky voice and that curious blue-black and creamy brilliance.

'But what's this, Bill? What's come over you? Standing there sulking, and then pretending to be jealous of that Rogers man, and then telling me you're crazy.'

'I was stupid, I know.'

'But that's no proper explanation, because, you see, you don't happen to be stupid.'

'I'm not so sure,' he told her. 'But if you want to know, I suppose I can explain. I was sulking here, simply because I wanted you out here with me and you would go on dancing. Yes, of course – you needn't say anything. Of course, it's babyish. Then I wasn't pretending to be jealous of Rogers. I wish I had been pretending. But unfortunately it was real. I *was* jealous of Rogers. He happens to be a chap I don't like, anyhow, but even if it had been somebody I do like, I might have been jealous. And that's why I admitted I'm crazy. You see, I seem to have suddenly gone crazy about you. Oh! – it sounds like one of those damned silly songs. But I think about you all the time.'

'But, Bill, I hadn't the ghost of a notion you were this way,' she protested. 'When did it start, anyway?'

'I don't know. Quite early.'

'Not that first date we had together,' she remarked grimly.

'No, perhaps not. Though – I don't know – it may have started then. Probably did. But it's been going on ever since. I've not felt like this about anybody for years, Terry – perhaps never before. And I never shall again. It's like a sort of enchantment, Terry. I'm lost in it. If I'm crazy, I'm crazy – but I've started now and you're going to hear about it.' And she did hear about it, for he went on and on, pouring out his heart.

When he came to a halt, she drew a long breath. 'Well, Bill, when you *do* start talking, you *start*. I wouldn't have believed it possible.' She looked closely, mischievously, at him.

All virtue had gone out of him now. He was back to earth, a burst balloon. 'All right,' he said shortly, gruffly. 'I suppose you've a right to be amused. But I had to tell you. Perhaps I ought to be thankful you're not offended.' He was very much the stiff little Englishman in his speech.

'So it's like that,' she said, in a husky mocking whisper. 'Poor Bill! And I thought you were thinking about your island all the time.'

She looked at him, smiling. Then she was in his arms and he was kissing her, with a fine certainty that surprised him. Her cheeks were cool, fragrant, and her lips had a faint salt taste, like the night itself.

She let her hands rest on the lapels of his dinner jacket for a moment, then pushed him away. 'No, somebody's coming,' she said quickly. 'I'm going down. Feel better now, Bill? Good-night.' And she fairly ran away.

'I saw you,' said a loud but indistinctive voice, 'I saw

you. But wha' the hell, tha's all right.' It was the Canadian
drunk, Forest, who came tottering up, his long figure all
grotesque angles. 'It's only Jim Forest – and wha's he but
a blurry old soak? Tha's all he is. Tha's all he is – *now.*'
He brought out this last word with such emphasis that he
nearly knocked himself down. So now he rested one hand
heavily on William's shoulder, and leaned, at a fantastic
angle, against the rail. 'I say – I saw you. An' I say – tha's
the stuff. Berrer than booze. You take my advice, kid,' he
continued, in a paternal strain, though actually he must
have been a few years younger than William, 'you stick to
tha'. Best girl on the ship – easily – *easily.* You're lucky
devil. I was once lucky devil, bu' now I'm Jim Forest – the
blurry old soak. Le's have a good, good yarn, shall we?'

William made it clear that he was not in favour of a
good yarn at that hour.

'You're ri', kid,' cried Mr. Forest enthusiastically. 'Who
th'ell wants good yarn. No, no, no. Le's go to bed.'

So William, still haunted by those kisses, put an end to
the evening by piloting and supporting Forest, who was
as difficult to manage as a six-foot concertina, in the
direction of his cabin. He did it too with great good-
humour. After all, in his own fashion, he was nearly as
drunk as Forest.

4

Now, when they had broken into the second week, the
voyage, which had been only a day or two before still new
and strange, seemed to have been going on for ever.
Their ordinary life on land belonged to a previous avatar.
Those people who had soon emerged as personalities
now stood out with dreadful distinctness. There were

changes in their universe. The Pacific was no longer like purple-black marble; it was lighter and gayer, changing from cobalt to the most brilliant emerald; its surface was being for ever broken by flying fish, sometimes solitary, sometimes in showers; but for the rest, it still remained the great emptiness it had been from the first. Now and again, the sky would darken so quickly that a hand might have pulled a dirty curtain across it, and then for an hour or so there would be a drumming downpour. The late mornings and the afternoons were hotter and stickier than ever, and people with tender livers began to show marked signs of temper. Terry and William agreed that the food, though looking as attractive as ever on the menu card, was beginning to lose its flavour. But Mr. Cantock still ate heartily, and Mrs. da Silva, who was an experimental feeder, plunged more wildly than ever, probably in search of something really 'pruddy' to eat. There were many uncomplimentary references to the steward who worked the panatrope, for the three tunes for which he had a passion were now on everybody's nerves. The interval between lunch and tea appeared to elongate itself daily, and merely to pass through it, unless you were a good afternoon sleeper, was like walking down a long dusty road. Only at sunset did they all become brighter and friendlier; and the nights came like a bene-diction.

This little world, like any other, hummed with news. There was a mysterious quarrel between the two Austra-lian women, Mrs. Matherson and Miss Stroud, on the one side, and Mr. Cantock, on the other. It was rumoured that Mr. Cantock, who was her neighbour, had made improper advances, late one night, to Miss Stroud. It was said that the captain had had to intervene. But nobody knew for certain what it was all about; and meanwhile, Mrs. Matherson, her eyes harder than ever, was saying bitter things about Mr. Cantock to select listeners in the lounge; Miss Stroud was looking more than ever down her long nose, still triumphantly virgin; and Mr. Cantock was busy keeping clear of the pair of them, inviting Mrs. da Silva, Terry, William, anybody, to more and more cocktails in the smoke-room, where he lost himself and his hearers in vast tangled forests of reminiscence, in which it was impossible to distinguish between Central Africa and China, and couriers turned into dancing girls and commissioners into monkeys. Mr. Tiefman wandered about, 'sked book' in hand, looking for somebody with whom he could compare itineraries, and was able to batten once or twice upon the little invalidish man, who appeared and disappeared like a ghost. But Mr. Tiefman was worried, and smoke-room gossip had it that either Burlecker or Jubb had sneaked into his cabin and stolen that famous third sock. A more likely explanation was that either the first or second officer had told him that the boat might be two days late in arriving at Wellington. Mr. Boothroyd, the genial fat starer, had achieved fame by winning two Jack Pots in one morning from the automatic gambling machine in the barber's shop. There were rumours of an affair in progress between Mrs. Kinderfield, who what with literature and drink and her determination to settle in Tahiti was obviously no better than she should be, and a very handsome brown fellow in the second-class, said to be a half-caste from Papeete. They had been seen together, quite late at night, in that little well of lower deck between the first- and second-class quarters. Moreover, the chap came into the first-class smoke-room, bold as brass. Mr. and Mrs. Burlecker had had a tremendous quarrel very late one night, after an unusually prolonged session in the smoke-room, and it was said that Mr. Bur-

lecker had been locked out of the cabin for a long time
and had hammered on the door and shouted insults. Mr.
What's-His-Name from South Norwood was now throwing
so cunning a deck quoit that he had twice beaten the
captain himself. Miss Settle, the brisk English spinster,
had had a wireless message from New Zealand to say that
her niece had given birth to a boy. Stock and Rogers were
hardly on speaking terms any longer, after having had a
long and bitter argument about the respective merits of
the Middle-West and Australia. The big rich American
woman, who always sat on a deck chair away from everybody else and was said to complain a great deal, had given
ten dollars towards the prizes for the stewards' boxing
contest. And the steward at the captain's table had made
the third officer look very silly in three rounds. Two
of the vague French passengers had turned out to be a
honeymoon couple, now on their way, via Tahiti, to some
very remote South Sea island, where they would have to
live for several years; and it was generally agreed that
nobody would have guessed they had such a romantic
destiny, for they looked such a skinny spotty pair. And the
captain had had everybody in turn up to his cabin after
dinner, for coffee and liqueurs, and had solemnly read
out riddles for them to guess, from cuttings out of New
Zealand papers. It was thought that Mr. Dursley, that
nice quiet Englishman, and Miss Riley, the very pretty
American girl, were 'thicker' than ever, though exactly
how 'thick' could not be discovered.

Actually, during the few days that followed their late
hour on deck, William and Terry were less intimate than
they had been that night. Nevertheless, their relationship
was not what it had been before; it grew quietly and
strengthened itself, out of sight; and now and again they
would exchange a short remark or two, or perhaps merely

a smile, that put them close together and quite apart from all the other people in the ship. To say that William was completely satisfied with this would be to libel him as a lover, but he was not painfully dissatisfied. The enchantment of her mere presence remained for him, and the hottest and stickiest afternoon could not stifle that cool magic.

They crossed the Equator, and Neptune held his court, and there was a great deal of screaming horseplay with red paint and black paint, lather made of oatmeal, and the ship's swimming bath, hideous with stewards very roughly disguised as mermaids. The sun bounded up the morning sky, to challenge them fiercely. The sea was a melting mirror. Clouds raced across the blue, let fall their thundering rain, then passed like a dream. The elderly Frenchman with the black béret took to sun bathing, up among the boats, and baked himself like a brick. A few birds came, to remind them that the first islands, mere atolls, were not far away. Forest disappeared into his cabin, and was reported to be under the care of the ship's old doctor, a yellow withered wisp of a man, and no mean tippler himself. Mr. Tiefman was observed examining his 'sked book' on the Tahiti page, for he would be spending a day there with the ship and of course had already planned to make the most of it. All the passengers due to land at Papeete, the port of Tahiti, began to talk vaguely of packing, but did nothing about it, as if the lotus-spell was already upon them. The assistant purser put up large facetious notices announcing a fancy-dress parade and dance for both first- and second-class passengers, with prizes for the best costumes. Down below, in his little oven of a shop, the barber overhauled his stock of fancy costumes, crêpe hair, false whiskers and noses, for sale or hire to the more ambitious masqueraders. The three stewardesses could be seen dashing in and out of cabins importantly, needles in their mouths and lengths of frivolous material over their arms. Women pinned things on one another. Men, looking mysterious, took stewards on one side and confided in them. For the passengers to Tahiti, this fancy-dress parade and dance was to be the last important event of the voyage. For them it was to end, symbolically perhaps, in carnival.

5

Not having donned fancy-dress these many years, William was at first disposed to keep out of it. Nearly all the other people, however, were joining in; Terry had howled him down when he had told her he was diffident about it; so he gravely considered this disguise and that and finally sought out the barber, with whom he had already had some friendly chat. Between them they decided that William should be a clown. There was a splendid clown's costume, complete with frilly ruff and little hat, in pink and green, and the barber had plenty of make-up. Having arrived at this decision, William discovered, to his astonishment, that somewhere in the depths of his being he must have long cherished the notion of appearing sometimes as a clown. He found himself looking forward to the prospect of clownage. There was something attractive, in a massive primitive fashion, about painting one's face white and then daubing on it, in the boldest crimson, a monstrous nose, grinning mouth, and fierce dimples.

We know only too well that there are times when everything goes wrong, but, in our haste to make the worst of life, we are apt to forget that there are also times when everything goes right. This night remained in William's memory as one of those times. A fancy-dress dance on board a smallish steamer on the Pacific does not suggest the carnival spirit in its richest manifestation, yet William asked for nothing better. It was one of those rare nights that ought to go on for ever, and in a queer way do seem to go on for ever, as if they had wandered into a new sort of time. It was like finding oneself, completely at home too, in an enchanting scene of a Shakespearean comedy. For an hour or two, the veil thinned, and immortal folly, beauty, friendship and love came shining through – or so it seemed to one romantic temperament. There were good reasons of course why William should have enjoyed himself: he was where he had long wanted to be, and on the eve of his island adventure; he was in love, and his lady, who, even if she was not in love with him, smiled upon him and was ready to be kind, would be there too, illuminating the scene; and there was abroad an easy friendly spirit, final product of the false camaraderie of shipboard life, to which he now eagerly responded; in short, all things conspired for his pleasure. But there was more than that in it. He had been, to outward appearance and address, William Dursley too long; and now not only was he William Dursley cut loose, adrift on the Pacific, but he was William Dursley transformed into a clown, and therefore not really William Dursley. It was a grand escape.

They made their first appearance at dinner. The dining-saloon had broken out into an extraordinary confusion of flags and coloured paper, and there was a fine idiocy about the whole scene. Most of the others were already there when William appeared, and he was greeted with a round of applause, the first he ever remembered having. There was a faint suggestion in this applause that they would never have guessed that Mr. Dursley had it in him.

Mr. Dursley for once found his vanity being tickled, and liked it. Terry was not down yet, but the other two at the table were, and Mrs. da Silva had achieved a vaguely Spanish effect with a shawl and a high comb, while Mr. Cantock, by a simple re-arrangement of his dinner-jacket, waistcoat and collar, had turned himself into a clergyman. 'That's good, Mr. Dursley,' he cried, in his queer squeaky voice, 'that's very good. So is this, I think. Don't you? I always do this. No trouble and very effective. Just before we got to Alexandria, we had one, and they said "No, you can't do that." Miss Watson and Mrs. Bates were particularly anxious about it. And I said, "Why not?" And they said, "Because both Mr. Reynolds and Mr. Falk *are* clergymen." "But they don't wear the clothes," I said . . .' And Mr. Cantock went meandering on.

'My!' cried Mrs. da Silva, with real enthusiasm. 'But ain't that pruddy! Oh! – it is pruddy.'

It was Terry – and she was a mermaid. Her shoulders and arms were bare, and she wore an almost skin-tight greeny dress that had a silvery scaly effect too, and then she came as near to possessing a tail as ingenuity and wire and painted cloth could bring her. Terry was pretty enough at any time, but Terry as a mermaid took away your breath. William surrendered his at once. There was a splendid round of applause, which William enjoyed as much as his own.

'Well, I think we're a swell table,' said Terry, sitting down, after some careful handling of her tail. 'Mrs. da Silva, that Spanish costume's sweet. You look the part, Mr. Cantock. And Bill – why, you're fine. You're the best clown I've seen in years.'

'Terry,' said William fervently, 'you're absolutely lovely. If I thought mermaids were really like that, I'd drown to-morrow.'

So they were all pleased with themselves, and they ordered champagne and drank it much too quickly, being excited and busy turning this way and that to see the others. Mr. Boothroyd, very imposing as a French chef, with an enormous white cap and a most convincing little moustache and beard, marched from table to table, flourishing a steel and a huge carving knife. Little Miss Settle had turned herself into a gypsy. The man who lived at South Norwood, suddenly showing the most unexpected enterprise, arrived as a tent, and nearly suffocated in his enthusiasm for the part. One of the younger Frenchmen was tremendous as an Oriental, of mysterious nationality but clearly of very high rank. Mrs. Kinderfield wore a white sombrero and a red shirt, and appeared to be a sort of cowgirl, a droopy literary cowgirl in *pince-nez*. She made William laugh, but she did not make him laugh so much as another fellow passenger did. What with the clown's costume and the general excitement and the champagne, William discovered that he was ready to laugh a great deal and very loudly, and suddenly he did. He leaned back, and laughed and laughed.

'What is it?' cried Terry.

William could only laugh.

'Donkey!' said the lovely mermaid, frowning at him, but ready to laugh herself. 'What *is* it?'

He did not point, but threw a coloured stream of paper in the required direction. It was Mr. Tiefman. Neither Mrs. da Silva nor Mr. Cantock thought him at all funny; Terry laughed, but chiefly because she had caught the infection from William; but to William the sight of Mr. Tiefman was irresistibly absurd. Mr. Tiefman's fancy-dress schedule, which may or may not have been provided for in his 'sked book,' was as simple as his other arrangements. He had left off his one tie, had turned the coat of his yachting suit inside out, and had attached, rather insecurely, to his large flat greasy face a most wildly unconvincing ginger moustache. It was as if this ginger moustache had been flying aimlessly about the room, and had settled just below Mr. Tiefman's nose for a few minutes. Clearly feeling that he had done his duty by this part of the itinerary, Mr. Tiefman, behind his preposterous moustache, was taking his ease, beaming through his thick glasses. To William, at that moment, Mr. Tiefman was the richest thing in creation. There was a simple but sublime idiocy about that costume and that moustache.

'So the guide said, "If you go in there, you can't use Chinese dollars." And I said "Why not?" And he said, "Because they won't take Chinese dollars." ' Mr. Cantock, most unclerically flushed with wine, was going on and on, though nobody knew what country he was in now, and probably would not have known even if they had been really listening to him all the time. 'And so I said, "Well, we want to go in there, whether they take Chinese dollars or not." And Mrs. Ferguson said the same thing. But this guide didn't want us to go in there. He wanted us to go in another place, further down the road, a place run by Russians. You see, they paid him a commission on the people he brought. But I said, "We'll go in here, Mrs. Ferguson. I've got some American money, if that will do." So we went in. And it was good – very good.'

William was now troubled by a sudden appreciation of the idiocy of Mr. Cantock's reminiscences, that mixture in them of the fantastic and the dull. He looked at Mr. Cantock's bushy grey eyebrows, his sharp nose, now a little red, and his clerical collar, and the longer he looked, the more absurd Mr. Cantock seemed. And then the absurdity of Mr. Cantock became mixed with the absurdity of Mr. Tiefman, and other surrounding absurdities joined forces with them both to assail him. He did not laugh aloud now, but he shook quite violently inside with laughter. This helped the champagne to go to his head, and he could almost feel it bubbling there, in a mounting tide of liquid gold. They all ate without knowing exactly what they were eating; they called for fresh bottles and pledged one another royally; they threw coloured paper from table to table; they shouted across the intervening spaces, and yelled with laughter; and the men were suddenly all handsome, ardent and gay, and the women all charming and beautiful. The amplified panatrope continued to fling among them, like a constant largesse of brass, its strains of amorous cynicism and sentiment. It was all a circus, and William, in his real clown's paint and frills, was happy in it.

When they were spilled fantastically on deck, they found a perfect night gemmed with stars and with a new moon like a great slice of cantaloup. On that little lighted stage, set in an expanse of purple-and black velvet, they played their parts. The first-class passengers paraded before the second-class passengers, and then the second-class passengers, who appeared to be even more determined and ambitious masqueraders than their social or financial superiors, paraded before the first-class. Among the seconds were several Island people, both half-caste and native, and these had boldly put on native costume, the gaudy red-and-white *pareu*, the grass skirt, the ornaments of shell. One native girl, saucy and giggling, would begin the famous *hula* dance, but then would suddenly stop the movement of her lovely brown body, give a scream of laughter, and scamper away into the shadows. And now William knew that this was indeed the South Pacific, that the magical islands were just beyond the horizon, and that the Southern Cross was planted in the sky. Never did he remember feeling so excited, so recklessly happy.

After the parades and between the dances that followed them, the company, like a toy bazaar galvanised into life, rushed into the smoke-room, where the elderly steward, in the profoundest despair, staggered out of his bar with trays loaded with drink. Everybody insisted upon standing drinks to everybody else, and they were all both gay and confidential, as if they were prisoners unexpectedly reprieved. There were many impudent, though not unfriendly, things that William had long wanted to say to a number of people in that ship, and now, bobbing up all over the place in true clown's fashion, he did not hesitate to say them. Nobody minded. The people who had seemed fairly decent before now appeared to be the best of companions. The rather amusing people were seen as the richest drolls. And even the people he had disliked now took on a fine absurd flavour, and could at least be laughed at. There was Rogers, for example. It seemed incredible that he could ever have been jealous of Rogers, now metamorphosed into a rough sketch of a Highlander, with short socks and prominent blue suspenders. Why, he had a drink with Rogers, and congratulated him warmly upon Sydney Harbour.

Clowns do not stand on ceremony with mermaids. If they want to dance with them, they dance with them. William would boldly descend upon his mermaid, seize her in his arms, and recklessly waltz her or foxtrot, just as the panatrope decided.

'I think this is a great night,' she told him, as they went twirling, just before the end.

'It's a marvellous night, Terry darling.'

'I'm glad you think so, Bill darling. And – say – I don't know whether it's those clothes you're wearing or the liquor you've had or what, Bill, but you certainly are dancing different. You're not the same partner at all.'

'Better?'

'Much, much better.'

'That's because it's a wonderful night in the middle of the Pacific,' he babbled, 'and you're a mermaid and I'm a clown, and I seem to be terribly in love with you.'

She laughed. 'Well, I like you a whole lot too, Bill.'

'I can't imagine why.'

'No, I can't.'

'What!'

'I'd thought you'd rise at that, Bill. Where's your beautiful modesty now? Well, I'm not going to tell you why I like you – not just now. But you can tell me why you think you're in love with me.'

'Not here, Terry. But let's stop dancing. I'm tired of dancing.'

'Are you? Well, I don't know that I am, young man.'

'Of course you are. Bored stiff with it,' he said masterfully. 'Come on, let's get out of this, and then I'll tell you all you want to know, and a great deal more besides.' He took her by the arm and they climbed to the little open boat-deck. There they sat down, away from everybody, and for a minute or two they were quiet, Terry looking dreamily out to sea.

William possessed himself of both her hands. He was not a clown any longer. 'You know,' he began, and then cleared his throat. 'I've never seen you – and I've never seen anybody – looking lovelier than you do this very minute.' And he meant it.

She smiled, but continued to look into the distance. William told himself she was thinking of that other man, that lover she had had, the fellow who had made her so unhappy. Probably at that moment, he reflected bitterly, she hardly knew who was by her side. He endured a minute of this self-torture, and then was stung into action. He pulled her towards him, held her close, and let her head fall into the crook of his right arm. He bent his head and then slowly brushed his cheek across her hair. Then he kissed her several times, quite violently.

She slowly opened her eyes, which seemed very mysterious in that half-light, and looked up at him. 'Why, Bill—' she began, as if in remonstrance, but did not trouble to say any more. Nor did she make any movement to escape from his arms.

'Oh, Terry!' he cried softly, rather like a child.

'Oh, Bill!' she murmured, dreamily mocking him.

'You know, I've thought I've been in love, but I've never been like this before,' he told her, in a somewhat cracked little voice. 'I'd begun to think people talked and wrote an awful lot of nonsense about it. I know better now.'

'Then it serves you right for being so unbelieving before,' she said sleepily.

'It's a sort of magic, isn't it? Sometimes it hurts like hell, and sometimes – like now – it's – oh! it's—'

'A million dollars.'

'Ten million dollars. But whatever it is – it's terribly important all the time. I've hardly bothered to think about Faraway and everything these last few days. I can't stop thinking about you. When you're not there, I have long, long conversations with you all the time, and talk much better than I do when you *are* here. Look here, you do at least like me, don't you?'

'Of course I do. I like you a whole lot. I wouldn't be here if I didn't.'

'No, that's true. Well, that's something, isn't it? I mean, it's a good start. For I love you, Terry, I really do. I – well, I'll say it, if it kills me – I adore you.'

'Dear Bill!' she said, and then suddenly flung her arms about his neck and kissed him with glorious abandon. They stayed like that, passionately close, straining, for an enchanted space of time that might have been two minutes or might have been twenty, for all William knew or cared. Then she freed herself.

'I'm hungry,' she said calmly, 'and I'm going down to grab a sandwich or two before they're all gone. And then I'm going to bed. Come on.' Her face, under the stronger light, revealed some crimson traces of that clown's painted grin, which he had partly imprinted upon her here and there. He was all the more surprised because he had forgotten for some time that he was a clown. But the night itself, as he somehow guessed as he followed her down the steps, he was never to forget. And even now, possessing it, he extended towards all those William Dursleys who had existed up to this night the genial patronage of a rich relative.

6

William did not seem to have been asleep any time before a bumping outside his cabin vaguely roused him. He might have fallen asleep again had he not felt that there was something queer happening, quite apart from the bumping. Things were odd; there was an unaccountable difference in their total aspect. Then he realised what it was. The ship was not moving. It was quite still, and nothing had ever seemed quite so still before as this ship was now. There was something so sinister about this stillness, which seemed to contradict the very nature of the ship, that for a moment he thought of disaster of some kind. Then he remembered. They were due at Tahiti this

very morning, and they must be off the island now. He
had a quick wash, smoothed his hair, put on a dressing-
gown, and went on deck, to find there a good many of
his fellow-passengers, also in dressing-gowns.

It was the hour of smokiness and cold light, just before
the true dawn. They were floating between two dark
green, misty shapes, one much smaller and further away
than the other. The larger was the island of Tahiti, the
other Moorea. William kept his eyes fixed on Tahiti. As
the sky paled and then was gradually flecked with faint
fire, the island did not dwindle, it grew and acquired
volume. It was nobly fantastic in outline, such an island
as a boy might hastily crayon. There were green peaks,
and one grandly out-topping the rest. Staring hard across
the brightening mirror of the lagoon, William could make
out valleys and high ravines, green places but still touched
with a smoky purple. It was like the landscape of some
long romantic poem.

His arm was squeezed. 'Good morning,' said Terry, her
eyes still hazy with sleep. 'We're here.'

'Good morning. I know we are. Isn't it grand? Isn't it
fantastic?'

'I'm sure it is. I haven't grasped it yet.'

'Neither have I, for that matter,' William told her,
'though I've been here for some time. It's like scenery in
a dream. My Lord! – if you could only *paint* this stuff.'

'I looked out of my porthole,' said Terry dreamily, 'and
saw the other one, Moorea. Have you seen it? You just
can't believe in it. It's too grand and crazy. You just feel
somebody's gone and made it up specially for you.'

'I know, I know,' cried William eagerly, delighted that
she should feel these things, too. It would have been a
disappointment if she had been cool and hard-boiled

about it all. But then, she appeared to have stopped being cool and hard-boiled.

'That must be Papeete,' she said, pointing, and they both stared hard. Yes, there was a town. They could see lights twinkling near the water-front. Various buildings began to thrust themselves out from the dim huddle.

'I can see coconut palms, miles of them,' Terry continued.

'I believe,' said William slowly and with relish, 'that I can see two very queer-shaped steeples in that town, and I believe they're red.'

'Yes, they are. And aren't they cunning!'

There were long flares in the sky, and they could almost see the light growing about them as fast as the magic beanstalk. They could hear noises across the water, tiny knocks and shouts from another world.

Terry put her pretty pert nose in the air, and sniffed hard. 'Do you notice it?' she cried to him.

'Notice what?'

'Why, the smell. You can't miss it, and it's quite different from any other smell you've ever known before.'

Solemnly, they sniffed together, inhaling all Polynesia. After the scentless days of sea, there was no mistaking this rich confused smell. It was not unlike that of some hot-houses. They were about to walk into a gigantic hot-house, with mountains in it. Very odd and exciting.

Now dawn broke, like sudden good news; the sea caught fire from the sky and became diamond drops and emerald gulfs; and every stem and frond and rock in the island quivered and leaped into life. It was as if a great orchestra had swept into some superb opening movement. Some boats were putting out, *chuff-chuffing* across the lagoon, and making for the pass to the outer sea, between the hidden ramparts of coral, that would bring them to the ship. William and Terry watched these boats for a while, then looked at one another and quite involuntarily smiled. Those smiles announced that they had landed in the South Seas.

CHAPTER VI

TAHITI

1

William had expected the Commander and Ramsbottom to look just the same as they did when they left him standing in Victoria Station. These two tropical personages were a surprise. The Commander was very brown, very trim, in a spotless white cotton suit and a topee. Ramsbottom's large flat face was now like underdone beef, and he seemed bigger and rounder and looser than ever in his cream silk shirt and white trousers. He wore a gigantic Panama, decorated with a band made of scores of coloured shells, and he looked as if he had been planting coconut groves and drinking rum punches in these parts for the last thirty years. And already he appeared to know quite a number of people, to be a personage on the island.

But if they were a surprise to William, Terry was a surprise to them. Not altogether a pleasant one, William guessed, to the Commander, who probably felt about her as William had done that first evening they met, so long ago, it seemed, in San Francisco. Ramsbottom had been equally astonished, but not at all displeased: he was clearly a man who liked a pretty face.

'Well, well, well,' he cried, beaming at Terry, 'you've right surprised me. Ah'd an idea you were an oldish chap with a yellow face and perhaps a chin beard.'

'Not a bit like me,' she told him.

'No, not quite. Well, happen you won't be as much use, but you'll be easier to look at. Mind you, there's some fairly nice-looking lasses here already – if you like 'em dark.'

'How d'you like 'em, Mr. Ramsbottom?' She was at her ease with him very quickly.

'So long as they're nice-looking, they can be any colour, for me. We do a good line in chocolate and bronze girls round here. But Ah'd give you the prize. And that's a compliment, make no mistake about it.'

'I won't.' Terry smiled at him, then gave William a lightning wink.

The Commander came hurrying back. 'You can go ashore now,' he announced. 'Then sometime to-day or to-morrow, you can go round and register with the police and get your permits. This way, Miss Riley.' A little fussy perhaps, but brisk and happy, the Commander led them towards the gangway.

There was a fine picturesque bustle on the landing-stage: native labourers, some of them beautifully muscular, went trotting to and from the ship, sometimes singing as they went; brown girls in bright cotton frocks were whispering and giggling and using to advantage their fine eyes; parchmenty old native women peered about or squatted in the nearest shade; there were some Chinese drifting about; and all the white men looked at a distance like romantic characters, simply because of their tropical clothes. Everything was as it should be. The best film producer could not have done more with the scene. But after the sea, William found the atmosphere very thick and rather trying. It was like being in a hot-house, but a very dusty smelly hot-house. There were too many smells. From the sheds there came a most individual sickly-sweet odour, and he was told that this was from the copra. Long before they had passed through the Customs shed, he had decided that he did not like copra.

They piled their luggage and themselves into two taxi-cars, of which there seemed to be no lack on the island, and drove off noisily.

'Did you get the latitude?' asked the Commander, who was sharing William's car.

'Yes. It's eleven degrees forty-seven south.'

The Commander repeated this carefully, then thought for a moment. 'I think it's just about where I thought it would be,' he remarked, finally. 'But we'll go into all that afterwards.'

'Where are we staying?' asked William, as the car left the quay behind.

'It's a newish place, just outside the town,' said the Commander. 'We tried staying in Papeete itself at first – it was cheap, and handy for the schooners – but it was noisy and rather messy, and too many people down there were interested in one's business. This place is much better. Reasonably clean, and the food's eatable, though of course our friend Ramsbottom doesn't think much of it.'

William grinned reminiscently. 'Not enough good stoof, eh?'

'Quite.' The Commander considered for a moment. 'You know, Dursley, I'm not sure Ramsbottom's the right sort of man for the tropics.'

'Don't you? Why?'

'He'll soon get too slack, if he's not careful. You've got to keep a tight hold on yourself in these places or you soon go to pieces. Lots of fellows here in pieces. Must discipline yourself or let somebody do it for you. As you know, I like Ramsbottom. He's a good fellow. It's just a matter of training, and he's not had it. Y'know, gives way to his appetites too much, whatever his appetite might be for. Got to keep out of hot countries if you're like that.'

'I'm beginning to wonder myself if I shall like this part of the world,' said William.

'Oh, you'll be all right. And you'll like it. Though it's not what people say it is, Dursley, not by a long chalk. Lot of damned nonsense talked and written about these islands. Life here's too slack. French are too slack.' The Commander seemed to be much more downright and forcible than he had been in England, perhaps because once more he had got something to do and was not rusting away. 'This girl – Miss Riley?' he now continued, doubtfully.

This girl indeed! 'I hope you don't mind her being here,' said William cautiously.

'Insisted on coming, didn't she? But she can't go to the island, y'know, Dursley? Quite impossible.'

'Yes, I told her that.'

'Well, as long as she understands that, it's something. Couldn't have a girl weeks and weeks on one of those schooners. No place for her. Matter of fact, it's a pity she's even come as far as this.'

'Oh, come now! Why?'

The Commander did not hesitate for a moment. 'I may seem old-fashioned, probably am, but in my opinion this place isn't fit for a decent white woman – especially a young girl – to visit. I don't mean there aren't any decent white women here. There are. But they live here all the time, married here. They understand it. But no place for a decent white girl. Too slack altogether. It's not as bad as it used to be, I admit, but it's bad enough. A girl like this now – well, she's American, of course, and they may be different – but she's a nice girl, isn't she?'

William assured him that she was.

'Looks it, too,' the Commander went on. 'Fine-looking, clean, healthy girl. Comes out here from decent surroundings, sheltered life probably, doesn't know anything about anything – well, a place like this isn't going to do her any good at all. Things going on here she won't make head or tail of, poor girl, and if she does, all the worse for her. Still, she's here, and it can't be helped. We must do our best to keep things from her, that's all, Dursley. A girl like that in a place like this is a great responsibility.'

William stole a glance at the Commander's earnest troubled face, and appreciated, somewhat wryly, the irony of the situation. He would have to warn Terry that she must not give this innocent gentleman a sudden shock. There was something lovable in his grave concern, and it had taken the edge off his sharp manner, which had begun to be too reminiscent of the quarter-deck. In fact. William had been wondering if action and sunlight between them were going to ripen the Commander into somebody not quite so lovable as that diffident personage he had discovered in Lugmouth, somebody who might indeed be rather a nuisance. But now he put the thought away quickly.

They had reached the hotel, which consisted of a large central bungalow, used as a dining-room, lounge, bar and office, and a number of small separate bungalows, all sprawling by the side of the lagoon. William made the acquaintance of the proprietor and his wife. M. Marot was a tall fat man with a large glistening face and a soft bovine eye, obviously French with some admixture of Tahitian blood. He had spent some time in the United States and Fiji and spoke English tolerably well. His wife, also French but with more native blood in her, was much smaller and darker, and as she spoke little English and was rather shy, she was content to smile at her guests and quickly disappear round corners, where her voice could be heard rating the servants in no uncertain terms. The Marots had only recently acquired this hotel, which was considered the most ambitious on the island, and so they were very anxious to please. They were mildly astonished by the fact that Terry and William, a handsome girl and an attentive man who arrived together and were obviously on very friendly terms, should want separate bungalows. Clearly that was not the way things were managed in Tahiti. The bungalows they gave them, however, were very close together.

The Commander and Ramsbottom shared the largest bungalow, nearest the road and about fifty yards away. The bungalows allotted to Terry and William were quite pleasant, and very tropical and romantic. Each consisted of a wide verandah, used as a sitting-room, a bedroom painted green and white, very cool, shaded, and a shower-bath. They were set in a garden, through which there wandered a stream that made a constant happy music among the stones. There were ponds filled with great lilies, many strange flowering shrubs, and here and there, at a fantastic angle, a coconut palm. In this garden, a Chinaman, wearing a hat as big as a cartwheel, worked methodically, never making a sound, never looking up, like a man in some old Oriental drawing. It was all very charming, and from their neighbouring verandahs Terry and William would interrupt their unpacking to tell one another how much they liked it. Beyond the dark stems and leaves, the lagoon was like a great blue diamond.

'You all right, Dursley?' asked the Commander, suddenly popping up.

'Yes, thanks. I like this place.'

'It's not bad. Pretty good quarters. Price is a bit stiff, of course. Much more than you pay in Papeete.'

'Oh! Do you know, I never asked. What do we pay here?'

'Ninety francs a day. Everything in, of course.'

William worked this out. 'No, it's not cheap, is it? I always thought you could live for next to nothing in these places.'

'You could at one time,' said the Commander ruefully. 'But not now. Unless you live with the natives, of course. Lot of sailors desert here still, and go and live up in the hills, with a native woman. It doesn't cost them anything to live. And if you wanted to pig it here, I suppose you could easily live on a few francs a day. But if you want to live decently, it costs you just as much to live here as it does to live anywhere else. That's how things are, y'know, these days.' And the Commander wandered into the bedroom, from which he returned to advise William to let down the mosquito-netting round his bed. There were, it seemed, plenty of mosquitoes in Tahiti, and this was the rainy season, when they began to breed. William regarded the mosquito-netting with disfavour.

'We might have a bathe before lunch,' said the Commander. 'I can hardly ever get Ramsbottom in, but you and Miss Riley ought to like it. Bathing's pretty good here. You ought to wear shoes, though.'

William had some canvas shoes. They arranged to bathe in a quarter of an hour, and Terry said she would come, too. A little before noon, they filed solemnly along the little jetty that ran out near the big central bungalow: a very stringy brown Commander; a small, compact, and somewhat self-conscious William; and a shapely, gorgeous, and entirely unself-conscious Terry. The water at the very edge of the lagoon looked uninviting, for the sand there was black; but further out, near the end of the little jetty, the lagoon had a wonderful sparkle and green clarity. And it was quite warm and very buoyant.

'Bill, look, look!' screamed Terry, in high excitement.

And William looked. The water was radiant with magical little fishes, hundreds and hundreds of them; fishes brighter than emeralds, turquoises, sapphires; fishes fantastically shaped and striped, like football teams or platoons of extravagant soldiery; and they all went swimming in companies, the black-and-white stripes with the black-and-white stripes, the flashing blue ones with all the other flashing blue ones. There were even tiny shoals of ghostly fishes, hardly opaque at all, like creatures cut out of thin celluloid. The Commander had a pair of diving goggles, and Terry and William took turns at wearing these and keeping their heads below water as long as possible to stare at the magical little fishes. It seemed incredible that one could ever be unhappy in a world that contained those fishes. If that was what Nature could do, William reflected, then somewhere in or behind Nature was an exuberant artist, shouting with laughter as he plunged his brush into his pots of coloured fire. Gay and grateful, William would have liked to have thanked and congratulated the little fishes themselves. Why could one do nothing but stare in this green silent world? Why couldn't a man talk for a minute or two to these little fishes, just exchange a brief message? Wasn't it in the *Arabian Nights* that the coloured fishes began talking in the pan? That was life in a fairy-tale. But then these fishes seemed to be in a fairy-tale, too. Yet William knew that he himself was not in a fairy-tale, even though Terry was swimming beside him and he was splashing South Sea water and Faraway Island was waiting for them all. There were probably good scientific reasons, he reminded himself, why the fishes were so enchantingly coloured and shaped. Was it possible for life to be magical, a fairy-tale, if looked at from one side, and at the same time to have good scientific reasons for itself, if looked at from another? He puzzled over this, as he lazily floated above the pageant of the fishes, a monstrous shadow in its sky. And for years afterwards, at odd moments, there would come a sudden sheen of unearthly blue, brighter than the flash of a kingfisher, and then the little fishes would go swimming through his mind, and he would be back in the lagoon, puzzling over their magic.

He enjoyed his bathe, but when he came out he did not feel, as he had always felt after bathing in less warm and luxuriant waters, as if his whole body had just been re-made for him. Nevertheless, it was pleasant to stand under the shower-bath in his bungalow, to dry oneself in the slowest laziest fashion, then to put on clean white clothes, the very thinnest possible, and stroll across to the big bungalow for lunch. Ramsbottom was alone there, drinking a cocktail. He insisted upon William joining him in another.

'We're not the only people staying in this hotel, are we?' William asked him.

'No, we're not. There's three others,' replied Ramsbottom. 'But they won't be in to lunch to-day. They're all off somewhere. Mr. and Mrs. Pullen have gone to see some friends o' theirs on the other side o' the island. They're Americans, and he's come down here for a bit 'cos he's been poorly. He's in the real estate business – as they call it – in Los Angeles. He's a quiet chap – he still looks poorly – and his wife doesn't make a lot o' noise either. Then there's an English chap called Crawford.'

'What's he like?' asked William.

'So far he's like a dummy, and that's about all you can

say. He goes and fishes with somebody, right out catching big fish; and that's about all he does do, barring eating and sleeping. He doesn't talk, and you can't make him. His name's Crawford. Happen he'll be in his forties. He's clean-shaved, but he's got a lot o' hair on his legs. He's knocked about a bit, been to India and China. And that's all you can say about him. It isn't he won't talk to me. He'll talk to nobody. M'soo can't get anything out of him. He might as well be an oyster with khaki shorts on.'

William laughed, for there was genuine indignation in Ramsbottom's voice. Then William glanced towards the other bungalows, which he could see through the open windows. The other two were not coming yet. 'How's the Commander getting on?' he enquired.

'Now Ah'll tell you,' said Ramsbottom, with the air of a man opening a big subject. He dropped his voice now. 'Commander's all right, and you know what Ah think about him. Ah think Commander's a grand chap. A credit to his country. But Ah'll tell you straight, Ah don't think these hot places suit him. They get him on his liver. These thin chaps are no good in a hot place, just for that reason – liver. Now this place suits me – Ah don't mean everything about it suits me, 'cos it doesn't – but Ah don't mind it being so hot and moist. But Commander's got his liver touched up, and it's making him a bit sharp, d'you see, Dursley? You may have noticed it yourself.'

William admitted cautiously that he had noticed something.

'Thought you would,' said Ramsbottom in a triumphant whisper. 'Mind you, Ah'm not grumbling. Ah wouldn't say even this bit of a word against Commander except to you. But he's got his liver touched up all right, and now you've got to mind yourself with him. And this place isn't his style, you see. If we'd been in one o' the English islands, with natives on one side o' the fence and white men on the other, sentries and policemen all smart as you like, and everybody a what's it – y'know – what they are in India – pukka Sahib, and not sitting about boozing with your collar off, and no little brown girls with flowers in their hair and the cheek o' the devil – well, he'd have been all right. But this place isn't his style at all. Too French. Too free-and-easy in the wine, women, and shaving departments. Too much *oo lah lah* for him. What's the result? He gets a bit short with you. We've had a few words already. Nothing, y'know, nothing at all. But still – well, there you are, lad.'

Terry came in, and the Commander arrived a moment later. They sat down to lunch, which was served by two Chinese waiters, to whom Ramsbottom continually said 'Catch 'em.' 'Catch 'em bread, Chung Ling Soo,' he would cry. 'Catch 'em whisky. You savvy?' And he was always so triumphant that you were almost persuaded that he had just been speaking a very difficult foreign language.

The lunch consisted of some nondescript little fishes, some rather tough meat with rice, and a salad made of sliced oranges and grated fresh coconut. Ramsbottom was not encouraging on the subject of food in the South Seas. 'Very little good stoof,' he declared, taking the floor. 'Too much eating out of tins. Native stoof's not what it's cracked up to be, not by a long chalk, it isn't. That bread fruit now. You can eat it all right, and if you was a shipwrecked sailor, you'd thank God for it, but for any chap that likes his stomach, it's nothing – not a patch on a good potato done in its jacket. Can't compare 'em. Then there's that purply root – taro or whatever they call it. Well, it looks like a kind o' cheap washing soap, and as far as Ah'm concerned, it tastes like it. They've got a

sort o' big banana they make into a vegetable, and that's
not so bad. But there's nothing you'd want to take away
with you. According to one or two books Ah read on the
way out, Ah'd got a notion there was things to eat here
right out o' the common for tastiness, but it's all my eye.
It's all eating out o' tins.'

The Commander cleared his throat. 'We'd better talk
business, I think. We have the place to ourselves, and it's
a good time.'

'Well, Ah'm not stopping you,' cried Ramsbottom.
'Let's get down to business, by all means.'

'I thought you might tell them what we've done,' said
the Commander, a trifle apologetically.

'No, you can do that. You've had most of it to do, so
far, so you can tell 'em about it. Besides, the schooner
business is right in your line and not in mine.'

'All right.' The Commander hesitated a moment, then
looked from William to Terry. 'You'll want to know what
we've been doing, eh? Of course. Well, as we agreed
before, the first thing to do was to see this island for
ourselves. You can't start taking a lot of labourers, tackle
and provisions before you've made certain the place is
there and that this stuff – and plenty of it, too – is there.'

They were all agreed upon this.

'What we wanted then,' the Commander continued,
'was a schooner that would take us to see the island, and
naturally we wanted to avoid the expense of chartering
one for the whole journey, from here to the island. That's
been our difficulty. We had to try and find a schooner
that could give us an ordinary passage for a good part of
the way, then we could charter it simply from its last place
of call to the island. You see what I mean?'

'Yes,' said William. 'You had to find a schooner that

was going in the direction of the island anyhow. We should save a lot on that, of course.'

'Of course,' said the Commander. 'There's quite a difference between chartering a vessel and booking a passage or two in her.'

'Ay, there is that,' cried Ramsbottom, 'even with these smelly little converted canal barges they call schooners. You'd be surprised what they want for the hire o' one o' these things, Dursley. You'd think if you showed 'em a pound or two, they'd give you one o' these schooners right off. But not they! And even for a passage, they're none so cheap. Ah call 'em expensive, mucky way you have to live on 'em.'

Terry contracted her brows, and looked sternly at the Commander. 'But how could you find a schooner that was going in the direction of the island, when you didn't know where the island was, not until you got the latitude?'

The Commander smiled at her. 'We were lucky in having the longitude. If we hadn't had that, we couldn't have done anything. But we knew the longitude, and knew the island was in the South Seas, and so it seemed to me that any schooner that was making for the Marquesas or the Tuamotus would probably serve our turn. As a matter of fact, the schooner we're thinking of taking goes round the more northerly Tuamotus. I haven't worked out the position of Faraway yet on a chart, and I can only guess very roughly how far she'll have to take us past her last place of call. It's a good way, of course; but we can't help that, and we do save a good deal by not chartering her all the way. They'll give us a passage, I think, for about five or six hundred francs a week, and we ought to get the charter down to about thirty-five hundred francs a week, or possibly four thousand.'

'It's quite enough for one o' them floating bug traps,'

observed Ramsbottom, 'but when all's said and done, if we see what we hope to see on that island, it's a fleabite. You agree, don't you, Dursley?'

William, who had been busy converting francs into pounds sterling, did agree.

'You've fixed up about a credit here, Ah suppose?' Ramsbottom enquired of William, rather anxiously. 'There'll be a lot o' paying out to do, and we're a long way from anywhere.'

'I've arranged all that,' William told him, 'with the Bank of Indo-China. That's all right. By the way, how long will it take this schooner to get us to Faraway?'

'Can't tell yet,' said the Commander. 'Several weeks, altogether.'

'What'll you do if the island's gone?' cried Terry.

'Gone?'

'Well, if it just isn't there. Don't some of these islands just disappear? My father told me they did. People say they've seen islands – quite big ones, sticking up miles out of the water – and then nobody is able to find them. What'll you do if this island's like that?'

Ramsbottom gazed at her with benevolent irony. 'Oh, we'll just have a good laugh. A little thing like that won't bother us, Miss Riley. We'll only have come a few thousand miles for nothing, and missed a fortune. We'll have a good laugh, and then have a game o' cards.'

'I believe that island is there all right,' the Commander declared emphatically.

'So do I,' said William.

'Oh well, so do I, for that matter,' Terry told them. 'I wasn't trying to frighten you.'

'Yes, you were,' said Ramsbottom, with mock severity. 'You were trying to take the 'eart out of us. It's your job to cheer us up – that's why we let you bring your pretty face here – and not to tell we're going after an island that's not there. Wait till you see one o' them schooners. It'ud break a man's heart to be in one o' them things for weeks – and paying good money to be tossed about day and night and fed on bits o' coconut and rice – and then to find it was all for nothing. So just change your tune, Miss Riley, or you'll not be allowed to attend another board meeting. And we may be off in less than a week's time.'

'In less than a week?'

'Yes,' said the Commander. 'Or about a week. So we haven't any time to waste. She's an eighty-five-ton schooner, with auxiliary power; belongs to some Chinese here; and she's called the *Hutia*. Skipper's one of these mixed fellows, part Tahitian, part French, and a bit of Scandinavian, I fancy. Funny, but there's quite a lot of Scandinavian blood down here, particularly among the skipper class. This fellow's supposed to be a good sailor, though he's temperamental, like the rest of them down here. But the point is, do you agree? Do you think we're doing the right thing?'

'I do,' replied William. 'I don't see what else we could do. Obviously, as you say, it would be idiotic to do anything but see the island first, to make sure the pitchblende is really there, and this is the best way of getting there, so far as I can see.'

'I don't believe any of you want my opinion,' said Terry, refusing to listen to their denials. 'But I'll tell you that I think you're doing right, too. And I want to have a look at that schooner. I don't see why I shouldn't come, too.'

'You will when you've seen the schooner,' said Ramsbottom grimly. 'How d'you fancy spending a month or so sleeping between me and a couple o' seasick Chinamen on a shelf full of beetles? Ah thought not. However, you come with us and have a look at the schooner.'

'What's the programme now?' asked William.

'Snooze – for an hour or so,' replied Ramsbottom promptly. The Commander nodded in agreement, adding that they had better go in to Papeete afterwards. They reached their respective bungalows just in time, for suddenly the sun was blotted out, the dirty curtains were pulled across the sky, and then the rain came thundering down, beating upon roofs and foliage with its quivering gleaming rods.

2

It was bright and hot again when they walked into the town. The air was heavy with the scent of the *tiare* and the daturas, gardenias and jasmine. There were butterflies liked winged patches of velvet. The peaks of the Diadem were coloured a fantastic blue. The deep upper valleys seemed to smoke in the sunlight. The universal green of the island was greener than ever, as if it had just been laid on. Along the edge of the road, where they walked, there went before them a curious grey flicker, and this, it appeared, was caused by a thousand or more grey land crabs all rapidly vanishing into their holes, from which they peeped, not unlike terrified little citizens during a revolution.

'This place,' said Ramsbottom, when they had reached the town, 'seems to me more Chinese than anything else. And by the look of them, they must breed like rabbits.'

There were certainly plenty of Chinese about. They saw Chinese stores, restaurants, tailors' and other shops. But the presence of these people and their places of business did not really make Papeete look Oriental. Bits of it, a small length of street, an official building, reminded William of a small French provincial town. The rest of it was like nothing but itself: an overgrown village smothered in luxurious vegetation, bright with hibiscus, from the palest pink to the deepest crimson, with white-and-yellow ginger-flowers, and multi-coloured cannas and zinnias, and here and there a flamboyant tree like a flaming sunset; a picturesque slum in a hot-house; an opening chorus of a musical comedy, but with real smells, real dirt, real sores; a place where the sound of the idle strumming of guitars was shattered every half minute by the unnecessary *honk-honking* of automobiles; a slack, messy, ridiculous, maddening, delightful hole of a place.

'I feel I must buy something,' cried Terry.

The Commander laughed. 'I know that feeling well. You always get it in these places. Well, why not buy something?'

'I have to, anyway,' she said pensively. After which, she disappeared into a store.

'It's not always as busy as this,' said the Commander, while they waited for her. 'This is boat day, so everybody's come in.'

'I want to get some cotton shirts and trousers,' William announced. 'Where's the best place?'

'Can't beat the Chinese,' said the Commander. 'You might try that place across there. I'll wait for Miss Riley.'

Ramsbottom accompanied William into the Chinese tailors', where three little smiling Orientals sat sewing and a fourth, who wore an even broader grin, stood behind the counter.

'Catch 'em clothes, savvy?' said Ramsbottom solemnly linguistic.

The Chinaman grinned harder than ever, and pointed

to Ramsbottom, who shook his head, and pointed to William, saying gravely: 'Catch 'em shirt, catch 'em trousers, eh?' In order that there should be no mistake, he poked a fat forefinger at William's shirt and trousers. The tailor called to one of his assistants, who dropped his sewing and picked up an enormous sheet of paper, on which he set down William's measurements as if he were designing a poster. The price, which was absurdly cheap, was agreed upon; the materials were chosen; and then, by some very brisk dumb show, a few 'catch 'ems' from Ramsbottom, and a reference to a calendar and a watch, they arranged that the things should be ready in two and a half days' time. William and Ramsbottom left the tailor nodding and smiling like a clockwork bronze toy. William was delighted: this was shopping in the grandest romantic manner; this was life in the South Seas.

A small boy sauntered past. He was a merry handsome boy, of an old-gold shade, and he wore nothing but a tattered pink cotton shirt, and he was holding in his two hands, the better to refresh himself, a slice of melon eighteen inches long and of an astonishing crushed strawberry hue. Then William remembered that Gauguin had painted on this island.

Terry was as delighted as he was. You could almost see her eyes dancing, across the street. She had a child's eagerness to enjoy everything, and this and her delight only seemed to intensify her radiance. Against this background, she shone like a creature from some more ethereal and luminous planet, and William gazed at her in happy adoration.

They all made now for the Cercle Bougainville, that very informal club about which both Terry and William had heard and read a good deal. The other P. T. Riley and old Uncle Baldwin had both spent a lot of time and money at the Bougainville, and it had played a considerable part in their anecdotes. In a street close to the lagoon, they turned through an open doorway, climbed a steep rickety staircase, and found themselves on a broad verandah. Everything there was unpainted, ramshackle, tumbledown. A deserted inner room housed the sad ruin of a billiard-table. The life of the club was centred on the verandah overlooking the lagoon, and this was crowded with people sitting at little tables, chattering, drinking, and throwing dice to see who would have to pay for the next round. It was a very lively scene, for already there had obviously been many rounds of rum punches and Rainbow cocktails in circulation among the tables.

'There's your ship,' said the Commander, pointing, as they seated themselves.

It was strange to see the *Marukai* still there, for it seemed to William days and days since he had left her. If he had thought of her at all, he would have pictured her far away somewhere. But there she was, looking enormous.

'She sails very soon,' the Commander continued, with a quiet air of satisfaction, as if he were partly responsible for this nautical regularity. 'She only has about twelve hours in port, I believe, this trip.'

'Bill, the gang's all here,' Terry announced excitedly, indicating the crowd at the neighbouring tables.

Yes, at least half the people there were from the *Marukai*. To his joy, William caught sight of Mr. Tiefman, who was solemnly sipping a rum punch, doing his duty by his 'sked book,' which had told him to have a rum punch at the Bougainville at this hour. The Burleckers and the Stocks were there, very flushed and noisy, and Burlecker was wearing a chaplet of flowers at a very rakish angle. Mrs. Kinderfield was there, long and droopy as ever but very happy and excited now, and at the same table were Jubb, the grim little American, and her half-caste gentleman friend from the second-class, a tall stout native woman, and several others. The second officer was with two pretty Tahitian girls. Rogers and a rather tight unshaven man, not from the *Marukai*, were entertaining several other native girls, who were flashing their beautiful white teeth and staring with lustrous eyes. Their late fellow-passengers waved and shouted to Terry and William.

A grave young Chinaman brought them four rum punches. 'Cheap enough,' said Ramsbottom, regarding his drink dubiously, 'but it's poor stoof. This French rum they have here's like sweet hair oil to my taste. Sickly. And this cocktail they serve here's worse still. A deal too sweet, and a deal too strong. All made o' liqueurs. You'd call it a woman's drink if any woman had a head to stand it. As it is, you might just as well ask somebody to fill your mouth wi' sugar and then give you a bang on the head with a sandbag, as drink a few o' them cocktails. Result would be the same. Isn't that right, Commander?'

'It's a miserable concoction,' said the Commander severely, 'but it suits these people. They all drink to get drunk as soon as possible. They don't drink because they've done their work and they're feeling happy, as men used to do. They drink because they want to run away from life. That's the American style.' Then he remembered Terry, and turned to her, with an apologetic smile on his fine lined face. 'Sorry, Miss Riley!'

She examined his face gravely for a second. Then she smiled. 'That's all right, Commander Ivybridge. You can't tell me anything about Americans drinking. You don't know the half of it. But I don't believe folks get soused because they want to run away from life. Now, in America,

it's because life's running away with them, and they want
to stop it, if only for a night. But give us a chance. This
isn't America, you know, though I do see quite a lot of
American thirsts putting in a good spell here.'

'I like this place,' William announced, looking about
him with satisfaction. The club itself was like some old
ramshackle ship, a sort of genial, boozy *Flying Dutchman*.
What it must have seen and heard in its time! Why, it
must have been the beginning and the end of thousands
of wild romances. Iliads and Odysseys by the score had
started to life on this broken-down balcony.

'It'll do,' said Ramsbottom, 'though for my part Ah'd
rather be having one in the Midland Hotel, Manchester.
But this is the best they have, and it's lively, that's one
thing. Now, just think of it – a ten-pound note would buy
all there is here that's worth anything, and for all that,
there's chaps looking forward to coming here from places
five hundred, happen a thousand, miles away. It serves a
big district, this does, you might say. There's nothing like
this for two thousand miles, Ah fancy, whichever way you
go. Hello, here's a friend o' mine.' A tall Tahitian girl,
wearing a bright yellow silk frock, and a white flower over
one ear, came up to them. She smiled at Ramsbottom,
who cried: 'Now, Hina love, can't you find a seat? Come
and sit with us. And what'll you have to drink?'

She sat down, smiling at them all, and Ramsbottom
performed a sketchy introduction. She and Terry looked
at one another for a moment or so with a frank and
fathomless curiosity; they might have been meeting on
the shore of a desert island. Their beauty was in sharp
contrast. That of the Tahitian girl was more gentle, more
deeply feminine, nearer the artless grace of an animal; it
was not difficult to imagine her being fashioned by the
sun, the tropical rains, the rich soil. Terry's almost met-

allic brilliance was startling, by contrast; she looked at once harder and yet more fragile; and the restlessness and spiritual challenge of her beauty were now emphasised. To William, looking from one to the other, the Tahitian girl was hardly anything more than part of the delightful romantic scene. Terry, whose every aspect caught at his heart, still seemed to him romance itself; all emerald Polynesia was only a setting for her.

The girl Hina, in very broken English, murmured something about one Tars Flock.

'That's the novelist, isn't it?' said Terry. 'I heard he was down here. You've read some of his books, haven't you, Bill?'

William had read one or two of Mr. Flock's popular stories, which were chiefly concerned with a mythical Wild West of handsome wild gunmen and cattle barons' beautiful daughters. 'What does he do, down here?' he asked.

'Fishes,' replied the Commander. 'Goes out in his little yacht and catches big fish. I had a word with him the other day. Rather a bounder.'

'Ay, and if this Tars Flock left,' cried Ramsbottom, 'it beats me what they'd find to talk about here. They talk about him and his fish morning, noon and night, till you get sick of hearing his name. You just take notice, Dursley. My word, he seems to have been a right godsend to this island. Ah thought when I came here Ah'd be hearing some tales that'ud make my hair stand on end – y'know, proper *Wide World* magazine stuff. But they talk about price o' copra, same as they talk about price o' cotton in Manchester; and a bit about boats; and then all the rest o' the time, they're on about this Tars Flock and his big fishes. Nay, Ah could write a book about him now myself, and Ah've been here no time.'

A few minutes afterwards, William and Terry were claimed by some of the *Marukai* people and were introduced to various island personages, and then William discovered, to his surprise, that Ramsbottom had hardly been exaggerating, for at every table somebody was saying something about Tars Flock and his fishing. Other names were mentioned, however, and one of them startled William. He overheard somebody at the next table say something about Garsuvin. Garsuvin! He had almost forgotten the existence of that strange personage, but now, when he heard the name again, his memory became very lively and quite disturbing. Try as he might, he could not help feeling unpleasantly conscience-stricken again. An image of that odd intellectual clown's face returned to him.

He turned to the man beside him at the table, a little middle-aged American agent called Waters, and said: 'I heard somebody talking about a man called Garsuvin. Do you know him?'

'Garsuvin? Yeh, used to see a lot of him here one time.'

'Does he live here now?'

'No. He's got interests here,' replied Waters, 'pretty big interests, too. Got a lot of money invested in these islands, all over the place. But he don't live here any more. Turns up in a yacht sometimes, that's all. You know him?'

'I met him in England – once.'

'Queer guy, Garsuvin. I can tell you some very funny stories about him. You ask me sometime.'

William, still feeling rather perturbed, said that he would. But that was mere politeness; he found that his one desire was to forget about Mr. Garsuvin, whose large melancholy eyes had not yet quite faded from the depths of his memory.

'Bill,' cried Terry, coming round from another table,

'here's something for you. I've just been introduced to somebody from Suffolk, England. Yes, Suffolk, England. Come along and I'll introduce you.'

William was not excited by the thought of meeting somebody from Suffolk, England, as Terry seemed to think he ought to be, but he followed her to a table near the far door, where an elderly man and a small neat woman were sitting together. The man was an Englishman, an old inhabitant of the island, called Dobson. It was the woman who came from Suffolk. Her name was Mrs. Jackson, and she was, it seemed, the widow of a New Zealand skipper. She had a pleasant open face, with grey eyes, a freckled snub nose, and a friendly mouth; not interesting, not pretty, rather mousey and faded, just a commonplace, honest, smiling, compact little woman of thirty or so. William was prepared to like her, but unfortunately she did not interest him, and having left home so recently he could not be as excited as she was by the mere fact of meeting somebody from the same part of the world. She had obviously been away for several years, with the result that she was delighted by this encounter.

'And you come from Buntingham, Mr. Dursley?' she cried, in very familiar and pleasant East Anglian tones. 'Well, I come from Ipswich. Yes, I was born there and I lived there all my life till I was twenty. Then I went to London, and I was there four years. And I've been out of England now for six years.'

'And she'd like to be back,' observed Dobson, who evidently did not share her views.

She nodded eagerly, and smiled, rather like a confiding child, at William and Terry. 'Yes, I would. I'm dying to go back. Mr. Dursley, you're going to make me more homesick than ever, if you stay here. But you'll promise to tell me all about Suffolk, about Ipswich and Buntingham and everything, won't you?'

'Of course he will,' said Terry promptly. 'You home folks will have to get together.'

William promised he would, but he could not help feeling embarrassed by this eager approach. He had fled from Buntingham to find the South Seas – and Terry. He had them both, and he found it difficult to work up the slightest interest in Mrs. Jackson and her passion for Suffolk. But he felt vaguely sorry for her. How faded, how dull, she seemed – poor girl – by the side of the radiant Terry!

She was only drinking an iced lemonade, and clearly was not at home in the Cercle Bougainville. It appeared that she had a bungalow and a small plantation about eight miles outside Papeete, had begun to take boarders and was thinking of enlarging her establishment and turning it into an hotel proper. This much William learned during the next few minutes, at the end of which the crowd on the verandah began to break up. It was time for the passengers to return to the *Marukai*. After receiving a hasty but cordial invitation from Mrs. Jackson to visit her place, William and Terry left her, joined some of their *Marukai* acquaintances, and, with the Commander and Ramsbottom in attendance, quitted the club for the landing stage outside, where a good many people had already gathered.

They all went aboard for a few minutes. William and Terry had a word or two with nearly all their old shipmates.

'Yes, *sir*,' cried Mr. Tiefman triumphantly to William. 'I've had a good day in Tahiti, and every darned thing worked according to skedool. Motor tour round the island this morning. Lunched off real native food out at

What's It's – you know, the place where everybody goes for native food. Out in a glass-bottom boat this afternoon to see the coral and native diver. Had a rum punch and a Rainbow cocktail at the Bugganvil. Didn't see the girls do a *hula*, but I guess that takes time to fix up, specially these days, when they tell me the girls don't dance it much. Well, I'm ready to call it a day. Yes, *sir*. Boat going off prompt to time too. Good-bye, Mr. Dursley. Been a great pleasure to make your acquaintance. One of the best things about taking a big trip like this is the number of nice folks you meet. Yes, *sir.*' And that was the last word William had from Mr. Tiefman, who carried his great itinerary and his 'sked book,' his overcoat-mackintosh-rug, his horrible tie, his three over-worked socks, into the unknown. Farewell, farewell, Mr. Tiefman!

And now the four of them had returned to the thronged landing stage, and were waving good-bye with the rest as the *Marukai* moved off. A vague feeling of sadness possessed William as he watched her go; as if she had been his home for years instead of a mere ten days. Terry must have been feeling this too, for she gripped his arm and squeezed it. Some of the Tahitian girls wept as they waved; not because the ship was carrying away anybody dear to them, but simply because weeping expressed the mood of the moment. A bugle rang out, with a kind of shrill irony, from the boat deck. Very cautiously, the *Marukai* turned, then headed for the narrow pass out of the lagoon. Once through the pass, she dwindled rapidly.

'And that's the last we shall see o' civilisation for a bit,' remarked Ramsbottom, as they still stood and stared.

Above Moorea, which was like a piece of black crumpled paper, the sunset sky was going mad, juggling with its coloured fires, lifting veil after veil of orange and carmine to reveal, for a few seconds, ineffable distances of pale apple green, showing the gates of heaven above the burnished jaws of hell. Then darkness fell on them, and the *Marukai* was only a little light. At once Papeete was mysterious and gay, and its life seemed to throb to the distant strumming of guitars. There was a maddening fragrance all along the road home.

3

When William had been on Tahiti for a week he felt he had been there for months. It was as if the humid atmosphere had shredded away the rest of the world to a few faded tatters of memory. It was not that the days were uneventful. Nor the nights; which he found long and rather miserable, for the heat and an increasing number of mosquito-bites tended to keep him wakeful, so that he had plenty of time to think and to discover, at his leisure, what a South Pacific island was like at various hours from one until four in the morning. And there was always the mosquito that contrived to get inside the netting, and there sang insolently. The days were long, for they were out bathing at seven and had finished breakfast before nine, and did not go to bed very early; but each had its own new sensations. There had been the necessary visit to the police department of the *Etablissements français de l'Océanie*, where he and Terry, giggling a little, had made their way to a tiny office so hot and damp and buried in tropical leafage that the clerk himself seemed to be rotting away there, like a fat white plant; and from which they had returned with their little permits, in which, among other things, were set down in a fine clerkly French hand the maiden names of their respective mothers. There had been a solemn visit to the schooner *Hutia*, that was to carry the three men to Faraway; a grand romantic vessel, but for the time being far too hot and smelly and messy with stores for comfort. William had made the acquaintance of the skipper with the mixed French, Scandinavian and Polynesian blood, Prettel by name, an enormous brown hairy fellow dressed in a dirty singlet. The Commander had described him as temperamental, and he certainly looked it. They told some queer stories of Prettel at the Bougainville, William was informed, though he never heard them. Indeed, he never heard any queer stories of anybody at the Bougainville; only rather dull anecdotes about Tars Flock and his big fish. The Commander, who was a great schooner man, had taken him to some of the neighbouring vessels, with whose skippers he had scraped up an acquaintance; dumpy two and three-masted boats that went in search of copra and pearls and were now busy taking in fresh supplies of stores and trade goods; very picturesque with their outlandish names, their Chinese super-cargoes, their Kanaka crews, their awnings and washing out to dry, their deck muddle, their blistered sides, their rich smells; very picturesque, very romantic, though William could not help noticing that the fourth he saw was somehow less picturesque, less romantic, than the first had been. He had seen a schooner come in, crowded with natives taking a deck passage from neighbouring islands, and he had seen a schooner go out, equally crowded with natives, who looked just like those who had come in; and each time there had been the same scene, the same laughing and singing and kissing and crying, for the islanders appeared to work as hard and consistently at this demonstrativeness as a well-trained opera chorus.

They usually bathed several times a day, though after the first day or two, Terry was not always there. To begin with, she had quickly made friends with the two Americans at the hotel, the Pullens (which is more than William could do with his fellow-countryman, Crawford, who was as reserved and remote as Ramsbottom had said he was); and the Pullens, who were friendly with other Americans dotted about the island, had taken a fancy to her and were always asking her to go on expeditions with them. sometimes William went too, but at other times he was not asked, and then, in spite of continual remonstrances with himself, he would find himself growing jealous and rather bitter, would decide to be cool with Terry when next they met, and then would instantly thaw at the sight of her welcoming smile. He was not, he knew, making any progress with her; in fact, he felt that they had been closer during the last few days aboard the *Marukai*; but this did not make him feel very uneasy, for he told himself that for the time being she was excited too much by the island life, which roused her enthusiasm to a much higher pitch than it did his, to bother about personal relations. So he took care not to press any claim. He felt that he was not losing her; she was always glad to see him; came eagerly to share her discoveries; grabbed hold of him in moments of excitement; and kissed him good night very sweetly. She was now on the liveliest chaffing terms with Ramsbottom, who entertained her greatly; and was at least friendly with the Commander, who saw far less of her. Both she and Ramsbottom were far fonder of visiting the Bougainville than the other two were. Ramsbottom liked the iced drinks, the gossip, and the pretty Tahitian girls who occasionally visited the place, girls with whom he mixed the paternal and the amorous in very nice proportions. Terry did not drink too much (but she drank more than William wanted her to drink, though he dared not tell her so), but she enjoyed chattering with the other

Americans there. The Bougainville, for what it was worth, was the social centre of the town, of the island, and Terry was nothing if not a social being. This fact gave William no pleasure. He was now making discoveries about himself, and one of them was that he was quite a possessive person. He wanted to take Terry away from them all, to hide her away for a time, to possess her in embowered solitude. So far he had not possessed her in any sense, a fact that would not have surprised him at home; but here it was different: you loved where you slept. In Tahiti the body is pampered royally; and William's, already a warm brown from sea and sun, reprieved at last from darkness and woollen underclothes, and turning arrogant, began to clamour: Why, why, why?

In spite of the flaws in this new scheme of things: the humid heat; the mosquitoes; the surprisingly dull aspect of all South Sea life during the long glaring afternoons; the unexpected monotonies; the lack of progress with Terry; William was happy. Sometimes there would come a moment of real ecstasy, like that first glimpse of the little fishes; the mad sunsets; a sight of Moorea, cut fantastically out of amethyst; a rainbow dropped from the purple crags of the Diadem, an incredible Wagnerian landscape; the first plunge into the cool stream above Loti's pool; that vision of the great waterfall far up the valley, where he and the Commander had suffocatingly climbed, to be refreshed at last by wild oranges and flying spray; exquisite moments, vast windfalls for the memory, to be recaptured over and over again, to light up a hundred future darknessess. Nevertheless, William's happiness, a truly romantic affair, was produced from within and not from without, and at the root of it were ideas and not reality. It was not Tahiti itself that was making him happy so much as the idea that he was in Tahiti. Terry herself was doing little or nothing for his joy, but the idea of her being there, so accessible, was doing a great deal. And the days were enriched and illuminated by a fine confusion of these two magics.

4

This was the last day before the *Hutia* sailed, and they had all agreed to make the most of it. Ramsbottom had invited his two partners, Terry, and Mrs. Pullen (Pullen had gone over to Moorea on business, and so was not available) to a grand native fish lunch out at Taravao, on the other side of the island. A Tahitian had kept a primitive hotel, famous for its native food, out there for many years, but it had just passed into the hands of an Englishman, Major Hockaday, whose third attempt this was to run an hotel in Tahiti and Moorea. Ramsbottom had met Major Hockaday in Papeete, and this had largely determined his choice of Taravao as their lunching place. They set out, in a hired seven-seater Buick, fairly early in the morning, for there was talk of bathing on the way, and it was forty roughish miles to Taravao. As they were passing through Papeete, Terry suggested they should pick up Mrs. Jackson, the young widow from Suffolk, and so complete the party. Ramsbottom had no objection, so it was agreed that they should call at Mrs. Jackson's place, some six or seven miles away. None of them had been there yet, but the driver knew it.

They found Mrs. Jackson outside a long low bungalow, very gay and fragrant with a flamboyant tree, scarlet-and-green crotons, and double-blossom hibiscus. Her rather pale round face flushed with pleasure when she saw them and learned their errand, and though she protested she ought not to leave her three boarders (an elderly French-man and a middle-aged New Zealand couple), it did not take long to persuade her to join them. Within five minutes, all neat and smiling, she was climbing into the car. Off they went then, the six of them, swaying and bumping along the one road that Tahiti can boast, dodg-ing the leisurely Chinese carts and the natives dreamily repairing the soft track. It was a smoking hot morning, and their road seemed to be made up of gold dust and purple-green shade. About half-way they found a little beach of white sand not far from the road, and there stopped and bathed, all but Ramsbottom, who preferred to smoke a cigar and look on, and Mrs. Pullen, a large damp bleached woman, smilingly indolent. It was a beautiful little beach, shelving very gradually into the glittering lagoon, where William discovered, to his delight, little fishes coloured and striped even more fan-tastically than those he had seen before. He also dis-covered that Mrs. Jackson was much less dim and mouse-like when bathing, for she was a good swimmer and had a very trim girl's figure. The four of them splashed about and dived to see the fishes, then came out and sprawled on the hot sand and watched the antics of the frigate-birds. And then William found that by turning his head a little he could stare at the down on Terry's right arm, glinting in the sun. So he stared, and lost himself.

Back in the Buick, they swayed and bumped into a shaggy Eden. They saw long slender cascades blown from the blue heights above the wilderness of giant ferns and bearded tree stems. There were caves fringed with hang-ing roots and holding black midnight. Gardens came blazing in orange and scarlet, burst like bombs and were gone. There was a grove of trees with trunks like columns and immense roots that seemed to be carved in stone, so that within this grove there was the ancient and twilit solemnity of a Gothic cathedral. The water-colourist in William alternated violently between delight and despair. There was too much of everything. This was the wild carnival of landscape.

The car had to stop a hundred yards or so from Major Hockaday's main bungalow, the one used as a dining-room, and Ramsbottom and William led the way to it on foot. From the interior, which looked quite dark from outside, there came the sound of music. Ramsbottom and William approached quietly, not wishing to disturb the musicians. When they reached the entrance they peeped in cautiously. In the far corner, seated close together on a basket lounge, were three persons, all strumming guitars, singing, and staring solemnly and idiotically at one another in the manner of all guitar strummers. One of them was Mrs. Kinderfield, who was wearing a chaplet of flowers on her cropped head, her *pince-nez*, a green shirt, and very short shorts, so that there seemed to be yards of thin white legs sticking out of them. Another was a small native girl, wearing only a scarlet-and-white *pareu*, and looking as fat as butter. And the third, and the most solemn, was Major Hockaday himself, a bandy-legged fellow of forty, with a broad, stupid, washed-out face, who was wearing a khaki shirt and shorts and exposing a great deal of thick hairy knobbly leg. Only the native girl seemed to be sure of the tune they were playing and singing, but what the other lacked in knowledge they made up for in diligence and concentration, so that they stared so hard it appeared as if their eyes were about to pop out of their heads. And as William stood in the entrance, looking at and listening to this absurd trio, he had a momentary conviction that life in the South Seas was neither beautiful nor romantic, but singularly futile and preposterous.

'Well, well,' cried Ramsbottom, with a dry emphasis, 'quite a turn, eh? Or it will be when you've all learned the tune.'

'Who's that?' cried Hockaday sharply, jumping up. 'Oh, it's you, Ramsbottom, is it? Good morning. Is all your party here? Splendid, splendid!' And Major Hockaday set his bandy hairy legs in motion and bustled about, clapping his hands and calling out various native girls' names, until very soon the place was in an uproar and seemed to be crammed with visitors bumping into one another and native girls, all giggles and shining coppery skins.

Mrs. Kinderfield, who appeared to be rather drunk, drooped above William. 'My work, Mr. Dursley,' she was saying, 'calls for the delicate ad-justment of many, many, psycho-logical problems. Es-pecially' – and here she fixed him with a very severe glare through the *pince-nez* – 'those many, many psycho-logical problems appertaining to sexual ree-lationships. Now I know what you are going to say, Mr. Dursley.' And she paused.

Here she had the advantage of William, and he remained silent.

'You are going to say, "How is the life here going to help you to find those delicate ad-justments?" I will try to answer that question in a few words. I believe' – and now she glared harder than ever, and in order to assist her argument, gave him a jab in the ribs with her guitar – 'that the universal uncarnscious can be ree-vealed by a study of a happy primitive unrepressed people, es-pecially in their sexual ree-lationships. You have that here, Mr. Dursley. And it's a warnderful, warnderful life. It's' – and she steadied herself – 'a revel-ation. And I'm staying

right here with the major till I find a bangalow of my
own.'

They were all talking at once now; even the Commander, who, after regarding Major Hockaday and his
ménage with some distaste, had settled in a corner with
Mrs. Jackson, who seemed to be very talkative. Mrs. Kinderfield now bore down upon Mrs. Pullen, and left William
free to join Ramsbottom, Terry, and Hockaday, who was
shaking a cocktail. Ramsbottom introduced William to
the major. They had not met before, but William had
heard a good deal about this fellow-countryman, who
supplied the Bougainville with gossip, not merely because
he kept trying to run hotels, but chiefly because what Mrs.
Kinderfield would have called his 'sexual ree-lationships'
were peculiar and notorious. When Hockaday had first
arrived on the island, he had married – in the Tahitian
sense – the eldest of a family of five bouncing brown girls;
but after a year or so, he had driven this girl from his
bed and taken in her place the sister next to her; and
now it was not exactly known at the Bourgainville whether
he was still with the fourth, had passed on to the fifth, or
was living with both of them. This probably explained
why the major had never been able to make his hotels
pay; and it also explained that stupid, washed-out look of
his. William, unlike the Commander, had no strong views,
and was not consciously prejudiced against Major Hockaday because of his conjugal experiments; but nevertheless
he did not like Major Hockaday. He did not like his face,
his bandy legs, his voice, his strumming, and the general
atmosphere of him. Hockaday was obviously one of those
temporary war officers who insist on trailing their brief
military rank into civil life, and William was heartily prejudiced against the whole breed. Fake officer and gentle-

man, he concluded very quickly, were written all over the major.

'Well, chin-chin!' cried Major Hockaday, raising his glass. 'Glad to see you here, Miss Riley. You too, Dursley. See you get a first-class Tahitian lunch. Just beginning to make improvements and haven't settled down properly, but hope to make a good show of it. At the same time, I want to keep all the old features – native life, y'know. You'll see. What d'you think of Tahiti, Miss Riley?'

'I just love it,' cried Terry, with genuine enthusiasm. 'I've heard all about it all my life, and looked forward to coming – and even at that, I'm not disappointed. It's grand.'

'You liking it, Dursley?' the major enquired, with more than a suspicion of patronage.

'Not bad,' replied William, with deliberate coolness.

'Not bad? My God! – think it isn't bad!' The major was horrified. 'Wait till you've seen the life here, really got to know it. Only place for a man to live these days. England! – not for me, no, no. You don't get me back there. Been tried – but no fear.' There was a suggestion here that high office, a peerage, or large sums of money had been offered in vain. 'I want sunshine, fresh air, beautiful scenery, freedom,' the major continued, rather as if he were ordering them at the stores. 'Fellow can live a man's life here. He can breathe. Excuse me. Must go and stir those lazy devils or we'll never see any lunch.' And off he bustled, and not without reason, for the picturesque damsels who composed his domestic staff – probably all relatives and friends of the sisters he was for ever marrying and divorcing – seemed to be occupying themselves with strumming, singing, weaving chains of flowers, dancing a few wiggles of the *hula*, and, of course, giggling.

It was rather late when Ramsbottom and his five guests

sat down to lunch, all looking rather self-conscious and foolish and smelling like hot-houses with chaplets and garlands of jasmine and gardenias, but they did not sit down to any mere snack. The first course was oysters, and there appeared to be thousands of them, as if whole ocean beds had been despoiled for them. William never remembered seeing so many oyster shells before; you could hardly see the table for them.

'Well, they seem to think we'll fancy an oyster or two,' remarked Ramsbottom, who, with his flowers at a sinister angle, looked rather like a Nero in spectacles. 'There can't be an oyster left i' these parts.'

'It looks an awful lot,' said Mrs. Jackson, the only old inhabitant at the table, 'but as a matter of fact, you can eat dozens and dozens of them – they're so tiny.'

'They are that,' said Ramsbottom, busy poking away with his fork. 'Nay, they're all shell and no oyster. It's a quarrying job, this.'

They all quarried away, until at last they had great piles of very thick and oddly-shaped shells in front of them, and a fishy taste in their mouths, but no solid conviction of having eaten anything much. There was no such Barmecide quality about the next course, however, which was lobster. The table was now as crowded with lobsters as it had seemed before with oysters.

'This is even fishier,' William told Terry, 'than that seafood lunch I had in the ship place in San Francisco.'

'It's like visiting with a mermaid,' said Terry, greedily exploring her lobster.

Apparently these two courses had been mere trifles to whet the appetite, for now the lunch really began. The relatives and friends of the sisters stopped strumming and giggling, and decided to serve a little solid food. They marched up with shrimps and rice, raw fish with coconut sauce, chicken and hot breadfruit and yams and sweet potatoes, baked feis, and all the fruits of the island, until the table began to look like a still-life in the Flemish grand manner. There was a sweet and rather strong Sauterne to drink, and, at the end of the meal, some sticky French liqueurs for those who wanted them. It was a tremendous lunch.

When it was over, Mrs. Kinderfield collared the three women and marched them off on some little tour of exploration. Major Hockaday had some long story to tell to Ramsbottom, who had had about twice as much food and three times as much drink as anybody else, and was now very flushed and beaming indeed. So William and the Commander went sleepily into the shaded verandah, overlooking an armlet of the lagoon, to smoke and gaze at the blue silken world.

Oddly enough, this was the time the Commander chose to be quite loquacious, and on personal topics too. 'That woman, you know, Dursley,' he began, with a judicial air, 'Mrs. Jackson – that's a good type of woman. The real sort. Good English blood.'

William, amused, wondering if his companion had fallen in love, merely gave an encouraging murmur.

'Notice the eyes – absolutely steady. You can't beat those steady grey eyes in a woman. She's gone through a tough time—'

'Oh, has she? Did she tell you all about it?'

'She told me something,' said the Commander, 'but even if she hadn't, I'd have known. She's probably still got a tough time ahead of her. But that won't matter. She'll come through all right.'

William laughed lazily. 'You seem very enthusiastic abut Mrs. Jackson all of a sudden.'

The Commander frowned, though not angrily.

'Because she's the kind I like. And you don't meet many of them here. Messy people, with no sense of responsibility, dodging their duties – that's what you meet here. That ghastly American female, the one with the eye-glasses, for instance – ugh! No backbone, no guts, no sense, no decency. And this major – as he calls himself – he's a sloppy bounder, Dursley.'

'I agree. I don't fancy the major at all, Commander.'

'I should think not. That's why I like this little woman, Mrs. Jackson. She's the best English type. Now you compare her with this American girl.'

William's attention was alert at once. This was serious. What about this American girl? Now steady, Commander, old man! Be very careful.

Quite unconscious of any change in his listener's attitude, the Commander went on: 'Shouldn't be saying these things, I suppose, but a fellow can't help noticing and drawing his conclusions. Now this American girl – she's showy – she's attractive – and no doubt she's got lots of good qualities—'

'No doubt,' said William to himself grimly.

'But, in my opinion, this quiet English girl is worth ten of her,' the Commander continued innocently. 'You couldn't depend on this American girl. Sooner or later she'd let you down—'

'How do you know?' demanded William, rather aggressively.

'I can tell. I've had to judge a lot of people's characters in my time,' replied the Commander firmly. 'You couldn't depend on her. Nothing solid there. No real bony character. Brilliant, but weak and unstable and bit rotten somewhere. Now this English woman, Mrs. Jackson – she wouldn't let a man down. She'd see you through if it killed her. And that's what you want, in this world, in the long run, Dursley. People who see what their duty is and go and do it, without a lot of fuss. People who know when they have obligations.' The Commander was very sententious, and William came rapidly to the conclusion that the lunch must have taken him that way. After all, he had had his share of drink, though he was certainly not tight, like Ramsbottom. 'These American women are all spoilt now. That's bad for them. Don't suppose this girl can help it. She's not a bad girl.'

'Of course she isn't,' cried William. 'And after all, you know very little about her. I know her much better than you do. And – with all due respect to you, Commander, I can't help thinking you're talking a lot of bosh. You're simply prejudiced. You understand English people, and you don't understand Americans. I don't pretend to understand Americans myself. There are a good many things about Terry – Miss Riley – I don't understand. But as for her being unstable and spineless and all that sort of thing – it's absolutely monstrous. I'm surprised at you, Commander. As a matter of fact, that's just where you're wrong. If there's one thing she has got – as I've seen for myself – it's backbone and guts, though that seems rather a foul way to talk about a lovely girl. But you know what I mean.' William's voice now lost its sharp protesting tone. He gazed out to sea, and continued, rather dreamily: 'It seems to me that America is producing an entirely new race of people. I noticed that in San Francisco. Physically they're different. Take Terry, for example. Now she seems to me to be beautiful in a new way. It's the mixture of races. She is an extraordinary mixture, as she once told me – Irish, Spanish, Jewish and God knows what. Of course the result of a mixture like that might be an awful mess, and I don't say I haven't seen some awful messes there. But it seems to turn out well, especially for the women. There's a fascinating piquancy about them. Look at Terry. And it stands to reason that with this new physical type, you'll get a new type of character, and because you don't understand it, you can't begin to make hasty judgments about it. Don't you agree?'

The Commander said nothing. William looked at him: he was fast asleep. For a moment, William was disgusted, angry, but then he smiled at himself. There was something ironical in the situation: here was a man who, to make conversation on the edge of a nap, denounces the girl you're in love with, and then, just when you are beginning to defend her, slips away into unconsciousness. So William continued the argument in his head, but it got dreamier and dreamier; and finally, he simply thought vaguely about Terry, savouring the essence of her. But he had eaten a good deal and the afternoon was very hot, and at last even Terry disappeared, along with all the bloom and glitter of Tahiti.

He awoke to the sound of voices, and so did the Commander. Terry, Mrs. Jackson, Mrs. Pullen, and Major Hockaday were there, laughing at them.

'Bill,' said Terry, 'where's Mr. Ramsbottom? We thought he was here with you.'

'Not here,' muttered William, getting up.

'He must be somewhere round here,' she continued. 'And Mrs. Jackson and Mrs. Pullen want to be getting back.'

'What, already?'

'You look at the time, Mr. Dursley,' said Mrs. Jackson, laughing. 'You've been snoozing there for hours. I wanted you to give me all the Suffolk news, and you haven't yet.'

'What's this?' said the Commander, suddenly brisk and alert. 'Can't you find Ramsbottom? Why, we left him with you, Hockaday.'

'He wasn't with me more than ten minutes,' said the major. 'Then he went off on his own somewhere. Thought he'd gone for a siesta. Looked sleepy, I thought.'

'He looked pickled to me,' Mrs. Pullen drawled, making a statement, and not criticising the absent one.

'He was a bit lit,' said Terry. 'Well, we've just got to find him, that's all. Come on, you two sleeping beauties, you've got to find him.'

'Make enquiries,' said the major. 'One of the girls or boys round the place probably saw him. Don't miss much, so long as it isn't work.' And he put his bandy little legs into action.

The others trailed in the same direction. It was still very hot, and everybody was feeling the effect of that enormous lunch. Nobody was actually snappy, but at any moment somebody might be. Hockaday returned to say that Ramsbottom had been seen going inland, walking by the stream up the narrow steep little glen. It was decided that Terry, Mrs. Jackson, the Commander and William should explore this glen in search of him. They found a narrow track, wandering between pandanus trees and enormous bamboos, then climbing among great ferns, wild banana trees, and the strongly smelling lantana, and up they went, finding the shade and the cool air above the rushing stream very welcome. After about twenty minutes' easy walking, they came to a little waterfall, and above the fall, a charming pool, dappled in sunlight and green shade, and hung about with dripping roots and maidenhair.

'Well,' cried little Mrs. Jackson, 'just look at his lordship.'

And there his lordship was, like one of the more disreputable antique gods. He was wearing nothing but his trousers, but the upper half of him was richly garlanded

with crimson-and-white flowers. A little native boy, naked
except for a loincloth, was sitting at one side of him, and
a little native girl, who might have been shaped out of
brown satin, was sitting on the other side, and both
of them were watching his face, with the solemnest black
eyes, and carefully fanning it with enormous leaves. And
the wreathed and fragrant deity himself was leaning
against a mossy bank, his spectacles almost at the end of
his nose, his mouth wide open, snoring with majestic
rhythm and sonority.

The four of them went up quietly and formed a semi-
circle. The two native children jumped to their feet,
flashed looks of enquiry at the newcomers, then grinned
and did not attempt to run away.

'Isn't he a picture?' said Mrs. Jackson softly.

'I'll say he is,' said Terry.

'Ah Ramsbottom!' William whispered. 'If Manchester
could only see you now!'

'Eh!' said Ramsbottom, without, however, opening his
eyes.

'Ramsbottom,' called the Commander quietly, 'it's time
you were up.'

Ramsbottom slowly opened his eyes, and blinked at
them; he carefully adjusted his spectacles, and stared
at them; a large fat smile gradually spread over his face;
then it gradually disappeared, and he looked puzzled.
The two native children now claimed his attention, and
there must have been something in his eye that alarmed
them, for suddenly they bolted and a moment later it
was as if they had never been there. This fact added to
Ramsbottom's bewilderment. He pushed the flowers away
from his forehead.

'Now wait a minute,' he began slowly, 'wait a minute.
Let's get this straight. Was there two kids here or not?

There was, eh? That's good. And what about that girl? Was she here?'

'Mr. Ramsbottom,' cried Terry reproachfully, 'you don't mean to say there's been a girl here too.'

'Well, that's what Ah want to know. Now wait a minute. Ah'm that mixed up, Ah don't know fairly if Ah've been dreaming or not, but if them kids was here, then Ah didn't dream them. And Ah don't think Ah can have dreamt rest of it.'

'Where are the rest of your clothes?' asked the Commander.

'Rest of my— Here, wait a minute.' He felt his bare garlanded chest in dismay. 'Ah started with a shirt and white coat on, Ah'll swear to that. And now Ah've lost them, and sitting here like a young flower show. Excuse me, ladies. But Ah must get up.' It was then that he discovered his shirt and coat, for he had been partly sitting on them. Asking the ladies to excuse him again, he vanished round the corner, returning a minute later clothed and ungarlanded.

'I think I liked you better just wearing the flowers, Mr. Ramsbottom,' said Terry.

'So did I,' cried Mrs. Jackson, who, rather to William's surprise, was enjoying all this immensely and getting quite giggly.

'Ah'll tell you what it is,' said Ramsbottom solemnly. 'Ah'm in a maze, as you might say. Ah'm trying to sort it out how Ah got here.'

'That's what we're wondering,' William told him. 'We heard you were lost and so came to look for you.'

'Mrs. Jackson here and Mrs. Pullen are anxious to get back,' the Commander added.

'Oh well, if that's it, Ah'm sorry. Let's be getting on,

and Ah'll tell you about it afterwards, when Ah get it sorted out.'

It was when they had got back to the hotel and were waiting for the car that he told his story. 'You see, Ah'd had a right good tuck-in at lunch and more than a toothful o'wine and liqueur, and what with that and the 'eat, Ah was feeling a bit muzzy and heavy and sleepy. But Ah thought Ah'd walk out a bit, 'cos it doesn't suit me to lie down and sleep straight after a heavy meal, Ah've got to move about a bit first, d'you see? So Ah thought to myself – when the major had done telling his tale, which was all something and nothing – Ah thought to myself Ah'd go and sit by that stream, for coolness' sake. Well, Ah started walking up that path where we've just been – taking my time, and, as Ah said, a bit muzzy – and Ah went up and up, till suddenly Ah bumps into as queer a looking chap as ever Ah set eyes on. To begin with, he'd long hair, and a beard that reached half-way down to his middle; and all the clothes he was wearing wouldn't have made two decent pocket handkerchiefs. And he wasn't a native – not he! He was as white as we are, was this chap, or he had been, for now he was all over a brick-red colour, and his hair and beard must have been quite yellow once, and now they were just turning grey. He was a big chap too, thin as a lath – you could count his ribs as easy as ninepence – and he had a great nose on him, jutting out like Flamborough Head. It takes a bit to surprise me, especially down here, but Ah'll tell you, that chap did. It was like bumping into Elijah in the wilderness.'

'He must be a nature man,' observed Mrs. Jackson. 'There are a lot of them, and they live by themselves, in little huts, just on fruit and stuff – no money at all. And they don't wear clothes. It's an easy way of living, though

I must say it wouldn't suit me. You just might as well be a sheep in a field and have done with it.'

'Well, wait a minute. This chap was no sheep. So Ah says hello to him, and he says hello to me. And we starts talking. He could speak a sort o' queer English, but as a matter o'fact, he was a Russian, and Ah fancy he said he'd been a count or a prince. Anyway, Ah asked him some questions, and he answered 'em, telling me how he lived, much as you said, Mrs. Jackson. And he asked me if Ah could give him a pencil, for he was wanting one badly, and as it happens Ah always keep a pencil or two on me, so Ah gave him one, and he was right pleased with it. He told me he only lived a step or two away, so Ah said Ah'd go up with him and have look. So we went a bit farther up, just above that pool where you found me, and he took me to a bit of a hut he had, a place nearly as bare as a bone. Now Ah may have been muzzy, but you see, Ah'm remembering it all right. Nay, Ah think it must have happened, all right. It sounds daft, but Ah can't have dreamt it.' Here Mr. Ramsbottom paused, and looked at his listeners.

'What did happen?' asked the Commander, rather impatiently.

'It's all right saying that, but Ah'm taking my time 'cos when Ah've done you'll call me a liar. So we squats down in this hut of his, and he talked and Ah listened, half asleep, and then he told me he'd spent years and years studying something or other – Ah know there was a lot o' meditation and concentration in it – a sort o' magic stuff – and he could do this, that and the other. Well, Ah'd heard these tales before, and Ah laughed in his face, sleepy as I was. That nettled him a bit, and he brought that great nose of his close to me, stared and stared with eyes like a cat, and said if Ah'd think of somebody Ah'd known well and tell him, he'd make 'em appear. Ah thought to myself this chap's gone dotty with living up here alone so long. However, Ah thought Ah'd humour him. You've got to humour 'em, haven't you?'

His audience agreed that you had to humour them.

'All right then. So, being a bit muzzy and sleepy and daft, Ah said to him, silly as you like, "Ah'll have another word with Maggie Armitage." Now this Maggie Armitage Ah hadn't set eyes on for nearly twenty year. She were an old sweetheart o' mine, and just about twenty year since Maggie and me had had one o' the grandest holidays any man ever had, at Blackpool. So, silly as you like, Ah said to him "Produce Maggie Armitage." He told me to think about her for a minute or two, and Ah did and he stared and stared. Then he told me to wait there a minute, and he went out. And Ah hadn't to wait long neither. Somebody came in.'

'It wasn't Maggie Armitage?' shrieked Terry.

'It was,' cried Ramsbottom. 'It was Maggie Armitage all right, and she might have just come off Central Pier, Blackpool, with me, twenty year since. No different at all. She walked straight in, said "Hello, Johnny lad," and came and put her two arms round my neck and her cheek against mine, just as she'd done many a time, and Ah can remember telling myself that if this was dreaming, Ah'd dream on a bit, 'cos Ah never liked anybody better than Ah did Maggie. Then she said, "Let's go and sit by that pool, Johnny," and she took me by the hand, and we went down and sat where you saw me – yes, we did, Maggie and me. She sat down close to me and put her head against my shoulder and Ah held her tight, and she asked me how things were with me and Ah told her and Ah asked how things were with her, and it was all so quiet and peaceful – nay, bless my soul! – Ah don't remember

when it was so quiet and peaceful. Then all of a sudden
– and Ah remember it as plain as plain can be – Ah gave
a sort o' shiver. No waking up or anything like that, just a
sort o' little shiver. But then Ah found it wasn't Maggie
who was there at all.'

'Wasn't there anybody there?' Terry demanded, looked
at him wide-eyed.

'Yes, Ah was holding somebody all right. But it wasn't
Maggie, it was one of these native lasses, all black eyes
and hair and brown skin. Not Maggie at all. Well, that
made me jump, and this girl – a nice enough lass, Ah
dare say – gives a giggle and a wriggle and rubs my cheek
with her hand – and then Ah felt that sleepy, all of a
sudden, Ah couldn't keep my eyes open. Just dropped
straight off. But Ah woke up once, and there wasn't a girl
there, but them two kids you saw, fanning me. And Ah
thought to myself, "Nay, lad, you're going daft," so
Ah went to sleep again, and next time Ah wakened up,
all you lot were there. And that's as true as Ah'm here.'

'I think you dreamt most of it, Ramsbottom,' said the
Commander.

'Well, happen Ah did,' replied Ramsbottom, puzzling
it out. 'But when did Ah start dreaming? Answer me that.
That Russian nature chap, did Ah dream him?'

'You didn't dream all those flowers you had hung round
you,' said Mrs. Jackson briskly, 'because we saw them
ourselves. I expect you dreamt all the Maggie Armitage
part, though.'

'You must have been very much in love with her, Mr.
Ramsbottom,' said Terry.

'That's what I think, Miss Riley,' said Mrs. Jackson.

'Well, Ah might have been one time,' said Ramsbottom
meditatively, 'and Ah must say Ah was right glad to see

her, this afternoon. She never told me how she got there, y'know.'

'I think you really met the Russian nature man,' said William, 'and that he was a magician. He conjured that native girl into Maggie Armitage for you for a time. And then it didn't work any longer, and you found out.'

'Clever Bill,' cried Terry, 'I believe you're right too. And the Commander doesn't. Do you? You think it was too much lunch. Well, here's the car.'

5

William and Terry spent that last evening by themselves. They dined, among heavily scented blossom and smoke and the sound of strumming, at the *Tiare*, and then went to Papeete's solitary picture theatre, where there happened to be a performance that night. They knew this, because just before reaching Papeete in the car from Taravao they had passed an open lorry on which several happy native youths were taking it in turns to whack at a drum. This was the usual method of giving notice that the picture theatre would open. There was a fairly large and very enthusiastic audience, which amused itself during the numerous waits, and even during the actual film show too, by making music with voices and guitars. The films were old silent ones, badly cut and not always even complete, but their producers' hearts would have been warmed by their Tahitian reception. Many of these islanders can have had only the vaguest notion what the films were all about, but they appreciated broad melodrama when they saw it, and they yelled like children at the chases and the rescues. Thus, they enjoyed themselves, and as the white members of the audience enjoyed their own superiority and found some entertainment in the antique films, enjoyment was general. But nothing that the pictures could show was half so picturesque and romantic as the scene outside the theatre during the interval, when all the members of the audience, American tourists, French planters and clerks, roguish half-castes, yellow fat old women, flirtatious girls, grinning lads, solemn Chinese, sauntered up and down under the flickering arc lights, and bought coloured drinks, little cakes, vast strawberry-tinted slices of melon, at the line of stalls. Not even with colour and sound and a million dollars had Hollywood ever achieved such a parade. Terry adored it; and William, adoring her, discovered in it a subtle double pleasure, and was happy.

And now it was all over, and they were walking back to the hotel. It was a lovely night, a night of the legendary South Seas, when the worst copra dump or most monotonous stretch of palm and coral suddenly becomes part of the Garden of the Hesperides; it had a silken and fragrant beauty in it; there was half a white moon and just a glimmer of stars; there was a soft little wind among the palms; and through this nocturne in purple and silver, this island symphony of distant booming surf, sighing wind, and cicadas, they walked slowly, arm-in-arm, close together. Now and then a car would pass them, sometimes carrying a load of beanfeasting, singing Tahitians, and offering a quick glimpse of flower-crowned dark faces. William was drunk, not with wine – though he had had his share of that – but with love and romantic wonder. All that he had wanted, more even than he had dreamed of, was his now. He tightened his grip on Terry's arm, as if he felt that to let it go would be the signal for her and all this magic of moonlight to vanish.

They did not talk much about themselves as they walked

along the road. They talked quietly about Faraway and what Terry would do while the three of them were away, about the Commander and Ramsbottom, and what they thought of the island life. It was all something and nothing, yet there was in it to William a perfection of harmony. There had been times lately when Terry had frightened him by suddenly appearing alien, and he had felt that he was losing touch with the enchanting Terry of the ship. But happily – for this would be their last evening together for some time – there was not the slightest misgiving now. This was the Terry he had always believed in, had always known was there. To leave her, if only for a few weeks, would be a heart-breaking business.

It was late when they arrived at the hotel, and all the bungalows were in darkness. They picked their way through the stream-haunted garden, where the daturas were giving out a very strong sweet smell. Even here they could still hear a distant strumming, probably from the servants' quarters, across the way. Between the black silhouetted palms, the lagoon was a bright silver. The moonlight mistily filled the great lily cups in the pond. Without stopping or turning, Terry climbed the steps to the verandah of her bungalow, and so William followed her. She did not switch on the light, but stood in the darkness of the verandah looking out towards the lagoon. He stood beside her in silence for a moment, then put out a hand and called her name softly, and she turned to him, slipping into his arms, and gave him kiss for kiss.

'Terry,' he said at last, after telling her, rather confusedly, what he felt about her, 'will you marry me?'

She put her cheek against his. 'It's sweet of you, Bill, to ask me. Where'd we live? In Buntingham, Suffolk, England?'

'Why, I hadn't thought about it,' he confessed. 'I suppose so. My business is there. Unless, of course, we make a fortune out of Faraway.'

'Do you think we shall?'

'I think we might. Don't you?'

'I've got a sort of hunch, Bill – I've had it all along – that we shan't. Somehow I just don't believe much in that island.'

'Oh! – I say, Terry,' he protested.

'Sorry, Bill. I don't mean I think the island's not there or anything like that. But somehow I've got a nasty little feeling it's not going to come to anything much. I guess I oughtn't to be saying that, though, just when you're going to start out and look for it.'

'No, and probably be away weeks and weeks. I'll hate being away from you, even though I know you're here and waiting for me to come back.'

'Right there on the quayside, Bill.'

'But you've not answered my question. Never mind where we're going to live. Will you marry me, Terry?'

'Oh, I wasn't very serious about the living part. But listen, Bill. I don't think I want to marry you – or anybody else – just now. I just don't feel like marrying, though I think you'd be an awful nice man to marry, Bill.'

'You really mean – you don't love me enough.'

'Perhaps so. I don't know. I don't think I know much about myself, these days. But I know I like you an awful lot, Bill.' And she kissed him.

'I shall be thinking about you every minute while I'm away,' he told her quietly. 'I think about you all the time here, now. I always have done, ever since about the second time I met you. Sometimes it's unbearable. It hurts, Terry. And I never realised before that I was capable of feeling so much about anybody. I'm not good at this sort of thing, I know.'

She laughed softly. 'Oh, but you are, Bill. And if you were any better, you'd be a darned sight worse.'

He caught her to him, almost roughly. 'Terry – my darling,' he groaned, as if he ached for her.

'Listen, Bill. You'd better go now.'

'Oh, but—' There was woeful disappointment in his cry.

'Then in five minutes, ten minutes, you can come back – if you want to. I'm tired of these clothes – or any clothes.'

'You mean—'

'Better make it quarter of an hour. I want to have a shower – so do you, I expect – and if you hurry, you get hot all over again. And don't make too much noise, Bill, even if this is Tahiti.'

When he returned, fresh from a cold shower and wearing his thinnest pyjamas, he was cool enough in body, but anything but cool in mind. And he was nervous. His heart, monstrously enlarged, knocked dreadfully in the still darkness of the verandah. But above that knocking he seemed to be able to hear mysterious night noises from miles away. There was one silvered square of moonlight on the floor of the bedroom. He stood for a moment at the entrance, his eyes searching the shade. There was an ivory shape on the bed.

'And if you're just going to stand there, Bill,' said the shape, very quietly, 'I'll close these mosquito curtains again. It's asking too much of any mosquito to stay away from here.'

He had just time to tell himself how astonishing, how cool, how oddly prosaic, women were, before he reached her side. The next moment, the curtains were closed behind him, her arms were about his neck, and their lips had met.

When he re-crossed that narrow fragrant strip of garden back to his own bungalow, the moon was dying in the sky and the night had a remote mild darkness. His feelings were oddly mixed, triumph jostling humility. He had taken possession of one Terry, but there were still a dozen others, smiling, beckoning him on, eluding him. There was still a hunger in his heart, though it was ready to burst with gratitude and tenderness.

CHAPTER VII

FIRST ATTEMPT AT FARAWAY

1

THE DEPARTURE of the *Hutia* was in the best South Seas tradition. William's contribution to the picturesque drama was very small: he shook hands with a number of Bougainville acquaintances, who had come along to see them off, chiefly for lack of something better to do; he said *au revoir* to little Mrs. Jackson, who suddenly turned up, pink and breathless, to remind him that she was still waiting for his Suffolk news; and he kissed Terry, who looked very beautiful, heart-breaking, and a trifle too calm. Ramsbottom added a little comic relief, for after being embraced by two pretty Tahitian sisters, he was then embraced by their mother, a woman even larger than himself and a complete stranger to him. But there were between twenty and thirty native passengers, of all ages and shades, and they had brought their bedding and food, as well as some strange odds and ends of luggage. The schooner was heavily loaded with cargo and stores, every inch of space being used, and she carried on deck some live-stock in crates, fowls and little pigs. It looked as if the *Hutia* were carrying a small expeditionary force. Captain Prettel, that temperamental man, who had now changed his singlet, was drunk, but by no means incapable, and happily spent his time bellowing at the crew or exchanging doubtful jokes and little embraces

with any presentable female who happened to be near.
All the friends and relatives of the native passengers and
crew were at the water's edge, laughing and crying. A
man in an antique yachting cap and a mustard-coloured
shirt played the accordion with passionate abandon, never
opening his eyes and never stopping. Sometimes the
crowd, mostly female and in pink cotton, sang to his
tunes, and sometimes it danced a little. Some of it just
stared, out of huge, dark, unfathomably tragic eyes. These
huge dark stares were returned by some of the passengers,
who flung themselves casually into the most expressive
attitudes, so that any one of them might have served as a
symbolic figure of exiled and doomed humanity. William
rather envied them in their capacity for such a rich
expressiveness of voice, gesture, attitude, for to give way
so easily to the emotions is to remain unbroken by them,
and even to find a histrionic pleasure in the worst of
them. He saw himself and the other whites as stiff brittle
people, who had cut themselves off from the natural easy
poetry of everyday life. Instead of standing there stiffly,
with a little smile frozen on his face, why shouldn't he
fling himself down and look at Terry as if doomsday were
breaking between them?

The *Hutia's* little engine began to splutter, for she was
going through the pass under power. The crew began to
cast off. The accordion wailed, and the women wept.
'*Haéré oé*,' they cried from the shore. '*Parahi*,' they cried
from the ship.

'Ah'll tell you what it is, chaps,' said Ramsbottom,
waving a hand, 'when you come to leave it, this seems a
right nice place. Ah'm beginning to wish now Ah'd let
you two do this surveying job by yourselves.'

As he floated away, William stared at the receding Terry
until his eyes ached. His heart ached a little too, for now

that he was actually leaving her he felt strangely depressed, far more depressed than he had expected to feel. Something whispered that it was bad to let her go like that. He was troubled by a sense of insecurity.

That little habitable strip round the edge of the lagoon, which had been his world these last days, soon vanished, and Tahiti was seen for what it was, a great jagged rock. It had a fantastic beauty now that it never had when one was on it, and as William remarked this fact, he remembered what he had said when he had looked down on San Francisco that night with Terry and the Viking and his wife. Wasn't it the same thing again? Was it always like that? Tahiti and Moorea, incredibly enchanting shapes now, mocked him as they dwindled and rose to the horizon.

That evening there was a stiffish sea running, and though the *Hutia* had a good broad beam and was almost loaded to the water's edge, she was pitching a good deal. This made William feel rather uncomfortable; not seasick, but vaguely uneasy in body and gloomy in mind. Ramsbottom more than shared his uneasiness and gloom, and did not hesitate to find words for them.

'What Ah feel,' he confessed, as they watched the fiery afterglow fade out of the sky, 'is a bit lost. Ah feel such a long way from anywhere – do you know what Ah mean? All this' – and he briefly indicated several thousand miles of the Pacific – 'gives me the creeps. It's so damned homeless. Now you don't feel that way, do you, Commander?'

The Commander didn't. They had noticed that the further they got out to sea, the more cheerful the Commander became. Already he seemed to love this schooner. 'Glad to get away. Can't you feel the difference, now we're out to sea. No more stuffiness. That island was stuffy. This is the life.' And he puffed away luxuriously at his little black briar.

'What's it going to be like, sleeping down there in that saloon?' Ramsbottom enquired.

'Not so good.'

'I'm sure it isn't,' said William, trying not to notice the pitching motion. 'I'm not at all keen on that saloon.'

'Don't sleep there then,' said the Commander briskly. 'I'm not – if it's fine to-night, I shall sleep up here.'

'Good idea!' cried William. 'I'll come up here, too.'

Ramsbottom's large round face, even in that wavering light, could be seen as the perfect expression of dubiousness, and the other two laughed. 'Cheer up,' said the Commander. 'You'll feel better after dinner or supper or whatever they call it. And you'll probably get quite a decent one to-night.'

'Ah expect they start off better than they go on,' said Ramsbottom gloomily.

'Of course they do. They can't help it. For three or four days, while the fresh vegetables and ice last, you'll live like a fighting-cock, Ramsbottom; but after that, you won't. You'll live on tinned stuff, coconut, rice and fish. Why, the people on these islands we shall see practically live on nothing but coconut and fish. That French fellow we've got with us, who's going back to one of the islands – he's probably lived chiefly on fish and coconut for years.'

'And he looks it,' said Ramsbottom. 'If you ask me, it's the thought o' that diet again that's weighing him down, poor devil.'

'Yes, but when you've been out to sea a few days,' the Commander continued cheerfully, 'you'll be ready to eat anything. You'll feel twice the man you do now.'

'Ah don't want to feel twice the man Ah do now. Ah want to feel about quarter of him.'

'Think about the island, about Faraway.'

That immediately set them talking about Faraway, though not one of them had anything new to say, for they had talked a great deal already about it, and the subject, in their present state of knowledge, was by no means inexhaustible. But as men will, when they have a common interest, they went round and round with the topic, like old circus horses. And from the deck forward, there came the droning sound of a native *himene* accompanied by the inevitable strumming, half fascinating, half irritating. Here it was blended romantically with the creaking of the rigging and the wash of the seas. There was no light anywhere now but on this pitching deck.

Gigantic, tousled and gay, Captain Prettel loomed before them to ask if they would join him in an apéritif in the saloon before dinner. Now that darkness had fallen and the saloon was a little lighted interior, it had a certain snug quality. The captain mixed gin and vermouth for them, and was very talkative. He insisted upon talking in English, which he spoke very badly, and concluded many of his most mysterious utterances with huge guffaws that were a trifle disconcerting. He had quite a respect for the Commander, a fellow-seaman and a man of age and dignity, but nevertheless appeared to think that the unknown and senseless expedition on which the trio was embarked stamped them as lunatics.

''Appee days, eh, Commandair?' he roared, raising his glass.

'Happy days,' responded the Commander, with grave politeness.

'You find treasor, eh? Gold. Ha ha – gold in de eart' – vairy vairy old, dees gold, eh? Peerats. Gold of peerats.'

The Commander assured him, as he had probably done before, that they were not in search of a pirate's treasure, but the captain could not be convinced, and the expedition seemed to him, at the moment, the best joke in the world. It lasted him until dinner, during which he told a very long, involved and incomprehensible story of some man or other he had known who had gone looking for treasure. He told it first in what he thought was English, and then told it all over again, very rapidly, in French with a mixture of Tahitian, to their fellow-passenger, the very quiet Frenchman who had lived so long on fish and coconuts. He was an excessively thin and watery man with a long drooping moustache. The three Englishmen were interested in the story, but could not understand it. This Frenchman could understand it, but was not interested in it. He did not appear to be interested in anything but the dinner and the red wine in front of him, both of which he attacked quite greedily. It seemed odd that so much solid food and drink should vanish into that ghostly interior, to be converted into more ghostliness. But the lack of understanding, on the one side, and the lack of interest on the other, did not impair the captain's good spirits. He made the most of the social occasion, and gigantically nodded, winked and guffawed. He looked more tousled than ever, and there was sauce on his singlet.

Before they had time to go on deck again, the rain came down, assaulting them with such fury that conversation was only possible at the top of the voice. William peeped out and found the intense blackness and its deluge quite terrifying. He regarded Captain Prettel with a new respect. The captain, with his nods, winks, guffaws, and sauce-stained singlet, was responsible for taking this overloaded, groaning tub through this drumming horror. Moreover, the captain did not seem to be at all concerned about it. He was now busy yawning, which he did on such a scale that he set them all yawning, and very soon they were in their berths, the captain in his own little cabin and the four passengers in the saloon itself. William was too uncomfortable to sleep for a long time. The saloon was smelly and stuffy; the pitching of the schooner was unpleasant; all his old mosquito-bites began itching again; and though he was really tired, he was still excited, and perhaps a little alarmed, by the novelty of it all; so he could not compose himself. Then the Frenchman, with rare impudence, considering that he was such a dim figure, began snoring, and shortly afterwards Ramsbottom added a droning bass to this Latin tenor. William moved restlessly in his berth, itself for ever moving, and cursed the pair of them. He was, he knew, in for a long wakeful night of idiotic discomfort, and very soon his thoughts would take on a deeper tinge and every bright image would desert his mind until finally, just before he dropped off to sleep, all would be death and desolation. He told himself sternly to make the best of it, and failed.

2

It was all different in the morning. They were moving through a smiling and limpid world. Clear in the sunlight and set in this immense frame of blue-green rollers and foam, the deck of the schooner, with its picturesque passengers and crew, its sails and awnings and drying clothes, its litter of bales and casks, was an enchanting piece of colour. Every minute, something – it might be a girl's satiny arm or the swelling, glinting torso of a Polynesian sailor – caught his delighted glance. Coming up on deck from that saloon was like entering a world newly made.

It was a merry one: the crew, mostly big fellows, sang, flashed their superb teeth, and roared with laughter; the native passengers happily chattered and strummed and flirted and played little games; Captain Prettel was still gay; and even Ramsbottom, who, much as he might dislike schooners, could not be miserable long if conditions were at all favourable, recovered his usual cheerfulness. As for the Commander, he was happier than William had ever seen him before. After breakfast, he pored over such charts as the captain possessed, then pottered about the boat, helped the crew to fish, and explained all manner of nautical and fishy matters to his two friends. Here he had a better audience in Ramsbottom than in William. Different as they were in so many of their characteristics, Ramsbottom and the Commander were alike in their passion for facts. They were quite content to hand one another long strings of facts for hours together. Now it was the Commander's turn. He told Ramsbottom all about giant rays and sharks and bonito and flying fish, and the pair of them would stare at the glitter and foam in search of a fin or the white flash of a belly. William was usually with them, but he was not always paying attention. He could handle facts well enough when it was necessary – as in his business – but he had not the same passion for them, for information of almost every kind. He was caught not by natural history, but by natural beauty. He soon became dreamy, as befitted a man in love. He would lose himself in long reveries, in which he was aware of nothing outside himself but the blue bubble of sea and sky. He thought a lot about Terry, but not sharply, passionately, only as a man might think of a distant lovely country, in which, because he had been happy there once, he planned to make his home. And the sunlight and the salt winds between them drenched him with a sleepy contentment.

Sometimes he was roused out of it. On the third day out, they were all thrilled. They passed quite close to a magnificent steam yacht, flying the Stars and Stripes and obviously bound for Tahiti. Everybody rushed to the side to look and wave at this white and glittering beauty, some three thousand tons of nautical luxury. The people in her seemed to be equally interested in the *Hutia*, for they, too, crowded to the side and waved.

'Belongs to some American millionaire, I suppose?' said the Commander to Captain Prettel.

'Feelms,' replied Captain Prettel, 'all for feelms. Holleevood – yais.'

'Oh, they've come from Hollywood, eh?'

'To Tahiti – yais – for feelms. 'Ave you not 'eard of dees? Yais – day make a Tahiti feelm – nativ lif – nice girls, eh? – *hula-hula*.' You could almost see the film they were going to make, as the captain said this. It appeared that this yacht was bringing out a whole film company, producers, directors, camera and technical men, and some actors and actresses (they were going to use some of the local people, too) to go 'on location' – as they called it – in Tahiti. Perhaps Captain Prettel was sorry he would miss the fun; perhaps the sight of so much luxury made him envious; perhaps the yacht reminded him of some secret sorrow; but, whatever it was, the fact remains that from this moment his spirits suffered a rapid decline and fall. Gone was that first gaiety; those roars of laughter were heard no more. Now he spread around him an immense gloom. The tiny saloon could not contain his vast despair. He drank innumerable tots of rum and gin, but they only induced in him a more profound sadness. The ironic caprices of Fate, the fickleness of Woman, the mutability of things in this world, these, it appeared, were his themes when he chose to talk; though once more, the English were interested but could not understand, and the spectral Frenchman could understand but was not interested, a fact that Captain Prettel, now that he was in the right humour, may have noticed with some appreciation of its irony.

'Nay,' said Ramsbottom, looking speculatively out to sea, 'he's right down in the mouth, skipper is. What's up with him?'

'He's temperamental,' William replied. 'The Commander told us that, right at the first.'

'Yes,' said the Commander, 'he's known for it. They told me all about him when I was first considering the charter. But he's a good sailor. A lot of good sailors are like that. You wouldn't expect them to be, but they are. Old Birston – Barometer Birston, they used to call him – was one of the best sailors I ever knew – I was with him two years in the old *Inscrutable* – and he could handle a ship like an angel, but you never knew what mood he'd be in, up and down, up and down, all the time. This chap's the same. Not my style, and I don't admire it, but it doesn't matter so long as they do their duty.'

'Well, from what I made out,' said Ramsbottom, not very hopefully, 'he's not so set on his duty just now. Doesn't care what becomes of him, he says. That's a nice look-out for some of us, isn't it? Here, what's that? D'you see it, out there?'

The Commander, who had extraordinary long sight, looked steadily in the direction Ramsbottom indicated. 'It's a wreck,' he pronounced at last. 'Looks like a big schooner. She's on a coral reef. We passed one yesterday, too. There are lots of wrecks round here. Very tricky navigation. Get on to one of those reefs and it's all up with you. And there are no lights round here, to warn you off. Taking a ship through these parts wants real sailoring. The charts are a bit sketchy, too.'

'Well, Ah call that a nice look-out,' cried Ramsbottom, raising his voice in righteous indignation. 'Here we are in a place where if you're not bothering your head off every minute, you're going to be wrecked and chewed up by sharks, and here's this captain, boozing away and telling you a chap might as well be dead as alive. Ah suppose by the time we're all in the water, with sharks round our ankles, he'll suddenly cheer up again. It's more than we shall. Nay, Ah'm not so set on this job whoever's in charge, but at least give me a chap that wants to go on living.'

'Don't worry,' said the Commander, smiling. 'Prettel's all right. And he's been sailing this route for donkeys' years. He's a good seaman, and so's that mate of his, that island fellow.'

'Happen so. But Ah'd sooner be on that yacht we saw. That's about my style. Ah think we ought to have made a film job of this, and then we'd have done it in style. And that's a queer thing, when you come to think of it. If we'd been three chaps pretending to look for an unknown island – just for the films – we'd have been doing it in style, but because we *are* looking out for an island, we've to do it like this. You make more out o' pretending now than you do out o' doing the real thing. Isn't that so?'

They agreed it was. 'Funny to see those film people, miles away from anywhere, like that,' said William. 'The world's very big and yet very small, both at the same time now. You can soon get a long way from anywhere, and yet you're not a long way from anywhere. You can still die of exposure in England – several people do, every year, I believe – and yet you can go to the ends of the earth and find a lot of people calmly taking films. I came across the Atlantic in the *Gargantua*, and the *Gargantua* is one of the boats that are fitted with telephones. You can ring up people at home and tell them how you are. I was thinking when I was crossing how queer it would be if the *Gargantua* was sinking, and you couldn't get off in the boats and there was no help near, and you rang up a friend at home and told him so.'

'Quite possible,' said the Commander, 'but I don't see anything very queer about it. I notice you're always thinking things are queer, Dursley. It's rather a habit of yours. Or a trick of speech.'

'And I'll tell you why,' said Ramsbottom shrewdly, looking from one to the other, 'it's 'cos Dursley here's a bit of a poet. Now wait. Ah don't mean he goes and writes poetry – though Ah wouldn't altogether put that past him, specially now that he's met Miss Riley – but he feels that way. Ah feel a bit that way myself, and more so than ever in these parts. Why – bless my soul! – there's so many queer things i' this world, Commander, that if you once start thinking about 'em, you're fit to burst.'

'There's a good island,' said William, pointing. The Commander brought out his glasses, and they all examined it in turn. It was not the first they had seen, but it was easily the largest. Tahiti and Moorea and the others in the Society group were not coral islands at all, but volcanic ones, really mountain-tops sticking out of the water. These Tuamotus were genuine coral islands or atolls, simply rings of coral, ten, fifteen, or twenty feet out of the water, surrounding a central lagoon. They did not look anything like so impressive as Tahiti and Moorea, with their great green slopes, blue fissures, and remote bare peaks; but on the other hand, they looked far more

like the Pacific islands of romantic sea legend, the islands
of shipwrecked sailors. At a distance there was not much
to see, just a thin dazzling line of beach and the green of
the palms above the smoke of surf and spray. But what
there was caught and held the imagination, surfeited as
it was with sights and sounds of the open seas; as if Eden
bloomed behind that distant feathering of green.

3

They landed on the larger island that William had first
noticed. Its shore seemed absolutely barren, but then he
discovered that the life on these atolls is away from the
thundering open sea, on the inner shore, round the
lagoon. And into this lagoon, in which pink forests or
coral fell away into glades of emerald water, the *Hutia*
cautiously entered, like a bewildered mortal tiptoeing into
some shimmering world of dream and myth. The whole
scene had an exquisite gauzy beauty, and carried with it
not the remotest suggestion of the wholesale trade in
vegetable fats, the margarine and soap industries, whose
enterprise had actually sent the *Hutia* into this dim pearly
fairyland. Ariel might have come whistling over the water
to them; Caliban might have been seen scratching himself
among the shells and hermit crabs; and Prospero himself, wand in hand, might have welcomed them at the
water's edge. Instead, they found a crowd of natives, some
lazy old ones and some very noisy and energetic young
ones, an old snuffy bearded French priest, and Mr. Drivnak, late of Seattle and once Czecho-Slovachia.

Mr. Drivnak was a small, round, bullet-headed man,
with lively little black eyes, a lively little black moustache,
and pores so large and open that he seemed in constant

danger of sweating all his features away. He pounced upon Captain Prettel, but when they had concluded their business and the captain went away with the priest, an old friend of his, Mr. Drivnak pounced upon William and Ramsbottom, first inviting them to have a drink at his bungalow, to which he marched them at a great pace, talking all the time. He had plenty of English, having been some years in Seattle, but he had a peculiarly thick and rasping voice. William had seen this place as a series of enchanting, luminous water-colours, and walking with Mr. Drivnak and listening to him was like taking these water-colours and rapidly tearing them up. Mr. Drivnak's bungalow was also the island store, and it was all neat and bright and business-like, but did not seem to be on the island at all.

'Id certainly is von big pleasure to me to meet you gentlemen,' cried Mr. Drivnak, mopping his face, then beaming upon them.

They said it was a pleasure to them, too.

'I been here nearly two years,' continued Mr. Drivnak, 'and how many fresh faces you think I've seen? How many? Now how many? Give a guess, just give a guess.'

They did not want to give a guess, but he was one of those tiresome people who insist upon your giving them a guess. So Ramsbottom said twenty, and William said thirty.

'Sigs,' Mr. Drivnak shouted triumphantly, starting fresh rivulets of sweat at every pore, 'just sigs and no more. Sigs fresh faces in nearly two years. Id isn't good, eh? No, no, no, no, id isn't good.'

'How's trade?' enquired Ramsbottom, with a glance towards the other room, which was the store and seemed full of things.

'No good. Never will be good here, never, never, never. Why? No business enderprise, no developmend.'

William stared through the open window, past the cool broad leaves, into a patch of sunlight where the dreamy coffee-coloured damsel who had just waited upon them was now gracefully reclining and doing something to her long, straight, black hair. She had a flat stupid face, not at all beautiful, but nevertheless at that moment she looked charming, idyllic. 'But did you expect any business enterprise and development here?' he asked.

Mr. Drivnak was astonished at the question.

'Ah must say,' said Ramsbottom bluntly, 'you came to a queer shop for it.'

'No, no, no,' said Mr. Drivnak with great emphasis. 'No shob ad all. I open this store myself. In Seattle I work in a big store. I take a course. Yes, gentlemen, I take a course. I prepare myself. I take a big business course – by correspondenz. Some money is left to me by an aunt in Czecho-Slovachia. Id is not too much, but id is enough. I want independenz. I want room to develop. I say to myself I shall find id here. And here I am – a man of ideas, gentlemen, who has worked in a big store in Seattle and has taken a business course. I come here with the ideas and the energy. In Papeete I said to them, "Show me a good beautiful island where there is room for developmend." '

'Well, you got it all right,' said Ramsbottom, giving William a wink.

'God id, yes. But nothing can be done here.' Mr. Drivnak seemed to glare at them through a misty cascade of sweat. Hastily he mopped his face, as if he was wiping it all out and starting with a new one. 'Ideas came ad once. Why sell the copra? We will deal with it ourselves. What about planting coffee? And why not elecdrig light? And tourism. Why not tourism?'

Mr. Drivnak paused, allowing the sound of voices in song to reach them. The islanders were idly chanting, it seemed. Mr Drivnak listened for a moment, then exclaimed: 'You hear? Filthy stuff. Filthy, filthy stuff.'

'Why,' said William, 'it sounds vaguely like a hymn to me. Wait a minute. It is. I believe it's *From Greenland's Icy Mountains*.'

'And we can do with 'em,' said Ramsbottom.

'The tune no doubt, yes,' said Mr. Drivnak hastily, 'but the vords – no. Native vords. Filthy, filthy. Yes, I think id is the von about the dirty fat woman. But what did I say before? Ah yes – about the tourism.' He jumped up, grabbed hold of them both, and promptly rushed them outside, where he began pointing this way and that. 'There, you see, gentlemen, a place for an hotel. An hotel there. Perhaps a casino – oh, just a little casino – down there, facing the lagoon. You have your factory – perhaps two factories, three factories – over there, on the other side. A place for your varehouse? Over there. Perfect. All perfect for every kind of developmend. I tell you gentlemen – this place robs of my sanidy. I have the ideas – I burst and burst with the ideas – and I have the enderprise and the business knowledge – and nothing, nothing, nothing can be done.' He set off now at a brisk pace, shouting as he went. 'Here is your Main Streed.'

'Where?' puffed Ramsbottom, staring at the vague track ahead of them, winding between little native huts and coconut palms.

'Just where you are. Made for id. Id would go straight from the hotel to the wharf, keeping quite clear of the industrial section.' He waved a hand towards seven palm trees and two huts. 'That would be over there.'

When they left, next morning, all the islanders were there to say farewell: some were in little boats; some standing on the dazzling beach; others, the youngest, were plunging into the liquid gold of the lagoon; behind them was a shore of bright pink patches and violet shadows; further behind still, beyond the palms, where the outer shore was, there was a faint mist of spray; and the sky was a piece of faded blue silk. It was, to William's eye, a scene of incredible, remote loveliness, and there in the middle of it, waving farewell with the rest, still beaming and sweating, but bidding them godspeed out of a great despair, was Mr. Drivnak.

4

From now onwards, a certain idyllic monotony descended upon the voyage. Some islands had lagoons into which there was a pass, so that the schooner could anchor there. Other islands had to be approached by way of the outer shore, and the schooner would have to stand off and then launch a surf-boat. This landing in surf-boats was at first quite a terrifying experience for William. Ramsbottom, a heavy man and a temptation to any shark, never overcame his dislike of it. The Commander enjoyed it, and was an enthusiastic admirer of the skill of the native crews. Though the islands were of many different sizes and shapes, there was hardly any other difference between them: they had the same brilliant white coral beaches, the same rows of rustling palms, the same huts and stores of copra. The native passengers were always changing, but they always seemed the same crowd of people. The ghostly Frenchman vanished, and his place was taken by a Mormon missionary, a cheerful, ruddy fellow, sociable

enough, but a dull talker, who appeared to have left the
Mormon of legend a long way behind. He conducted
services at two or three of the larger islands *en route*, and
William attended one of them. The men sat on one side,
the women on the other, and they all sang lustily enough,
and sometimes chattered during the service; but on the
whole it was a dull affair. They had now grown accustomed
to schooner life, though its discomforts tended to increase
as the voyage lengthened out, for more and more cock-
roaches and copra bugs found their way into the saloon,
the supply of fresh water was very scanty, so that for
bathing purposes, almost for ordinary washing purposes,
they had to depend upon the occasional pools they would
find in a reef, and the food, mostly rice and fish and red
beans, was very different from the comparatively luxurious and varied fare of the first few days. But though they
talked longingly sometimes of what they would order in
a decent restaurant, the next time they found themselves
inside one, they submitted fairly cheerfully to this monotonous diet, just as they did to the various discomforts of
the voyage.

It would have been a very different matter if they had
been sailing in the schooner for pleasure; but they were
nourished by the thought that every day brought them
nearer to Faraway Island. They felt they were making
progress with their adventure. Night after night, as the
Hutia moved spectrally in a world of stars, they would talk
about it, and round and round it, so that there was
nothing even remotely connected with pitchblende and
uncharted Pacific islands that they did not discuss at some
time or other. The Commander was still the happiest of
the trio; but William was reasonably content, and
Ramsbottom did not grumble as he had done at first.

Ramsbottom, however, had a poor opinion of life on

these coral islands, and did not hesitate to say so. 'If you ask me,' he declared, without waiting to be asked, 'there's more goes on down any street you like to mention in Lancashire, than there is in two thousand miles round these parts. Ah can understand a chap coming out here for a rest – he'd get that soon enough – but Ah'll be damned if Ah can see why anybody should come out here for an adventure. All you can say for this place is that it's a long way from anywhere, and if that fact keeps you excited, well and good. But it wouldn't me. Ah like to see something going on, a bit o' life. Ah'd pine away here waiting for something to happen.'

Oddly enough, the very next day something did happen to him. They had landed on a small island, populated only by clouds of terns, for the natives had recently deserted the place. Ramsbottom had wandered away on his own, towards the reef, where there were a great many pools in the coral. William the Commander had lost sight of him, and concluded that he was having a solitary bath somewhere. While they were smoking and idly dropping a word or two to one another, they were suddenly surprised to see a naked figure, pink in the bright sunlight, coming their way, and hopping and skipping in the most extraordinary manner. It was Ramsbottom. On he came, with his shirt and trousers in a bundle under his arm, and gradually his pace became slower and his movements less fantastic, until at last he tottered up to them, panting, exhausted, and flung himself down on the beach beside them. They saw then that one of his legs was bleeding.

'If you've got that on the coral, Ramsbottom,' said the Commander, 'better get it washed at once. What's happened?'

Ramsbottom opened his mouth to reply, but thought

better of it and kept his mouth open in order to recover his breath. There was a wild look in his eye.

'What's the matter?' asked William, in some concern. For a moment, he thought that Ramsbottom must be suffering from sunstroke.

'Did you see me running?' Ramsbottom panted. 'Ah was chased.'

'Chased?' They stared at him. They had not seen a soul near him.

'Ay, chased.' Ramsbottom made a great effort, said no more for a minute, then sat up. 'And Ah never was more surprised in all my born days. Believe me or believe me not, but Ah was chased by a damn great eel. Oh, you can stare, but it's as true as Ah'm here. Ah can never look an eel in the face again. You see, Ah went to a pool up there and took my clothes off, and it was deepish, so Ah sat on the edge, you see, and dangled my legs in the water, just as Ah used to do many a time when Ah was a kid. All of a sudden, something long and dark came and made a snap at my legs. Ah couldn't believe it at first. "Here, steady," Ah said. But next minute, before Ah could get my legs away, it had nearly got its teeth into 'em, and tore the skin as you can see for yourselves. Ah jumped back and stood on the edge to see what it was, and – my goodness! – it came right out o' the water at me. It was a damn great eel, and it must have been five or six feet long and twice the thickness of my arm. And teeth! – rows of 'em. It jumped right out o' the water at me. You'd think it'ud hated me like poison for the last twenty years and had just been waiting for this. "By God, Ah'll get you, Johnny Ramsbottom," it was saying. "Ah'm keeping away from you," Ah said, and Ah backed away, towards the next pool. It came right after me. It did. Ah'm not lying. That eel came right out of its pool and after me, snapping its teeth like a mad dog. "Ah'm off," Ah said, and off Ah went, as fast as Ah could go, and how far it came after me, Ah don't know, 'cos Ah didn't stop to enquire. And if you'd been there, you'd have done the same thing. Ah tell you, that damn great eel hated the sight o' me, and it'ud had me torn in ribbons in two two's. Damn me if Ah ever want to see an eel again, not if it's only in a jelly in a tureen. And now call me a liar.'

But when he heard of this adventure, Captain Prettel, who roared with laughter and kept slapping Ramsbottom on the back, was ready to confirm the truth of it, and said it was a ferocious large eel called a moray that had taken such a dislike to Ramsbottom. And the story was fortunate enough to restore the mercurial skipper's spirits for several days. He began singing again, and took to drinking rum instead of gin, a sure sign that he no longer wished to be consoled in an evil and hostile world.

Then there was the island where the Commander involuntarily made a conquest of a young lady called Wonderful Storyteller. On most of these islands, the natives were very friendly and not at all shy. They would salute the strangers, and sometimes make a pleasant fuss of them. Once William wandered away from the village, to stroll along the edge of the lagoon, and a young and handsome girl, with a shining face and huge melancholy eyes, landed from a tiny canoe, walked straight up to him, and put her hand in his, murmuring some unknown word of greeting. For a minute they stood there, hand in hand, unable to exchange a word, but smiling at one another. Then the girl nodded gravely, and returned to her tiny canoe, leaving William with a whiff of coconut oil, and a queer mixed feeling of delight and embarrassment. But the young lady whom they discovered afterwards to be called Wonderful Storyteller made much more direct advances to the Commander, for whose lean face and clear blue eyes she seemed to have conceived an instantaneous passion. At the very first encounter, she laid a caressing hand upon his arm and gazed with wondering delight into his eyes. The Commander was terribly embarrassed. He was not an amorous man, and did not want to encourage her. On the other hand, he was nothing if not chivalrous, and could not brush her aside. In a vaguely paternal 'There, there!' fashion, he patted the detaining hand, and then contrived to escape. Not for long, however. Wonderful Storyteller, having decided that this was the man for her, would not let him go. She ran away, only to return with several little presents, polished shells and the like, and when he stopped to examine them and to thank her, she put a smooth brown arm about his neck and laid her cheek against his, to the uproarious delight of Ramsbottom and Captain Prettel. Gently the scarlet Commander disengaged himself. But there is not much chance of hiding on one of these small low islands. For the next hour, the onlookers were entertained by a comedy of flight, pursuit, capture, that ended with the Commander hurriedly returning to the schooner, leaving Wonderful Storyteller standing at the water's edge, a small desolate figure.

'Nay, nay,' said Ramsbottom, 'Ah thought you knew how to treat a lass better than that, Commander.'

'We're not all old lechers like you, Ramsbottom,' retorted the Commander good-humouredly.

'Old! Old! Steady on a bit. You can give me a good few years,' cried Ramsbottom. This was true enough, though William was surprised to find how often he idly thought of Ramsbottom as the older man. Lean and frosted though he might be, there was something youthful, almost boyish, about the Commander. You did not feel that he was too old to respond to Wonderful Storyteller's, or any other girl's, advances, but not old enough; which was absurd, seeing that the man was sixty or so. There was something distinctly virginal about him; in comically sharp contrast to Ramsbottom, whose great fat carcase had missed nothing in this life.

'Possibly,' said the Commander, not over-pleased at this reference to his years. 'But you're old in sin, Ramsbottom; and you're going to be a nasty, greasy old man long before your time.'

'Well, Ah'll have had what fun's been going,' said Ramsbottom. 'And if some of it's been what you're pleased to call lechery, well, Ah'll have leched with the best. Ah like women – they were meant for man, and man was meant for them – and Ah only wish they liked me a bit more. Not that Ah do so bad, considering. An' Ah'll say this for these South Seas – they may not be all they're cracked up to be, but women's women down here, with no damn nonsense about 'em. Mind you, women at home are just like these really—'

'Nothing of the kind,' said the Commander sharply. 'These women are just animals – pleasant to look at, just as some animals are – but animals. Women at home – decent white women – quite different.'

'You make me laugh. You do, honestly; you make me laugh. Different! Course they're not different. Only difference is that down here they've got the lid off, that's all. They're natural here. Our women are just like these, once you get 'em quiet indoors or put two or three glasses o' port in 'em—'

'Rubbish! And disgusting rubbish, too!' The Commander blew out his breath sharply, then walked away.

Ramsbottom looked after him, with a droll expression

on his enormous round face, then gave William a wink.
'Ah've upset him, Dursley.'

'I believe you have,' said William. 'I've noticed before,
he doesn't like that sort of talk about women.' William
was not sure that he himself enjoyed it very much either.
There was a world of difference, he felt, between Terry
and these island creatures. And at the thought of her,
his mind lit up, like a twilight landscape under summer
lightning.

'He's one o' these worshippers-from-afar, the poor old
Commander is,' said Ramsbottom. 'Coming out here on
that French boat, we'd time to talk about everything there
is to talk about – and then hours and hours to spare. And
one night, we got on to women and love and such-like,
and he told me the story of his life, if you can call it that.
Anyhow, you could get it on a postcard, poor devil. He
went and fell in love with the wife of another naval chap
– at Malta or somewhere – and he just managed to say
something to her once, and then ran away and worship-
ped-from-afar. And from all Ah could gather, this other
chap was a rotten bad husband and this wife of his was
as miserable as sin, but of course the Commander
couldn't do anything but worship-from-afar. A lot o'
people think that's what women like. So they do, up to a
point. They like nothing better than this worshipping-
from-afar, my-star-of-eve stuff as a bit of an extra, as you
might say. But they want something a damn sight better
to be going on with, as a regular thing. They want a chap
on the other side of the fireplace of an evening and a
chap that'll land himself in bed with 'em, and if they like
him enough, they'll soon see that's where he is, and not
worshipping-from-afar and all that bunkum. Down here,
as Ah said, you see 'em with the lid off. They look you
over, pick what they fancy, come up and wiggle their

behinds at you a bit, and then say, "Here, Ah want you."
Well, they're doing that at home, just the same, only
quieter. Trouble there is, you can't see what you're getting.' And Ramsbottom laughed coarsely.

Ignoring these later remarks, which were not altogether
to the taste of a man romantically and idealistically in love,
William asked a question or two about the Commander.

'No, he never did anything,' replied Ramsbottom. 'Ate
his heart out in suffering solitude, as they'd say on the
pictures. Ah don't think he ever got further than having
her photograph in a silver frame at the bottom of his tin
trunk – if he got as far as that.'

'Poor devil,' said William.

'Ay, no doubt. But, mind you, Dursley – and you're old
enough to know this for yourself, though I doubt if you
do – there's a lot o' good sympathy wasted on these chaps
like the Commander, who go on calling women their
guiding stars and angels and what not, and never go and
put a good supper and half a bottle o' something into
'em and then put their arms round 'em. It seems to me
these chaps get about as much as they want. If they wanted
the women themselves – the real flesh-and-blood lumps
o' stuff, and not the guiding stars – they'd go and get
'em. Ah tell you, women themselves have no patience
with it, except as a bit o' fancy-work from men they're
not so struck on, just to raise their opinions of themselves.
There's none o' that nonsense about them. What they
want, they go and get.'

William laughed. 'But I think you've missed the point,
for all that, Ramsbottom. I don't believe you understand
a man like the Commander. I'm not very much like him,
but I understand his point of view. The point is, he's got
a definite code, and he sticks to it. He might want a

certain woman terribly badly, I believe, but if it was against his code, he wouldn't be able to do anything about it.'

'Something in that,' Ramsbottom admitted. 'Ah know what you mean. But what that amounts to is that he likes his code better than he likes his women. So he can't grumble.'

'He could, if he wanted to. He could grumble because the one woman for him he couldn't have because it just happened she was married to somebody else, and he felt he couldn't do anything about it. That's bad luck for him.'

'But do you believe in this one woman?'

'Yes,' said William promptly, thinking instantly of Terry.

'Well, Ah'm surprised at – a chap your age—'

'It's nothing to do with ages,' William put in hastily.

'No, perhaps not,' said Ramsbottom meditatively. 'Age is nothing without experience. Well, Ah don't believe in this one woman stuff. Ah doubt if any particular woman will make a man happy longer than a month or two. On the other hand, there's hundreds and hundreds – perhaps half a dozen down the same street – that'ud suit him as well as another. The Commander stuck to this one – in his mind, simply 'cos he couldn't get her, and so he thought she was a lot better than the ones he could get. Just contrariness, that is, like fancying strawberries in December. The Commander's got a lot of that in him, and happen you have, too. Ah haven't, Ah'm glad to say. And what's the result? For all his talk and worshipping-from-afar and all the rest of it, the Commander doesn't like women, and they've got nothing out of him. Whereas Ah do like 'em, and they've had plenty out o' me. As for you, Dursley, you're about half-and-half, Ah fancy, somewhere between us. But watch out, lad, watch out.'

'What do you mean?' demanded William.

'Ah've seen you with our friend, Terry Riley there,' said Ramsbottom coolly. 'Don't think Ah've got no eyes in my head. And Ah wasn't born yesterday. Well, she's as grand a lass to look at as Ah've ever set eyes on. But take it easy, take it easy. And no Commander work, remember. No star-of-eve stuff. Take what you can get and let it go at that.'

'Here, wait a minute,' William protested. But Ramsbottom, shaking his head, went waddling towards the saloon. William did not follow him, but remained on deck, thinking of Terry and trying to find her image in the huge embers of the sunset.

5

'On dees,' said Captain Prettel, pointing across the lagoon, 'you find Englishman.'

An Englishman! They were interested at once. They had not found a fellow-countryman yet on any of the islands.

'Yais – Eenglishman. Vairy, vairy old. Perhaps he die. Cap'n Jary he is called. He see and 'ear *tupapaus* alvays. He is like a *tupapau.*'

Something stirred in William's memory. What was it? Then he remembered, and was back again in the study at Ivy Lodge, his uncle's papers before him, and there was the ghostly snapshot of the thin old man, with his uncle's writing on the back: *Cap. Staveling up in the Manihikis just after hearing his big-headed Tupapau knock on the roof. Last time too. Never saw poor Cap. again.* It gave him a queer sensation to remember that. How far away from all this he had been then, and how he had clutched at its magical possibilities! And now here he was. But this was Captain

Jary, not Captain Staveling, who must have died years ago. These islands seemed to have a fair supply of antique and spectral captains who were in the habit of seeing ghosts. But then it was natural for seamen to retire to these islands, and it might be equally natural for them to see ghosts, if they lived here long enough. Probably their imaginations came in time to be dominated by the imaginations of the islanders, who went in terror of the *tupapaus*. Then again, perhaps there *were* tupapaus, and you had to live a long time in these quiet remote places before you began to notice them.

There seemed to be only about a dozen huts on the island, but one of them was much larger than the rest, and was indeed a bungalow with a corrugated iron roof. But it was very shabby. It was a curiously shabby island, without any of the idyllic prettiness of most of the others. Even the palms had a very ragged and barren look, though they must have been fruitful enough, for there was a fair store of copra waiting for the schooner. The lagoon was unusually sombre in tint, and the coral of the place was rough and rather colourless. The name of this shabby island was Tapuka. On the beach, not far from the bags of copra, were three dead sharks, with their jaws all cleaned up and fixed wide open, ready for sale. They looked as if they were sardonically amused at life. Although there did not appear to be many inhabitants, yet the beach was alive with children, bobbing and splashing and screaming. At first, there was no sign of Captain Jary. A large native, who was wearing nothing but a pair of cotton shorts and a taxi-driver's cap, was in charge of the copra. When William and the others landed, however, a figure came tottering out of the bungalow with the corrugated iron roof. This obviously was Captain Jary. He was wearing patched old drill trousers and nothing else.

He was an astonishing and rather repulsive figure, for he was very tall and horribly thin, had long white hair and beard, and a greyish mat of hair on his chest. Captain Prettel rushed forward to shake him by the hand, and the old man at once returned with Prettel to his bungalow, taking no notice at all of the three strangers. They concluded, correctly as it afterwards appeared, that he had not seen them. They hung about the beach, watching the loading and unloading of the copra and trade goods, and the antics of the children, and then, after an hour or so, Prettel, reeking of his own store of liquor, came along and asked them to pay the old man a visit in his bungalow.

At close quarters, Captain Jary looked even more dimly patriarchal than he had done at a distance, and not unlike a faded water-colour sketch of a prophet that had somehow acquired real hair. His eyes, a washed-out blue, were the dimmest thing about him, and this gave him a curiously unreal appearance. William never remembered seeing anybody before who looked quite so old. Nor had he ever seen any place before that seemed to remote as this bungalow. It was very neglected and littered with dusty odds and ends. There was the wreck of a mandolin; there were the remains of a set of dominoes; some carpenter's tools; a model ship with broken masts; three bound volumes of the *English Illustrated Magazine*, Lytton's *Last Days of Pompeii*, a Bible, and some books without backs that might have been anything; two long German pipes, half a flute, some ancient playing-cards, several springs for clockwork, and a stuffed monkey in a very unpleasant state of decay. In this dust-bin at the end of the earth sat Captain Jary, welcoming his fellow-countrymen. He wore a tattered blue coat now, but did not attempt to button it over his thick mat of grey hair.

'Yes,' he quavered rustily, 'Grimsby was my town. I left

it in Seventy-Eight, and that's a tidy time since, gen'l'men, a tidy time it is. I was a Grimsby man, and my father was Grimsby before me. I was in sail for forty year. All over I was, in sail. None o' you gen'l'men been in sail?' He turned upon them his queer faded eyes, which were not quite sightless, and yet seemed as blank as the windows of an empty house. He did not wait for any reply. 'And then I was master of a steamer for fifteen year. And I came here – retired – twenty year ago, or more – I don't just remember. Came here to die, twenty-five year ago. And I've raised another family since then – got grand-children here.' He produced the thin ghost of a chuckle. 'This is the third family I've raised, gen'l'men. I've got one in Wellington. But I don't come from New Zealand, not me. I'm a Grimsby man by rights, though I left in Seventy-Eight. Any o' you gen'l'men know Grimsby?'

Here there was a pause long enough for two of them to say that they knew it slightly.

The captain took no notice of them. 'If you didn't know it,' he continued, with a certain faint relish creeping into his tone, 'you never will now. Grimsby's gone. Hull's gone. Scarborough's gone. And they tell me Yarmouth's gone, though I don't rightly know about that. You haven't to believe all you hear. But I know them others has gone.'

'What d'you mean – gone?' demanded Ramsbottom, looking at him in astonishment.

'Smashed up, blown up, set fire to, burned out, beaten down, gone,' replied Captain Jary. 'All that coast's gone, you might say, for there's not one brick standing on another, they tell me. All done in this big war they had. Russians or Germans came along and smashed it all up, half the north-east coast, and they've never bothered to build them places again. No good me going back, even if I wanted to, is it? I'm a Grimsby man, and if there's no

Grimsby, then there's no place for me to go to. That's right, isn't it, gen'l'men? That's sense. And they tell me half London went at the same time, though I didn't care about that, for I never took much stock of London. I ha'n't been there since Nought Two.'

William and the Commander said nothing, for it seemed useless to try and put that wandering old mind right; but Ramsbottom could not contain himself. 'Nay, who's been telling you all this stuff?' he said, rather sharply. 'It's a lot o' nonsense. Grimsby and Hull and Scarborough are like they always were.'

Captain Jary shook his head, with good-natured contempt, like a man correcting a child. 'They're keeping it from you. You're not a Grimsby man, are you? Or a Hull man? No, I thought not. Well, there was this big war, you see – Russians and Germans and Dutchmen and so on – and they all came across and smashed up all them parts. I've not seen 'em myself, but I've talked with them that has. All gone. No fishing round there these days, that's all gone. You could get good fish out o' the North Sea too, one time. Better than you can get here – a lot better – more tasty-eating. I was always partial to a bit o' mackerel, even if it was a dirty feeder. And a nice fresh herring. That's all gone. And I've seen the day when you'd find more fish in Grimsby of an early morning than would keep 'em all for a week from here to Fiji. And tasty fish too. But I left Grimsby in Seventy-Eight. That's a tidy time since, gen'l'men, a tidy time it is. I was in sail for forty year.'

It seemed as if his talk was trapped in a circle, and that unless they broke away they would stand there listening to him going round and round. He returned now to his account of the desolated north-east coast of England, and William began to feel that if he heard it again, he would believe that Grimsby and Hull and Scarborough really had gone. Even as it was, he would have liked to have had a quick glimpse of them to reassure himself. Captain Jary did not mention *tupapaus*, perhaps because the fact that they were English had imprisoned him in this Grimsby circle; but he had no need to talk about ghosts to be ghostly. And quite suddenly, without giving any sign that he was about to stop talking, he did stop, and quietly fell asleep. When they tip-toed out, they might have been leaving behind them a dead man, he was now so quiet, so still, so bloodless. And the glare and bustle of life outside the bungalow was incredible; they might have been plunging into Piccadilly on a June morning, the contrast was so great.

'Poor old boy,' said the Commander, as they walked away. 'He must be ninety, if he's a day.'

'And better dead, if you ask me,' said Ramsbottom. 'He can't grumble. He's had a ripe old age, even if he's rotten now. He said he'd raised a family since he was seventy. There's plenty of time for you yet, Commander. But Ah'll tell you one thing. If you going to live to be that old and wrong in the head, you're better off here than at home. Nobody much to bother you, plenty o' sunshine, and the bit of fish and coconut you get to eat is about all you want, anyhow. Make a note of it, Dursley lad. When you're getting old and silly, see you make for one o' these places. Never mind about the ghosts.'

'I don't think you would,' said William. 'You're a ghost yourself then. It was all ghosts with that poor old captain.'

'Ay, he'd even turned Grimsby into a ghost,' said Ramsbottom. 'And that takes a bit o' doing.'

6

'Only one more stop, and then we shape a course for Faraway,' the Commander announced.

'Have you worked out how far it is?' asked William.

'I've done my best. From here, it must be about sixteen hundred miles, rather more or less.'

Ramsbottom shook his head. 'You know, chaps, it frightens me. It does. It frightens me. We seem to be just about the other end of nowhere here, and if we go nearly another two thousand miles further on, God knows where we'll be. Ah admit, when Ah get there, Ah'll be all right, 'cos wherever you go, when you get there you find it's a place and not so different to any other place. It's thinking about it that frightens me – these thousand miles you talk about as if they were couple o' hops and a skip.'

'That's all they are, at sea,' said the Commander. 'Why, the Elizabethans went out into the unknown and found themselves sailing round the world in ships no bigger than this and not so well equipped. If you've got a good supply of fresh water, and food, and a stout little ship, it doesn't matter how far you go at sea. You can go ten thousand miles as easily as you can go ten miles.'

'Ah dare say you're right,' said Ramsbottom. 'But you've been in the trade and that makes a difference. When Ah take a look at these charts and Ah see we're just a pinpoint, a thousand miles from anywhere, Ah get a homeless, lost dog sort o' feeling.'

'Well, you can't complain so far,' the Commander told him. 'We have hardly been out of sight of land for days. But once we make for Faraway, we shall. We'll be out in the open sea again, and a good job too. It's navigating these reefs that frightens me. It's really ticklish work among these islands, but Prettel knows his job.' The Commander glanced at the sky. 'I wonder what he's going to do now.'

'Why?' asked William.

'I fancy there's a storm coming up,' said the Commander, 'and I wonder if he's going to try to run for shelter into this next lagoon or wait outside here. She's moving. But look at the sky.'

The sky was dropping and thickening. All the deep blues and vivid greens were being rapidly drained out of the sea, which had a long sullen swell on it. Light faded from the horizon. The steady breeze, which had bowled them along so merrily for the last few days, sank to a sigh, then for a space the air was uncannily still, until at last there came an uneasy prowling little wind. They heard the *plug-plug-plug* of the engine, going at full speed. Captain Prettel was risking it, making for the pass into the lagoon as hard as he could go. There was a reef quite near at hand; they could hear the dull booming of the breakers along it. But they did not hear it long, for soon the rain fell upon them, a vast tumultuous obliteration. Ramsbottom hurried down into the saloon, and William soon followed him. They had it to themselves, for Captain Prettel was more than fully occupied running his schooner through the pass, and the Commander had evidently decided to remain on deck. Above the drumming rain, they heard the crack of thunder. William caught sight of Ramsbottom's face, suddenly illuminated by a glare of lightning. It had lost a lot of its colour, and its thick lower lip was wobbling a little. 'He's terrified,' William told himself, and then found that he himself felt a little better. Nevertheless, he knew that one wrong twist of the wheel, and the coral would rip the side out of the *Hutia* in half a minute, and down they would all go. He remembered the astonishing number of gins and rums that he had seen Captain Prettel swallow in that saloon.

'I'm going back on deck,' he shouted to Ramsbottom.

'Then Ah'm coming with you, lad.'

They found the Commander there, peering anxiously over the side, and soaked to the skin. 'We're going through now,' he roared; and a moment later the schooner gave a lurch that sent them staggering back. For a minute or two she was pitching badly. There were cracks of thunder and a long red stab of lightning. 'We're through all right,' the Commander told them. 'This is the lagoon.' The downpour continued as the schooner moved on, rather jerkily, through the gathering darkness. They went below to dry themselves, and to wait for their evening meal, which was a long time coming. The skipper did not appear, and from the shouts and stamp of feet it seemed as if he was having some trouble with his anchorage. When at last they had swallowed their fish and rice, beans and coffee, they were so tired that they turned in at once, and slept heavily until morning.

Telling one another that this would be the last time they would set food on land for many days, William and Ramsbottom went ashore early the next morning, though there was nothing to see that they had not seen before. There appeared to be only about a dozen natives living on this island, and though they were cheerful friendly souls, they were shyer and less interesting than most of the other islanders they had met. But it was pleasant to sprawl on the beach, and drowse away the blue and sparkling morning. But they were not allowed to dream it all away, however, for they had not been ashore two hours before they saw the Commander hurrying towards them. His very pace told them something was wrong. They sat up, looked at him, looked at one another.

'What's up?' cried Ramsbottom.

Vexation and disgust were written all over the Commander. 'He refuses to take us.'

'What do you mean?'

'The captain won't take us to Faraway.'

'Why, what's the matter?'

'He says he can't depend on his auxiliary power, and he says he won't go all that way without it. A torn hawser has fouled the propeller. There's that diver in the crew trying to clear it now. And he says there's a leak in his tank. And there's something wrong with his engine, and he doubts if they can put it right. It's no use. I've argued and argued with him, but he won't budge. He's not going all that way and back, with all this copra aboard, just under sail. Too risky, he says, and it would take too long. He daren't chance it.'

'But he contracted to take us, didn't he?' said William. 'You definitely arranged to charter the schooner.'

'Yes, but he's within his rights in refusing the charter now. It's no good. I even offered him extra money, but I can't tempt him. I can't blame him, under the circumstances, but it's damnably unlucky for us.'

'It is,' said Ramsbottom slowly, 'though Ah must say, Ah'd rather wait than drown.'

'We shouldn't drown,' said the Commander contemptuously. 'These schooners have been from here to San Francisco under sail before now, and not so long ago either. It might be very slow, that's all. But if he won't go, he won't go, and there's an end to it. We shall have to go back to Tahiti with him, and try again in another schooner.'

'But look at the time we're wasting,' said William irritably.

'I know, Dursley, I know,' said the Commander sharply.

'You needn't tell me that. If I don't know what time we're wasting, who does?'

'And you're sure he won't have a pop at it?' asked Ramsbottom.

'Try him yourself if you think you can do any better, Ramsbottom,' the Commander told him.

'All right, all right, keep your temper.'

'I am keeping my temper. But – damn it! – when a fellow's been arguing and pleading for an hour and more, and with a pig-headed devil who can only understand about half of what you say – it's not pleasant to be told you've probably made a muck of the job. If you think you can persuade him, Ramsbottom – or you, Dursley – well, go and have a try. I'll give you my blessing. But I can't do any more, and I don't think you'll shift him.'

'It's rotten bad luck,' said William, with a vision of their returning to Tahiti and of Faraway more remote than ever.

'And Ah suppose we've got to pay him now to take us back to where we started from,' said Ramsbottom grimly.

'Oh, about that, he's behaving decently. He says he'll only charge us for our food back to Tahiti, and that won't be much. Because the charter's fallen through, he doesn't ask us for passage money back to Tahiti. Actually, it's not going to cost us a lot more – unless we're a long time in Tahiti finding another schooner to take us to Faraway.'

'It's not the money, obviously, it's the waste of time that's the nuisance,' said William. 'So far as I know, we're the first in the field with Faraway. I don't believe anybody else knows about the pitchblende being there. But I suppose there's always a risk of somebody collaring the island – and then where are we?' And he suddenly remembered Garsuvin, who had not been in his thoughts for some time. Oh – this delay was maddening.

Ramsbottom was philosophical about this. 'Well, we took a chance on that when we decided to come out here at all, and Ah don't see a few weeks is going to make a lot o' difference. All Ah'm mad about is all this schooner work for nothing. Ah might have been taking it easy in Tahiti all this time. Still, there it is. Ah suppose we'll have to make the best of it. When are we off back?'

'To-night,' said the Commander, 'with any luck. And we're only calling at two islands on the way back.'

But it was the morning after when they actually sailed. The sea and sky were like one great hollow pearl, smokily flecked with fire, but nobody cared about that. The captain was still worried about his engine. The Commander and Ramsbottom were inclined to be irritable. William was now the best-tempered; it was disappointing to turn one's back on Faraway like this; but his face was turned again towards Terry. She would probably laugh at them when they told her what had happened, but that did not matter. She would be there, that was the great thing. And William, holding her steadily in his thoughts, was able now to consider the beauty of the morning.

CHAPTER VIII

THE SHIP OF MAKE-BELIEVE

1

THERE WAS Papeete again, and here, dominating it, was the steam yacht they had passed on the voyage out. They could read her name: the *Sapphira*. At close quarters, she looked more luxurious than ever. The *Hutia*, loaded in every available space with copra and carrying a tatterdemalion crowd of native passengers from her last place of call, crept past the yacht like a limping pauper. There were the usual idlers, with the usual gathering of friends and relatives of the native passengers, to watch the *Hutia* being tied up. But Terry was not there. William knew very well that there was no reason why she should be, for she was not to know that he was arriving that afternoon, yet he had had an unreasonable conviction that she would be there, the first to wave at them, and he could not help feeling disappointed. Her absence somehow made the whole scene seem shabby, even though the island itself, after the innumerable flat atolls they had seen, towered in fantastic splendour, with a theatrical and almost insolent beauty.

'I hate that damned yacht,' he said to Ramsbottom, as they waited to go ashore.

'Ah wish it were mine. But what's it done to you?'

'Oh – I dunno. It spoils things here. What do these Hollywood people want to come here for, anyhow? They make the place look all wrong,' he continued, as if he were a grumbling old inhabitant. 'Why can't they keep to their own wretched place?'

Ramsbottom gave him a droll look. 'By the way, where's our American partner? Ah don't see her in this crowd.'

'Neither do I. But she wouldn't know we were coming back.'

'Perhaps she's on this yacht, having a good time with all the other Americans. Can't blame her if she is, can you?'

William said he couldn't, but nevertheless found himself blaming her hard if she should be doing anything of the kind. He also told himself that he would be glad to escape Ramsbottom's company for a week or two, if possible. Ramsbottom was all right, but one could easily have too much of him. He was really worse than the Commander, for he would keep on talking all the time, whereas frequently the Commander either kept silent or went off to meditate in solitude.

They went back to the same hotel, and William at once enquired about Terry, only to learn that she had not been there for the last two or three days, though most of her things were still in her bungalow and she had not definitely quitted the hotel. M. Marot thought she was somewhere with the film people, for she had been seeing a good deal of them. But two of the film people, he went on to say, were staying with him now, having taken the bungalow formerly occupied by the Pullens: a Monsieur Jubb, a very quiet one, and a Monsieur Ennis, very talkative. At this piece of news, disappointment visited William again, and this time brought with it an odd little feeling of sickness. He told himself not to be a fool, returned to the same bungalow he had had before, had a very long shower bath, put on some beautifully clean fresh clothes, then went in search of Monsieur Jubb, who was obviously the sardonic little man he had met on the *Marukai* coming down.

He found the verandah of what had been before the Pullens' bungalow occupied by a long lean man, who was sprawling across two chairs. 'Is Jubb here?'

'Jubb's out,' said the long lean man, turning a bright eye upon his visitor. The other eye, the lid of which drooped heavily, did not appear to work. This gave his face, which was as long and lean as the rest of him and began in the shadow of a lock of black hair, sported with a heavily veined nose that pointed somewhere in the direction of his right shoulder-blade, and ended in a long blue wedge of chin, an appearance half-sinister, half-droll. He was wearing crimson pyjama trousers, green carpet slippers, and nothing else; and he was smoking a corn cob pipe, from which hung strands of tobacco that fell off from time to time and made him give a jump and slap his bare chest. 'I'm Pat Ennis. Anything I can do for you?'

'I just wanted to see Jubb. He was on the boat with me, coming down here. My name's Dursley.'

'I've heard about you. You were staying here before, and went off on a wild expedition. Isn't that right? Well, come along in and have a drink, for God's sake. I've got everything here you'd want to drink – and some you wouldn't want to drink – and I've even got some ice.'

After William had accepted a drink and they had chatted for a few minutes, he ventured a question about Terry.

'Miss Riley? Oh, she's down on location with the outfit. They were shooting something about twenty miles down the coast, and either they're staying there or they might have gone back to the boat for the night. Yes, she got friendly with two or three of them down there, and Meisen – he's directing this picture – took a look at her and said she could play a small part that was going begging. She's easy to look at, isn't she? Nice kid too, I'd say. All right so long as she don't take it seriously. But she wants to keep out of this picture racket.'

William knew nothing whatever about this picture racket, but hastily and with complete sincerity he agreed with Mr. Ennis. He found this news of Terry singularly disturbing, even though it was comforting in a way to learn where she was. If he could not immediately run and find her, then he wanted to keep her out of his thoughts. He tried to do this by asking Mr. Ennis questions about himself.

Mr. Ennis, it appeared, had once been a newspaper man, but for the last few years had been writing scenarios in Hollywood, not, as he explained carefully, because he liked writing scenarios, but because he had a wife and seven children, from whom, so far as William could gather, he was separated. Terry was very fond of using the expression 'hard-boiled,' and now William had a fair idea of what it meant. It meant, among other things, Mr. Pat Ennis. As a newspaper man and then a scenario writer, Mr. Ennis had been jeering and yawning behind the scenes so long that when he met a member of the audience he did not know whether to cry or be sick. William was no film fan, but he sometimes visited the Buntingham Picture Theatre, and he could not help showing some interest, even a trace of excitement, when he learned that on the yacht, the *Sapphira*, was the great Joseph Sapphire himself, whose films, with their trade mark of the turning flashing jewel, he had often seen in both London and Buntingham. Joseph Sapphire was one of the few remaining emperors of the film world. William remembered the fuss there was in the newspapers when Joseph Sapphire came to London. And here he was, just round the corner.

William hated the thought of Terry with these fascinating and, no doubt, sinister people, but he could not help being thrilled by this news. Ennis, a figure of disillusion, regarded him with pity, though, like most people in such a position, he contrived to make the most of it, enjoying the glamour with which the films invested him, and then going on to enjoy the superiority of his own attitude in refusing to recognise the glamour.

'That's why I'm staying here, and paying out good money to do it,' he explained. 'I'm supposed to be on that yacht like the rest of 'em, but the minute we touched land, I beat it like hell. That yacht's Hollywood – wherever Sap-hire is, it's Hollywood – if you went with him to the South Pole it would be Hollywood – and I want to get out of it. This suits me. When they want me, they've got to send for me. I told 'em I'd got to be quiet, to work, and they swallowed that. You can't be quiet on that yacht, it's the most God-awful bug house you ever knew. Matter of fact, I could do what I've got to do on the mezzanine floor of a boiler factory, but I don't tell 'em that. Why should I?'

'Did you write this picture they're doing now?' asked William.

'Most of it,' said Ennis, blowing out thick clouds of smoke. 'And do you know what it is? I'll tell you. It's the most startling revelation,' he chanted nasally, 'of what happens to the sophisticated lover in regions where only primitive passion holds sway, of what happens when a spoiled beauty of Chicago's rich younger set finds herself lost among the islands of Romance, of what happens when Lake Shore Drive meets the South Seas. It's a wonder picture of adventure and romance and love, in which you can hear the great heart of modern woman-hood beating. So far we have made for you pictures, good pictures, but this is not a good picture – it is *the* picture, the picture that you will never forget. In other words,' he continued, with a startling change of tone, 'it's the usual hokum.'

William laughed. 'And you were really beginning to make me feel excited about it.'

'God help us all,' said Ennis, stretching out his long legs another six inches. 'You ought to know the picture by now, if you ever see pictures. I know I've written the darned thing often enough. A beautiful rich girl, tired of all her admirers and the idle luxurious life she is leading – blast her eyes! – I'd like to put her behind a truck drivers' quick-lunch bar – goes into the wilds, and there she meets the handsome young native and falls good and hard for him – but alas! – he's only a native. She's got to go out of his life. He's got to go out of her life. They've both got to go out of one another's lives. But wait a minute. Is he native? Is your grandmother? Why, he's a Phi Beta Kappa, with assorted pennons from Yale, Harvard, Princeton and the Oswego Technical High School. Everything's O.K.'

'I do seem to know that picture,' murmured William.

'I'll say you do. Let's give the devil his due, though. We're making pictures – and lots of 'em – that are a bit better than that, but this is what we depend on to gross big and get the dollars. Well, they wanted a part for Carlos Diverga, and they wanted a part for Avril Paxton, so we did this all over again. I was going to locate it down in Arizona one time, then they changed it to Mexico, and then they thought it looked too much like an ordinary Western, so they moved it down here and gave Sap-hire a excuse for a trip in his yacht and a chance of looking over the *hula-hula* girls. Have you seen Avril Paxton?'

'The name's familiar,' said William, trying to remember,

'but I don't think I have. I may have forgotten, though. Most of these film-star girls look alike to me.'

'Well, if you think they *look* alike, you ought to know a few of 'em, and then you'd see. They *are* alike, only some are dumber than others. They're not as dumb as they used to be, in the silent-picture days. The whole place isn't as dumb as it was then. Somebody's got to have a bit of intelligence now. But Hollywood's duller than it used to be in the old silent days, when the money was easy and the place was just a gold-plated three-ring circus. Oh God! – it's dull now. It makes me tired to think about it. The only excitement left there is wondering when they'll take that brass plate with your name on off the door. And they can fire me when they like. I've been thinking of telling Mr. Joseph Sapphire a few things, and then letting him sail home without me – he'll do that anyhow if I tell him what's on my mind about him – and staying here and writing a few short stories. But I won't fire myself. He's got to fire me. I owe that much to the wife and kids.'

'Is Mr. Sapphire dull too?' asked William, who was genuinely interested.

'He's getting dull,' replied Ennis gloomily. 'I've had too much of him. You get sick of any comic if you see too much of him.'

'What is he? I mean, where does he come from, what's his background?'

'What is he? I'll show him to you to-morrow, if you like. Sapphire – that's not his real name, of course – God knows what his real name is – is some kind of Polish Jew from the East Side. Say, I believe he made good in pictures because he can't talk. There isn't a language he knows how to talk in. You can laugh, but that's so with a lot of those birds. They forget their Polish or Yiddish or whatever it is, and they can't talk English properly, so they haven't a language. That sends 'em into pictures. Joseph got in on the ground floor, and they've never been able to turn him out. And now he sits there, smothered in Yes Men, dropping things so they'll pick 'em up. I tell you, he's the Grand Duke Sapphire now. He doesn't know it, but he's a better comedian than any of the comics he's got on the pay roll. If only we could make a picture out of him! I'd do my part in it for nothing.'

'These men – like Sapphire – do they believe in the pictures they make?'

'Now that's where they're clever. They can't do – they must know, after all this time, that it's all boloney – but do they let on? They do not. I could give you ten good financial box-office reasons why we're making this picture, and old Joseph knows 'em better than I do. But if you went to him now and said, "What about this picture?" he'd tell you – and – my God! – he'd look you straight in the eye while he was telling you – that it's the finest picture that he or anybody else had ever made or ever thought of, and by the time he'd done, you'd be thinking he was ready to lose his last dollar making this picture. But whether he kids himself or not, I've never been able to find out. That's where you've got to hand it to him. He leaves you guessing. Well, he's got that, and I suppose he knows his stuff at the financial end – but when you've said that, you've finished. If he knows one damn thing about anything else – and that includes making pictures – it's missed me, and I've worked hard enough sometimes looking for it. Ignorance on the scale of his ignorance isn't a gift and a talent – my God! – it's genius. Hollywood's helped, of course, because if you live in most other places, you've got to learn something some time. But even at that, Joseph's a genius at knowing nothing or knowing it wrong. He's supposed to have slept about a bit in his time and he's used enough sex appeal in his pictures to have populated Siberia, but if he told me to-morrow that babies are found under gooseberry bushes, I wouldn't be surprised. If I went down there now and told him I was taking a motor-boat to run over to Arabia for the day, he wouldn't turn a hair. If you told him William the Conquerer was your Queen Victoria's uncle, it'ud be all the same to him. Say, I doubt if he can read and write. He can't talk, not properly, he can't. He can only just walk. But he's made ten million dollars out of pictures, and he can hire and fire fellows like you and me by the score, before he's had his morning coffee. And that's Joseph Sapphire. And if he still remembers his proper name or knows how old he is, I'll be surprised. Let's have another drink.'

While they were having this drink Jubb arrived. 'Why, hello, Dursley! Didn't know you were back from the wild parts.'

William asked him if he had seen Terry.

'Sure. She's in the Bougainville right now, sitting in with some of the boys and girls.'

'I think I'll go down there,' said William, who did not care by this time whether they all thought he was crazy about Terry or not.

'If you'll wait a minute we'll come with you,' said Jubb. 'I've got a car waiting there now. Say listen, Pat, you'd better come right along and talk to Finberg. Oh, Sap's put him up to it all right. You'll have to talk to him. And Meisen talks about pulling out now. Says he's shot all he wants here, and the light's hell anyhow, with this humidity. Just cover them rotten bones of yours with a shirt and pants, and let's go.'

Ennis uncoiled his long lean self, and sauntered into the bungalow. Jubb made himself a cocktail and promptly poured it down his throat. 'I can't get used to not drinking it quick,' he explained. 'I bet I pull a face too when it's going down. Can't get out of the habit. Well, where did you get to?'

William told him, more or less, and by the time he had finished, Ennis was ready and they made for the waiting car.

'And any hour now, Tom,' said Ennis dreamily, 'I may tell old Joseph what's on my mind.'

'Either he'll fire you – plunk! like that—'

'And that's all right with me,' Ennis put in quickly. 'If my contract's to be torn up, this is the place for the tearing.'

'Or he'll give you another contract at more money,' said Jubb grinning.

'Hell! – that's what frightens me. I'd have to take it too – for the sake of the wife and kids.'

'Papeete again,' and it escaped from William almost involuntarily.

'Yeh,' said Jubb, looking about him with no enthusiasm. 'Always reminds me of a set we used to have on the old R.O.V. lot. Do you remember that tropical town set, Pat?'

'I do,' said Ennis in a deep voice, 'but it was better than this. More like a tropical town. But then I guess it cost more to build than this. Quite right too. This is only for real people, to live in. What the hell!'

2

What a crowd there was on the Bougainville balcony now! Some of them looked like film people.

'Terry.'

'Why, Bill. This is a surprise.' Yes, she was glad to see

him. She was not terribly excited, to be sure; but she was genuinely glad. They did not kiss. William was too shy with all these people about, though if Terry had given him a lead he would have followed quickly enough. She was looking lovely; perhaps a little more made-up than when he saw her last; but then that was probably her film work. She made everybody else on that balcony look muddy and only half-alive.

They managed to get away by themselves for a minute or two. 'When did you get in?' she asked, and before he had time to answer, followed it with: 'And did you find the island? And have you brought me back a fortune, Bill? Come on, tell me the news.'

He began to tell her.

'What, do you mean you never got there?' she cried, more amused than alarmed or annoyed. 'Well, aren't you a lot of saps! You went that far and never got to the island? I told you I'd a hunch nothing was going to come of that island.'

'Give us a chance,' he protested. 'It wasn't our fault. The skipper wouldn't take us any further. But we're not giving it up as a bad job now. Naturally not. We've only just begun. We're going to find another schooner as soon as possible.'

'Well, good luck to you,' she said easily. It seemed to William quite plain from her manner that she had not been bothering her head very much lately about Faraway and their expedition, that she no longer saw herself as one of them. Other interests had claimed her. The film, of course. You could hardly blame her. Nevertheless, William felt anxious and a little hurt. The smile he gave her when he told her that he had heard about her new film work was rather strained: he could feel it cracking on his lips.

'It was dull on the way back,' he told her, 'though it wasn't really dull for me because I knew I was coming back to you, Terry. I only mean we didn't see anything much. Going out was quite interesting. You'd have enjoyed it.'

'And later on, you're going to tell me *all* about it,' said Terry brightly. 'We'd better get back to the crowd now.'

The crowd, which by this time had seated itself round two tables put together, was almost entirely composed of film people. Ennis, Jubb, a Mr. Finberg, a Mr. Forman, a Miss Garraty, a Mrs. Jarvis, a fat man called Pete, and a synthetic blonde referred to as Georgie. The rum punches and Rainbow cocktails were in brisk circulation. Ennis, now comfortably filled with liquor and looking at once more droll and sinister than ever, dominated the company. They were talking about pictures and Hollywood. All these people, as William soon discovered, made it plain to you that they were sick of pictures and Hollywood, but for all that, they never seemed to talk about anything else. They themselves were such stuff as films are made of, and their lives were rounded with a little celluloid.

'That was the time that poor little guy, Hatch, thought he was playing the Emperor Nero,' Mr. Forman remarked reminiscently, 'and he came on the lot all dressed up for it.'

'Yeh – the poor little ham,' said Jubb.

Georgie found her voice. 'Wasn't he the feller that committed sooicide in the studio?'

'He was.'

'I was with the old R.O.V. at the time,' said Ennis, swivelling his one bright eye and instantly commanding their attention. 'Poor little Hatch blew his top in just outside the old-time saloon in the Western set – you remember it, Jubb? You too, Forman. He was through. He'd had too many kicks in the pants. Yes, he was a ham all right – and too much even for the old R.O.V. studio – but he thought he was a great actor. It wasn't just losing the dollars he cared about – it was his art – yes, sir. When you found yourself in a corner with little Hatch, you had to listen to him on his art, and he'd tell you with tears in his eyes.'

'That's so,' said Jubb. 'He come crying to me many a time, right at the end. Griffith ought to have signed him up just for his tear apparatus.'

'The last few weeks there wasn't a God-awful trick that those rough-necks in the R.O.V. didn't play on him, and old Lastein – he was head then – knew all about it and never interfered. They gave that little ham a bad break. But he had his revenge all right. And he had it after he'd committed suicide. That's the queer thing. There aren't many people in Hollywood know this story, because the heads of the R.O.V. had it hushed up. Believe me or believe me not, but Hatch haunted that studio.'

There were shrill cries of interest and excitement from the women. The men made more sceptical noises, indicating that either they didn't believe in ghosts or didn't believe in Pat Ennis.

'He haunted that studio all right,' Ennis continued solemnly, though that drooping eyelid of his seemed to droop harder than ever now. 'And he haunted it in a new way, the way a film studio ought to be haunted. It cost the R.O.V. a packet before they could rid of him too. Oh – it was very neat. You never heard a ghost having a better idea.'

'What was it?' asked somebody.

'Pat Ennis,' cried Miss Garraty, 'I'm just not going to believe a single word of this.'

'Suit yourself,' said Ennis. 'But Jubb here will bear me out. It started this way. About two or three weeks after little Hatch had shot himself, Jimmy Morgan came rushing up to me and said, "Who put Hatch into *The Diamond Trail*, d'you know, Pat?" I told him I didn't know, and I didn't know Hatch had been in it. "Neither did I," said Jimmy, "but he's there all right. I've been going through the rushes with Lastein and Hatch is there all right, and Lastein's raving mad." So I went along to see those rushes – I'd done most of the scenario – and there was Hatch, not doing anything big, and not helping on the picture at all, but pretty prominent, for all that. Well, Lastein tried to get to the bottom of it, but everybody swore that he'd never put Hatch in. Nobody could remember him being there when they were shooting. The result was, they had to cut that picture to hell, and two of the sequences had to be shot all over again. The next picture we finished was *His Frozen Bride*, and this time I went with Lastein and Morgan and one or two of the others to see it run through. Hatch was in it again. I thought Lastein would go mad. You couldn't get rid of Hatch. He popped up every two or three minutes, and did his ham stuff. Lastein cursed the whole God-damned lot of us, said he'd fire us all, and had a conference on the Hatch question. Every man there who'd had anything to do with *His Frozen Bride* – and I was of of 'em – swore to God that little Hatch had never been near the lot. Lastein said it was a conspiracy. We were all in it together, he told us. The veins were sticking out of his forehead like blue ropes. I was sorry for him, though I was a damn sight sorrier for the rest of us. He said he'd get to the bottom of it if it cost him every dollar he had and he had to wreck the whole organisation. We weren't going to make a fool of him. And all the rest of it. Then one of the chief camera-men

– I forget his name, but he was a queer devil – got up, pointed a long yellow finger at Lastein, and said: "Mr. Lastein, you can't get to the bottom of this. There is no conspiracy. It is not natural but supernatural. This little actor went and destroyed himself because he was not given his chance here. Now he is haunting us – not the studio, that would be too easy for us – but the films themselves." Lastein told him to go and see a doctor. Somebody said: "Let's go and see some more rushes." Lastein agreed, after a bit of persuading, and we all went over and saw about half a picture we were shooting then, called *The Bull On Broadway*. Was Hatch in it? I'll say he was. Got a better part this time, too. Lastein jumped up and screamed with fury. "Mr. Lastein," said this camera-man – and I can hear his voice now, very quietly coming out of the dark – "Mr. Lastein, you forget. All these scenes have been taken since this man died." It was true. We all knew it. I tell you, folks, there wasn't a sound in that room for the next sixty seconds.'

'Mr. Ennis,' said Terry earnestly, fixing her beautiful eyes upon his long melancholy face, 'this isn't true, is it?'

'Miss Riley,' he replied solemnly, taking out his corn cob pipe and pointing the stem at her, 'this is a ve-ery curious world, as you'll learn later. Queerer things than this might be happening on this balcony to-night. I could tell you of other things quite as queer.'

'I'll say you could, Pat,' said Mr. Finberg, grinning.

'Tell 'em the rest, boy,' Jubb commanded.

'Well, that settled it. We went into conference again, and Lastein said: "Vell, boys, I guess I've been blaming you for nothing. Now that fellow Hatch is dead, he seems to have found some vay of giving himself parts in all our pictures." Wogenberg, head of the publicity, spoke up then. "Yeh," he said, "and – oh boy! – what a story he's given us. I can make this story break into every front page from here to Rhode Island." Lastein, who knew his stuff, wasn't having that. "You can," he said, "but take it from me, Vogenberg, you're not going to. You're going to keep it under your hat – and that goes vith all of you. This has got to be kept quiet, or it'll be all up vith the R.O.V. And vy. I'll tell you. Either the public vill believe it or not. If they believe it they vill feel there's something queer and nasty about R.O.V. pictures. If they don't believe it, then they vill laugh at us for trying to pull something too raw. Ain't that right?" We agreed it was. Then old Lastein appealed to me. "The question now is, vat is to be done? Ennis, you're a writer, you ought to know about ghosts and such things, and you knew Hatch ven he vas alive, vat you think ought to be done?" I thought a bit, then told 'em. I argued this way. Hatch – or his ghost, anyhow – had the drop on us. We couldn't fight him, or we'd be cutting every picture we made to hell. We'd got to give him what he wanted – *once*, and then there was a chance he'd be satisfied and turn his ghostly attention to something else. Therefore, I said, the only thing to do is to let him stay in this picture and put his name among the featured players. I admitted that was taking a chance, because little Hatch's ghost might see that as a sign of encouragement and want to star in the next picture. But if he was just doing it out of cussedness, well then, it might stop at that. It took some time to make Lastein see it, but we all worked hard on him, and in the end he agreed. Hatch stayed in the picture, and if you dig up *The Old Bull on Broadway*, you'll find Roderick F. Hatch among the featured players in it. And the trick worked. Believe me, folks, Hatch never popped up in another picture.'

'*That* is the only part I do believe,' said Mr. Finberg, speaking for the company.

Every now and then, while Ennis had been talking, William had looked at Terry, to exchange that secret little glance of understanding which is the delight of lovers in company. At first it had seemed to him that she had responded, but as the talk went on, he caught her eye less often, until finally it escaped him altogether. And then he saw her smile, and not at him, and there was in that smile all that he was looking for; it was that authentic quick flash of intimacy, as unmistakable as a caress. She was looking at a tall young man who had just arrived and was standing behind Ennis and Jubb. He stared jealously at this new arrival. It was horrible. He felt sick with apprehension.

'Hello, Don Carlos,' somebody cried. 'Get a chair.'

So this, then, was Carlos Divega, the film actor. He nodded and smiled, and contrived to seat himself at the crowded table with an easy grace that was almost insolent. There was indeed a kind of insolence about his body, though his eyes, very large and black, looked a trifle anxious and rather stupid. He was evidently a half-caste, probably from Central or South America. His carefully waved hair was blue-black, curiously metallic. He had a long olive face, with a fine straight nose, but with a rather thick, insensitive mouth. He was handsome enough, but in what seemed to William, whose gaze greedily devoured every detail of his appearance, a wretched shoddy fashion. Such distinction as he possessed had been roughly stamped on from without, and nothing but stupidity was coming from within. That is how William saw him, and William promptly loathed him. He represented nearly all the things that William disliked in a man, though actually some of these things, that tall figure, that graceful insolent carriage, that animal vividness, were what he had long secretly desired. And with the terrible clarity of the jealous lover, William saw at once what probably nobody else at the table had noticed, that Terry and Divega were arriving at that stage of intimacy when every new glance and smile is exciting and a fresh little revelation. And he, William, felt utterly helpless. Every minute now, he was growing smaller, more insignificant, stupider, gloomier, more and more like a man that a woman would desert for a shoddily handsome, glorious rotter of a half-caste film actor.

When they broke up, Terry explained to him, with an easy kindness that he found hard to bear, that she had been invited to dine on the yacht with the others, but hoped to see him sometime the next day. She would stay the night on the yacht, for they might be filming early in the morning. And she sent her love to Ramsbottom and the Commander. There was not time to say much. If she noticed anything wrong with him, she did not refer to it; and as he felt he must either say a great deal or keep quiet, he kept quiet. He returned to the hotel with Ennis, who went straight off to his bungalow and stayed there. William dined with Ramsbottom and the Commander, talked a little about schooners, and then went to bed early. This second stay in Tahiti had begun badly.

3

The next morning, Ennis, who appeared to have taken a fancy to William, asked him if he would like to see them filming. This would probably be the last day. William agreed at once. His principal object was to see Terry as soon as possible, but he could not help being interested in the filming too. So they hired a car, and arrived at the place, which was twenty miles down the coast, about the middle of the morning. The company was assembled at the picturesque entrance to a little valley, on a small stretch of beach where there was white sand. It was an odd scene. There were two vans from the yacht, each containing cameras and sound-recording apparatus. The great panjandrum himself, Joseph Sapphire, was there, dressed in a striped yachting suit and lolling in a special chair that had his name painted on it in white letters. He was surrounded by his staff, the Yes Men. Sometimes these people would dart away, presumably to convey his commands. William had an obscure conviction that on these occasions somebody was immediately executed. If they weren't, then the business was mismanaged. It was absurd if Sapphire should be denied the power of life-and-death over his subjects, for his state was so obviously Roman and Imperial. Then there was the director of the film, Meisen, and his staff. Meisen was extremely ugly, not unlike a blanched frog; he wore a green béret and a green silk shirt; never stopped smoking a pipe; and did not seem to speak to anybody except the two men at his side. You felt, however, that he was a personality. Ennis said that Sapphire had paid an enormous fee to tempt Meisen away from the Ufa Company and his exciting life in Berlin, into the wilderness of Hollywood. There was something about Herr Meisen – perhaps a mere turn of the head – that suggested he had a contempt for the whole Sapphire organisation. He was a frog who had agreed to make a film for tadpoles. Then there was a small crowd of islanders who were being used in the film, and who clearly took the very sensible line that acting in a film was simply an amusing way of earning a few francs and a new species of picnic. Mr. Sapphire must have dimly realised this, and it must have annoyed him, for he was continually sending out messengers to the man in charge of the island 'extras,' and no doubt would have had a dozen of them strangled or beheaded if he had had all the powers that properly belonged to him. Miss Avril Paxton was there; a quite unreal person, a sort of rough sketch in oils of a pretty woman, when you were close to her; but changing at once into a vivid lovely creature, the personage of the screen, when she fell back, diminished, into a scene illuminated by a sunlight that was a passable substitute for studio lighting. So was Carlos Divega; very handsome, exotic, shoddy, detestable. There were a few other players, and among them, eager, excited, and heart-breaking, Terry. The crowd was completed by the camera and technical men, and an outer ring of native spectators, who had brought with them food and drink, children and musical instruments, and an easy frivolous attitude towards the whole business that must have wounded Mr. Sapphire.

When the cameras were actually working there was quiet, induced by the bellowing of half a dozen men with megaphones – 'Silence, everybody.' The moment each little scene was done – though the same scene appeared to be taken time after time – there was a tremendous din, for all these people, except Meisen, seemed to be fond of issuing commands and airing their opinions, and they all had very loud voices. The islanders, not to be outdone by these Americans, contributed their fair share of noise, roaring and screaming with laughter. William was fasci-nated by these alternations of quiet and bedlam. The whole scene was lunatic, and, like Ennis's queer face, was half-droll, half-sinister. William saw people all over the world, millions and millions of them, being lured to their seats and then chained there by these oddly brittle bits of make-believe, Mr. Sapphire's charades under the blue sky. Here they all were, in Tahiti, its lagoon sparkling on one side of them and its hills mounting in green and purple grandeur on the other, and yet at the same time they were only pretending to be in Tahiti. They were determined that millions of spectators, thousands of miles away, should be enchanted by the picturesque and romantic qualities of life in Tahiti, yet Sapphire and Meisen and the rest were not in the least concerned themselves with those picturesque and romantic qualities, had no time to spare for the life in Tahiti, had hardly yet lifted their eyes to the coroneted peak of the Diadem. As Ennis explained, they were simply 'on location': this was merely an extension of the studio and Hollywood. It was all very odd. The modern world, William reflected, was becoming more and more simply something to be filmed; this was primarily the age of celluloid; and soon it might be impossible to distinguish between reality and film stuff, so that you would not know if you were witnessing an historical event or a scene arranged by a film company. Indeed, the two might soon be the same, and nations might go to war with the active and benevolent co-operation of Mr. Sapphire and his colleagues.

Mr. Finberg, who was one of the most prominent of Mr. Sapphire's staff officers, came across to them. 'Mr. Sapphire wants a word with you, Pat.'

'What is it this time?' enquired Ennis, in disgust. 'Has he got another new idea?'

'That's it. He's got an idea for a new ending.'

'Thought so.' Ennis was quite pleased to discover that his worst fears had been confirmed. 'All right. I'll be along. You come along too, Dursley, and I'll introduce you to the great man. And this,' he continued, as they walked along, 'is where I get myself well and truly fired.

You watch. This is going to let me out into the daylight with a gold-plated alibi.'

Mr. Sapphire, who had a small twisted nose, a long slit of a mouth, and an astonishing number of tiny wrinkles all over his face, was affable, if a trifle condescending, to William. 'You seen plenty of our pictures in England, Mr. Leslie?'

William, feeling rather odd as Mr. Leslie, said that he had.

'Good pictures we make, eh?'

William said they were. He would have found it difficult to say anything else, even if he had wanted to. You could easily go away and laugh at Mr. Sapphire, but there was something imposing about his actual presence. He had an imperial manner. He took it for granted that you would agree with him. William had a suspicion now that Ennis would not do anything and had merely been boasting.

'Vell,' said Mr. Sapphire complacently, 'you're seeing the biggest picture ever planned by the Sapphire Studios being made right now. You take a good look at everything.'

The audience was over. William retired a pace or two, and felt that he ought to have salaamed, saluted, bowed, or touched his forelock.

'Vell, Ennis,' said Mr. Sapphire, 'I got a big new idea for the finish – came to me this morning. We'll have a speed-boat race. You could easily alter the story to bring that in. A speed-boat race – just vat the picture vanted. It's a big idea.'

'It's a swell idea,' cried one of the staff.

'Makes a sure-fire finish,' cried another.

'Vat you think of it?' enquired Mr. Sapphire, with no perceptible trace of anxiety in his tone.

Ennis's drooping lid seemed to droop more than ever. He turned one bright sardonic eye upon the uplifted face of Mr. Sapphire. 'I'll tell you what I think of it,' he announced in a loud voice. 'It's lousy.'

The short silence that followed seemed to be thickly studded with exclamation marks. Before anybody else had collected enough breath to say anything, Ennis continued: 'Say, listen, if you want to put some speed racing into this picture, you go ahead and do it. But hell! – why stint yourself? Let's have some more swell ideas while we're about it. We could work something good in about a submarine or an airship. What about some big bombing planes jazzing round the sky? Hire a couple of elephants and let the picture finish in Africa. Let's build a Noah's Ark and make it a Bible story. Let's have a football game in it – you never seen one yet in a South Seas picture. Tahiti beats Yale and Harvard combined. Let's finish with the Empire State Building on fire. Swell ideas! I'll give you some swell ideas. We'll finish the picture with a big scene showing the annual convention of the Kiwanis and Knights of Pythias – fifteen thousand of 'em in costume – all swimming here from Los Angeles. Only don't ask me to go jack-assing round with you on this picture any more. I'm through with it. You put your own speed-boats in. You can't make the picture much worse than it is already. It's more like some God-awful crossword puzzle now than a picture. It's like a Marx Brothers picture with the Marxes left out. If you can catch me doing anything to this story again, you'll catch me doing it with an axe. And that's that, Mr. Sapphire. Your idea's lousy.'

Mr. Sapphire was curiously calm. 'I'll have a vord with you alone, Ennis,' he said, and rose majestically.

Ennis shot a glance at William that said: 'This time I'm fired all right.' Mr. Sapphire led him away, apparently to fire him in private. The others stared after him. William went in search of Terry.

'And now you can tell me all about that trip,' she said brightly, not unlike an efficient hostess.

He looked at her dumbly. She had receded miles from him. He had left one Terry and had returned to find another. She had been closer to him than this long ago, in San Francisco. He was even ready to hate this Terry, who looked at him so impersonally. Why couldn't her face and her voice have changed too?

'Well, don't you want to tell me all about it, Bill?' she said.

This was a little less like an efficient hostess. He melted at once. 'Of course I do. It's the one thing I've been thinking of for days. But there doesn't seem to be time now. When can I see you alone? We've hardly had a minute together yet, you know.'

'I do know. And I'm sorry, Bill.'

This ought to have pleased him, but it didn't. It seemed to him that she was too sorry, and not really sorry because they had had no time together, but sorry for him; and he did not want her to be sorry for him. He wanted her to be in love with him, and he knew very well that women in love are not sorry in this fashion. Miserably, he kept silent, and found time in that silence to despise himself for not having the courage to tell her what was in his mind.

She looked at him steadily. 'Well, if you don't want to tell me now, you can tell me to-night. I'm coming along to the hotel, before dinner. And don't you forget, Mr. William Dursley, that Miss P. T. Riley is one of your Faraway Island co-directors and demands a report on the first expedition. What do you think of me as a movie actress?'

'I don't know, though of course you ought to be good. But I haven't seen you do anything much yet.'

'And you won't – not in this picture.'

'Do you like it?'

'I love it.'

And obviously she did. He regarded her gloomily, feeling out of it, and then, seeing himself as a stupid depressing creature, tried to be less gloomy and failed. They talked for a few minutes more, but it was not a success. Even he was glad when she was called away. He would see her that night, at the hotel, and then it might be all different.

Ennis had returned from his private conference with Mr. Sapphire. 'Well,' said William, 'did he fire you?'

'Now you're a reasonable fellow, Dursley,' said Ennis, who seemed to be somewhat irritable. 'What would you bet that I'd just been fired?'

'I don't often bet, but I should think that a pretty safe one.'

'You certainly would. And why? Because you're a sane man. But nobody's sane in this picture racket. Fired? Not me.'

'What, you haven't been?'

'Don't you see what I went and did?'

'From what I saw and heard,' said William, 'you were simply asking for it. And, to be quite candid, I didn't think when it came to the point that you would have the nerve. You know, there's something rather impressive about your Mr. Sapphire. I suppose it's because he's had so much of his own way these last few years, just like one of the old despots.'

'He's impressive all right,' cried Ennis in deep disgust. 'The Metropolitan Museum ought to buy him and have him stuffed. But – what the hell! – it's my own fault.'

'Well, what happened?'

'I'll tell you what happened, and I'm telling you God's truth. I'm not making up a word of this. I couldn't. I haven't the power of invention. You saw him take me on one side? "Vell, Ennis," he says, "I tell you this. Your manners is lousy. We don't vant any more of that rough-neck stuff in the picture business. We got to talk to each other like proper gentlemen now it's a big industry. And you can take that contract of yours and tear it right up because you're through with it." So I told him that was O.K. with me. As you know, that's just what I wanted, that very thing. I'd got a grand alibi. I could spend the next six months here getting over that torn contract. So I began to pat myself on the back. But just then old Sap begins to do some patting, too. He pats me on the arm. "But ven you've torn that contract up, Ennis, I'm going to give you a better vun." I looked at him. "What!" I shouts. And I'm not sure I didn't say "Vat!" "You spoke your mind, Ennis," he says, purring like an old tom-cat. "You're an honest man, and you got the interest of the Sapphire Pictures at heart, else you vouldn't talk that vay to me. And that's vat I vant. That's real service. You didn't like that speed-boat finish, and you said so. I guess you're right." You see what I did? I went and overshot the mark. I laid it on too thick. If I'd only said half what I did say, he'd have given me the air. Now I've gone and got a better contract, and I'm sewn up with Sapphire for another two years, unless they certify me and put me away before it expires. But can you beat it?'

William could not beat it. He admitted that it was all rather fantastic. 'But won't you find the job easier,' he continued, 'now that Sapphire has decided to listen to you?'

'Listen to me!' Ennis shook his head over such ignorance. 'He'll not listen to me again for twelve months. By to-morrow, he'll be wanting that speed-boat finish again. That is, if he hasn't thought of something worse. Aw – what's the use of talking! These big movie men have you licked from the start. You can't handle 'em. Have you ever been left alone to look after a baby, Dursley? You haven't? Well, you don't know anything yet. You can't handle a baby – it's got to do what it damn well likes. And these fellows like Sap are just babies that weigh two hundred pounds and have five million dollars to spend. If you could take down their pants now and again and belt their behinds with a slipper till they promised to be good, you might get somewhere. But as you can't, you're licked. They win every time. But do what Sap said, Dursley. You take a good look at everything now. You're seeing a bit of Hollywood. Take a good look at it. You'll never see its like again.'

4

Once again they were on the verandah of Terry's bunga-low, with night around them. There was a distant strum-ming that cut through the sound of the streams and tiny cascades in the garden. Between the black silhouetted palms the lagoon was still a bright silver. The scent of the daturas below was as strong and sweet as ever. The great lily cups in the pond were faintly luminous. Yet now it was all different. It was rapidly shrinking into a mere huddle of canvas scenery. William's misery was growing and growing, a black cloud blotting everything out. He stared through it at Terry, with hot pricking eyes.

'Well, I must say, Bill,' she was saying, in what seemed to him the ugliest voice he had ever heard, with a rising whining peevish note in it, 'I must say I don't see what right you have to take it that way. I thought you were different.'

'Different from what?'

'You know what I mean.'

'No, I don't.' Oh God! – this was hateful. They weren't talking; it was simply their voices that were going on and on, answering snap with snap, whine with whine.

'Well, what right have you to talk to me that way? Hasn't a girl got any independence of her own? If you were my husband, you couldn't be acting worse.'

'Acting worse! Oh, Terry, how can you talk like that? It's such rubbish. It's so false. You must know it is.'

'There you are! Look at the way you're talking now. I'm not responsible to you for everything I do.'

'I never said you were.' But this was not good enough. He swept it all away. 'Yes, you are. Of course you are.'

'Well, you needn't shout, Bill.'

'You're responsible to me,' he continued, lowering his voice and not controlling it very well, 'because I love you. Everything you say and do is terribly important to me. You've got the power and therefore you've got to accept the responsibility too. You can't dodge it. And that's your trouble, Terry. You want to dodge it.'

She tried to take this lightly, but failed. 'You just can't make it that way, Bill, and you know you can't. If you do love me, I can't help it, can I? Have I ever pretended to be in love with you? I'll admit I've been very fond of you, Bill, and am yet and always will be. I think you're a lovely person. We've had the swellest time, and we've been fine friends—'

'We haven't been friends at all,' he cried, 'and you must know very well we haven't. It's not been friendship at all. I fell in love with you. I'm still in love with you. I think I always will be now. What's friendship got to do with it? Don't pretend, Terry. Be honest, for God's sake.'

'It's all very well, Bill, to say "Be honest." What do you want me to say? The only honest thing I can say to you, Bill, is that I'm sorry. No, listen. I'm sorry, I'm really sorry. I am fond of you, Bill. I like you no end. But I can't marry you. It wouldn't work, honest it wouldn't. It's sweet of you to ask me. Don't think I don't appreciate that. But I just couldn't. And I've got to go. You do understand that, don't you? Mr. Sapphire's given me a contract – and everybody says it's a very good contract for a beginner – and I'd be a fool to refuse it. I'd love to stay on here with you, Bill, and see what happens about the island and everything, but I just can't refuse this. You do understand, don't you?'

'What I do understand,' said William bitterly, 'is that you're falling for that film fellow, Divega. I saw that as soon as I came back here.'

She did not reply, and then it seemed as if the pair of them were doomed to everlasting silence. William's voice went on and on inside his head, alternately pleading and heaping reproaches upon her, but the mechanism of speech appeared to have failed him. The silence had thickness and weight now; it seemed to push back the words into his throat. You needed a sentence like a hammer to smash it. William hadn't one ready, and neither, it appeared, had Terry.

She turned away and looked out over the garden, and he could see the creamy curve of her cheek and found it almost unbearable. When that little curve had gone, half the world would go with it. He was ready to hate the Terry that would take it away from him, a cold, thieving Terry. And then there was a moment when he pierced the mystery of this romantic love. His adoration was not for this girl standing here – for here was somebody he could hate and was even now disliking – but for a girl that only Terry could help him to create, with the unique materials of her mind and body. If his Terry were entirely his own creation, then the loss would not be so great. But she was not. It was a double creation, and now that she had turned away from him – and possibly was busy creating another Terry for another lover – he was left with only a bitter sense of frustration, worse off than an artist robbed of his paints, brushes, canvas. Something of this he saw at that moment, but then the presence of this Terry, so poignantly like his own, with the same creamy curve of cheek, plucked him out of this momentary detachment. He disliked this girl beside him no longer. She was his Terry, or if not now, could be this next minute. It had all begun in magic. Was there not some magic to help him now?

'Don't go, Terry.' He went closer. 'You can't go, you can't leave me now. I love you. I think I fell in love with you that very first night in San Francisco, and I've never stopped falling in love with you since. It isn't as if you didn't care for me at all. You must remember I've been away. None of this would have happened if I hadn't been away, if we'd been here together all the time. Think of that last night we had before I sailed for the island. It would have gone on like that, Terry. It could do now. You were happy then – I know you were – you could be happier still. Terry, don't go.' But though he was terribly sincere, he discovered a sort of ironic echo to his voice, and it was to drown that echo that he went on adding sentence to sentence. Now, as if clutching in despair at concrete reality, he seized both her hands and turned her towards him. But through some trick either of darkness or nerves, he only saw before him a lovely dark image as wavering as a reflection in moving water.

'It's no use,' she said, a troubled voice coming remotely from this vague fluid beauty. 'Poor old Bill. I'm sorry. You're terribly nice, Bill. If I'd been a girl in Buntingham, Suffolk, I'd have just made one big grab at you and not let you out of my sight. But there it is. We've had a great time, haven't we, Bill? We'll let it go at that.'

'How can we let it go at that?' And, saying no more, he put his arms round her, kissed her several times, and held her close, and there was a wonderful and heart-breaking sense of familiarity, of being completely at home, in the shape and weight of her body in his arms. She did not resist him at all, but nevertheless she was not as she had been before; she was not entirely passive; but there was something, an inner response, missing; and the feeling of loss grew upon him, gradually curdling the delight of holding her in his arms again, until at last it made him release her.

She put her hands upon the lapels of his coat and looked at him dubiously, her eyes gigantic hollows of night. 'You don't hate me now, do you, Bill?'

'I don't see that it matters whether I do or not,' he replied sulkily, sounding and indeed feeling rather like a small boy.

'Yes, it does. I'd just hate to go away thinking you were feeling like that.'

'That's really being greedy, Terry. You want to go on to something else that amuses you more, but at the same time you want to feel that I'm left behind still comfortably adoring you. What does it really matter to you what I'm feeling now or going to feel? You oughtn't to care a damn.'

'Well, I do. And you mustn't be so bitter.'

'Why shouldn't I be bitter?' he demanded idiotically. 'You're taking enough away with you, God knows. Surely you don't want to take everything. At least let me be bitter if I want to be bitter.'

'Bill, you're talking like a fool now. You don't mean a single word of it.'

'As a matter of fact,' he told her, 'I don't hate you. I seem to be still in love with you. How long it'll take me to get out of it, I don't know, but I suspect it's going to take some time. But that's up to me. Don't worry, Terry. I'm not going to complain any more or even to suggest that you haven't a perfect right to leave this place in as great a hurry as you decided to come to it. No, let me say what I have to say. I shall probably be cursing you now and again, for making yourself so important to me – or allowing me to make you so important – and then slipping away. But I've no right to grumble, I see that now. I was talking like a silly boy a few minutes. Now I'm talking like a man, or trying to. You've given me a lot, Terry, even in this short space, and I ought to be thankful for it. I am, you know, my darling. Look, I'm thanking you now. And if we do have the luck to make a fortune out of Faraway, I shall come and give you your share myself.'

'Oh, Bill, when you talk quietly like that, I just can't bear it.'

'You won't have to. I'm going. Good night, Terry. Or is it Good-bye now?'

'No, not till noon to-morrow, please. Bill, I'm so sorry. You're the sweetest thing. And I'm not the least bit of good.' She kissed him.

It was not so bad at first when he reached his own bungalow. That last long speech of his had left him with a certain glow of noble romantic self-approval, and it was only when that glow had faded that he began to feel desperately sorry for himself.

5

It was much worse next day. All the morning, Papeete buzzed with news of the immediate departure of the *Sapphira*. The Bougainville was crowded with the film people and all their island acquaintances, and the poker dice were for ever being thrown to decide who should pay for drinks. William, who had gone there with Ramsbottom, drank with the rest, but unlike them did not soon turn hilarious and drunk. There was something numb inside him that resisted. Terry, with some of the other girls of the film company, only popped in and out of the club, for they were all busy buying presents and souvenirs. William only exchanged a few words with her all morning. He and Ramsbottom sat steadily in the shade of the Bougainville verandah, with Ennis, Jubb and a few of the others. Ennis was very drunk.

'That's right, boys,' he told them, his one bright eye brighter than ever and his long sardonic nose now the very symbol of genial disillusion, 'I'm lit, pickled, or soused, and I propose to stay that way for several weeks. I'm not going to wake up, cold sober, till I've been back in Hollywood long enough to get it into my system again. By that time, I shan't believe a damned word about these islands, anyhow. I'll be back in the old gilded cage.'

'Unless your liver rots to pieces on the way up, Ennis,' said Jubb grimly.

'It went long since. We're building up a new race without livers, Jubb. That's what Prohibition's done for us. It's the survival of the fittest all over again. Why, even now some of our boys can drink spirits of shellac and like it. The next generation will be able to drink anything – *any-bloody-mortal-thing*.'

'*Whoopee* – Ennis!' someone shrieked from the next table.

'Whoopee yourself, whoever you are!' muttered Ennis. 'This whoopee stuff makes me tired. See the new Pat Ennis dictionary for definition of same. *Whoopee* – a what-is-it word—'

'Be yourself, Pat, you can't just say a what-is-it word. What kind of a dictionary's that, anyhow?'

'Leave me alone and I'll dig out what I mean. I've got it. *Whoopee* – an onomatopœic word, expressing high spirits, in favour in the United States during the later Nineteen Twenties. Probably imitated from the sound of a factory buzzer. Dropped out of favour during the Great Slump, except among film actors and soused camera-men. How's that?'

'Good! Very good!' cried Ramsbottom, now filled with iced rum and good fellowship. 'And if Ah hadn't something very special to do down here, nay – hang me if Ah wouldn't come back to Hollywood with you, lad.'

'We could use him, couldn't we, Jubb?'

'We could. We could feature him in short comics, with some bathing beauties.'

'That'ud do me nicely.' And Ramsbottom leered hugely. 'What do you say, Dursley?'

William managed to find a rather stiff little grin and said nothing.

'He's not feeling himself this morning, chaps, my partner here isn't,' Ramsbottom explained, to William's annoyance. 'And Ah think Ah know why. One of our syndicate's deserting us, and Ah've noticed he's been sweet on her for some time. It's Miss Riley – and she's going back with you lot.'

'That so,' said Ennis, swivelling round that bright eye. 'Nice kid, too.'

'Nice kid and easy to look at,' said Jubb. 'She ought to make good.'

'Oh – for God's sake, Jubb, how can you talk that way? You're not in conference now. And if you're feeling like that, Dursley—' and here the lighthouse eye focused itself on William, who could feel his face getting hot – 'All right, boy. We've all been through it. Even Jubb here has, though you wouldn't think so to look at him. But I've known the time when even that alligator heart of his was melted and tamed and generally kicked round the studio. What was the name of that little red-head we had on the lot last year, Jubb? You know, boy, the one you fell so hard for.'

'Fell nothing! I was sorry for the kid, that's all.'

'You heard him? He was sorry for the kid, that's all. Let's have another round after that one. That's the way. If they think you're tough, they start by making you feel sorry for 'em. If they think you're not tough, they just belt you over the head with the first thing handy. But they get you, just the same. They get you all right. Well, Dursley, forget it, just forget it. Once that kid gets aboard that tinpan yacht, she's lost; she's not real any more; she's grease paint and celluloid and press cuttings; she's just another one gone to the beautiful bloody kingdom of make-believe, where Sapphire sits on his golden throne and Jubb and me are First Silver Dish-Washers. I tell you, it's all make-believe. You think that yacht's real, don't you? Like hell! That's make-believe, too. The captain and the crew are only small character parts, only they don't know it yet. Look at her. Isn't she a pretty picture? My God, she ought to be – for that's all she is. Put these drinks down, boys. They're real, though they wouldn't be if we stayed here much longer. Dursley, Ramsbottom, here's luck to you both, and may God make you His featured players. Not stars, mind you – that's no damn good; you're here to-day and gone to-morrow; no, just featured players. And here's to Jubb—'

'And you, Pat.'

'And me – First Silver Dish-Washers in the Kingdom of Make-believe. And I'll tell you a secret, boys. Old Sapphire has been trying to beget a son for years and years now. That's why he keeps changing his wives – like your old Henry Eight. But he can't do it. How the hell could he? Having a son's real, and he's not real. He's not found a make-believe formula yet for having a son. But he'll do it yet. He'll call a big conference, and we'll all put our heads together and make-believe as hard as we can and spend a million dollars we haven't really got and the end of it'll be that old Sap will have a son – in natural colours and with sound by the Western Electric.'

'Come on, Pat,' said Jubb, grinning, 'it's time I got you aboard.'

They were all moving now. William's head ached and he felt slightly sick. It was very hot along the crowded water-front. The yacht was standing out in the lagoon, and only her passengers were being allowed to go out to her in the various launches. William and Ramsbottom went with Ennis and Jubb to their launch, shook hands, and waved them good-bye. It was then that William saw Terry, who was hurrying from the town, loaded with parcels. She was rather flushed, obviously excited, and looked glorious.

'I've only got a minute, Bill,' she cried. 'Listen, you'll write to me care of Sapphire Pictures, Hollywood, or to the old address in San Francisco, won't you? Tell me what happens about the island. And listen, if you come to California again, you've got to come and see me, now promise. And I promise if ever I find myself in England,

I'll come to Buntingham, Suffolk, to see you. That's a promise. We've had good times, haven't we, Bill?'

'Yes,' he said, trying to be cheerful. 'And the best of luck, Terry.'

'And the very best to you, Bill darling. There. Good-bye.'

That was all. He watched the launch take her away, and saw her, a diminished but easily recognisable figure, climb into the yacht and wave in his direction. And now her going, which up to this moment had only been a sort of unpleasant threat, was achingly real. He stood dumbly among the shouting, singing, waving crowd, keeping his eyes fixed upon the *Sapphira*, which made the ponderous and curiously leisurely preparations for departure that can be remarked in all ships. At last, after an interval in which time appeared to have been replaced by a thick hot eternity, the yacht gave a triumphant blast or two and slowly began to turn. The crowd about him yelled and waved harder than ever, but William neither moved nor raised his voice. The ship of make-believe glittered for a few more minutes in the lagoon, and then found the open sea and rapidly began to recede, until finally she was only a tiny patch of white and a trail of smoke.

'Good morning, Mr. Dursley,' somebody cried softly. 'I expect you're sorry to see that yacht go, aren't you? I know I am. She brought a bit of life into the place, didn't she?'

It was the young widow from his own part of the world, that Mrs. Jackson whose very existence he had almost forgotten. He made some reply, but could not have said five minutes afterwards what it was. She said something then, looked at him with friendly eyes, nodded and smiled and went away, much to his relief. The *Sapphira* was now only so much fading smoke. He stared at it for another minute, then wandered away. Tahiti and the whole South

Seas were nothing now; stupid blank sunshine and a wilderness of blue water; even Faraway did not really matter; for what was there here that could happen to a man that could possibly lift him from the mere routine of living and make him happy? Nothing, nothing. William stared before him in despair. His whole life seemed to have narrowed to one dull ache.

CHAPTER IX

MRS. JACKSON AND THE SECOND ATTEMPT

1

THEY HAD now to find another schooner that would take them to Faraway Island, and this meant a schooner that was bound either for the distant low islands, like the *Hutia*, or for the Marquesas, which formed the best jumping-off place of all for Faraway. But such schooners did not leave Papeete every day or so, and as they did not work to a time-table there was no telling when one of them might turn up. There was nothing to be done but to keep one's eyes and ears open on the water-front. This was the Commander's job, and he enjoyed doing it. He was in and out of schooners, asking for news and listening to skippers' gossip, half the day. It was fortunate that he had something like this to do, for he disliked the ordinary life of the island. He bathed every morning and sometimes went fishing, but the rest of his waking time was spent schooner-hunting, and William and Ramsbottom saw very little of him. And this arrangement pleased all three of them.

A few days after Terry's departure, William felt the loss of her even more than he had done the first day. It was like facing a death. The very sunlight seemed different. The days were simply so much time that had to be passed. He could have told himself that he would soon get over it, but the trouble was, he did not want to get over it.

When he had got over it, he felt, a vital part of him would be dead. So he passed the time, shovelling the hours away like so much rubbish. He had lost now all his first delight in the romantic picturesqueness of the island. Some beauty remained, of course. It was still good to watch the sunsets flaring above the incredible crags of Moorea, to stare up at the misty Diadem in the early morning. But his sense of wonder was no longer excited merely by his being there. He did not walk about the streets of Papeete and tell himself that this was romance itself. Indeed, he rather disliked the streets of Papeete. And now a schooner was a schooner and nothing more. Terry had gone and taken with her the mainspring. His spirits were lumping and leaden, and of their own accord would not rise: they needed the assistance of a few drinks. Sometimes, after these few drinks, things would be almost amusing or have a faint significance, but there was always the danger of having a drink or two too many and then feeling nothing but maudlin pity for oneself and a horrible emptiness when complete sobriety returned. This emptiness inside was matched by an emptiness outside, for more and more William came to feel that behind the charmingly shaped and coloured foreground of this South Seas life, the little stir and clutter of its easy human existences, was an enormous vacancy; and there was something sinister about this vacancy, as if it was in the field of vision of a baleful deity. No wonder that this Polynesian race had been dwindling for centuries, that beneath their laughter and singing and love-making there was a deep melancholy. This emptiness had its eye on them, and they knew it. Everybody, white men and brown, tried to pretend it was not there, to be aware of nothing beyond the rich garlanded foreground, but if they were all sensitive they knew, they knew. Sometimes you caught an islander, with huge sombre eyes, staring into it, as if into Doomsday. Probably that was why, if you stayed on a year or two, you could never drag yourself away. It would not let you go. You pretended it was the satiny arms of the girls or the wreaths of jasmine and *tiare* that kept you there, when all the time it was this sinister vacancy that held you prisoner. Perhaps the vast antique empires, which legend said were drowned in those seas, had cast a spell, this being the air that had known and still quivered with their horror. There were times now, and not infrequent either, when William hated the place.

So in company with Ramsbottom, William haunted the verandah of the Bougainville and had his few drinks. Sometimes they went on picnics or visited distant bunga-lows, and there, too, they always found a few drinks. William discovered very soon that not only was he miser-able in mind when he had not had his drinks, but also physically uncomfortable. On several mornings he got up feeling rather sick and dizzy, and it was not until he had renewed his acquaintance with iced rum or gin that he had felt even moderately comfortable again. He had sense enough to realise that he was really not well, but for the time being he had not sufficient interest in being well to bother about it. It simply did not matter now that Terry had gone. There was Faraway, of course, and that was important, but in a week or two they would have got their schooner and would be on their way there, out of all this, so there was no need to worry about Faraway. He had to pass the time, to escape regret or boredom at all costs. Not being a fool, he saw exactly what he was doing, but he could not help taking a certain pleasure in the part of the man who did not care, a not unfamiliar romantic figure. At the moment, until they sailed for the island, this was the only romantic stuff left to him, and so he made the most of it. No, not quite the most of it, for so far he had not claimed for himself one of the pretty and amiable half-caste girls whom he met at the Bougainville or on one of the picnics. For a day or two after Terry had gone, he had had no eyes for them, but then suddenly, though still in despair about Terry, he found himself all eyes for them. Until now he had not realised how attractive they were. The tall grave Hina, plump little Pepe, the luscious Teura, the merry teeth-flashing Revatua: it was exciting to see them, and to meet them was almost maddening. Every shining surface they had, every curve, every velvety glance, seemed to suggest that they could do more than a few drinks could to give a man forgetfulness and heart's ease. But William, unlike Ramsbottom, who was completely at ease with the pretty creatures and chaffed, patted, and slapped them as he pleased, was still shy and slightly uneasy in their tantalising presence. Nevertheless, every day he was less shy and uneasy.

They came close to having a quarrel with the Commander. 'I might as well tell you,' he began, just after breakfast one morning, 'that I think you fellows are playing the fool. Instead of standing up to the place, you're giving in to it. You've got to stand up to the tropics, if you don't want to go under.'

'Under where?' asked Ramsbottom.

'You know what I mean, Ramsbottom.'

'Well, Ah think you'd better explain yourself a bit, hadn't you?'

'All right. I will. In my opinion, you're both slacking about and drinking too much. I've been to these places before and you fellows haven't. I told you at the first what could easily happen. Now it's happening.'

'Don't be ridiculous, Commander,' cried William. 'You

sound as if you thought we were turning into beach-combers or going native or something.'

'That's not so ridiculous either,' he retorted, with a sharp frosted glance at the pair of them. 'I've seen that happen a good many times.'

'Well, you're not going to see it happen with us, so you can make up your mind about that,' said Ramsbottom sharply. 'What's your complaint? You seem to have got one.'

'I have. You're slacking about and drinking too much, both of you. And you can't stand it. You're not looking too well, Ramsbottom—'

'Never better in my life, thank you.'

'And as for Dursley here, he's looking rotten, a sick man. You're fools to yourselves and you're not playing the game with the job we're here to do. You've got to keep fit for the sake of the island. After all, we didn't come here to sit about in Papeete boozing.'

'Well, a chap's got to do something.'

'That's nonsense, Ramsbottom, and you know it. There are plenty of ways of passing time here, without sitting about all day boozing with a crowd of wasters and native girls.'

'All right, uncle,' Ramsbottom jeered.

This made the Commander angry. 'Drop that, Ramsbottom.'

'Drop it be damned! Why should Ah drop it? You've said your bit, let me say mine. Fact is, Commander, you're one o' these people who won't let other people spend their own time and money in their own way. Because you don't fancy a thing yourself, nobody else has got to fancy it. Ah've met a lot like you in my time, and well Ah might, for England's full of 'em. Live and let live, Ah say. This fishing they do round here that you've tried your hand at once or twice – it seems to me the safest way of spending time Ah could imagine, but it's not doing any harm to me, and if you like it, well, get on with it – Ah wouldn't try and stop you. "That's what he fancies," Ah say to myself, "so good luck to him." Well, what Ah fancy is sitting in with a few good chaps and perhaps one or two jolly girls and having a drink or two and a talk and happen a bit of a sing-song. That's not your cup o' tea, and so Ah've got to chuck it. Nay, Commander, it's not reasonable.'

'I agree,' said William quickly. 'And I don't see why you're taking this high line, Commander. After all, you didn't come here as our tutor or governor or anything. We're quite capable of looking after ourselves.'

'That's just what you're not capable of doing.' The Commander snorted. 'You come straight out from home, with no experience of this sort of life, like a pair of snotties who've just joined. You're both telling me as plainly as you can that it's no business of mine. But the point is, it is. I wish it wasn't Then I needn't interfere. But we didn't come out here for a jaunt. We came here to find that island and see what we could do with it. And all my expenses are being paid—'

'You needn't bring that into it,' Ramsbottom told him.

'But if you fellows slack round like this much longer, you'll not have the guts or the energy to do what you came to do. And then where are we? Look at my position then. And sooner or later, you'll turn round and tell me I ought to have stopped you going on like this.'

'Not me. If that's your idea, then you don't know Johnny Ramsbottom. Ah never told anybody, never in my life, that they ought to have stopped me. Ah can do all the stopping that's wanted, thank you.'

'I see your point, Commander,' William told him, 'but

you're exaggerating, you see. And why should we blame you? We don't think you're in charge of us.'

'Look here, Dursley, let's talk sense for a minute. Do you imagine you're a fit man? Because you don't look it.'

'I don't feel bad,' replied William, not quite truthfully. 'I feel the heat rather, and I don't sleep too well, that's all. But from the way you talk, you might think I was about to suffer acute alcohol-poisoning or delirium tremens or something. We're not tight all day, you know.'

'I know you're not, but you ought to chuck the whole thing and look after yourself for a week or two. Look here, go and see a doctor, and then do what he tells you to do.'

'Certainly not.' William disliked seeing doctors. 'Why should I? There's nothing wrong with me. He'd simply talk twaddle, pocket my fee, and laugh at me.'

'Well, Ah don't know, lad.' And Ramsbottom eyed him speculatively. 'You're not a good colour. You might just pop in and have ten minutes' doctoring. It wouldn't do you any harm.'

'It might, quite easily. I've known people,' William continued, though he could not have said when or where he had known them, 'who popped in for ten minutes' doctoring and went on being heavily doctored for the rest of their lives. No, I'll see a doctor when I feel ill, and I don't happen to feel ill.'

'Please yourself, lad. Ah'm not going to interfere. But look here, Commander, why don't you brighten up and enjoy yourself for a week or two. We'll have to leave it soon, when we start for the island, whether we like it or not. So come and have a bit o' fun with us.'

'I don't like your idea of fun, and I think the pair of you are acting the goat.' And the Commander, without another word, marched out of the dining-room.

Ramsbottom watched him go and stuck out his fat under-lip. 'Well, Ah'd just as soon act the goat as the donkey; what do you say, lad?'

'I think the Commander's talking like a prig.'

'It's what Ah told you when you first came here. The 'eat's finding him out and touching up his liver. This place doesn't really suit him. He'd never have gone on like that in England. Feeling his age too, and doesn't like it. Well, it looks as if he's going one way and we're going another, till we set off again on our travels. What's the programme to-day, lad?'

This remonstrance, being a failure, produced the inevitable result. The two erring partners spent even less time in or near the quiet hotel. Their few drinks began to be poured out for them about the middle of the morning and were still to hand quite late at night. They made a new acquaintance at the Bougainville who almost immediately became their chief ally. This was a young Frenchman called Broisat, who arrived on the boat from Marseilles one morning, after being away from the island for eighteen months, and began at once to buy drinks for everybody. He was a jovial young man, with a broad pale face and rather glassy eyes, whose father manufactured cars just outside Paris and appeared to give his son a very generous allowance, probably preferring that the young man should play the fool for a year or two in Tahiti than in Paris, where folly is apt to be very expensive. Broisat had been educated in England, spoke very good English, and seemed to prefer the company of the English and Americans on the island to that of his fellow-countrymen. He had a large bungalow outside Papeete, and was indeed a neighbour of the young widow, Mrs. Jackson, who was still waiting for the East Anglian news that William had promised to give her. This bungalow Broisat had let furnished during the time he was away, but now it stood empty and he immediately took possession of it. Things would happen, it was generally agreed, at Broisat's place. They did; but for William they began and ended with a party that the enthusiastic Broisat improvised one night.

William and Ramsbottom, flushed and hot after their few drinks, were dining among the flowers and smoke of the *Tiare* Restaurant, and there Broisat discovered them. He was with Waters, the little middle-aged American with the unchanging grin, and they were both in that condition, not drunk, but not sober, which tells a man that the ordinary sensible routine of life is the most damnable tyranny that must be smashed at once. In short, they were ready to do anything but talk quietly, stop drinking, and go to bed.

'We must have a party,' cried Broisat.

'When? Where? How?'

'To-night. Out at my place. Yes, we must have a party. What a pity it is not my birthday! Is it your birthday, Waters? Or yours, Ramsbottom, Dursley? No? What a great shame!'

'That's all right,' said Waters. 'Must be somebody's birthday, I reckon.'

'How clever of you! Yes, it must be somebody's birthday, and no doubt we know that somebody. It should be celebrated. What do you say, boys?'

'Ah quite agree,' said Ramsbottom solemnly. 'It's a damn shame the way these somebodies' birthdays come and go, nobody taking any notice. Let's celebrate, Ah say.'

Broisat was now inspired. After all, a man must take something in life seriously, and Broisat saw himself as a giver of good parties. His eyes flashed; he made rapid decisive gestures; his plans were ready at once; he was like a born cavalry general who had been ordered to raid enemy territory. 'Marvellous! Listen. You have your car here, Waters. I have mine. We can get everybody in those cars. There are four of us here, and I will ask Denis Blum – that makes five. Then we want some girls. You know the girls, Waters.'

'Sure I know the girls. Who d'you want? Hina, Teura, little Pepe and her sister, Turia, Revatua, Vahine?'

'Marvellous! I leave the girls to you, Waters. You know more about them now than I do – they change so much in two years. You bring all the girls along in your car. I will take these two and Blum with me, and also take along some more wine and things. How is that? Good – let's go.'

Thus William and Ramsbottom, with Blum, a plump, curly-haired fellow from Alsace, found themselves in Broisat's car, bumping along what seemed to be a narrow green tunnel decorated with pandanus and palm and bread-fruit tree leaves. Less than an hour later, they were sitting on the verandah of Broisat's large bungalow, waiting for the rest of the party, having a few more drinks, and looking out upon the silver and deep violet of the lagoon.

2

William had lost all count of the hours. Time, like many things, had been annihilated. The eating and drinking, the chaffing and laughing, the dancing to the gramophone, and above all the strumming and soft chanting of the girls, had been going on and on for ever, Some of them had bathed, and now the girls were wearing their red-and-white *pareus* so that the lamplight fell exquisitely, tenderly, upon their bare shoulders. William brooded

over these shoulders, their beautiful texture, their beautiful contours; they had the perfection of some strange
fruit; they made him feel happy and sad all at once. The
faces of these island girls were very charming, in their
soft darkness; their eyes were neither shining nor dull,
but had a sort of smoky brightness about them; they had
purple lips; and the white star-like flowers above their ears
were very fragrant, though their scent was not sufficiently
strong to drown the smell of the coconut oil on their
long straight black hair. But it was their shoulders, so
cunningly moulded and coloured in the lamplight, that
fascinated William. It was monstrous and marvellous
that they should have such beautiful shoulders and arms.
These were the shoulders and arms of goddesses; traps
for a wandering Ulysses.

He could not decide whether this ceaseless strumming
and soft chanting – only interrupted by screams of laughter when the girls had plunged into an unusually obscene
Tahitian ditty and had then caught each other's glances
– was the most irritating or the most soothing noise in
the world. Sometimes it seemed to be one, sometimes the
other. Also he could not decide whether he was drunk or
not. True, he had had a lot to drink, more than he had
ever had before, and he felt queer, very queer – but was
he really drunk? He thought not. For a long time, things
had behaved very well to him, even though some people
might have thought them rather obtrusive, for what they
did was to stand out at him, to shriek their shapes and
colours at him, to batter at his eyes and ears and nose.
Some people might object to things behaving in that
fashion, but William rather liked it. He sat among them
like an emperor. His companions were emperors and
empresses. Very early in the party, he had come to the
conclusion that he was lucky, very, very lucky, to know

such wonderfully good fellows. Nearly every remark they made was astoundingly good, if not wise, then very witty, and frequently both. And how lucky to find himself with such lovely and amiable girls! Some fellows said that these were the best girls in the world. He did not agree – even now he did not agree – for you could not compare them with Terry. But then Terry was different. The whole thing was different. And he had lost Terry. But had he? No, he hadn't. Yes, he had. He had lost the one woman in the world he could ever love, and he was a sick man – yes, he was a sick man, for he hadn't felt very well lately and the Commander had definitely said that he looked a sick man – and though this was a fine party, a party that well deserved the golden light that seemed to illuminate it, yet it could not make him happy again. Nothing would ever make him happy again, he told himself with mournful pride. Meanwhile, this party was great fun. He had not had enough of this sort of thing. He was beginning to feel a trifle sick and dizzy. and there was far too much coconut oil about, and perhaps that strumming and chanting did get on one's nerves, but nevertheless this was all great fun. This was the island life as it ought to be lived, the South Seas of happy legend.

No, he was not drunk, not at least the innermost central part of him; but this essential self had withdrawn itself further than usual from the rest of him, with the result that the rest of him took on an independent existence. To the mild surprise of William, that is, of the essential detached self of William, the rest of him was immensely one of the party: it made remarks in a loud voice and roared with laughter; it sang a little; it went on helping itself to drinks; it danced with the girls and occasionally hugged them. And now things had stopped assaulting him with their shapes and colours and sounds. Every face there no longer stood out in sharp relief. A haze, touched with gold, crept into the room, softening the edges of things. Faces became rather blurred and distant corners were quite misty, so that it was all like a party in a dream. It was as if through a veil of gilt-spangled gauze that he saw Ramsbottom's head sink back and his mouth fall open while Hina and another girl added more flowers to those already crowning him; that he saw Broisat, Waters and the flashing Revatua shaking the poker dice, and the ripe and russet Blum trying to play the guitar at the same time as the smiling luscious Teura; that he saw little Pepe making large eyes at him and coming at last to perch on the arm of his long cane chair.

Somebody said something about dancing, and the next moment the gramophone was on again. Ramsbottom was still asleep, with his mouth wide open and petals lodged here and there on his vast moon face. The others all danced. William danced – or at least stumbled not unhappily about the room – with a giggling Pepe. She seemed to him then an entrancing person to hold. She was just the right size and shape. Among much that was vague, fluid, drifting, this exquisitely comfortable shapeliness and solidity of Pepe stood out as a grand fact. After the dancing, he found himself back in his chair with both her arms about his neck and her cheek pressed against his. Neither the arms nor the cheek were at all cool, and it was a warm night, but nevertheless it was very pleasant to have Pepe as close as that. No, it was more than pleasant, it was exciting. But he was thirsty, and said so. For a moment there were no arms about him and she was there holding out a glass and smiling at him. He drank, smiled at her, then finished the drink. To his surprise he heard the glass break on the floor. The room began to recede and then to waver and melt in a rather disgusting fashion, so he glared hard at it and by an effort of will pulled it nearly back to its normal appearance. But then he relaxed, and immediately the place began to bend about and run like a candle at the fire's edge. Voices, too, turned idiotic, blaring out and then fading, as if they were being played on trombones. It was all sickening and rather sad, particularly as behind these treacherous appearances there was really a beautiful party happening. In fact, if only one could steady oneself and the whole thing and find time to think clearly, one would discover in the very heart, the golden and fiery heart, of this night's festivity a great secret, something that might change a man's life entirely, a clue to lasting happiness, a panacea, the philosopher's stone, the fountain of youth. It was there, right in the heart of this night's companionship, but a man would have to think clearly to find it. Then William had a sudden and most passionate desire to get out of that room, out of the bungalow, and to sit on the beach outside. But Pepe would have to come with him. He told her so, rather elaborately if brokenly, in a mixture of French and English. He staggered to his feet.

Pepe laughed. '*Maururu vau.*'

He glared at her. He had to do that to keep her steadily in focus. 'What's that, Pepe? I don't understand Tahitian. Matter of fact, little Pepe, I don't understand anything much. But I'd like to. I'd like to understand everything – everything there is to understand – d'you see?'

She laughed again. 'Yais, I come wit' you.'

The night was so large, cool, tranquil, comforting, that he sat down at once upon the sand and wept a little. He did not want to cry, he just cried. It might be weak, but still it was splendid to be there, crying a little, in that large and beautiful night. There was a tickling on his left cheek and a strong scent of the *tiare*. That was Pepe, rubbing flowers against his cheek. He made a grab at her, but she was not there. Vaguely he heard her giggling in the darkness. He called her and she came closer. This time she did not escape, though she did not try very hard. Now the only real thing in this wide vacancy of night was her sweet solidity. She rubbed herself against him, like an affectionate little animal. He was happily drowning in the mixed odour of the *tiare*, frangipanni, coconut oil, and in warm flesh.

He woke up to find himself in another world altogether, perhaps in hell. He was still lying on the beach, only a few yards from the bungalow verandah, but Pepe had vanished. Night had faded, but it was not quite dawn. He had time to notice so much before the first great black wave of nausea swept over him, darkening all his senses. Many a morning lately he had found himself feeling sick and dizzy, but never as sick and dizzy as this. It was horrible, terrifying, as if he was coming all to pieces. He put his head forward, resting it on his arms, but that only made him feel worse. Slowly, creakily, he got up and stumbled a few paces until he reached one of the supports beneath the verandah. Then he was really sick, and afterwards, for several minutes, he went on retching dreadfully. He was cold too, not healthily cold outside, from being in the open all night, but cold inside, as if icy fingers were groping in his belly and entrails. The retching stopped at last, but instead of feeling warmer he felt even colder. As he laboriously climbed into the bungalow, his teeth began to chatter and every limb he had was aching and shaking. He wanted a drink of water. He wanted some brandy. Inside the bungalow it was still dark, and stuffy, smelly, stale, a beastly hole. He could hear snores and thought he saw one or two figures stretched out. After infinite swaying and stumbling – for there were moments when it seemed as if his body was drifting away from him – he found his way through to the front of the bungalow, with some vague idea in his head of resting outside instead of waking anybody. But there he collapsed, sinking through dark shafts of weakness and nausea. 'Oh, God, I do feel rotten,' his voice kept saying, behind those chattering teeth, 'I do feel rotten.'

It was lighter and he could distinguish a movement somewhere. Painfully he kept his eyes open and raised his head a little. Above him was an enormous face that swayed about like a yellow captive balloon. A Chinaman; one of Broisat's servants; perhaps the gardener. He couldn't be real, with a face that size, and a face, too, whose expression never changed.

'Get brandy – cognac – and some water,' William whispered. 'Very sick. Tell master I'm very sick.'

For an age, it seemed, the vast yellow face floated there without a wrinkle being disturbed or an eyelash moved. He felt like screaming in horror. It was like being dead and knowing that you are dead, the final illogical terror that haunts all men. But then at last the face gave a sign. It bent lower, muttered something, then moved away. William felt that he could do no more. Somebody else would have to look after him. Whether he lived or died, it would have to be somebody else's affair now.

3

William now spent some time in a fluid and gaseous world. It was not a pleasant life. Something was injected into his arm, in which they seemed to make quite a large hole; there was a reek of iodine; and a bulbous hairy face had a part in this event. This face, which really was too bulbous and hairy, appeared several times, and it spoke French. Once it roared '*C'est la logique, madame,*' and a longish and scratchy fingernail, presumably belonging to it, drew lines across William's chest and hurt him a little, to the accompaniment of any number of *Voicis* and *Voilàs* and much vague passionate talk of *la physiologie.* A woman was about a good deal, and she was white, English, and not entirely unfamiliar. She had a steadier image than most of the others who appeared. It was all very confusing and unpleasant. That Ramsbottom and the Commander should make an appearance, staring at him with great eyes, was all very well, but why should Uncle Baldwin turn up, too? William might be ill, but he could not be deceived. Uncle Baldwin was dead, wasn't he? Well then, what was he doing here? And Terry, too. Terry was not dead, of course, but she was no longer on the island; she had gone on that yacht, back to California. Perhaps the yacht had turned round and had brought her back to him. Once she came in and put her arms round his neck and her cheek to his, and was very quiet and kind, quieter and kinder than she had ever been. But then another time she came and pointed a long finger at him and laughed quite cruelly. It was unfair of her to do this. William told both Uncle Baldwin and his friend Greenlaw of the Grammar School about it, and they agreed that it was unfair. He talked a good deal about this and other matters, but most of the people who came did not take much notice of him. That Englishwoman listened to him, but did not seem to understand, which was very stupid of her. And all the time William felt hot, thirsty, and generally uncomfortable, and was tired of the way people and even things were behaving, never keeping still, wavering, advancing, receding, glaring and fading. If life could not do better than this, a man might as well die. This was a silly sort of existence.

He woke up one morning and found himself back in the ordinary sane world. He was very tired, as if he had just returned after a long journey. Everything round him looked a little tired, too. It was all very pleasant, peaceful, sensible, but rather dim and worn. He was not in his own bungalow at the hotel, but in a strange bed-room, and after some reflection he decided that he must be still in Broisat's bungalow. There were one or two large photographs hanging on the wall, and they looked like photographs of French people. Through a half opened shutter, a shaft of sunlight was piercing the room, but even that seemed a trifle faded. They were all tired, the whole roomful of them.

Somebody came in. It was little Mrs. Jackson, the young widow from Suffolk. And he had never given her the news she had asked for, never had the talk he promised.

'Why,' she cried, coming at once to the side of the bed and looking at him intently, 'you're a lot better this morning.'

'I've been ill, haven't I?'

'I should think you have been ill, Mr. Dursley.'

'What's been the matter with me?'

'I couldn't tell you exactly. It's been rather mysterious. A sort of fever, I think, due to something wrong with your liver. You'd a temperature of a hundred and five a good part of the time. Doctor Dombois says it began with your liver, but you can't really tell, because he's mad on livers. He'll put you on a diet now and tell you you haven't to drink anything but Vichy water and lime juice for months and months. He always does. He's famous for it.' She smiled at him, and it was a nice intimate smile, suggesting that the two of them were there together, looking down

on the doctor and his little fads. She really had a very
pleasant face, and William felt that it did him good to
look at it.

'I must take your temperature now,' she said briskly,
and at once stuck a thermometer in his mouth.

'What is it?'

'It's sub-normal now,' she told him.

'It feels sub-normal. Everything looks sub-normal –
except you, Mrs. Jackson.'

'I shall take that as a compliment whether it is one or
not,' she said gaily. 'But don't think you're going to be
better all at once. You'll probably feel very depressed and
weak for several days now.'

'I feel tired.'

'Then you mustn't talk—'

'Oh no—' and he was quite alarmed – 'don't go. I
don't feel too tired to talk, and there are several questions
I want to ask. If I don't have them answered, I shall be
worrying about them for the rest of the day, and that will
be very bad for me.'

'Artful, aren't you?'

'Tell me – this is Broisat's bungalow, isn't it?'

'Yes, of course it is. And I live just next door. You were
taken ill quite suddenly, after one of his silly parties. I
expect you drank too much. I do think men are silly. You
can't have been feeling very well before that.'

William admitted that he hadn't been feeling very well.
He also admitted that it was all very silly, and meant it
too, for now there seemed something quite idiotic and
indefensible about his recent antics. In the face of Mrs.
Jackson's cool bright sanity, there was nothing to be said
for them, and the sooner they were forgotten the better.

'How long have I been here?' he asked.

'Four days. And I'm not surprised you can't remember. You were delirious most of the time.'

'But I remember you vaguely,' he told her. 'You were here a lot, weren't you? It was awfully good of you, Mrs. Jackson, and I'm very grateful. Why did you do it?'

'Oh, I rather like nursing people. I've done a bit of nursing in my time. And I was near and there was nobody else, and I was glad to do it. I was only sorry I couldn't have you in my own bungalow, but you couldn't be moved, you see.'

'I believe I owe an awful lot to you, Mrs. Jackson,' he said gravely.

'Well, I did what I could, and I'm not going to pretend it didn't matter, because it did. But you needn't bother to thank me or make a fuss, because I really liked doing it. It's fun looking after people when they're ill, especially when they pull through so nicely, like you. And I wanted something badly to break the monotony, I can tell you. So there! And now you ought to stop talking, and keep quiet till the doctor comes. Do you want something to drink?'

He did, and she gave him some Vichy into which some limes had been squeezed. It was bitter but most refreshing. She looked at him speculatively. 'You ought to be washed, you know.'

'I know I ought. I feel very scruffy. If you could get me some soap and water, I could do it myself.'

'You couldn't,' she cried, quite indignantly. 'Don't be ridiculous. You're not to move. Don't think you're well yet, because you're not, Mr. Dursley. I could wash you – but perhaps you'd rather the Chinese boy did it now, would you?'

Hesitating a little, William decided for the Chinese boy, and the Chinese boy it was who washed him and generally tidied him up. Mrs. Jackson left before this toilet began, and did not return when it was finished. William sank into a doze, and it was not until the doctor arrived, later in the day, that he was fully awake again. Mrs. Jackson was with the doctor, whom William recognised as the owner of that bulbous hairy face which had haunted him during the last few days.

Dr. Dombois was one of those massive Frenchmen who combine, in the unique Gallic manner, gusto with complete disillusion, a combination apparently impossible to members of the Anglo-Saxon or Teutonic races. He did not enter the bungalow, he exploded into it, and once there he roared and gesticulated and clowned about, but all the time he looked at everybody and everything with shrewd little eyes. Now he pounced upon William as if they had agreed to do a comic acrobatic act together; at any moment, it seemed, he might throw William up to the ceiling, catch him, and then hurl him out of the window. He never stopped talking. He would begin with faulty English, change to slow French, and then toboggan into rapid colloquial French that left William and Mrs. Jackson far behind. His principal theme, as Mrs. Jackson had predicted, was diet. William had come out to the tropics – very well, one must come out to the tropics sometimes – and for a little season the tropics were very pleasant and of an interesting nature; but the body of William, the liver, kidneys, bowels, and blood of William, were not accustomed to the tropical life, and meanwhile William must eat the rich food, the red meat, and drink the strong wines and the spirits; and with what result, if you please, my friend? – the liver has too much work to do, far, far too much work to do, and it makes its protest, not once, not twice, but many times, it makes its protest – for it is a patient and long-suffering servant; but, my old one, there comes a time when it can do no more, it is tired of you, for you work it too hard, so it begins to poison you, and then your temperature flies, your heart is worked too hard, there is a bad crisis, and here you are; and now, no red meat, no wines, no spirits, but a little fish, a little chicken, vegetables, and plenty of Vichy water and limes. A little medicine – oh yes, you must have a little medicine, or you would not think you were ill – but it is the careful diet that will do the trick. And he could be removed – perhaps to-morrow – to Mrs. Jackson's bungalow. Mrs. Jackson was an excellent nurse and wise young woman; she understood about the diet. Yes, it would be a good idea for William to be Mrs. Jackson's boarder. The doctor then departed, leaving behind a surprising amount of empty and silent space, which William contemplated for a few minutes and then lost in sleep.

4

It was pleasant and at the same time rather odd being a guest at Mrs. Jackson's bungalow. The oddity of it was due to the fact that here the South Seas had an East Anglian flavour. It was as if he had a finger or two and one ear back in Buntingham. There were only two other guests now, a quiet, middle-aged New Zealand couple called Atkinson, who had come from Wellington to have a long restful holiday in Tahiti. They bathed and slept a good deal during the day, and William saw very little of them at first, but later he and Mrs. Jackson used to play a rather sketchy sort of bridge with them. They were nice dull people. Mrs. Jackson ran the place very well, and William was more comfortable than he had been at Marot's hotel. The first few days were spent in the dreamiest stage of convalescence, and he did nothing but drowse, chat a little with Mrs. Jackson, and try to read a detective story. He was allowed a visit, however, from the Commander and Ramsbottom, who told him that there was a good chance of their finding a passage to Faraway on a schooner that was leaving for the Marquesas in about a fortnight's time, the *Rose Marie*, Captain Peterson. Meanwhile, he was to stay there, be quiet, and get better, otherwise he would not be able to go with them. This would not do at all: he swore that nothing would prevent him from going with them. He was very eager now to push on with their expedition, for all the holiday spirit had vanished and the island never left his thoughts for long. It was, he felt, all that was left to him. Terry had gone; he had seen the South Seas; there was only Faraway.

Once he had passed the first dozing stage of convalescence, he spent hours and hours talking with his hostess. He gave her every scrap of information he could muster about Suffolk, and whether he was talking about people, the state of trade, the motor-buses, the picture theatres, the new hotels and shops, the great frost of two years before, or last summer's short heat-wave, she listened with delight, as if it was all an enchanting tale. She was never tired of asking questions. The moment she came in and sat down beside him, her clear grey eyes seemed to brighten, and there were times now when she looked quite pretty. He felt rather ashamed of himself these days because he had once thought her a mousey and faded creature of no particular interest. It showed him, he admitted, how easy it is to misjudge people. She was increasingly pleasant to look at, he found, with her open face, wide honest eyes, and soft friendly mouth. She was very much a real person. No wonder that everybody

appeared to respect her and like her. The Commander
had been quite right about her.

   She told him all about herself. He learned how she had
left Ipswich to take a job in an office in the City and there
had met Captain Jackson from one of the New Zealand
boats, a man much older than herself, but a fine handsome fellow, very kind but desperately shy, how they had
married and she had gone with him to Wellington, how
he decided to leave the sea and settle on one of the South
Sea islands, and how they had come here, only to find,
suddenly, dreadfully, that he was rapidly wasting away with
a cancer of the stomach. After his death, she had tried to
carry out his scheme for this bungalow and its plantation,
was still trying, and only just making ends meet. By the
end of the first week, he knew a great deal about her. He
knew why she had never felt at home in Wellington, what
had happened to her sister Grace, why she preferred blue
for her dresses, what her favourite joints and puddings
were, her opinion of London offices and tea-shops and
theatres, why her uncle Ernest had never left them anything in his will after all, what she would do if she were
very rich, and a thousand and one other things. And it
was not mere politeness or loneliness that made William
listen to her, and listen to her with growing interest. She
was one of those people – and they are usually women –
who do not seem to have much imagination, who have a
sense of fun but little humour and no wit, who appear to
be completely cut off from the stimulations and graces
and ecstasies of the arts, who have never entertained an
idea in their heads and have no notion of what is happening in the world, and yet in some mysterious fashion give
the impression of being ripe personalities who live full
rich lives. True, he did not listen to her as he had listened
to Terry; these stories of Ipswich and Wellington were not

lit by the same sun and moon as Terry's stories of her life in San Francisco, which once or twice he remembered now with a queer mixed feeling of regret and irony. Here there was a growing interest, but no enchantment. Nevertheless, the longer he listened to Mrs. Jackson the more he respected, admired, and felt an increasing affection for her. She was a real woman, and a fine one. And she seemed to him a much more solid character than he was.

'Your name's Margery, isn't it?' he said to her, one evening after dinner. 'In future I shall call you Margery.'

'I wish you would,' she replied briskly, with no fluttering of eyelashes and nonsense of that kind. 'I know your name's William. So I'll call you William.'

'Good! That means we're friends, doesn't it?' he said, but not at all sentimentally.

'Of course it does. And I'm going to tell you something. I've hoped we should be friends – really good friends – ever since we first met – that night at the Bougainville. Do you remember?'

Yes, he remembered. And what a lot of things he remembered all at once!

'Funny meeting you there,' she mused, 'because I don't often go. There's nothing wrong with it, but it's not my style. But it's nice to go in on boat days, just to see a few fresh faces. That's why everybody goes there then. They pretend not to, most of them, but they all live for boat days. Silly, isn't it? I mean, living in a place where you're waiting for boat days. But I made up my mind then that if there was a chance, if you were stopping here, I'd try and make a friend of you. I'd almost stopped thinking like that about people. You get out of the habit, you know.'

'I know you do. I've been rather like that myself these last few years.'

'Have you really! I'd never have thought it. But you nearly always think of people being a lot grander than you are yourself, don't you? Well, it's easy to get to know people here – and I never go out of my way to avoid them – why should I? – but that doesn't mean you make friends. The more you live inside yourself – you know what I mean – the harder it is to make friends. But I remember thinking I'd like to have a good try with you. So there, I've given the game away now.'

'I'm glad. But, Margery, what was the reason? Was it because you liked the look of me or because I reminded you of home?'

'A bit of both, I suppose. But never mind what it was.'

'All right, I won't. After all, we're here, aren't we? And I owe an awful lot to you.'

'No, you don't, William. We've had all that out before. Besides, if you bring that in every time, I shall think you only consider me a sort of nurse.' And she laughed, but not very heartily.

He looked at her steadily. The light was not very good, but he saw her eyes meet his fearlessly for a moment or two and then, as it were, cloudily escape. There was something significant about that. He was aware of a growing suspicion while he replied to her. 'Well, I don't. As a matter of fact, I rather dislike nurses, or I think I do. No, I think of you as the one good friend I've made here, and easily the nicest woman on this island.'

'Now that American girl has gone,' she said softly. They stared at one another for a moment. Then before he could say anything, she cried: 'No, no, I don't want you to tell me anything. I'd much rather you didn't, really I would. And I'm sorry I spoke. Let's talk about something else – quick! Wait a minute. Oh dear! – you can never think of anything when you want to badly, can you? I know. Did your friends give you any news yesterday when they came here?'

'Nothing very much.'

'Oh, but I forgot – that's a secret, isn't it?'

'What do you mean, Margery?'

'What the three of you are here for. Everybody here knows that it's some sort of secret business, looking for treasure or something like that.'

'Do they? Do you mean, they all talk about it?'

'Of course they do. Didn't you know? You've a funny idea of what happens on this island if you didn't know that. Do you think that three of you can come here, go round talking about chartering schooners, then go off for weeks and come back again, and all the time not tell anybody what you're doing, and not set people talking? They've all been gossiping like mad about you. Of course they have. They would. They're terribly nosy here. You can't blame them, when there's so little happens and they must have something to talk about. You've been a nice change for them from Tars Flock and his big fishes and that little mess, Hockaday, and all his native girls.'

'I suppose so. And they think we're treasure-hunting, do they?'

'Some do, and others don't. They have to think something, you know. Is it really a secret? How exciting! Just imagine coming here all the way from Buntingham with a secret! You had an uncle out here once, hadn't you? Yes, I know that much. But what's going to happen now?'

'When we left Tahiti before,' William replied carefully, 'we went in search of a certain island. We didn't find it simply because the schooner had to turn back. Now we're going again, probably in about a week's time. With any luck we ought to get there this time.'

'Are you coming back here?' she asked very quietly.

'Yes, I hope so. I mean, we're planning to return here with the schooner. We shall leave most of our things here.' And as he said this, he saw her face brighten, and he knew that she was immensely relieved.

'Well, I'm glad, and I'm not going to pretend I'm not. I didn't want you to go away for ever now, William. As it is, you've made me feel homesick.'

He arrived at a decision. 'Can you keep a secret, a really important secret?'

'I can keep a secret. I may talk a good deal, but when I want to I can put a big padlock on my tongue. Really I can. But, mind you, William, I'm not asking you to tell me – I haven't been fishing – and if you don't want to tell me, I shan't mind. At least not much. Of course I'm curious. Who wouldn't be?'

'I'll tell you,' he said, lowering his voice.

'I've never heard of such a thing,' she cried, when he had finished. 'I've read about them in books and magazines, but that's all. And you needn't be afraid. You can trust me.'

'I have trusted you,' he said gravely, and then he caught her hands and smiled at her. It was a purely friendly gesture on his part, but for a moment it seemed as if her response to it would be more than friendly, as if she was lifted towards him by some great wave of surrender, as if a misty warmth darkened her eyes. But then she released herself, made some excuse, and left him.

The days passed dreamily. Dr. Dombois had taken a last look at him, advised him to continue some time on a light diet and to avoid spirits and the heavier wines, and had given him a final dig in the ribs. He had been twice into Papeete with Mrs. Jackson, to buy a few things and to see the Commander and Ramsbottom and the *Rose Marie*, a two-master now laying in her stores and trade goods. He had begun bathing again, and fortunately there was a little stretch of sand in front of Mrs. Jackson's bungalow and the lagoon there was just right. So he renewed his acquaintance with the magical coloured little fishes. For the rest, he idled with a book on the verandah, played sleepy bridge with the other three, or talked to Margery Jackson. These talks had now taken on a new character. The suspicion he had entertained before had ripened into a certainty. He knew now that she was in love with him. It would have taken him much longer to discover this – indeed he might never have discovered it – if his affair with Terry had not left him far more sensitive in this direction than he had ever been before. He was almost certain that during these last ten days she had been going through those states of mind that he had experienced on the *Marukai* with Terry. It was the same enchantment, only this time it was going out from him and not being felt by him. He knew – or if he did not know, he told himself, then he was the most conceited ass in the South Pacific – exactly what was happening to her behind the smiling eagerness, the entranced looks, the sudden doubts and hesitations. He was the magical one now. Yes, there could be no doubt about it. If he had not liked her so much, this discovery would have made him feel uncomfortable and he would have taken himself off as soon as possible, for he had as little sexual vanity as it is possible for a man to have and still remain a man. But he liked her, admired her too, enormously, so that this discovery warmed and enlarged him and seemed to deliver huge new tracts of good life into his hands. His interest in her was quickened at once. She became immediately much more of a woman. Very definitely now she had arms, legs, breasts, cheeks and lips. Perhaps because she was desirous, she became what she had never been before – desirable. But not urgently, achingly so, only pleasantly; it was easy and restful to be with her, yet always now there was a little flicker of excitement there, too. Sometimes for nearly a whole day he never thought about Terry.

Just before he left, the occasion conspired against her self-protection. The Atkinsons had been away all day and were not returning until late that night. Margery had been busy most of the day, but at sunset she joined William at the lagoon's edge and together they watched the western sky turn into smoke and flame, plumes of amethyst and orange, islands of palest blue and green, while below the fantastic peaks and crags of Moorea were transformed into the castles and mad towns of Gothic folk-lore. Whatever his current opinion of the islands might be, William never wearied of this colossal daily spectacle, in which for the time being he always lost himself. On this occasion they watched it together, in silence. When it had burnt itself out and Moorea was only a sullen mass and there were cold lights in the darkening lagoon, they turned away from the water's edge and strolled through the shadowy plantation. When they reached the garden in front of the bungalow, the scarlet crotons and the pale yellow and pink hibiscus flowers were being swallowed by the swift tropical nightfall, but the whole place was almost sickly sweet with the fragrance of the jasmine and gardenias. It was now a typically beautiful South Seas evening. They passed through the bungalow and made for the verandah, which overlooked the lagoon. Beyond the lighted radius of the two oil lamps all was deep violet. Ten thousand tiny moths came to explore the lamplight and remained as a kind of vague scribble in the air. The usual lizard, high up on the wall, made lightning passes with his tongue and sometimes with the whole of himself, making a sharp flicker of green up there. A few stars appeared, mild as the evening air. There was the familiar blended sound – the distant dull shock of the outer sea against the coral walls of the lagoon, the dry rustle of the palms, and a faint strumming from some native hut. William lit a cigarette and idly absorbed it all. He felt strangely content.

'It's a lovely night,' he remarked lazily. 'It may be just dull and hot here during the day, but I do think the early mornings and the sunsets and the nights are marvellous. Just look at it now. I know there isn't much to see, but it's got a wonderful atmosphere, you know, Margery.'

'I suppose it has,' she said.

She sounded very grudging, and he looked at her, wondering if she had just had a sudden change of mood. 'I'm still new,' he said lightly, 'so I haven't got used to these evenings yet.'

'I have. And I'm sick and tired of them.' She was quite vehement.

'Not tired of this?'

'Yes, sick and tired of it. I know it looks very nice, and I suppose once I was back home I should talk for hours about it, but just now I could scream at it. Yes, I could. I could scream and scream at it. I want to go home. What's the matter with us English people, anyway? Why have we to be always going away when we've got the loveliest little place in the world? Yes, we have. I don't care what you or anybody says about cold and rain and fog and all the rest of it, England's the loveliest place. I've got one of the nicest gardens on this island – anybody will tell you that – and I'd gladly exchange it all just for one little wet primrose.'

'Oh well, so would I,' cried William, his imagination suddenly delighted by a vivid image of a little wet primrose. 'Or for that matter, for a cowslip or two, or some kingcups, or daffodils—'

'Or English violets. I'm sick of these big showy sticky sickly flowers. Those little wild flowers we have at home that come peeping up in the woods and the hedges when it's still cold and wet – there's something in Shakespeare about that, isn't there? – we used to learn it at school – but it's all true, too – a handful of them's worth more than all this sickly tropical stuff put together. And then the green, green fields – not like the green here, but all fresh and sweet – with the daisies and dandelions and buttercups in them!'

'And the soft skies,' cried William, the water-colourist in him remembering with ecstasy. 'The soft skies, with their delicate lovely gradations. And the haze over the fields and the hills on early summer mornings. And the queer golden glow in autumn.'

'Yes, and the long, long twilights – not like these quick stupid things here, light one minute and dark the next. Summer evenings going on and on. And the smell of hay – Oh, William – the smell of hay. And the bluebells I used to see in the woods out Hadleigh way. And all the little birds singing and singing and singing. Why, if I heard a blackbird now I wouldn't know what to do with myself.'

'But, Margery, that's all very well,' he said, with a judicial air, 'but you can't condemn this simply because it hasn't got all the English things in it.'

'Yes, I can,' she replied wildly. 'Because I'm English and I want the English things, all the lovely little English things. They go to your heart, and nothing here goes to your heart. It's all too sloppy and *easy* here. Yes, easy. You know what I mean. The sun just shines and shines and when rain is wanted it comes pelting down for an hour or two, and that's that. There's no cold wind, no frost and snow and sleet, no mists and fog. They call it a human paradise and all that, but I don't want a human paradise. And, anyhow, this isn't one, except for sloppy lazy people who don't want to make an effort. There's such a thing as making it too easy for everybody. Look at the flowers. Those little English spring flowers have a hard time; they have to come through the snow and sleet and east winds; but when they do come they've got something none of these flowers have got. You know that's true.'

As he agreed, he was telling himself that he would never have thought her capable of this impassioned outburst.

'This isn't our place. We're not at home here. It's all too sloppy and easy on the surface and somehow too queer and rather cruel underneath – just the opposite, I'm sure, of England, where all the hardness is on top and underneath it's all safe and kind and friendly to you. They make a fuss about these natives here. They're not bad people at all – I know them quite well now – and often I feel sorry for them because they're all dying off in some queer way – but all the same, they're an irritating lot, just like big brown babies, who must either be playing and laughing or crying. These girls – oh yes – I know what men say about them – but it's all a lot of silly nonsense, just sailors' talk. Any decent white girl is worth ten of them to any decent white man, a man who wants a real woman by his side and not a pretty little brown animal. I know there are some very nice people – I mean, white people – on the island, but a lot of them are just sloppy fools who think they're being very grand and romantic when they're just being lazy and cowardly, coming here to run away from life, that's all. The people who first came here may have been different – I don't know about that – though it's always been a favourite place for lazy runaways.'

'Like me,' said William, half teasing and half in earnest, though he did not expect her to catch his serious meaning.

'No, not a bit like you, William. Don't be silly. If you're going to make fun of me, I'll stop talking. Perhaps I ought to stop, anyhow.'

'No, no, please don't stop, Margery. So you really do want to go home?'

'Home? I should think I do. I know what they mean now when they talk about being home-sick. That's it exactly. I could cry when I think about it. And don't think I'm making a mistake about England and imagining it's all violets and daisies and summer evenings and skylarks. I want all the rest of it just as badly. I'd give anything, anything, just to go for a walk up the Woodbridge Road on a cold wet Saturday afternoon in November or March, with the trees all bare and water in the fields. I'd come back to a nice bright fire and tea and buttered toast, and all the shop windows would be shining through the rain, and there would be boys selling papers, and people going to the theatre. And think of Christmas. And the snow sometimes, falling so gently and covering everything, so that you look out of the window one morning and everything's a queer blue and white. Then spring coming, and everything quite different. It's never really different here – one month is the same as another. And all the nice sensible English people—'

'A lot of them, you know, are neither nice nor sensible. You'd soon find that out.'

'Perhaps I would, but if you'd been away as long as I have, you wouldn't be talking like that. Besides, think of the children – children with enormous blue eyes and rosy cheeks, round rosy cheeks like apples – honestly, William, there isn't anything here as good as an apple—'

'Margery, I must inform you,' he said, with mock gravity, 'that you're sentimental.'

'Well, if that's being sentimental, I suppose I *am* sentimental. Why shouldn't I be? Is it wrong or something? I've got feelings and I'm not ashamed of them. I'm not a dummy, and I'm not going to pretend I am a dummy, just to please people who think you ought not to be sentimental, as they call it. I'm sick and tired of this place, which isn't my home and will never make me happy, and I want to go back to where I belong, and every time I really think about it – and I try not to – it all seems so lovely and far away—'

'Far away?' He gave a short laugh, but there was no hint of amusement in it.

She stared at him. 'Well, it is far away, isn't it? I know it seems so to me. And I know if I really begin to think about it, I want to cry. And don't think I cry easily, because I don't – I'm not one of those weepy females. Oh – but I've talked too much already. I'm getting all silly and excited. If I'm not careful, I shall be crying in a minute.' And there were tears in her voice.

'Why, Margery,' he said, feeling a tenderness for her he had not expected. He put his hands on her shoulders and then a moment later she was in his arms, silent, pressing her cheek against his. He kissed her forehead; she lifted her face, and he kissed her on the mouth; and then she returned his kisses with a passion that surprised him. Finally, after resting in his arms again for a minute, she slowly withdrew, looked at him steadily, and said in a very small voice: 'You're not to bother about that, William. I suppose I asked for it, in a way. Though I didn't mean to.'

'No, of course not, Margery. I – well, I understood what

you felt – and I was sorry – and, you see, I'm very fond
of you—'

'Are you? I'm glad of that, anyhow. But you needn't say
any more, William. Really you needn't.'

'I don't know what to say. The fact is, I'm all mixed up
just now—' His voice trailed away. She nodded, and then
waited in silence, her eyes fixed on his. Then he came to
a sudden decision, and, taking hold of her hands, said
gravely: 'Listen, Margery. I'm going away, to find that
island. I don't know how long we shall be away, but I shall
come back here. Will you be here?'

'I will if you want me to be here.'

'You'll wait?'

'Yes, of course I'll wait.'

She said it very quietly. It would have been just the
same if she had merely nodded. He knew instinctively
that this was a woman who would if it was necessary wait
for a man she loved not simply a month or two, but half
a lifetime. All the film companies or any other companies
could descend on the island, and it could be overrun
with young men like demi-gods adoring her, and yet those
steady grey eyes would still be fixed on his image and she
would wait. It was wonderful and terrifying. Even now he
knew what he was going to say to her when he returned
to Tahiti. That was inevitable.

5

The *Rose Marie* was slightly larger and much older than
the *Hutia*, but otherwise there was not much difference
between them. There was the same picturesque huddle
of native passengers and goods on deck, the same picturesque and dramatic departure. Margery was there to see

them off, and endeared herself to the whole syndicate by presenting it with a large basket filled with good things to eat. She and William said good-bye to one another quietly enough, but he watched her dwindle to the tiniest visible patch of white. This time, even Ramsbottom was not sorry to be leaving Tahiti. All three were glad to be moving again. Ever since Prettel had refused to take the *Hutia* out of her usual course and they had been compelled to turn their backs on Faraway, they had never rid themselves of a feeling of frustration, and it was chiefly this that had made them so short-tempered with one another. Now that they were moving towards Faraway again and no more time was being wasted, this feeling of frustration left them, they were united by a common purpose, and they were almost as eager and friendly as they had been at the very beginning.

There might be little difference between the *Rose Marie* and the *Hutia*, but their skippers were very different. Captain Peterson of the *Rose Marie* was an elderly Dane, a massive fellow with a magnificent hairless red-brown torso, over which he rarely wore a shirt. Perhaps he shaved his body, for it was always entirely smooth, and if it had not been for the fine play of muscle in it, it would have looked uncommonly like sausage. This naked hairlessness gave Captain Peterson an odd – and at first even sinister – appearance. His face was very square, enormous, and seamed, and would have been intimidating if it had not been for his mild and innocent blue eyes. Peterson had a thick accent, but his English was quite fluent; indeed, after a day or two, both William and Ramsbottom discovered that the captain's English was too fluent, and they began to wish he had known nothing but his native Danish. For Captain Peterson, though an excellent fellow with thirty years' experience in this trade, was a bore. It was not long before they began to dread his 'Exgooz me, pliz,' which always preceded his interminable talks at them. He had a passion for Scandinavian history and he combined this, not unskilfully, with a passion for talking about his family. The Danish-Prussian War of the 'Sixties was one of his favourite themes, and he would rumble on about it for hours. They would be chatting idly on deck or down in the saloon after dinner and then suddenly there would come this 'Exgooz me, pliz,' and the gigantic Norseman would be there, holding before them a faded photograph. 'These are all cavalry ovvizers of the Danish Army in the war wit' Brussia. That one there is my uncle Axel, who was galled the bravest man in the whole Danish Army during the war wit' Brussia. I will show it to you in the hisdory boog of the war wit' Brussia.' And out would come a very large shiny illustrated history of the war, and very slowly Peterson would turn its pages to find the references to his famous uncle Axel. There was nothing apologetic or appealing about Peterson. Once he had said his 'Exgooz me, pliz,' he felt that you were his history class and he spared you nothing. He explained everything at great length and always he spoke very slowly, though not always distinctly, and as it was impossible to listen to him with any interest for more than ten minutes and as he rarely let you off with less than an hour, and as there was no escape in the limited space of the schooner, he soon became an intolerable bore. He was bad enough on the subject of the war wit' Brussia, but he was much worse, being still longer-winded and not even having any photographs to show, on the subject of early Scandinavian history and the Vikings. He seemed to carry whole long lectures in his head, for he would instantly begin one talk where he left off the last. 'Exgooz me, pliz,' he would say, in that tremendous deep voice that could not possibly be ignored. 'When Harold Hardrada virst set sail, he had wit' him dree hundred vighting men, only dree hundred, but these men were the best vighting men that had left ever the shores of that gountry. And they set sail wit' Harold Hardrada. . . .' The Commander did not mind these talks; he liked Peterson; and so he would sit there, sucking away at his pipe and nodding sagely, or sometimes quietly dozing, while the happy captain droned on and on about his Vikings. But to Ramsbottom and William it was intolerable, and they devised all manner of schemes for dodging that fateful 'Exgooz me, pliz,' with the result that in the end it became a sort of game for them and passed the time not unpleasantly. There was something gloriously incongruous to William about passing the hours in a schooner in the South Seas trying to dodge Harold Hardrada and his Vikings.

Meanwhile the schooner was gently rocking itself across the wide space of empty ocean between the Society Isles and the Marquesas. The days followed one another in a dream-like sequence, gliding without event from one flare of sunset to the next. William would lie by the hour on deck, idly watching the fine antics of the birds or the regular advance of the long rollers, and his thoughts would be as shifting and inconsequent as the pattern of foam he saw there. Sometimes whole hours would pass without apparent thought at all; he would not be asleep then but sunk deep in some huge vague reverie. At such times he was neither happy nor unhappy, but in some dim drowned state of mind to which either happiness or unhappiness meant nothing. He only thought about Faraway itself as a distant and inevitable goal. He might have been on his way there for ever. Ramsbottom fell into the same gigantic mood, and for days shed most of his natural loquacity. Only the Commander, perhaps because he was proof against this hypnotic effect of the wide sea, was his ordinary self, ready to discuss plans, to talk about a passing big fish or odd flock of birds, or to listen cheerfully to Peterson's dreary sagas.

There came an evening at last, however, when Peterson set aside the Vikings and the Danish-Prussian War. 'To-morrow,' he announced at dinner, 'we gome to the islands. You begin to see the Marquesas. After you see something you never vorget.'

'I've never seen them yet,' said the Commander, 'and I've always wanted to, especially since I read Melville's *Typee* and *Omoo*.'

William had read Melville too, and said so.

'You have read Melville's boogs about the Marquesas?' cried Peterson. 'So have I. Very good. Oh yes – good boogs. We'll drink his health.'

'But it's all different now, isn't it?' said William.

'Yes, all different,' Peterson replied, with gathering mournfulness. 'These islands they are the most wonderful, the most beautiful islands in the world – and the saddest. Yes, they are the saddest. Soon there will be nobody left on them – nobody at all. These Marquesans, they die off. Even in my time, I see them die off – one by one – two by two – they go. Elephantiasis, leprosy, syphilis, and – worsd of all – tubercolosis – kill them off. When I come here firsd, long ago, there were many more of them, and fine big men, but I heard them – at night I heard them – cough, cough, cough. I would stand on shore and it would be night, wit' a moon and big stars, and all so beaudiful, but it would be spoiled for me because all the time I hear them – cough, cough, cough.' And the captain's mild blue eyes suddenly looked quite hollow and his face was a large tragic mask.

'They were a fine race too, weren't they?' said the Commander.

Peterson drew himself up at once; his naked chest expanded; his whole figure seemed to grow; and his eyes blazed. 'They were,' he shouted, and he banged the table with his great fist. 'They were the best race in the Pacific – the biggest, the strongest, the bravest, the greatest fighting men. They were the Vikings of the Pacific. Yes, they were the Vikings. They would go in their canoes to the Low Islands or to Tahiti, and where they went they conquered. They were fine men. And now they are finished. All the great races are finished. The Marquesans, they go, but the Chinese, they come, they stay, they breed like – like—'

'Rabbits,' suggested Ramsbottom.

'All right. Like rabbids. Little yellow men adding up figures or scratching the ground,' Peterson roared, with immense scorn, flashing a glance at the Chinese that seemed to turn them into insects. 'Soon you will see – the Pacific will belong to the Chinese. They work hard, they save their money, they breed like rabbids. The Marquesans will have gone like the Vikings. I hope they meet in Valhalla – all the big fighting men. When I think of these things, I could cry wit' tears. What is to become of the world, I say, when these great races all go?'

'Ah think the world'll get on very nicely without 'em,' said Ramsbottom coolly.

'I don't,' said the Commander. 'I agree with the captain. The great races – the races that produced the strongest and bravest men and the most beautiful and virtuous women – are finished now. It's only number that counts. Crowds, mobs, swarms, hordes – it's their turn now. Very soon I expect the entire land surface of the world will be covered with people, little people all alike, running in

and out of factories, going round and round like white
mice in cages. One country will be just as good as another.
It won't make any difference where you are then. It'll all
be just one damned great beehive or ant-hill. You might
live to see it, Dursley. But I shan't, thank God! And neither
will the captain here. We shall be dead, won't we, Cap'n
Peterson, and glad to be out of it.'

'Yes, much bedder,' said Peterson, wagging his great
head. 'You and me, Commander, we die quick and perhaps go to Valhalla. We live too late. One hundred years
ago, perhaps, we come here to the Marquesas, like Melville, and we would be happy. We would drink wit' the
big fighting men and the minstrels and we would sit and
watch the beaudiful girls dancing in rows and they would
come and put flowers on our heads. Now it is too late.
Cough, cough, cough. You can hear it yet. Cough, cough,
cough. Commander, I drink your health. Now exgooz me,
pliz, there is something I wish to do and then I go to
sleeb. I think I am very sad.'

6

Tahiti and Moorea had at once captured William's imagination. These Marquesas did not capture his imagination,
they stunned it, so that afterwards, when they had shaken
themselves over the horizon and he found himself once
again in the green-blue bowl of sky and ocean, he could
hardly believe that he had really seen them. Tahiti and
Moorea were picturesque and romantic islands, perhaps
the most picturesque and romantic islands this world
could show. The Marquesas simply did not belong to this
world at all. They were like the ruins of some nobler
planet. They transcended any possible order of the pictur-

esque and romantic. They did not compete with other places, and it was absurd to begin comparing them with other places. These were the landscapes of dark and splendid dreams, of *Macbeth* and Beethoven's Fifth Symphony. Black crags, pinnacles and tortured promontories had been flung out of the water and piled up in wild confusion; there were jagged peaks lost in cloud, and high smoky valleys; forests were hanging in the air, dripping and glittering; and rising sheer from the green depths were immense dark walls where innumerable white threads of waterfall were swaying and a hundred thousand white birds went circling. Every island seemed to have just been plucked from the very heart of the sea, so that it still dripped with salt water. They were black mountains and dark green woods for ever seen through a mist of spray. They were the Gothic castles of the deep Pacific. They were the fairy transformation scenes in some grim pantomime of drowned men. They were a hundred little infernos and paradises jammed together. They were terrifying, beautiful, and incredible. And the *Rose Marie*, now a toy boat, moved cautiously from one to the other of these incredibilities, carrying with her, for their delight, a good selection of cheap tobacco, tinned meat, cotton goods, imitation jewellery, patent medicines, household utensils, fishing tackle, soap, scent, and a few discreet cases of gin and Tahiti rum.

Peterson had been right about these islands. Just as they had not the easy prettiness of the other island, so, too, they had not merely the same vague graceful melancholy: there was a deep sadness at the very heart of them. The population, now a mere handful, could play the part of merry islanders well enough, and it was here that William and his friends saw the best dances that the South Seas showed them. Even the convicts were cheerful fellows. Nevertheless, these people had the air of being survivors who knew they had escaped one catastrophe only to be inevitably doomed by the next. It was impossible to ignore the frequent signs and marks of disease, chiefly elephantiasis and tuberculosis. Here and there, among the few elderly men, William could see the surviving skeleton or shadow of that great race, but it was obvious that it had almost perished. Such of the islanders as they met they liked, and the Commander was stoutly of the opinion that these Marquesans were easily the best natives they had known in the South Seas. Ramsbottom preferred the gayer and more sophisticated Tahitians, while William hesitated between the two. But afterwards, whenever he began to think about the Marquesas, it was not any of the natives who troubled his memory, not even the grand old chief smiling above the monstrous ravages of his elephantiasis, nor the six girls who, at Peterson's request, performed for them the graceful sitting dance; nor was it the old French priest, who had also acquired this air of being one of a doomed race, or the learned and enthusiastic commissioner, or any other of the few public figures of the islands; it was his solitary fellow-countrymen there he remembered and once again he would be listening to the voice of Simon Hulberry. You could not possibly call Hulberry a Viking; he did not suggest in any way that great race mourned by Peterson and the Commander; yet ever afterwards he returned to William's memory as a figure oddly characteristic of the Marquesas.

The schooner was being loaded with copra; Ramsbottom and the Commander had wandered away together somewhere; and William was idling alone on the shore, at the edge of a grove of palms, now watching the boats, now turning away to stare at a hole in the rock through which the tide came roaring, to send up great sheets of spray. After half an hour or so of this pleasant idleness, he noticed that a rather unusual figure of a man was approaching him. When the fellow drew nearer, William saw that he was wearing a tattered khaki shirt and shorts, was immensely tall and thin, and had a good deal of thick black hair everywhere except on his face. He did not lounge up, as most white men did on the islands, but came across to where William was sitting with a sort of delicate deliberation. Once there he addressed William in excellent French, to which William made the best reply he could.

'Oh, but you're English of course,' said the stranger, speaking English. 'I beg your pardon. I don't exactly know why I should beg your pardon, but one always does when one mistakes an Englishman for a foreigner. I suppose our national ego demands it.' He spoke with precision, but with a certain high drawl and he exaggerated all his sibilants, and William, who had not heard these accents for a long time and certainly did not expect to hear them in this place, set him down at once as one of the more learned graduates of Oxford or Cambridge. He had heard such voices, elaborately condescending to him, over the wireless at home. But it was astonishing to hear such a voice on this extremely remote island. He stared with frank curiosity at the speaker, who had bushy brows, rather dim eyes, a long inquisitive nose, and a small, delicate and disappointed mouth.

'Yes, I'm English,' William told him. 'I've just come off that schooner there, the *Rose Marie* from Papeete.'

'Ah yes,' said the other, screwing up his eyes and staring rather disdainfully at the schooner, 'I believe she comes here once or twice a year. She's brought me one or two things, I think. By the way, you haven't such a thing as a

German dictionary with you, have you? If you have, I'd like to buy it from you. I want one rather badly.'

William could only soften the blow by offering this strange donnish person a cigarette, which he readily accepted, sitting down by William's side to smoke it. Then they exchanged names.

'Dursley?' said Hulberry, looking rather sadly at his excessively long, thin, hairy legs. 'I think there was a man called Dursley at New College in my time. I was at Balliol.'

William told him that this Dursley of New College was no relation. They talked easily for a quarter of an hour, mostly about Tahiti and the Marquesas, William having given the impression that he and his two friends were simply tourists trying to escape from the usual tourist routes. All that William gathered from Hulberry was that he had had a fellowship at Oxford, had lectured there and done some writing, and then, having inherited a little money, had given up everything and had come out here and bought a small plantation. This seemed to William a very odd thing for such a man to do, and he said so. 'Do you really like being buried away like this?' he asked.

'No, I don't enjoy it very much,' replied Hulberry, after carefully considering the question. 'The life here is very monotonous, though I don't think it is quite so stupid as life at home. But of course I didn't come here in search of romance or any nonsense of that kind, not being a writer of trash for the popular magazines. I came here to be quiet and to think, and I chose this place because it's so remote and the climate is reasonably healthy and pleasant. Naturally I don't want my thinking to be conditioned by some failure in my metabolism or anything of that kind. And I wanted to remove myself as far as possible from what we call Western civilisation without plunging myself into some other civilisation, such as that of the East or the new experimental one in Russia.'

'I see,' said William, who was not sure that he did, but had no desire to have his perplexities carefully disentangled by his companion. 'I suppose it's all right if you want to be quiet and away from everything disturbing. But I'm sure I couldn't be happy living here.'

'Where could you be happy?'

Where indeed? William had to think quickly. 'I don't know – perhaps nowhere, except at odd moments. But I think I shall be reasonably contented when I settle down again at home.'

Hulberry shook his head and screwed up his little mouth so that it almost disappeared. 'This seems to me an age of destruction,' he announced. 'The only people who can adequately express themselves in it are the people who wish to destroy. Look at what has been done in Russia. The destructive work was colossal and most thorough, and compared with it the more recent and constructive work there has been trivial. It is the same in Asia, especially in China. May I beg another cigarette? Thank you.' Having lit it, he let the smoke dribble out until it wreathed his head, then he stretched out his long thin body even more luxuriously, while William watched the white tropic-birds and the fairy terns skimming and flashing against the blue. 'Yes,' Hulberry continued comfortably, 'our industrialism is, of course, dying of over-production and the lack of big new markets to exploit. The rapid development of machinery is throwing the whole system out of gear, because while machinery produces goods in ever-greater quantities, it also throws more and more men out of employment and makes it impossible for those goods to be purchased. Unfortunately, machines consume so little.'

'Yes, I understand that argument,' said William.

'Some people,' said Hulberry, who was a lecturer rather than a conversationalist, 'imagine that communism or some form of socialism could settle this problem. A communist state could, of course, regulate production, and could save us from the idiocies of industrial America, where mass production is so artificial that it has to spend most of its time creating a demand for itself. But communism cannot save Western Europe. Russia provides no sound argument, simply because Russia was not living in this century at all, and it is playing with machinery like a child with a new toy. It may succeed finally, however, if it carries most of Asia with it, as I think it will, in destroying such civilisation as there remains in Western Europe. That, I think,' said Hulberry, speaking with cheerful precision, 'is more than likely. You will live to see it, Dursley, though how long you will live *after* you have seen it, I would not like to say.'

William felt like thanking him ironically. He did not trouble, however, being too busy entertaining a little vision of the ruined world, which vision was most oddly framed by the beautiful realities, the blue air and strong sunlight and the diamond sheets of spray, of the morning itself.

'Man has undoubtedly taken a wrong turning,' Hulberry continued complacently, 'and unfortunately he is travelling down it at a break-neck speed. My own problem is to discover, if I can, exactly when he took that turning. So far I have gone back to the eighteenth century, to the Middle ages, to the great Greek and Chinese civilisations, all of which, of course, are nothing but historical influences now. You appreciate the position. Every year there are more and more people in the world and we are all running in the same direction, although the wisest of us know that there is nothing for us there but disaster. But then something has gone wrong with man's consciousness.'

'Has it? What?' William demanded bluntly.

'He has eaten too greedily of the fruit from the Tree of Knowledge. He is trying to live without illusions. That is why he is so busy now, either savagely destroying things that may have taken centuries of effort to build up, or simply drugging himself. He wants to escape from the empty amphitheatre of his self-consciousness. His nature clamours for magic in a world that he has discovered to be non-magical. At first, of course, the discoveries themselves, whether they were chemical, physical, biological, psychological, or psychoanalytical, had a certain magical charm – I have noticed that all genuine research workers live in a kind of fairy tale, and that is why they are happier than other people – but that did not last long. To be thoroughly disillusioned tickles one's vanity for a time, as I myself have found, but that soon wears away. Civilised man has arrived at a period of complete and sterile self-consciousness. His relation to life is that of an elderly invalid, who has kept himself for years on a strict diet, to food. If he could immensely enlarge the scope and change the pattern of life, all might be well. But he can't. All the so-called enlargements and changes are trivial, of course, part of the mere mechanics of living. We can travel at colossal speeds, for example, and can communicate with one another over vast distances, but our reasons for travelling and the nature of our communications remain roughly the same. No, the scope and pattern of life cannot be altered, in spite of all this talk of conditioned reflexes, and our only hope, it appears, is to raise the level of consciousness, so that we do and do not know why we do, are the victims of illusion, and find ourselves back in a world filled with magic. And I do not see how that is to be done, my dear Dursley. Religion might do it, but you cannot invent a god. He must arrive like a thunderbolt. I don't think he will arrive. We're doomed to perish of self-knowledge. I anticipate an era of universal suicide. When people have no more institutions to destroy, they will begin to destroy themselves.'

'But look here,' said William desperately, 'you can't know all about yourself else you'd know why you felt so miserable knowing all about yourself. I mean, the part that feels miserable is still unknown. I don't believe we're completely self-conscious ever. And another thing. Perhaps the point is that all this self-knowledge you talk about just isn't true and is simply another illusion and a wretched one at that. I believe,' he declared sturdily, 'that we're stuffed with a lot of dubious half-knowledge; that's all. I've noticed that people who know an awful lot about anything – the people who really know more than anybody else – are not a bit depressed about it and are not just puffed up with conceit either, but think their particular subjects – whether it's the digestive system or the stars in the Milky Way – very grand and mysterious and exciting.'

'That is no argument at all, my dear fellow. By the way, might I have another cigarette? Thanks. No argument at all.'

'I know there's something wrong with a lot of us nowadays,' William continued earnestly, mopping his face. 'I know there is with me. Somehow our imagination tricks us into discontent. Perhaps we expect too much, want more than we're worth. I don't know. I shall have to think about it. But all the same – if you don't mind my saying so, Hulberry – I believe you're a bit of a humbug. You came out here and now you find, when somebody like me turns up and you want to talk, that the only way to make the best of being here and to be superior about it is to appear superhumanly detached and very pessimistic and grand. The fact is, there are all sorts of things happening in the world that people like you never notice. You think everything's going one way when actually it's changing direction. It's like these stories of the future in which everything that's happening now is simply carried to extremes. But things never happen like that.'

'I never said they did,' Hulberry pointed out, 'and I have no brief for authors of fantastic stories. But your point of view, Dursley, though it's naïve, of course, interests me. You're evidently a man of illusions. That's why you're here, I imagine. You're finding us all very romantic, aren't you?'

'I believe everybody's romantic, up to a point,' said William slowly. 'If they're not romantic about other people, they're romantic about themselves. You see yourself as a romantic figure just because you've come here from Balliol – probably throwing away a good career – and sit under these palm trees very grand and detached and philosophical—'

'You forget that I'm writing a book.'

'That doesn't make any difference. You could have written the book equally well, perhaps better, at home. You didn't really come here to write that book, Hulberry. You came here because you're wildly romantic about yourself, and as for being disillusioned, you're no more disillusioned than I am – less, in fact.'

They wrangled amiably about this for the next five minutes, and of course arrived nowhere.

'But honestly, Hulberry,' said William at last, 'do you really *like* being here?'

'No, I don't – not much. But I like it just as much as I

like being anywhere else. And that's not a gesture, it's the simple truth. If there were occasionally more people to talk to, I'd vastly prefer being here. As it is, I stay on quite cheerfully. I look like raising a family here, which is all wrong of course – but there you are. Yes, a very pretty, healthy, industrious, and quite charming native girl keeps house for me.'

'That's interesting. Tell me – are you fond of her?'

'I didn't think I would be, but actually I'm very fond of her. She's the only woman I ever remember being fond of – I never liked women much. She has plenty of intelligence but no intellect. She's never had an idea in her head; but then I've had far too many. And then most of the people I've known have had intellect but no intelligence, ideas but no *sense*, so she makes a pleasant change. Sometimes I almost recover my animal faith in existence. I think you said you hadn't a German dictionary?'

'No, sorry – I haven't. I wonder if there's anything I can give you.'

'I don't imagine so. Look here – you can stay here with me if you wish. I've enjoyed our talk. Stay here for a few months.'

'Sorry, but I can't. We're not here just looking round; we're on our way somewhere – on a species of treasure hunt.'

'That's foolish of you. It would be much more sensible to stay here and talk quietly for a few months. Your treasure wouldn't be much good when you found it, and then again, it's most unlikely that you will find it – nobody ever does. However, it's good for us who are both members of dying races – I count myself a Marquesan now, you know – to meet. I sometimes wonder which of us will be snuffed out first. Good-bye, Dursley.'

When the schooner was actually departing, a very tall thin figure suddenly appeared among the little crowd of waving shouting natives. 'Is that the English chap they said was here?' asked Ramsbottom, pointing.

William said it was and told them something about his talk with Hulberry.

'I hope he stays here,' cried the Commander indignantly. 'Detest that type of fellow. Ought to be allowed to prosecute a fellow for talking in that strain. Far too much of it at home now. Takes the heart out of people. I hope he stays here until he's got more faith in life.'

'But that's just what he *wants* to have,' William protested.

'Then why doesn't he get it?'

'Nay, Commander,' said Ramsbottom, 'that's easier said than done. And that's what you won't understand.'

'He shouldn't be slacking about here,' said the Commander sharply. 'He shouldn't be running away from life. He should go and do his duty. That's the trouble with all these young intellectuals – no duties, no sense of obligations. Do nothing but make other people as unsettled as themselves. I'd rather have any of these islanders – poor devils – than a fellow like that. And you're tarred a little with that brush, Dursley, if you don't mind my saying so.'

'I don't mind your saying so, Commander,' said William, staring at the grim majesty of the island which rose before them, in all its splendour of pointed glistening peaks and thick-folded robe of forest, as they drew away from its shore. 'I'm tarred with a good many brushes. You can say what you like. I'm so confused about myself I shan't contradict you.'

'You should stop thinking about yourself, lad. Ah did a long time since, and Ah've been a lot more cheerful ever since. Ah can quite surprise myself now and give myself a treat. Well, is this last o' these mad islands or have we a few more before we set off for our own wild goose?'

'Just one more, I believe,' replied the Commander. 'And then – we shape a course for Faraway.'

'That's if we don't come another bust-up. For God's sake, Commander,' said Ramsbottom earnestly, 'keep your eye on this chap, for if we've got to turn back again, Ah'm through with the job. Let's make no mistake this time, chaps.'

7

This time there was no mistake. Captain Peterson set a course for a point on the chart roughly indicated by latitude eleven degrees forty-seven minutes South and longitude one hundred and twelve degrees thirty-six minutes West, a course almost directly east from their last place of call. And now that they were on their way there, it seemed a formidably long distance to William. They were now literally launched into the blue. Notwithstanding his talk of the Vikings, Peterson did not show any great eagerness and enthusiasm for this voyage of discovery. His owners had accepted the charter, after consulting with him, and he had no sound reason for refusing it now, but there were times when he looked as if he would have given a good deal to have found that reason, in spite of the fact that he was being handsomely paid for the voyage. If they could have shown him the island on the chart or in the South Pacific Directory, he would not have been so dubious; but they could only tell him a deplorably vague story of an accidental discovery. His chief trouble was concerned with a supply of fresh water, for even on the ordinary voyages between the various groups of islands, these schooners often ran dangerously short of water, and now the *Rose Marie* was faced with fifteen hundred miles in which there was not one drop of fresh water to be found. They assured him, on the word of William's Uncle Baldwin, that Faraway itself had water on it, for Uncle Baldwin had been emphatic on that point. But unfortunately Captain Peterson had doubts of the very existence of the island. He knew dozens of stories about islands that were seen once, actually visited and explored, and never found again. The Commander himself, who knew some of these stories too, had to admit that his attitude was reasonable. Thus Peterson was confronted with the problem of carrying water for both the outward and return voyages, and he and the Commander spent hours, before they left the Marquesas, trying to settle this problem satisfactorily. They settled it finally by leaving behind three of the crew and part of the cargo of copra on the last island, to which they would have to return at once from Faraway; by taking aboard the largest possible supply of fresh water; and then by working out a scheme – over which the Commander smoked many a happy meditative pipe – of very severe rationing. If the three passengers had just arrived from England, they would have found this meagre rationing a real hardship, but by this time they were used to dwindling supplies of water on these schooners and had long regarded washes and shaves aboard ship as rare luxuries and not necessities.

Even then Captain Peterson, forgetting the Vikings, did not like this business. He insisted upon being paid for the charter – as he had a right to do – before setting out, and even drew up a long complicated document of his own for them to sign. Like Captain Prettel, he was convinced that they were in search of pirates' treasure, and as he did not even believe in the existence of the island itself, he was sure that they were wasting their money and his time. Now and then he would treat them as if they were queer invalids, giving them pitying glances and lowering his voice when he spoke to them. He was disappointing to William, who had imagined from the gigantic old fellow's talk that he would have welcomed this adventure and fairly charged into the unknown. Hang it all! – Ramsbottom, the retired wholesale grocer from Manchester, had more enterprise than this romantic-looking skipper of a South Sea schooner. He told the Commander so – for during these long empty days there was time to tell everybody everything that came into one's head – but the Commander, who had shown no sign of irritation when Peterson raised his various objections, did not agree. He understood and sympathised with the skipper's caution, which was natural, he declared, for the responsible master of a ship. Peterson, he pointed out, had to see them through, whereas Ramsbottom hardly knew yet what he was in for.

Actually, Ramsbottom began to express doubts himself about the existence of Faraway. 'These tales about islands that aren't there,' he admitted, as he and William watched the long smooth Pacific rollers go past, 'are getting me down a bit. There's far too many of 'em for my taste. Ah'm not saying your uncle didn't land on this island – Ah'm sure he did, from what you've told me – and anyhow there's that bit o' pitchblende to prove it – but whether we'll find it, there's another story. And this chap's not going to spend a lot o' time looking for it either, and you can't blame him.'

'I'm convinced it's there. From what my uncle said, it's a good solid lump of island, not at all the kind that's here to-day and gone to-morrow.'

'Well, we'd look soft if it had gone to-morrow. However, we're here and we'll have to chance it. Only Ah wish Ah could hear a few tales about islands that stay where they are – that would be a nice change. One thing is – we're having good weather. It's a shame this weather isn't rationed out a bit better, for Ah'll bet they could be doing with it badly at home, while Ah'd give a pound or two just for a bit o' snow or a good shower of 'ail.'

'We're making very good speed,' said William. 'But there's an awful lot of this Pacific, isn't there? I seem to have spent months and months now, just looking at it, all empty like this.'

'Ah never thought there was so much water in the world,' cried Ramsbottom. 'Nay, it's practically all water. You can see than when you take a look at a map, but you never believe it. But Ah believe it now all right. And Ah used to wonder why sailors carried on the way they do once they get ashore, but now Ah know. Fact is, they're right surprised with themselves to find they *are* on shore and that there is a shore to be on. It's worth getting drunk for, that is.'

They would ramble on like this for hours, but at other times they would watch half a day go by almost without speaking a word. William would find himself sinking into a vegetable mode of life; he would sit staring at the sea until at last he seemed to exist only in a dim dreamy world of shifting foam, with no more consciousness of what was outside it than a piece of floating seaweed; he would look at a distant faint haze of cloud until he was no more than a bubble rising and falling above the water and was at last lost in blue air and drowned in sleep. But then there were hours when he would lead a vivid dramatic life inside himself, when sharp-pointed memories of people and places, of Terry and Uncle Baldwin and

Margery, of San Francisco and Lugmouth and the upper deck of the *Marukai*, would start up to trouble him. He would go back and back into the past, feel again the sting of a cold morning on his cheeks as he ran from Ivy Lodge to the Grammar School, catch the smell of the cut grass in the old cricket field down by the river, wander into a rich dark Christmas of thirty years ago, find himself drowsing by his mother's side in some cavernous railway carriage of the remotest ages, go running and prattling among huge smiling ghosts. In the middle of this vacancy of sea and sky, a vague grey on one side and a deepening blue on the other, he would sit musing over this bright pitiful little epic, his life, in which he could find neither meaning nor even the hint of any pattern. It seemed to him that he had always been hurrying through the present to dive into the glorious future; he had always been like a man flicking over the pages of a book to reach some great passage; and even now, though he could look back upon his immediate past, the voyage from San Francisco to Tahiti and the first days on the island, and find that he had really lived and not waited for life to begin, he was still hurriedly consuming the days, rushing through the mere prelude again, until the moment arrived for the curtain to rise. Now, when that curtain did rise, it would show him Faraway Island. Life began again with Faraway.

It arrived when they were having lunch, which had long ago declined into a tasteless mess of tinned stuff, for which none of them, except Peterson, had any appetite. They charged up from the saloon to see a faint thickening upon the eastern horizon, over which the afternoon haze was settling. There was no mistake, however; and into the vast saucer of ocean there crept, a little uncertainly like a short-sighted beetle, a lump of rock. The glasses showed them an unmistakable island, small but massive, with jagged edges.

'That's it, you fellows,' cried the Commander, his face alight. 'That's it, Cap'n Peterson. You see, we were right after all.'

'Yes, that must be your island,' said Peterson, staring so hard at it that he looked as if he were ordering it not to disappear. 'To me it loogs just a rog. But maybe you only want a rog. Let hus hobe there is good water there, eh? And to-morrow if there is a place to land, then you land on it.'

'Not to-day?' said William, who couldn't wait.

Peterson shook his head, and explained that he would have to move very cautiously once they got near the island. All these waters were uncharted; there might be reefs; and the *Rose Marie* would have to creep up to the island, and only do that in daylight. To this the Commander instantly agreed. It was dangerous work approaching unknown islands. In one minute the schooner could easily be ripped open and sent to the bottom before they knew where they were. At sunset the island was only a few miles away, and they had a good view of it. Uncle Baldwin's description of it could not be quarrelled with: it was nothing more nor less than a huge lump of rock sticking out of the water to a height, at its highest visible point, which was almost in the centre, of several thousand feet. There appeared to be some vegetation on the lower slopes, but it was very sparse. It was anything but a pretty island. Even when its upper walls of smooth rock caught a reflected glow from the huge orange glare above the western horizon, it still looked desolate, savage, incredibly remote from humanity. But it was Faraway, the treasure house that had brought them across the world. The three adventurers stared at it, talking excitedly all the time, convinced now that Uncle Baldwin's story had been true in every detail. The schooner was riding at anchor, and it was not long before the island faded from their sight. Then, and not until then, they went below to join Peterson, who in honour of the occasion had opened his last bottle of liquor. They toasted him in it, and found that they had never tasted liquor so rare and potent.

CHAPTER X

FARAWAY FOUND AND LOST

1

THEY STOOD on Faraway Island. Three human arrows, shot from Buntingham and Lugmouth half round the globe, had at last found their target. It was a great moment, and if they had been children of an age that could adequately express itself in great moments, they would have embraced one another. As it was, they merely stared at one another and grinned. Here they were, they said idiotically.

There had been quite an exciting little journey, over roughish water, from the schooner, which Peterson was keeping far out, to this small sandy cove. The boat did not stay, but immediately returned to the schooner. Evidently Peterson meant to send his water party ashore later. Some obscure feeling made all three of them turn to watch the boat depart.

'I think,' said the Commander slowly, looking at the horizon, 'there's some dirty weather blowing up. We may miss it. Then again, we may not.'

The other two could see no signs of dirty weather, though this was not one of the usual brilliant blue mornings. It was very hot; the coarse black-and-grey sand beneath their feet was quite warm already; and the heat was bouncing off the sharp slopes of rock above. But it was not a clear morning; there was a thin haze over everything, and this haze dimmed such colour as there was on the island. Out at sea there was a sulky restlessness. The sky was neither cloud nor blue distance, but a pricking hollow of blended light and heat, which the eye met with reluctance. Faraway itself was quietly baking.

'Well,' said Ramsbottom, 'we're here. And the question now is – are we making a right start?'

'I'm certain this is where Dursley's uncle landed,' said the Commander. 'It's the obvious place. There doesn't seem to be any other on this side of the island.'

They consulted the rough plan, a few thick pencil scrawls, that Uncle Baldwin had given William, and while they were looking at it and talking, William found himself visited by a most vivid memory of his uncle. Only half of him was there on that tiny patch of sand in the middle of the Pacific; the other half was back in the study or the bedroom at Ivy Lodge, seeing his uncle arrive again, the raindrops still glistening on his ulster, or watching the old man in bed, purple and bulging-eyed, fighting for breath. And here they were on Faraway. Where was Uncle Baldwin?

'That's what's so strange,' said William, involuntarily speaking aloud.

They stared at him. 'It seems pretty plain to me, Dursley,' said the Commander. 'What's the difficulty?'

'I don't mean the plan,' said William. 'I was thinking about my uncle. Where is he? It's so ridiculous that we don't know. Think of it. We can find our way from England here. We know the weight of the sun, the size of distant stars, and for all I know – or care – the size and shape of the whole universe. We know all that, but yet we don't know what's become of my Uncle Baldwin. We don't know if he's just nothing or if he's carrying on somewhere else.'

'We do,' said the Commander. 'Or, at least, if you're a Christian you do.'

'Nay, you don't, Commander,' said Ramsbottom. 'Ah attended our Congregational Chapel for twenty year, and they never let on to me. But if you want to know what Ah think, Ah'll tell you. Ah believe your uncle's nowhere – snuffed out – finished. Where was he a hundred years since? Well, he's back in the same place. Nowhere.'

'But it's so ridiculous that we don't *know*,' William told them, his voice rising in indignation. 'What's the good of knowing all the nonsense we do know, when we don't know that? I tell you, it's monstrous. Sorry to drag this in, but I couldn't help thinking about my uncle—'

'Quite right,' said the Commander approvingly. He would have thought less of William if William had not remembered his uncle at this moment. The Commander was a man with a passionate sense of obligations. It was William's uncle who had discovered this island for them, and he ought to be remembered now.

'And I want to know where he is,' William continued, frowning in exasperation. 'It's maddening, this ignorance. I'm prepared to face it reasonably cheerfully – I mean the prospect of being snuffed out, as you call it, or the prospect of going on in some queer dim way – but I do think there might be some chance of knowing which it is. They can tell you how long the light takes to travel from Sirius, but nobody knows what's become of your father and mother.'

'If you turn spiritualist, lad, they'll soon tell you,' said Ramsbottom, grinning. 'Ah once went and they turned my father on for me and he said he was very happy where he was and life was very beautiful. And so Ah said, "Well, whoever that is, it's not my father – unless he's gone daft. If he's anything like what he used to be, he'd be hanged, drawn and quartered before he'd talk like that. And," Ah, said, "if he's not anything like what he used to be, then he's not my father." That settled 'em. Ah was never asked again, though if Ah had been, Ah wouldn't have gone. But we'd better be making a move.'

'We had.' The Commander, narrowing his eyes, looked at the plan and then looked up at what could be seen of the island. He pointed to a possible route from the cove. 'If we get to the top of that ledge, we ought to be able to see where we're going then.'

Ramsbottom made a dubious sort of noise, something between a sniff and a snort. 'Who's going to work on this job when we get started? It looks to me as if we'll have to take on a lot o' trained goats.'

'Oh, the natives from any of the mountainous islands wouldn't think anything of this,' said the Commander. 'We can work all that out later.'

'By jingo, it's hot,' said Ramsbottom, wiping his large face. 'Minute you get on land 'eat falls on you like a ton o' bricks. Well, who's carrying what? Don't forget that old Johnny Ramsbottom's got himself to carry, and that means about four stone more than either o' you.'

They divided up their load, which consisted of enough food and water for the day and a few small instruments, including an electroscope like that which William had seen at the Radium Institute. They had all agreed that it would be lunacy to make any definite plans about the island without making a thorough test of the black ore they might find on it. There was a fairly stiff little climb out of the cove, but at the end of it they found themselves on a broad ledge of rock, where they had an extensive view of the island, which went back in a series of irregular ridges.

'What a place!' cried William, when they halted.

'Ay, Ah wouldn't call this a beauty spot,' said Ramsbottom grimly. 'They won't have to complain of Bank Holiday litter here for a good long while.'

'It reminds me a bit of some of the coast of Arabia,' said the Commander. 'Colour's quite different, but it has the same barren desolate look.'

'Well, Ah've never seen the coast of Arabia,' said Ramsbottom, 'but if it's anything like this, you can have it. This fairly frightens me, Ah can tell you. It looks like the last place God ever made – that is, if He'd anything to do with it.'

There was certainly nothing very charming and hospitable about Faraway. It was, as Uncle Baldwin had said, simply a vast rock. It was not entirely without vegetation, but such vegetation as there was only added to the arid desolation of the place, for it appeared to be composed, most inhospitably, of cactus, thorny shrubs, and a few stunted and twisted trees, themselves as much like rock as it is possible for living things to be. In brilliant sunshine there might have been a play of colour along the various surfaces of stone, but now, in this grey unpleasant light, there was hardly anything to catch the eye. A few birds, probably finches, moved here and there, only throwing into relief the grim repose of the interior. The island looked indeed what it probably was, a remote peak of some incredibly antique world, whose every grace had long been submerged in the depth of the ocean. The three who stared at it knew only too well how far it was from anywhere, but now it looked infinitely further still; the known world had rushed away to the very edge of oblivion; even the schooner, their one link, chanced to be hidden from them at the moment; and there was nothing but these spiny and thorny growths, the mounting wilderness of rock, and a dim half-ring of sea that seemed to dissolve into stellar space itself.

'We might almost be on the moon,' said William, staring, fascinated by this savage remoteness.

Ramsbottom shook his head. 'Nothing in my line, this,' he observed, as if he had suddenly been offered the island as a job lot. 'Ah like a place to look a bit 'omely. If we do find this stuff and can get some human goats to cart it away – well and good. But if it's all a take-in, you two's going to hear something from me, bringing me to this island. It's like a slag heap that's been shoved into an oven. And where do we go now? Ah'm going to sit down while you chaps puzzle it out.'

The chaps did puzzle it out and decided to strike up to the right, where there was a gully comparatively free from boulders and prickly shrubs. But even here it was bad-going. The way was rough, over very hard and sometimes slippery rock; it was often steep; the heat of the morning increased; and all three of them, after so many idle days at sea, were distressingly out of condition. First their feet began to ache, then their legs and backs, until very soon they seemed to ache all over. Ramsbottom was in the most pitiable plight. After they had been going half an hour, he could no longer be considered a solid body, being almost dissolved in sweat. He complained that he could not see, for his face dripped perspiration and it made his spectacles useless. He staggered on behind his two lighter companions, groaning and cursing, and at one time they lost him altogether and had to go back to look for him. Soon after this they called a proper halt. They were now close to what seemed to be the main ledge of rock, several hundred feet above the sea and about a mile inland.

For a few minutes they said nothing, they were too hot,

breathless, tired. William's feet felt like raw pulp, and he found that his legs were bleeding a little from the long thorns. He pulled about a couple of dozen thorns out of his trouser legs. Ramsbottom was still busy mopping himself and groaning, while the Commander, who looked rather drawn, compressed his lips and gingerly touched or rubbed his aching limbs. When they had cooled off, the Commander, who was in charge of this department, allowed them to sip some water.

'Well,' Ramsbottom groaned, 'Ah call this a hell of a job. It's fair murder. Nay, nay, if Ah'd known what we were in for, you chaps could have done this part on your own. Ah'd have taken your word for it, whatever you'd found. 'Ere,' and he looked indignantly at William, 'did your uncle say anything about all this? How did he get here?'

'No, he simply said he came ashore to explore the island and then happened to come across the pitch-blende.'

Ramsbottom blew out his breath. 'Just came ashore for a bit of a stroll before dinner, eh? Just to stretch his legs, eh? What was this uncle o' yours? A mountain goat? Was this his idea of a bit o' fun? Nay, it beats me how a chap could get as far as this if he wasn't looking for something.'

'Not at all,' said the Commander. 'It's rough-going, but I've wandered about in places rougher than this, Ramsbottom, just out of curiosity, like Dursley's uncle. It's not so bad really. We're not in training, that's the trouble. You and I are old crocks, and Dursley here has just been ill. What can you expect?'

'Ah can tell you what Ah expect. Ah expect to set eyes on something that has the making of a fortune in it, and it's least a chap could expect after this lot.'

'Well, let's push on and see.'

'Oh dear! Oh dear! Now Ah've got down, Ah can't get up.'

'Would you like to stay here while Dursley and I go on?'

'Not me. Nay, Ah've come so far, Ah might as well be one of the proper exploring party and have done with it. Give me a hand, lad. That's better.'

'If it's there at all—'

'Ay, and that's a fair question. If we've been had on, Ah'll go straight back to England and find every relation Dursley's got and call 'em names.'

'You're welcome to,' William told him.

'Well, if it's there at all, it shouldn't be far now,' said the Commander, and moved on.

He was right. They were on the summit of the ridge shortly afterwards, and then they found themselves on a fairly smooth broad ledge, partly covered with a small shrub that had thick leathery leaves. Behind it was what looked like an irregular wall of rock, about a hundred feet high, going back in most places at an angle of about forty-five degrees to the continued base-line of the ledge.

'That's it,' shouted the Commander triumphantly.

They made straight for it, slipping a little among the leathery leaves, at what might be described as a quick hobble. It looked as if part of a hillside had been sheared away with a sharp knife. All the lower part of this cliff, as far as they could see to left or right, seemed to be composed of a seam, from ten to twenty feet thick, of black stuff.

William pointed to it. 'Pitchblende.'

'Must be. Looks just like the piece you have.'

They were there now. They could lean against the stuff, and promptly did lean against it, to take breath.

'First thing to do is to test it.'

'Break some off. You've got the hammer, haven't you?'

William brought out his electroscope and had charged it before the Commander had a piece ready for him. But the electroscope, having a whole wall of pitchblende in front of it, did not wait for any single specimen: if it could have burst, no doubt it would have done: its behaviour announced very plainly that here was pitchblende in God's plenty. Later, they tested several specimens in the usual manner, but this was a mere formality now. This was a seam of pitchblende. There was no flicker of doubt about it. The question now was how much there was of it. Leaving Ramsbottom with their belongings, William went off to the left and the Commander to the right, to discover how far the seam extended. The Commander was back first, for on his side the pitchblende disappeared after about two hundred yards. There was at least a quarter of a mile of it on William's side.

'That's grand,' cried Ramsbottom, who was now himself again. 'And then we don't know how thick it is.'

'It may not be any thickness at all – I mean only a few feet.'

'It can't be less than that, and it's just as likely to be a lot more. And – bless my soul! – if it's only five foot thick, you've got thousands and thousands and thousands o' tons here. Ah don't know how this stoof goes to the ton—'

'Fairly heavy, I should say.'

'Well, you can work it out for yourself. There's at least two thousand feet of it this way, isn't there? It'll average ten foot high, won't it? And we'll say it's only five foot thick. Well, that gives you a hundred thousand cubic feet o' the stoof, right off. And that might just as easily be two hundred thousand or three or four or a million. Lads, old uncle has turned up trumps. We're made men. Let's get comfortable, if we can, and have a bite o' something. We've earned it.'

2

A short distance from the pitchblende there was a great boulder, and in its shadow they ate their tinned meat, beans, fruit and chocolate, and washed them down with the tepid water they carried. All the time they talked eagerly, beginning soberly enough with a discussion of ways and means of getting the ore out and then removing it, and of the probable cost of labour (including the maintenance of the men, for every scrap of food would have to be brought to the island, and possibly water too), and transport. But soon it was as if that fantastic and almost everlasting radiation buried somewhere in the heart of this great black mass began to have its effect upon them, just as it did upon that tiny telltale wisp of gold-leaf in the electroscope. At last they knew the intoxication of victory. They had converted a wild legend into reality. They had flung themselves across the world and hit the centre of the target. Bells rang and flags were waved. With this intoxication of the mind there came also that languorous intoxication of the body that follows, after rest and refreshment, any physical ordeal, the test of effort, sweat and pain. An hour or two ago they had been pitiful little toiling creatures, victims of the sharp or slippery rock and the thorns and spikes, less than men, the clumsiest sort of insect. Now they were more than men; they were gods, sprawling there in the shade. Their remoteness from the world was itself godlike now; they possessed a secret that was like some gift of magic; power was theirs. So, as they talked all the difficulties vanished, as easily as a creditor's figures from a sponged slate; what remained to be done appeared the simplest routine; and more and more they ignored it, to concentrate upon other and godlike matters, blossom and fruit of this great hour. As they raised their voices, to catch and express the triumph at higher and higher levels, they opened their hearts and minds. Intoxicated as they were, they were now more themselves than they had ever been before together. High above their heads a wind came shrieking, snatching and riving at the hillside, and the sky was like an old bronze plate, but even the Commander did not bother his head about such trifles. They talked like three beings who had just made a planet and were wondering what to do with it. By this time, the pitchblende at their command had past the millionth ton, and ounce after ounce of radium, far more than the world had ever known before, was being plucked out of it. The question was, What should be done with it?

A few words from them, and what a commotion there would be, down there, in the world of ordinary folk! What a fury of wirelessing and telegraphing and typewriting and printing and telephoning! That would be amusing, but not so good as this hour to themselves, when they were alone with the grand secret. Now was the time to talk of what they could do and would do. Gifts of Arabian genii were in their hands. How and where should they bestow them? That was the question to be debated, and each man spoke for once out of his heart, for the intoxication of the hour was such that it swept away all thoughts that might clog and confine and left the mind free to rise and soar.

Ramsbottom had no doubts. 'Now, chaps,' he cried, 'let's have no silly nonsense about this business. This stoof's worth a fortune, and we're going to see we make a fortune out of it. We take it to the best market, and we sell it for as much as it'll fetch. We took the chance, and we've got to damn well see we get the benefit of it. If we don't, somebody who's done nothing but sit on his behind in a big chair while we've been on this job, he'll get the benefit of it, and we'll be the mugs. Ah know, chaps. You can't tell me anything about this world.'

The Commander had other views. 'I've thought about this a good deal, you fellows, but I didn't want to say anything until we'd made certain the pitchblende was all right. Look here, I don't want to make a patriotic speech. Not my style at all. But we're all three of us Englishmen. You can't get away from the fact that we owe a duty to our country. And it's our duty to see that England gets this stuff.'

'You're forgetting Miss Riley, anyhow,' Ramsbottom reminded him drily. 'She's got a share in it, and she's not English.'

'She could be bought out,' replied the Commander shortly. 'What do you say, Dursley?'

William thought for a moment. 'I don't agree with either of you. Of course, we've got to be reasonably paid for our risk and time and trouble—'

They hastened to agree.

'—But then, I think it ought to be put at the disposal of everybody. Yes, we'll give it to the whole world. We're Englishmen, yes, but we're men, plain human beings, creatures of this planet, first of all, and we ought to act on that basis and only on that basis. Don't you agree, Ramsbottom?'

'Not me. Ah think you're both talking like a couple o' school kids. Now listen to me a minute or two. Ah'm older than you, Dursley, and though Ah'm not older than you, Commander, Ah know a lot more about things

than you do – and Ah'll tell you for why – 'cos you've
spent your life in the service, with your board and lodging
and pay guaranteed by the government – and you just
might as well have been at school for all you could learn
about real things. You've got to scrap about for a living,
to go down into the market-place to find out how much
you're worth, before you really begin to learn. And Ah
don't fancy you've done so much of that, Dursley. All
right then. Now don't take offence, either of you. What
Ah'm telling you is for your own good. Now listen, you
both of you are feeling grand and noble; Ah can see it in
your faces. Well, when we've got the biggest price we can
get for this stoof, and you've got your share and Ah've
got mine, there's nothing to stop you giving away every
penny. But first we're going to look after Number One.
If we don't nobody else will. You say, Commander, you
want England to have this pitchblende or radium. You'd
make the government a present of most of it, like. What
for? Do you think they'd thank you for it? Did you ever
know a government or a country grateful to people like
you and me? No, and you never will. Suppose we'd gone
to 'em and told 'em what were after, how much help do
you think we'd have got – from the British Government
or any government or the League of Nations? You know
as well as Ah do, they'd have laughed in our faces. Suppose we get in a mess, as it is, do you think they're going
to help us out? Not they. Look after yourself first, Ah say.
If they want this stoof, let 'em pay for it, and pay good
and hard – they've always money to throw away on other
things. If you ask me, people get too much already for
nothing, these days, and what they get for nothing they
don't value. Let 'em pay. They won't think any better of
you for handing it all to 'em on a tray. It's a mistake lots
o' chaps, inventors and suchlike, have made is that. They

don't look after Number One, and then before they've finished, they find folk saying, "Look, there's that silly old devil coming again. Always talking about what he might have made if he'd wanted. You can't believe a word he says." That's what you get for giving 'em something. Ah don't believe in England and humanity and all that stoof. Ah believe in Johnny Ramsbottom and you two and my friends wherever they are, and them's the folk Ah'm going to look after. If we don't, nobody else will. Don't run away with the idea Ah'm a mean grasping sort o' chap, 'cos Ah'm not. But Ah want my own first, and then Ah can do what Ah like with it. And if we've a bit o' sense in our heads, we'll do nothing silly with this stoof. We'll sell to the highest bidder right to the last ounce.'

'But that might mean it would all go to some foreign country – perhaps Russia,' the Commander objected.

'Then let it go. More shame to England they couldn't raise the money,' said Ramsbottom. 'Ah tell you, you get nowhere by being sentimental on a job like this. Be sentimental afterwards, Ah say, when you're sitting on your pile, and you've got some good stoof inside you. Make certain o' that first, and then you can buy and give away as many Union Jacks as you like, lad. This is a trading job like any other, and it's up to us to find the best market.'

'I don't agree,' said the Commander warmly. 'I don't blame you for having it, Ramsbottom, but I must say I don't like your point of view. We're not shopkeepers and snivelling little hucksters, trying to sell twopenn'orth of nails for threepence. This is too big for that. This is an extraordinary, a wonderful discovery, and it's our duty to put it at the disposal of our own country. If England wants this – and we know she does – then England's got to have it. You talk, Ramsbottom, as if you were born nowhere, just as you, Dursley, talk as if you were born anywhere or everywhere. If all three of us belonged to different countries, I couldn't talk like this – but we don't. We're English. And let me tell you this, if Englishmen, our fellow-countrymen, hadn't gone on for centuries putting themselves and their discoveries at the service of their country, the three of us here wouldn't be the fellows we are now. We might not have been able to get here at all. If Dursley's uncle hadn't gone back to his own country at last, we'd never have heard of this island. I'm here because Dursley's uncle considered I did him a service. But I really did it because he was a fellow-countryman, that's all. There isn't one of us who wants to live anywhere but in England. We've taken all she's given us, with both hands – and – by heaven, gentlemen – now that we've a chance of paying her back, by giving her a monopoly of this stuff, we've got to leap at it. It ought to be our pleasure; but whether it's our pleasure or not, it's certainly our duty. I'd be ashamed of myself if I went to market with something as big and valuable as this and put it up for auction. I'd feel a common cheapjack. Ramsbottom seems to think that we owe a duty to nobody but ourselves, but if he found himself in a tight corner he'd soon discover that he thought his country owed a duty to him. Well, you owe one to her. You, Dursley, seem to think we owe a duty to everybody, just because we've all got two legs and can talk. I don't understand that. A duty to everybody is a duty to nobody, it seems to me. If you don't see the difference between what you owe the people in your own country and what you owe, if you owe anything, the Russians or Spaniards or Chinese, then I can't begin to talk to you. To me it's plain enough. This international talk is all twaddle. Fellows who talk about loving all the world are simply fellows who don't love anything, except their own conceit of themselves. A man who says he has an obligation that extends from here to Greenland is only a man who doesn't intend to acknowledge any real obligations at all. He's dodging, that's all. He doesn't intend to put himself out for anybody. Sorry, Dursley – I'm not getting at you, of course – but I don't think you realise where this easy talk leads you. As for you, Ramsbottom, you're only pretending to be cynical, to show you're a man of the world and we're not. You don't mean it.'

'Never more serious in my life,' declared Ramsbottom.

'Actually, as you must know, it's our duty to claim this island for the British Empire. And it's equally our duty to reserve this pitchblende – or the radium, if we should turn it into radium – for our own country and countrymen. Either we love our country or we don't. Do you?'

'Ah do that.'

'So do I,' replied William promptly.

'Then for God's sake,' shouted the Commander, who by this time had worked himself up into a fine state of excitement, 'do something for her for once in your lives.'

'Rer-hule, Bree-tan-ya,' sang Ramsbottom, 'Bree-tan-ya rer-hules the waves—'

'That'll do, Ramsbottom,' said the Commander sharply. 'It's not funny.'

'All right. Anything to oblige.' Ramsbottom winked at William. 'It's your turn next, lad. Stand up and say your piece.'

'No fear.' Actually, however, William did begin talking, and he had not been on long before he did stand up. 'I don't agree with either of you,' he told them earnestly. 'This seems to me our great chance – the only one we shall ever have – to do something for the whole world. I'm for offering the whole lot to an international trust, controlled by the League of Nations. We'll have to be compensated, of course, for our outlay and time and trouble, but that could easily be assessed. I'm dead against selling it to the highest bidder. If this stuff is valuable to humanity, then you can't let a gang of financial brigands corner it and then make monstrous profits out of people's suffering. That's what it amounts to – and it's foul. It's just as if you went running for a doctor and he sat there, deciding how urgent it was and then putting up his fee accordingly.'

'Well, Ah've known 'em do that before to-day.'

'Yes, and the fact that it sticks in your mind, as a damned contemptible exception, shows that it isn't what you expect from a doctor. I like money as much as you do, Ramsbottom, and I certainly insist on our being decently paid for what we've done, but we can't run this on a purely financial basis. It's too big. It's too important.'

'I agree,' said the Commander. 'Come, you must see that, Ramsbottom.'

'No, Ah don't, and Ah've told you for why. Ah say – get your money first, and then start being noble philanthropists and benefactors o' the human race afterwards. As Ah told you – there's nothing to stop you giving away all you get.'

'But then we've lost our chance and the mischief's been done,' cried William, jumping to his feet. 'We're dropping back into the same old dirty dreary track. It would be a rotten end to a fine adventure. I do that sort of thing in my office, but I came here to do something a damned sight better. Circumstances have been generous with us. We've got to be generous now. We might make fools of ourselves? All right, let's take the chance. That's the only way we can make any progress at all, by risking making fools of ourselves. When we decided to come here in the first place, to look for the island, we were risking making fools of ourselves. But, mind you, I don't agree with you, Commander. If this is too big a thing to be just an affair of buying and selling, it's too big a thing too to be restricted to one nation. That's where we've got to use our imaginations. Cancer doesn't know anything about nationalities, and if they want radium to defeat cancer, then radium hasn't got to know anything about nationalities either. It's not a matter of Englishmen and Frenchmen, Englishwomen and Italian women, with a thing like this; it's a matter of men and women, plain men and women – and damn the writing on their passports. This discovery of ours is going to help science, and science is international – thank God! And another thing. Every time you ignore national boundaries – yes, you can grin, Ramsbottom; no doubt I'm ranting on like some political tub-thumper; but I don't care – here's something I believe – there isn't much I can believe in nowadays, but I believe in this – and I say, every time you ignore national boundaries, you bring the possibility of a sane, happy, peaceful world a bit nearer. We know now what happens if you let the national nonsense have its head. The war showed us that. Half the world wrecked, millions of men slaughtered, and now nobody knows what the devil it was about. I'm an Englishman and I love England, just as you do, Commander. I owe a lot to England. But I owe still more to the world. I'm all for English people being English, and French people being French, and Chinese being Chinese. I loathe cosmopolitan people, who haven't any roots anywhere. But all that's just fun – if you see what I mean. It has to do with the sort of hats you wear and the sort of puddings you eat and the kind of beds you sleep in. There are some things too big and too serious to be national. They belong to mankind itself. All the things that are really important don't acknowledge any sort of frontiers. If we hand this over to an international trust, operated by the League of Nations or some international organisation of scientists, then there's one more thing that the nations have in common, and one more reason for not playing the military fool. You say, Commander, let's do something for England for once. But I say, for God's sake let's do something for civilisation for once. We've got a great chance. Let's take it. Let's go back and show them something. Let's make a grand gesture, even if it lands us in the workhouse. What do you say?'

'Rats,' replied Ramsbottom.

'And I say that I still don't agree,' said the Commander.

William looked at them in silence. The only sound now was the shrieking of the wind above their heads, and there was in it a disturbing suggestion of irony. They had disagreed; they had talked; they still disagreed; and the wind blew. That was that. William had not yet recovered from the emotional strain of those last days in Tahiti and the illness that followed them, and the exertions of the morning had taken a good deal out of him, so that now, having worked himself up to a tremendous state of excitement, he could easily have broken down and wept. But he didn't. Suddenly, to the astonishment of the other two, he burst out laughing. The tears that had been waiting for him to break down saw their chance, and went rolling down his cheeks.

'What the devil's the matter, Dursley?' said the Commander.

'I don't know,' cried William. But it was some time before he could stop laughing.

3

'Look here,' said the Commander, 'we must get back to the schooner at once. We've been here too long. It's blowing up. Come on, you fellows, we've got to hurry.'

When they left their little sheltered place, between the great boulder and the wall of rock, they found that the wind was far more violent than they had imagined it to be. It cooled the air, so that movement was not so unpleasant as it had been during the heat of the morning. Moreover, they were rested and had less to carry, and knew where they were going, with the result that the return journey was fairly easy. They went in silence, for the high wind made talking difficult, and anyhow for the time being they had said their say. Each retreated into the still impregnable fortress of his opinion. The shared triumph of the discovery had united them for a time as they had never been united before, but the subsequent difference of opinion had shattered that triumphant trinity and now, though not out of temper with one another, they were essentially three separate individuals, soberly dodging the thorns and spikes and sharp edges of rock, and bending before the wind. It was not until they were halfway down the gully between the two ledges that the Commander halted and began to examine the wide stretch of sea before them. The shore itself was hidden behind the ledge of rock below.

They all stopped. 'What's up, Commander?' asked Ramsbottom.

'I'm looking for the schooner,' replied the Commander. 'She was anchored out there before, in a line with that knob of rock there. She's not there now. I can't see her. Can you, Dursley?'

William couldn't. In that high wind it was not easy to

stare out to sea, and the sea itself seemed to be very unsettled, with a good deal of spray blowing about; but William had to confess that there was no sign of the schooner.

'Well, perhaps he's come further in, down here,' said Ramsbottom, pointing in the direction of the hidden shore.

The Commander shook his head. 'Peterson wouldn't do that, even if he could find deep water. If it was too risky early this morning, it would be riskier than ever now. There's a big sea running, I fancy, though it's hard to tell from here. What's more likely is that he's been compelled to raise anchor and run for the open. He was very nervous about being close in, and you can't blame him.'

They reached the ledge, crossed it, and found a good viewpoint from which they could see the shore. The schooner had certainly vanished. And a very big sea was running. Gigantic breakers were rolling up and smashing themselves against the rocks, over which vast sheets of spray went flying. Further out, it looked very ugly. The water was a dull green and very tumultuous. The horizon had disappeared. This was the Pacific in one of its rare moods of wrath and destruction. Now it added a thundering bass to the shrill treble of the wind. Both wind and water appeared to have taken a dislike to Faraway Island.

'That's what he's done,' the Commander shouted. 'He's pulled up and run for the open.'

'And what about us?'

'It's unfortunate, but we'll have to wait, that's all. You can't expect him to wreck his schooner for us.'

'Here,' cried Ramsbottom indignantly, 'what's going to happen to us, that's what Ah want to know? Ah've just realised what's on here. Nay, we sit up there, talking so grand about what we'll do with this stoof, and arguing about who's going to have it, and all the time we've been left on a rock two thousand miles from anywhere. Why – damn it! – we could pine to death in a few days here.'

'He may have left us something,' said the Commander, who seemed to be quite cool.

'Ah should hope so. It never struck me before, but this here's a right death-trap. What a place to be left in! There's nothing here but a drop o' slimy water and some prickles. We'll look well if we're left with a hillside full o' pitchblende, a chance of a fortune, and nothing else. If he never came back for us nobody'd be any the wiser. Who's to know we're here. Honestly, chaps,' he added, in genuine agitation, 'Ah, don't like the look o' this at all, Ah don't. Marooned, that's what we are, and we've gone and picked out the worst island we could find for it. There isn't enough stoof here to keep a couple of rabbits alive.'

'We'll hurry down to the cove where we landed,' said the Commander, preparing to move.

There was not much of that little patch of sand to be seen now. The tide was pounding away, high up the beach, and the air was filled with driven foam. At each side of the cove the cliffs seemed to be shivering under the impact of the rushing mounds of water. Once down there they realised what an ugly sea it was. It had a murderous movement and sound; it was bent on destroying them.

'What's that?' cried William, pointing.

'Probably supplies,' said the Commander; and they hurried across to a flat-topped rock, at the head of the cove, well out of the tide's reach. There they found a small cask of water, some tins of meat and biscuit, and a note from Captain Peterson, who informed them apologetically that he had been compelled by the gathering storm to run for the open, for fear the schooner should be blown ashore, and had no time to find them and summon them back. He would return as soon as he could.

'That's all right then,' said the Commander cheerfully. 'We shan't starve, Ramsbottom, with all this good stoof. This storm ought to blow itself out to-night, and Peterson ought to be back to-morrow or the day after. We'll have to make the best of it, that's all. It'll give us plenty of opportunity to discuss ways and means of getting that pitchblende away.'

'Suppose the storm gets worse?' said William, who tried to feel as confident as the Commander appeared to be.

'It will get worse. It's getting worse now.'

Ramsbottom groaned. His large round face had lost a good deal of its colour. He kept moistening his lips.

'But that means it will blow over all the sooner,' the Commander continued. 'There's nothing to be worried about. We may have an uncomfortable night, but that's about all it will amount to.'

'Unless, of course,' said William, 'something happens to the schooner.'

'Ay, and what then?' Ramsbottom looked anxiously from one to the other.

'If anything happens to the schooner,' said the Commander, slowly, gravely, 'then it won't come back here for us, and we shall have to wait until a ship does come.'

'And when it does come,' said Ramsbottom grimly, 'all it'll find here will be three very nice skeletons and a few empty tins. Well, Ah haven't done any praying for a long time, but Ah must say, Ah feel like putting in a word or two for that schooner. And next time Ah go on an island – if Ah'm ever daft enough, once Ah'm out o' this – it won't be an island that nobody's ever heard of – it'll be an island with a regular service o' steamers – something like the Isle o' Man.'

'Sensible fellow,' said the Commander, who was in excellent spirits. 'Well, we'd better look for some lodgings. It'll be dark soon, and there may be a thunderstorm and some heavy rain. Look at that sky.'

They looked at it. William never remembered seeing a more unpleasant sky; it seemed to be bulging darkly with sinister intentions; and somebody somewhere had only to pull a string, it seemed, and that sky would be rent across and would drop on them anything from filthy water to red-hot cinders. He thought, with passionate longing, of the mild and tender skies of Suffolk. He had had more than enough of these melodramatic regions. Once and for all – damn the tropics!

Not far from where their supplies had been left, there was a shallow cave, piled high with sand and shells. The tide had once been there, but there was no evidence that it had been there for a long time. There they removed their precious little cask of water and the food and their other belongings, and then they sat at the entrance, and William and the Commander smoked and Ramsbottom nibbled at a biscuit.

'Only an hour or two ago,' said William slowly, 'we were arguing – quite heatedly too – about what we should do with the pitchblende or the radium we made out of it. And now—'

'It's a different story,' said the Commander.

'Ay, we look a bit soft now,' said Ramsbottom. 'Trouble with all of us folk is we never know when we're well off. We're never satisfied. But just let me get out o' this, and my travels are over. If you want to find Johnny Ramsbottom, you'll find him at home. Ah'll be content to sit in an easy chair – with a bit o' good stoof doing nicely in the oven – and read books about all this. From now on, Ah'm one o' these arm-chair travellers. And if you ask me, you

see a lot more. Ah've got more out o' travel, reading
books and going to the pictures than Ah've done being
on this job.'

'Well, you're going to see something in a minute,
Ramsbottom,' said the Commander grimly, with a glance
at the sky. 'You're going to see a first-class tropical thunderstorm.

They watched the sky curdle and darken.

4

It was a brilliant morning. The day before, their second
day on the island, had been like the first day, except that
they had watched the stormy weather ebb away instead of
gather force. Now it had completely vanished. The sky
was a tender blue and the sea one vast twinkle. The sand
in their cove might have been diamond dust. William felt
better than he had done the day before, which had been
a miserable long day, only broken by another visit to the
pitchblende. Yesterday morning, after the storm, they had
crept out of their shallow cave feeling cramped, sodden,
and cross. If the Commander had not quickly recovered
himself, taken charge of the party and brought sense and
cheerfulness into it, they might have all quarrelled or at
least spent most of the day sulkily avoiding one another.
Now, though they looked more like castaways than ever –
for their beards were beginning to sprout, and their thin
cotton clothes had suffered from the unequal struggle
with storms, spikes and thorns, and razor edges of rock –
they felt better. While they breakfasted off biscuit and
tinned meat, they told one another that the schooner
would return for them at any moment. And the sea

winked at them, as if it had taken part in a friendly conspiracy to give them a day or two's adventure.

'You wouldn't think,' said Ramsbottom lazily, as they stretched themselves out on the sand, and William and the Commander smoked their pipes, 'you wouldn't think them shoes belonged to a chap that could put his hand on a fortune. Ah never saw three pairs o' shoes so far gone.' And, indeed, their soles, white canvas ones with thin leather soles, were in a wretched condition, and obviously would not hold together much longer.

'Wouldn't it be frightfully ironical if, now that we've found the pitchblende, the schooner didn't come back and we just starved to death here? Nobody would ever know about the pitchblende either.'

'We should have to do something about that,' said the Commander gravely. 'We should have to leave a message of some kind to tell people what we'd found. Sooner or later a ship would call here. But you needn't worry about that. It's a hundred to one against Peterson losing his ship – if he's got a fault as a seaman, it is too much caution – and he ought to be back here any time. He knows how we're situated just as well as we do.'

'What do you think we ought to do, this morning?'

'I suggest that we explore the island a bit more,' the Commander continued. 'The higher up we are, the better chance we have of seeing the schooner in good time. And Ramsbottom if he likes can stay here, in case Peterson arrives before you and I get back. What do you say, Ramsbottom?'

'That'll suit me, Commander,' said Ramsbottom cheerfully. 'Ah can pass a morning nicely here, taking it easy, and doing a bit o' quiet thinking. Ah'd like to think about a meal or two Ah'm going to have at Simpson's the minute Ah get back to London.'

'Good stoof?' enquired William.

'Good stoof,' replied Ramsbottom solemnly. 'And you must admit, we could do with it. No oysters, and no fish – not even Dover sole. No, Ah'm all for a bit o' dry land tack now. Ah don't want to see the sea – or to eat what's in it – not for a long long time, Ah don't. You can have too much of a good thing, and Ah've had it. Since we started on this job, Ah've never been out o' sight o' the sea, and Ah seem to have had a salty fishy taste in my mouth for months and months. No, what Ah want's a good plate o' tomato soup, or pea soup, or ox tail, and then a right good saddle o' mutton, with roast potatoes and turnips, or a thick rump steak and chips, or sirloin, underdone, with Yorkshire pudding, roast potatoes and cauliflower, or happen an Aylesbury duckling, with new potatoes and green peas; and then a nice gooseberry tart with cream, or a slice o' plum pudding with a drop of rum on it, or a mince pie with a little warm brandy poured into it, and then perhaps a Welsh rarebit, or a crumb or two o' ripe Stilton with Bath Oliver biscuits; and a glass of Bristol Cream Sherry to start off with, and a glass of Warre or Cockburn's best port to finish off with; and Ah tell you, chaps, the minute we get back to London, you come with me to Simpson's and we'll have a bit o' good stoof.'

'You're making my mouth water, Ramsbottom,' said the Commander, smiling.

'You're making me feel sick,' said William. 'I feel I've eaten too much already. But what if there isn't any Simpson's? What if all the Strand's being burned down? Do you realise that it's weeks now since we heard any news from England at all, that we've been entirely cut off from the world, and that anything might have happened? Plague, Fire, Revolution, War,' he chanted, 'anything might have happened at home and we shouldn't know a thing about it.'

'Jugged hare,' cried Ramsbottom, as if a great light had suddenly illuminated the dark of his mind. 'Jugged hare. Ah knew there was something. Done in good red wine. It's not a thing you want often, Ah'll admit. But when you haven't had it for a long time – by jingo, it's rare eating! How do you feel about jugged hare, chaps? There's rich gravy for you. Ah suggest mashed potatoes with that and Brussels sprouts. What do you say?'

'There may have been a great financial crash,' William went on, 'and perhaps people at home are queueing up to get their rations of tinned meat and biscuits. You never know. There's no security in the world any more. Turn your back for a minute, and something frightful might happen.'

'And another thing.' Ramsbottom held up a large fat forefinger. 'Ah wouldn't say No to a rice pudding if it was properly made, with plenty of milk and an egg or two in it. What's matter with most rice puddings is that they're too dry and too lumpy. You see, if a thing looks simple, folk won't take trouble with it, and it's never done well. A rice pudding's a case in point. It's a sloppy last-minute job. Just the same with frying eggs and bacon. There's a right and a wrong way o' frying eggs and bacon. How often do you get an egg that's fried properly?'

Ramsbottom went on to develop this theme, but William did not listen carefully. He found himself contemplating the whole wide scene, the Pacific with its islands that were no more than grains of salt spilled on a large dining-table, the solitary enduring peak of rock that was Faraway Island, and the three of them here, marooned in the blue, with their pitchblende and their grandiose plans for it and their chatter about fried eggs. He found himself detached from it, and regarding it as one regards on waking the mixed splendour and idiocy of a vivid dream. There was some unknown reality, into which the mind retreated at these moments of smiling detachment, and from the standpoint of this unknown reality it seemed as if this real life, as we call it, was no more than a dream, only a few shades more solid and consistent than the dreams of the night. He told himself, too, that it was in no mere mood of idle romancing you felt this. Danger was here, death was here, just as they had been near him in the war, yet he could feel this now, just as he had felt it then. There was something brittle about the whole scene. You could, you felt, poke a finger through it. But what would you see through the hole you made? What was this other and deeper reality? You never looked about in it, you only looked out of it, to smile at the tissue-paper drama of ordinary reality. William stared hard, quite absurdly, at the sea, the dazzle of sand and rock, his companions, as if to discover if they were solid or merely wavering images, and asked himself if he was being mystical, philosophical or simply a trifle light-headed. Meanwhile, his staring showed him that Ramsbottom's face was not quite as full and round as it had been, but was tending to hang in folds, and that the Commander did not look at all well. His face was somewhat yellow and much too finely drawn.

When they had left Ramsbottom and were climbing out of the cove, he could not help saying something.

'Well? Of course I'm well.' The Commander was rather testy. He always resented any suggestion that he was not in the prime of life. 'Why shouldn't I be?'

William muttered apologetically that he thought the Commander was looking a trifle off-colour.

'Don't be absurd, Dursley. I'm all right. You can't expect

a fellow to look very spick and span after two days on this island. You ought to see yourself, my boy. You've got the makings of a very handsome black beard on your chin, but the rest of you isn't living up to it. No, I'm all right. Never better in my life. This sort of thing suits me better than it suits you fellows.'

William did not believe him, but he saw that it was useless to say anything more. As if to prove that he was the better man, the Commander led the way at a brisk pace, and as the sun was now very strong, it was warm work climbing. Once on the first broad ledge, they did not make for the gully they had used before, but moved along to the left, where the ledge bellied out towards the sea a little and provided them with a good view-point. There was no schooner to be seen. But there was something on the horizon, vague on the far blue shimmer. It looked to William, who saw it first, like a smudge of smoke.

'My God, you're right, Dursley,' cried the Commander excitedly. 'I believe it's smoke. If so, that can't be the schooner. Besides, Peterson wouldn't return from that quarter. Unless we're being deceived by a bit of cloud low down, that must be a steamer of some kind.' He whipped out the pocket telescope he always carried, and announced at once that it was certainly smoke. 'Look here, you wait here. I'm going up there to have a good look at her. No, no, I can manage it easily.' And off he went, telescope in hand.

He was making for a great overhanging rock about a hundred yards back from where they stood and about a hundred feet higher than they were. It did not look a difficult climb, and ordinarily William would never have thought of warning the Commander not to attempt it. For a few moments, William hesitated, not knowing what was best to do. The Commander so quickly resented any interference that suggested weakness that William did not like to insist upon accompanying him. On the other hand, William was convinced that the Commander was not his usual alert self. So he hesitated, walked a few steps after his companion, stopped, then moved on again, slowly and irresolutely. The Commander, who was all eagerness, had begun his ascent and did not seem to be finding it difficult. William sauntered in his direction, occasionally glancing back at that faint smudge out at sea. He had nearly reached the bottom of the slope when the Commander fell, some fifty feet, his final roll landing him only a few yards away.

His eyes were closed; all the colour had left his face; and he lay perfectly still. William, bending over him, sick with apprehension, thought at first he was dead. But very soon there were tiny signs of life in him. It looked like concussion. He must have hurt the back of his head badly. A horrible baffled feeling of helplessness descended upon William. What do you do with concussion? Vague phrases about 'keeping the patient's head low' and 'loosening his clothes' came to William, but did not seem very helpful. The Commander's head was low enough, and his clothes could hardly have been looser. Would Ramsbottom know? Could he risk leaving the Commander, to fetch Ramsbottom? He stared at the motionless figure beside him as if it might suggest some wise course of action. It remained almost irritatingly inert. Then William remembered something about chafing and rubbing the hands, and found himself idiotically grasping the Commander's hands, which were rather long and knobbly and at this moment disturbingly cold, and trying to chafe and rub them. Wasn't water always a help? About fifty yards away there was what remained of a small brackish pool, and now William ran and dipped his handkerchief in its green slime and then dabbed rather feebly and hopelessly at the Commander's face, which did not resent the indignity, though William felt all the time that the Commander himself, who was somewhere else, helpless, would have resented it bitterly. Finally, he ran back to the nearest point above the cove, and yelled at Ramsbottom, who was staring out to sea. Ramsbottom naturally thought these shouts referred to the object on the horizon, and indicated by large gestures that he had seen it, too. William had to go nearer before he made the other understand that he was wanted.

Together they carried the Commander into the shade, and there they felt the ugly bruise at the back of his skull and contrived to wash it with some thoroughness.

'Oh, it's concussion all right,' said Ramsbottom, sticking out his under-lip ruefully. 'And Ah doubt if a doctor could do anything for him. Either he'll pull through it or he won't – poor old lad.'

'Isn't there anything else we can do?'

'Only thing Ah can think of is to keep his head a bit lower than his body. That sends the blood down, do you see? Let's turn him round.' They turned him round. 'Ay, that's better. Now either he'll wake up or he won't.'

'My God, Ramsbottom, it's awful.'

'Nay, you needn't tell me that. Ah know that well enough. He never ought to have tried climbing anything this morning. He wasn't looking so grand.'

'I know. I told him so, and he was annoyed. I didn't want him to go up there.'

'Oh, Ah'm not blaming you. He's an obstinate old devil. It's a bad job, this.'

'Shall we try rubbing his hands again?'

'Better than nothing.'

It was several minutes before the Commander showed

any further signs of life. Finally, however, he returned to this world, not without reluctance. He opened his eyes; he groaned several times; and then he was very sick. After that he wanted a drink. There was nothing fit to drink up there, and as Ramsbottom had an idea that it would be good to wash the wound in sea water, they decided to carry him down to the cove. In the glare of the tropical sun, which was reflected by all the hard surfaces of rock, it was a murderously hot and tiring business carrying an almost unconscious man along that ledge and then down into the cove. But they set their teeth and did it, arriving exhausted and almost blind with sweat. The Commander had to be attended to then, and they gave him some water and washed his head and made him as comfortable as possible. By this time, he was fully conscious and apparently in no great pain, though still a trifle dazed.

'What was it?' he asked.

'What was what?'

'Out there – the smoke.'

Oh! – the smoke. They had forgotten about that smudge of smoke on the horizon. There was nothing to be seen, though the view from the cove was considerably restricted.

'It must have been a little dark cloud,' said William gloomily.

The Commander, not without difficulty, shook his head. He was sure it was not a cloud. A steamer must have passed within a few miles of them. It was maddening. Meanwhile, where was the schooner? William, who had flung himself down on the sand, when there was no more to be done for the Commander, wearily promised to go up and look round as soon as he had had a little rest. Ramsbottom was completely exhausted, and of course the Commander himself could hardly move a finger. Where was his pocket telescope? William did not know; he had forgotten all about that telescope, which must be lying, probably broken, where the Commander dropped it in his fall. The Commander closed his eyes and grimaced; his face had a faint greenish tinge; and he seemed to be feeling sick again. Ramsbottom puffed and blew and continually wiped his dripping face. William, tired, dejected, idly grasped handfuls of the warm coarse sand and let it dribble through his fingers. The immense relief he had felt when the Commander returned to life seemed to have left him now, but on the other hand he could still feel the effects of the first shock itself. For the time being, he had nothing more to say on any subject, and neither had Ramsbottom. The Commander, ironically enough, appeared to be struggling with a good many thoughts, presumably important, but was too weak to express them aloud. So they recuperated in silence.

This silence was destroyed most fantastically. Out at sea, there was a single sound, louder than a *pop* but sharper than a *boom*; a sort of *poomp*. It was followed by another sound, a trailing sound through the air, which William recognised at once; and it shot him upright. Then came, from somewhere high in the cliffs above, the inevitable crash. A single stone clattered over the rocks and then fell into the sand, only a few yards away. For a moment, in the tremendous silence that arrived then, they simply stared at one another.

Then Ramsbottom, indignantly: 'Here, what's that?'

'A shell,' cried William.

'A shell!'

'Yes, a shell,' said the Commander, speaking with care. 'Probably a four-inch, with a light charge. Go and see, Dursley. You're all right. They won't send another over.'

He was back within ten minutes. 'There's a warship out

there,' he gasped. 'Not very big – with two funnels – looks like an old cruiser – but don't know what country. And I think they're sending a boat. And that's not all. There's another ship further out, coming nearer. Looks like a yacht.'

'Two of 'em!' cried Ramsbottom. 'Nay, what the heck! Anyhow, we shan't starve.'

'No,' said the Commander, very slowly, 'we shan't starve. But will we get that pitchblende?'

5

William had stopped trying to make any sense of it all. He was prepared now simply to let things happen without question. These events were not springing out of any kind of life known to him; they might have been commanded into existence by an emperor on Mars. If there had been a dream-like unreality about themselves and their island earlier this morning, what could be said about things now! That cruiser riding at anchor, full in their sight, not half a mile away. That steam yacht, its white hull and single crimson funnel vivid in the sun, gradually approaching the cruiser. These little brown sailors, armed as if for a raid, now landing from a launch in this very cove. There they all were; the glare of the sun made that certain; they were solid, they were real; there was no arguing them away; and also there was no explaining them. William did not try. Anything might happen now. Nevertheless, he was not entirely passive. He stood up, felt ready to move, but did not stir, then waited, the muscles of his legs quivering a little as if they had an independent judgment of situations and had decided that this demanded instant flight.

There were about ten little brown sailors, and an officer or two, and now they bore down upon them. 'Chilean,' said the Commander. 'Yes, I'm sure of it. Chilean.'

They were Chilean, then? Well and good. If you pop up like that, out of nothing, quite unreasonably, you might as well be Chilean as anything else. One of them had an extraordinary broken nose, and William found himself wondering what size and shape the man's nose must have been before it was broken. The officer in charge of the party had a smart white uniform and little curly black side-whiskers, like bits of Astrakhan. He was addressing them now, and doing it in an unknown, hoarse and lisping tongue. Probably Spanish. Neither William nor Ramsbottom knew any Spanish, but apparently the Commander, whose eyes glittered feverishly in his long pale face, had a slight acquaintance with it. He listened carefully to what the officer had to say, and then stammered out a few syllables himself.

'As far as I can make out,' he told them, 'we're arrested.'

'Ah thought as much,' said Ramsbottom grimly. 'They don't look like chaps that have come to join us on a picnic and brought their own sandwiches. But what have we done wrong?'

'They're taking us aboard,' said the Commander, putting a hand on William's shoulder, for he was still very shaky. 'Come on, we might as well go at once.'

Two sailors, at a word of command, picked up their possessions. All the party climbed into the launch, and no time was wasted. Very soon the cruiser was towering above them. It was not a large cruiser, but William had seen nothing but schooners and native canoes for some time, so that it seemed enormous. It was called the *Maibo*.

'Second-class cruiser,' the Commander remarked. 'We

built her for them over twenty years ago. She's practically a sister ship to one I served in in 1911, though her armament's smaller and of course she's not so well kept. But she's old and out-of-date now, and I suppose they only use her for rough work.'

'Like this, Ah suppose,' Ramsbottom grunted.

'Yes, there's the Chilean flag,' and the Commander pointed.

There seemed to be a white bar and a red bar, and on the white bar a blue square in which there was a white star. Not a convincing flag, William reflected; the sort of flag you might invent for yourself in an idle moment; a vague, Ruritanian flag. But there was nothing phantasma-gorical about the cruiser herself. They could see the grey blisters of paint on her side now. Her company was very curious.

'You might think,' said William, rather bitterly, for he had suddenly taken a dislike to the *Maibo*, 'that they'd just captured three desperate outlaws or rebels or something.'

'They probably think they have,' said the Commander, producing a grin that appeared to hurt him and nearly succeeded in hurting anybody who looked at it.

'Ah'll tell you one thing, chaps,' Ramsbottom was sniffing hard, 'there's a grand smell of onions. Ah think they're doing a bit o' frying for their dinner.'

Among other things they appeared to have been frying was the little fat officer who met them on deck. His officially white tunic was richly larded with sweat, and his round yellow face might have been swimming in oil. He was not at all a good-tempered little fat man, and he seemed to take a strong dislike at once to the three captives. Their lack of Spanish was apparently in his opinion a suspicious circumstance. He spoke passionately to the officer who had brought them aboard, and if the glances he gave them meant anything, he must have been complaining because they had not been shot out of hand. Fortunately, this unpleasant little fat man hurried away, to give place to a broad oldish officer with a red face and white hair, whose English, though strange, was a great deal better than the Commander's Spanish. It soon appeared that this was the doctor. He pounced upon the Commander, felt his skull, looked into his eyes, gave him a little poke here and there, and then took him away. As they went, William heard the Commander proclaiming his own rank in the British Navy.

The little fat man returned, accompanied by an officer who was clearly the captain. He was tall, aloof, dignified, and melancholy, and in front of him William, to his disgust, unshaven and tattered as he was, felt like a guttersnipe visiting the local philanthropist. The little fat man gave the impression now of being in favour of torturing them. The captain touched him on the shoulder, smiled sadly, then moved majestically away. The little fat man gave them a final vindictive glare, then followed his superior.

'Ah make nothing o' this,' said Ramsbottom. 'What do you make of it? What are they after?'

'God knows! Perhaps they take us for some other people. Hasn't there been a revolution or a rebellion or something in Chile lately?'

'Nay, don't ask me. Life's too short to bother with everything. Ah take an interest in a right lot o' things, but there's some Ah can't be bothered with at any price. China's one. And Chile's another. Ah know roughly where it is, but that's about all. But if you ask me, they've gone and claimed the island. And that leaves us in a pretty pickle, unless we can do a deal.'

They were both leaning against the rail, and the sailors

who had brought them aboard were lounging close by. William turned round and was surprised to discover how near the yacht was. She was dropping her anchor. He could read her name quite easily: the *Isabella*. She was not so large and luxurious as Mr. Sapphire's yacht, but nevertheless she was handsome enough, and just now she was casting a charming reflection in the water. He could see two or three white figures on her upper deck, and they seemed to be looking in his direction, probably through glasses.

'Look at that yacht,' he said, nudging Ramsbottom. 'I wonder what she's doing here. Do you think she's come along with this cruiser?'

'Don't ask me, lad. Ah don't know where Ah am or what Ah'm doing yet. All Ah do know now is that Ah'm getting right peckish. We've had nothing to eat for some time, and that smell of onions has set me off.'

'I wonder what's become of the schooner. That ought to be here now.'

'Unless that little fat chap's gone and torpedoed her. He might have gone and done it himself – he's in a lather o' sweat, and he seems to hate the sight of us. Never mind. It's no good bothering our heads. Wait till the Commander comes back. He'll have found out something. And Ah must say Ah thought battleships were tidier than this. They could do with a good spring clean here, couldn't they? What do they use that contraption for, do you think?'

'Here's the Commander. He'll tell you.'

The Commander had his head bandaged. He looked very weary. He quickly dismissed his injuries. 'The point is,' he continued, speaking with a certain amount of effort, 'I understand now why they're here and why we're here. Faraway Island has been claimed by Chile. They took possession of it about a year ago. It didn't seem to be worth anything, of course, and so nobody cared whether they had it or not. They didn't care themselves.'

'Maybe not,' said Ramsbottom, sticking out his fat under-lip, 'but we do. Ah think that's a mess.'

'It's certainly a nuisance,' said William ruefully. 'It never occurred to me that one of the neighbouring states might have found it and claimed it. Still, it might be worse.'

'I've a lot more yet,' said the Commander. 'The schooner's gone.'

'The schooner's gone!'

'Yes, they stopped her and told her to get out of it. They learned something about us from Peterson, of course, but they didn't believe most of what he told them. And they had the right to order him out of these waters, if they wanted to, and apparently they had special instructions. There's been some trouble in Chile, and one or two of the revolutionaries got to Easter Island – they may have been exiled there, for all I know – and then they escaped to Tahiti. So they jumped to the conclusion that we were these revolutionaries. You can't blame them. It's a fairly reasonable conclusion. So they told Peterson to get out of it, and he had to go. They told him they'd attend to us. They'd had some special instructions about Faraway because of this yacht that's here.'

'Wait a minute,' cried Ramsbottom. 'Has that schooner gone of with our stoof? We'd all got some luggage on there, and now we've nothing but what we stand up in, and what we stand up in wouldn't fetch fourpence altogether.'

'I'd forgotten about our kit. I'll have to ask them about that. Peterson may have handed it over. If not, of course he'll take it back to Tahiti with him. After all, most of our possessions are still in Tahiti, aren't they?'

'Well, it's a mess.'

'But they must realise now we're not revolutionaries from Chile,' said William. 'I mean – look at us. Do we look like revolutionaries from Chile or Easter Island or wherever it is?'

'Well, we do look a bit suspicious, you know,' said the Commander.

'Something in that.' And Ramsbottom wagged his head drolly. 'Ah don't know what Ah look like, but you two look a nasty piece o' work just now, Ah can tell you.'

'But I've explained roughly what we're doing here – nothing about the pitchblende, of course – and I expect the doctor will make the captain understand. I soon proved to him – I mean the doctor – that I was a naval man myself, and that ought to help. Though there again, of course, it looks a bit suspicious.'

Ramsbottom was indignant. 'And here we are then – stuck on a silly old battleship in the middle o' the Pacific, and if we don't like it, Ah suppose we can go back on the island and live on spikes and mussels. Seems to me they've done us in properly.'

'Never mind about us, for the moment,' said William. 'The point is, what about the island? Even if it does belong to Chile, that doesn't mean we can't do anything with it. I suppose we might have to pay them something, but it needn't be much. Can't we get a concession or whatever they're called? We could tell them we simply want to develop the resources of the island. That ought to be enough.'

'Yes, that's right,' said Ramsbottom, looking from one to the other hopefully. 'It'll take time, Ah dare say; but that'll be all right. We might be better off, in fact, now that the island belongs to somebody, 'cos we might get government help, if we go about it in a right way. We could make Chile our headquarters and work things from there.'

'But the trouble is,' continued the Commander wearily, 'that somebody's already got a concession.'

'Have they? Are you sure?'

'I know,' cried William. 'The people on that yacht.'

'Yes,' said the Commander, 'the people in that yacht. I'm not certain of my facts, but I gather that they've something to do with Faraway, and of course that's why they're here.'

'Do they know what there is on the island?'

'I've no idea. I don't see why they should. On the other hand, if they don't, why are they here, bothering about the island at all?'

'You don't know who they are, do you?'

'I did hear the name, I think. I seem to remember it was something foreign – Spanish perhaps. But I won't be sure.'

'Commander, it wasn't Garsuvin, was it?' The name had just jumped to William's lips; and he had asked the question before he had had time to think why he should ask it.

'Garsuvin?'

'Yes.'

'Do you know,' said the Commander slowly, staring at him, 'I believe that *was* the name.'

William did not reply for a moment. He stared back at the Commander. But he had to say something. 'I'm sorry – but I believe we're dished.'

A sense of inevitable defeat weighed upon him. He felt hopeless. He had not been thinking it all out; there was no evidence yet that Garsuvin knew what was on the island, or even knew that this was the island; it was not that. Before the Commander had given him a proper reply, he had known that it was Garsuvin who was in that yacht; and no sooner had he known that it was Garsuvin than he knew, too, that it was all hopeless and that the pitchblende was lost to them. He had not given in to something outside himself: it was as if something inside had immediately opened the gates, simply on hearing that name, which carried with it a strange fatality. For a long time now a secret little fear, like a rat behind the wainscoting, had been scratching and gnawing; he had wakened in the night to hear it. Garsuvin had to win. It had been Garsuvin's pitchblende ever since – yes, ever since he, William, had destroyed that bit of paper in his study at Ivy Lodge and had afterwards refused to speak to Garsuvin over the telephone. He had dodged, hoping for a bit of magic to help him. There had been no magic; he could dodge no longer; here, inevitably, was Garsuvin. Absurd to feel like that, but he could not help it.

'I'm sorry,' he stammered. 'I think – it's hopeless – I'm awfully sorry.'

They could not make him out.

He told them he would explain. He leaned over the rail, and they came closer. In a low voice he told them about Garsuvin, hiding nothing. But he could not make it sound so important as it seemed to him, though he tried hard enough.

'Ah must say you ought to have told us all this before,' said Ramsbottom severely, 'though Ah don't blame you for taking no notice o' that paper. Ah'd have done the same myself.'

'I wouldn't,' said the Commander simply and without any suggestion of priggishness, 'and I don't think you ought to have done, Dursley. You ought to have had it out with this fellow. That was the only honest thing to do.'

'Yes, I think it was,' said William miserably.

'On the other hand,' said Ramsbottom, 'Ah don't see it's hopeless at all. It doesn't begin to look hopeless to me. He can't know what there is here.'

'I don't see how he can,' William admitted. 'But I also don't see how he comes to be here at all. How does he know that this is my uncle's island?'

'Perhaps he doesn't.'

'Well, if he doesn't now, he soon will do – don't you see? No, I can't believe it's a mere coincidence his being here. Only I'm sure he doesn't know about the pitch-blende. All he knows – or suspects – is that there's something valuable on the island.'

'Nay, surely to goodness he must do a bit more than suspect,' cried Ramsbottom. 'If he takes the trouble to get a concession or whatever it is and then comes all this way in a yacht, he must have a pretty good idea o' what he's after, unless he's got more time and money on his hands than most folk. Still, you never know. Hopeless be damned! Happen we can do a bit o' bluffing yet. Are they sure this chap himself is on the yacht?'

'Yes,' replied the Commander, and pointed. 'Who's that in the launch that's coming from the yacht? Is that the fellow?'

'Unless I'm greatly mistaken,' said William slowly, 'that's Garsuvin. You will be able to see him for yourself in a few minutes.' And as he watched the boat draw nearer, William felt like a man who had slipped across half the world to escape the police, only to be arrested in some remote jungle. The boat steered a swift straight course, her wash a broad arrow of Nemesis.

6

The clothes were different, of course, and William was surprised, now that he saw Garsuvin dressed in white, to discover how closely associated his image had been with that former suit of bright checks in the foreign fashion. But that astonishing face had not changed in one of its innumerable tiny lines and wrinkles. The high, bald, almost pointed head; the dark glinting eyes beneath their vast lids; the missing eyebrows; the nostrils sharply cut upwards; the long, thin but flexible mouth; the same air of a melancholy intellectual clown, with the same suggestion of decayed and unscrupulous aristocracy. Once again, William felt small and unimportant, and was angry with himself for giving in to it. Garsuvin showed no surprise, no resentment, no pleasure, no feeling of any kind, at meeting him there. He was elaborately polite, just as he had been before, and that was all. They might have run across one another in the lounge of a London hotel instead of at this queer end of the earth. The Commander and Ramsbottom were introduced. Garsuvin extended to them the same formal politeness.

'Excuse me, Mr. Durss-ley,' he said, in that queer voice of his, harsh and sibilant, commanding yet never loud, 'I go to speak with my friend the captain. Just for two minutes. Then we will talk.'

'All right, Mr. Garsuvin,' said William, trying to be nonchalant. 'And you might please explain to him that we're not revolutionaries from Chile or anything of that sort – if he's not yet convinced.'

'Of course, of course.' Garsuvin waved a large brown hand. 'Your crime is a very little one.' He searched for a word. '*Traspaso*, eh?'

'What? Trespassing – on that rock?' And the Commander laughed scornfully.

Garsuvin smiled. 'So absurd, eh? But we must remember the official mind. You understand that, Commander? You have known it. But that will be all right. Excuse me, please. In two minutes we will talk.'

'So that's the chap,' said Ramsbottom speculatively, looking after him as he walked quickly along the deck. 'Well, he's a queer one, is that chap. Of course he's foreign, but even when you take that into account, he's still a queer one. You wouldn't know in a month o' Sundays what he'd got up his sleeve.'

'I believe I've seen him before,' said the Commander, staring into the past. 'A long time ago. But I can't think where. He was quite a young man then, but it's the same fellow. I wish I could remember where it was. But my damned head aches too much. It'll worry me for weeks now. When you've been all over the place, as I have, and you meet fellows here, there and everywhere, from Chatham to Shanghai, faces you've seen before are always turning up again, like scraps from old letters – faces, faces, hundreds of 'em. It's very tantalising.' He said this almost piteously, like an old man.

'That chap's not here for fun,' Ramsbottom continued, as if the Commander had never spoken. 'You can bet your boots on that, Dursley. And he's going to take a bit o' bluffing.'

Garsuvin was soon back, and now he proposed that they should return with him to the yacht, where they could talk in comfort. To this they agreed; and it was while they were in the launch that Garsuvin first mentioned the island to William.

'They have a name for it now in Chile,' he announced casually. 'They call it *Isla Leona*. It was our friend there, the captain of the *Maibo*, who thought of that, for he thought that at a distance it looked like a crouching lioness. I have not seen that myself. Have you, Mr. Durssley?'

William gloomily replied that he had not noticed any resemblance. This affair of the island's name was no doubt a comparatively trifling thing, but nevertheless the fact that his Faraway Island was now officially *Isla Leona* in Chilean records and would soon appear as such in charts and maps, depressed him. It made him feel that he had lost the island and all that it might contain. There was something definite about this change of name. Now there was no Faraway Island; there was a Leona Island, and it was here, towering above them, its many faces of rock deeply wrinkled in the light of the rapidly declining sun; but there was no Faraway Island any more. Already it was part of a fading legend. It had gone where Terry had gone, not the last Terry, who sailed away in Sapphire's yacht, but the other one, who had vanished during their first voyage in search of the island; and William told himself that that Terry could live on Faraway, and he swept the pair of them into an idyllic South Seas that was becoming part of a fading legend, too. And having played, not happily, with these fancies, William looked up to find Garsuvin's dark glinting gaze fixed upon him. There seemed to be irony in it, but from what knowledge this irony had been distilled, William could not imagine.

Under an awning above the upper deck of the yacht, four persons were sitting round bottles, syphons, and glasses. Two men, two women. The large man seemed vaguely familiar. But it couldn't be? Yes, it was. That noble brow, that Roman nose, that jutting chin, that grand senatorial figure – yes, undoubtedly they belonged to the other Commander Ivybridge, the Coming Man of

Imperial Unity and Malay Fishing and Australian Domestic Service. And surely one of the women was the secretary girl, she of the tall slender form, the pale triangular
face, the enormous swimming violet eyes? Yes, it was; only
she seemed to be less secretarial now. William gaped at
them idiotically; they were not people, they were a conjur-
ing trick; and who had performed it? Garsuvin? Certainly
it was Garsuvin, who was now busy introducing everybody.
It was all done very quickly, and William had only time
to give a glance at the other two, one a slim, very dark,
prettyish girl, and the other a leathery middle-aged fellow
with a bushy grey moustache, both of them apparently
South Americans.

'We meet again, Mr. Dursley,' this new Commander
Ivybridge intoned in his magnificent baritone. 'You
remember calling to see me, eh?'

'I remember it very well,' said William, trying to make
this simple statement sound rather sinister. 'I didn't
expect to find you out here.'

'No, I can well believe that.' Commander Ivybridge
produced a very loud and nearly jolly laugh. 'But we are
here!'

There was no time for more. Garsuvin took charge of
them now, and, after making excuses to his guests, he
asked his three visitors to accompany him to the saloon;
and a very comfortable and handsome saloon it was too,
making William and his companions feel like ragged out-
casts. Garsuvin ordered the steward to bring cigars, cigarettes and drinks. Then he wasted no more time.

'Pardon me, gentlemen,' he said to the Commander
and Ramsbottom, 'if I do not address myself to you. But
I do not know your standing in this affair.'

'They are my partners in this business,' said William
promptly.

Garsuvin gave them a little bow. 'But I shall address myself to you, Mr. Durss-ley, for very good reasons. You came here, in a schooner from Tahiti, to prospect this island – is that not so? All right. You did that because your uncle, my old friend, Baldwin Totten, had told you of this island. But you are too late. This island is not yours to prospect. It was claimed by the Chilean Government—'

'We know that,' William told him.

'Good! You know that. Also, perhaps you know that I have made a little arrangement with the Chilean Government which gives me the right to do what I like with the island, on payment of a certain percentage.'

'You've obtained a concession.'

'A concession, yes – if you like to call it that. I have had business with Chile before, and I have friends in the government there. I can count on its support. That may be necessary with a place like this – so long a way from anywhere. Your uncle, you will realise, Mr. Durss-ley, had no rights in this island.'

'I'm not so sure about that,' said the Commander quickly.

Garsuvin gave him a polite nod. 'I shall be pleased to hear your views a little later, if you don't mind. To me it seems simple. This was anybody's island – no more the island of Baldwin Totten than of anybody else who knew how to find it. Now it is different. It is Chilean territory, and for purposes of development and commerce it is really my property. You cannot even land on the island without my permission or the authority of the Chilean Government. That is the position now. You see, Mr. Durss-ley, you are too late. I gave you your chance when I was in England. You would not take it. You were too greedy, my friend.'

William did not reply. At this stage, it seemed to him

dangerous to say anything. Evidently, Ramsbottom did not share this view, for he tapped the table, looked hard at Garsuvin, and said: 'Well, you seem to have gone to a lot o' trouble about all this. What d'you think you're going to get, now you are here?'

'I think I can get all that my friend Totten hoped to get,' Garsuvin replied softly.

'Well, you think wrong,' Ramsbottom told him, giving bluff for bluff.

Garsuvin smiled. 'The gentleman you met just now – not your countryman – the other – is a great, what you call it – you know – for gold and silver and copper – minerals, yes – he knows all about them—'

'A mineralogist?'

'That is it. Thank you. Yes, he is a great mineralogist from Santiago. I do not think your uncle, Mr. Durss-ley, could be called that.'

'No, he couldn't. But then he didn't come here prospecting, you know.'

'Of course. He came here by accident. But he found something, my friend, and I think that what he found in that island he found in the rock, because there is little else but rock there.'

'You seem to have a great faith – or to have had great faith – in my uncle's judgment.'

'In this affair – yes. I knew he had a great secret. He told me so, more than once. It had to do with this island. Mr. Durss-ley,' he continued, with no suggestion of anger, but with a profound melancholy in his voice, 'I asked you, over there in England, to let me share in this. I had a right. Your uncle had agreed to that. That you must have known, Mr. Durss-ley.'

'My uncle warned me against you.'

'That was because we had quarrelled. He wished to get

out of our agreement. He was not then as he had been. He was old and sick and so was capable of behaving not like an honourable man. There was an agreement between us, and each had a paper. He told you nothing of it, I suppose, and destroyed his paper.'

'No,' said William very quietly, 'he didn't destroy it. I destroyed it.'

Garsuvin lifted his heavy lids a little higher than usual, with an astonishingly impressive result. For a second or so, his eyes seemed enormous and devouring. But he showed no trace of anger. Only his melancholy deepened, as if this had brought him the millionth or some other round-numbered proof of the corruption of this world.

'I must tell you, too,' William continued, 'that these two gentlemen knew nothing of this until this afternoon. I only found the paper after we had made our arrangements to search for the island. It seemed too late then to bother them with it. So they didn't know until today. And one of them, I know, disapproves of what I did.'

'And that one's not me,' said Ramsbottom sturdily. 'Ah objected to not being told, but Ah think Dursley did quite right, and Ah'd have done the same. An agreement o' that sort looks fishy anyhow, and then his uncle – whose wishes he was trying to carry out – had warned him against you. Ah think he did quite right.'

'I don't,' said the Commander.

'Neither do I now,' said William. 'I think I ought to have had it out with you, Mr. Garsuvin. I was wrong in refusing to see you afterwards. I think I have been feeling that, somewhere at the back of my mind, for a long time.'

'I can quite understand that, Dursley,' the Commander told him gravely.

'Well, if you ask me, Ah think it's a lot o' fuss about nothing,' was Ramsbottom's verdict.

'You cannot say that,' Garsuvin observed smoothly. 'Unless of course you think this affair of the island is nothing. For if Mr. Durss-ley had talked to me instead of destroying the paper and then sneaking away, then I, too, might have been his partner, and I venture to say I might have been a very useful partner – more useful, for example, than you have been, my friend. As it is, you have come all this way, you have been put to much trouble, much expense – and see – you have no island. A few sailors come and take you away – and that is the last you will see of the island.'

This annoyed Ramsbottom, who stuck out his great under-lip. 'Ay, but wait a minute. Don't be too clever all at once, Mr. Garsuvin. You've gone to a deal o' trouble and expense yourself – a lot more than we have, if you've had to do a bit of bribing government officials and what-not and then had to bring this yacht. And how do you know you're going to get anything? You've got to find something first, haven't you? How do you know your mineralogist is going to help you? You're only guessing. We're not guessing, d'you see? We *know*. We learned a thing or two before we started on this job.'

Garsuvin nodded. 'You think I do not know what you came here for, eh?'

'Ah'm sure you don't,' roared Ramsbottom.

'Steady, Ramsbottom,' said the Commander.

'And you, Mr. Durss-ley, do you think I don't know?'

William looked at him steadily. 'Yes, I think you don't know.'

'If you did know, Ah've an idea you mightn't be bothering your head talking to us now. Mind you, it's only an idea.'

Garvusin smiled. 'I will be frank with you, gentlemen. I do not know. But I have a good suspicion. And if Totten

could put his hand on the treasure here – whatever it is
– it will not take me long, with such skilled assistance.'

'Perhaps my uncle was lucky. I think he was. You'll
think so, too, when you come to explore the island.
There's more of it than you'd think, and it's difficult-
going.'

'Gold,' said Garsuvin, giving them a sharp look, 'is
never found in easy places.'

They did not speak. They simply looked at him, trying
to make their faces completely blank.

'I have noticed that always. God has decided that gold
shall be found in deserts, in mountains, among the snow
and ice of the Klondyke – or on a rock like this, a long
way from anywhere.'

'That's interesting,' Ramsbottom remarked dryly.

'So,' and Garsuvin gave each of them a sharp glance,
'it is not gold, eh?'

'Isn't it?'

'Well, we shall soon find out,' said Garsuvin, briskly
now. 'To-morrow we go to work, and the island gives up
its secret for us.'

'Perhaps,' said the Commander.

'Ay, *you* might not be lucky,' said Ramsbottom. 'You
know, you've had rather a lot o' luck already, and it has
a trick of giving out. For instance, you were lucky to fasten
on to the right island, weren't you?'

'If you say so – yes.'

'That wasn't altogether luck,' said William slowly, staring hard at Garsuvin as he spoke. 'It's been puzzling me,
but now I think I know how it was done. Commander
Ivybridge – no, not you, Commander – but the other one,
on deck.'

'I've been wondering how that fellow came to be here,'
said the Commander grimly. 'It was rather too much of a

coincidence for my taste that the only two Commanders
Ivybridge in this world should meet just off this island.'

'Well, how does he come into it?' asked Ramsbottom.

'One moment, gentlemen, if you please,' said Garsuvin,
smiling at them. 'No doubt this is for you a most entertaining question – but not for me, and as I wish to talk now
with my friends on deck, I will leave you for a little time,
if you will excuse me. And I beg of you to stay to dinner.'

'Thanks very much, Mr. Garsuvin,' cried Ramsbottom
at once. 'Ah don't mind telling you, Ah've been worrying
some time about my dinner. You see – to start with – we
don't belong anywhere. We're right up a gum tree. You've
sent our schooner away—'

'Not me, please.'

'Well, them chaps on the cruiser have. And – damn it
– we've got to live, whether this island belongs to Chile
or you or Woolworth's. We can't starve, can we? And we'll
have to come to some arrangement with somebody.'

'For the present then – with me – for dinner. Afterwards
we can talk of further arrangements. Excuse me.'

The moment he had gone, they brought their heads
closer together and unconsciously put on a conspiratorial
air. 'Chaps,' whispered Ramsbottom, 'before a word's said
– not a syllable about what's there on the island. There
might easily be somebody listening in to this. Ah believe
that's an old trick – to leave you alone and then listen in
to what you're saying. It's not got to be mentioned, that's
all.'

They agreed at once.

'What do you think of our chances?' William asked.

'Not much,' replied Ramsbottom. 'Our only hope is to
bluff him for a share. We know something that he doesn't
know, and we might be able to sell him that.'

'How big a share?'

'What we can get, and that's not going to be much. But how did they come to spot the island? Where does this other Commander Ivybridge come in?'

'My uncle's letter, with the longitude in, went to this other Commander Ivybridge,' said William. 'You remember, Commander, I called on him and he gave me your address. And I believe Garsuvin called to see him that very same morning.'

'Why should this chap call on him?'

'Because he must have heard my uncle talk about a Commander Ivybridge – it's just what my uncle would have done – and as Garsuvin knew something about the island – I mean to say, he knew there *was* an island and that there was something valuable on it – he thought this Commander Ivybridge might be able to help him. And they must have put their heads together. You see, this Commander Ivybridge knew the longitude of the island; I know that because I saw him jot it down on his blotting-pad.'

'A thing he'd no right to do,' cried the Commander angrily.

'I agree. But I couldn't stop him, could I? You can see what happened after that. They put their heads together – two birds of a feather. They've got the longitude. They find that Chile has just claimed a newly discovered island with the same longitude. True, the latitude might be different, but they have to take a chance on that. Besides, the latitude of this Chilean island is roughly where Garsuvin expects the latitude of my uncle's island to be. Garsuvin goes to the Chilean Government, which probably thinks the island worthless, and gets permission to do what he likes with the place. Then he asks this Ivybridge to join him on this yacht, collars hold of a mineralogist—'

'He might be a mineralogist,' said Ramsbottom meditatively, 'and then again he might not. That might be bluff.'

'Possibly. But that's what he does, and so here he is. It all fits in.'

'And smart work too, if you ask me,' said Ramsbottom. 'If we'd had that chap on our side, Dursley lad, we'd not have been looking so soft now. As it is, we're almost sunk.'

'I've told you, Ramsbottom – I'm sorry. And you admit, you'd have done the same yourself.'

'Ah'm not so sure now. Ah think if Ah'd known that chap, Ah'd have kept him on my side. But it's done now. And what we've got to do is to make the best of it.'

They said no more, for now the other Commander Ivybridge, looking at once trim and gigantic in his white yachting suit, entered the saloon. 'Look here, you fellows,' he began in his usual large, somewhat patronising style, 'who's the man of business in this partnership of yours? Mr. Garsuvin suggests he talks to him and makes an offer.'

They looked at one another, and then William and the Commander nodded. Ramsbottom was the man to conduct negotiations, they agreed. He stood up.

'You'll find Mr. Garsuvin on the upper deck,' said Ivybridge, and made way for Ramsbottom to pass. Then he lit a cigarette, advanced into the saloon, and sat down.

7

The two Commanders Ivybridge looked at one another. William glanced from one to the other, immediately aware of the sharp contrast between them: the newcomer, so big, sleek, prosperous, important, not unlike a handsome actor playing the part of a public man of affairs; his friend, with his torn, stained clothes, his bandaged head, his deeply lined face, still showing traces of the morning's accident. They made an odd pair, and seemed to be staring at one another out of two different worlds.

The younger man was the first to speak. 'Well, Commander,' he said heartily, 'you don't seem to have managed this very well, do you? I gather that you thought the island still uncharted and unclaimed. Well, well – can't be helped, eh? Let's see, we've never actually met before, have we? But our letters have been mixed up sometimes.' He spoke, as always, as if he enjoyed the sound of his fine baritone voice.

The Commander gave him a frosty look. He found his voice with difficulty, as if it was rusty. 'Yes, they have,' he said grimly. 'And that's how you come to be here, Commander. I'm going to tell you now that you behaved like a cad.'

'What!' He bristled enormously. Obviously nobody had spoken to him like that for years.

'I say, you behaved like a cad. You've made use of information that wasn't yours to use. It came to you purely by accident.'

'I don't know what the devil you're talking about.'

'I'm talking about the longitude of this island. A letter intended for me fell into your hands. It gave the longitude of this island; you made a note of it; and then you used it.'

'Oh, that!'

'Yes, that. And you only make the matter worse by pretending it's of no importance.'

'Don't talk nonsense. Look here, Commander, you can't start pi-jawing me in that manner. I did make a note of the longitude – merely out of idle curiosity—'

'And then afterwards the same idle curiosity brought you here, I suppose.'

'What brought me here was an idea, the chance of developing something good. I'm interested in development. I'm a man of ideas. That's why I left the service.'

'It seems to me that His Majesty's Navy, which had tried to teach you to behave like a gentleman, was well rid of you.'

'I was well rid of them. But kindly drop this sort of talk. If you were a younger man I wouldn't take it from you.'

'When I was a younger man,' said the Commander in a melancholy tone, 'there weren't fellows like you in the Navy. They were on the stage or running bucket shops or tub-thumping at street corners, but they weren't in the senior service. We were all just plain simpletons who merely tried to do our duty and fulfil our obligations and act like gentlemen and not like mountebanks. Oh – I know all about you. When a man happens to have both the same name and the same retiring rank as yourself, you can't help taking an interest in his public activities.'

'Very good of you, I'm sure. Only please remember that I don't happen to be trying to win the approval of a few old shellbacks who've been forcibly retired and sit grumbling in hole-in-the-corner seaside towns. I'm proud to have their disapproval. It shows I'm alive and moving. I was glad to have it when I was in the Navy. And I'm glad to have it now.'

'Well, you've got it – so far as I'm concerned. Only why not call yourself something else, in future? Some of us don't like to see or hear about a Commander Anything making such a poor show, such a mountebanking ass of himself. And naval officers don't make use of private information in the way you've just done.'

'Naval officers of the kind you admire don't make use of anything except their hands and feet.'

'It's better to be stupid than clever in the wrong way,' cried the Commander, his voice rising in anger.

'I don't agree at all. It's a crime to be stupid. But there, it's no use arguing, my dear sir,' the other continued, having now entirely recovered his temper. 'We shall never see eye to eye about this or anything else. I know your point of view only too well, for I had enough of it when I was serving. I couldn't convince you I was right, not if I tried for a month; I know that; and so I'm not going to try at all. It doesn't matter. I'm not interested in your generation. Your world's finished.'

'I believe that's true,' said the Commander sombrely, 'I believe that's true. And it's time some of us went out with it, and left you to be as clever and slim as you like, and then you can all read one another's letters and advertise yourselves like cheap and nasty patent medicines and strut round like actors and behave like cads, just as you please. I've no doubt you'll make a lot of money and quite a name for yourself. You'll be somebody in this grand new world, where a man who tries to do his duty is just a damned fool. The only thing is, that it won't be a world worth being somebody in. It'll only be something between a brothel and a thieves' kitchen. And then a fresh set will come along, a bit smarter and even less scrupulous than you lot, and they'll steal your limelight and your loot, and then there'll be nothing left for you, far less than we've had left, for we've had the satisfaction of knowing that we had a good code and were trying to stick to it.'

'I didn't know oratory was part of it,' the younger man told him. He was annoyed, but contrived to keep his temper.

'It isn't.' The Commander managed the ghost of a

smile. 'But a fellow can't help getting worked up sometimes. I've talked too much. Sorry, Dursley.'

William shook his head. He had been plunged deep
into a vision of two worlds defying one another, and he
himself was not in either of them. He liked one of the
two commanders far more than he liked the other, but
that did not mean that he could accept the older man's
point of view. It was, he considered, altogether too narrow.
On the other hand, he could not possibly ally himself
with this other Commander, a figure he heartily despised.
So he was left in mid-air, and far from comfortable there.

The grand public Ivybridge nodded to them both, then
marched out, leaving behind much welcome space. The
yacht's electric lights were on now, and the open port-
holes were circles of purple velvet. It was hot down there
still, and they were tired and hungry. They sat in a sad
silence until Ramsbottom returned.

'Well, we've had a good set-to, and Ah've had to bluff
like hell and watch my step too, Ah can tell you. He offers
us ten per cent of the first three years' profit if we'll tell
him all we know. He says it isn't worth it, but he'll offer
that much because your uncle, Dursley, spotted the island
first. And it's either that or nothing, he says. That's all my
eye, of course, because he doesn't know what there is on
the island and he may not find out in a hurry. And he
admits he wants to save as much time as he can. It takes
time getting here, no matter where you start from. Well,
what d'you say, chaps? Ten per cent.'

They thought about it. The Commander shook his
head. Ramsbottom looked at William. 'Not good enough,'
said William.

'That's my opinion,' said Ramsbottom briskly. 'Ah'm
all for getting more out o' that chap. He's got such a
conceit of himself. That other chap may be a mineralogist

or he may not – he looks like a retired organ-grinder, but that proves nothing. Shall we bluff it out? What we going to ask for?'

They decided they would demand at least forty per cent. After all, they told one another, William's uncle had first noticed the island; they had had the ore tested; and they themselves had reached the island before Garsuvin and his party, none of whom had yet been ashore.

'We'll tell him so after dinner,' said Ramsbottom. 'He ought to be in a better frame o' mind by then. Ah know one who will, anyhow, and that's Johnny Ramsbottom. They're setting the table out up above, and the captain o' that cruiser is joining us. He's on his way now. So that's that. And let's see now if we can get a bit of a wash and brush-up. Ah don't know if you remember, but there's two very nice-looking young women in this party, and one of 'em's English. Let's put a good face on it, chaps. We're not sunk yet.'

8

They had dinner up on deck. It was an excellent dinner and the deep tropical night and the lighted deck together provided a beautiful setting for it. But William and his two comrades did not enjoy themselves. Ramsbottom fell upon the food and swilled away at the wine with great heartiness, but he did not say much and was not at all his usual cheerful garrulous self. The Commander did not even do justice to the food and drink; he only spoke when compelled to answer a question, and he looked pitifully tired and worn, a sick old man. William felt uncomfortable and depressed. He had no great hopes of their negotiations, and whatever happened now, it seemed as if the pitchblende had completely passed out of their control. It was not the loss of a possible fortune that troubled him – and he realised now how little he had cared about the money that might be made out of this adventure – but the knowledge that the island and its treasure were no longer theirs and the growing conviction that their quest was coming to a dreary sordid end. There was always a chance, of course, that Garsuvin, baffled, might turn to them and offer them a half-share or something considerable, but it seemed to him now a very poor chance. So he sat glumly in the shadow of these depressing thoughts, and there was nobody there to rouse him and take him out of it. He felt that it was impossible for him to get on easy terms – or even the semblance of easy terms – with Garsuvin, though that gentleman, who was playing host in the best traditions of Latin aristocratic hospitality, did not appear to be aware of the fact that there was anything wrong. He disliked both the younger Commander Ivybridge and his swaying and violet-eyed secretary or mistress or whatever she was. He was prepared to like the others, the mysterious dark young girl, the leathery Chilean who was supposed to be a mineralogist, and the captain of the cruiser, that imposing, melancholy personage, but unfortunately they had no English and he had no Spanish, and he was in no mood to make experiments with gestures and odd scraps of language. But these people had plenty of talk among themselves, and sometimes Garsuvin conversed with them in Spanish, when he was not talking English with Ivybridge and his girl. Moreover, William, like his two friends, felt too ragged and unshaven to be at ease in such spruce company. They might be all at the end of the earth, but nevertheless they were acutely conscious of their chins of stubble and their stained and torn white clothes. His barber and his laundryman had given Garsuvin an immense advantage in this game they were playing. And if he had wanted a good ally, he could not have found a better one than the violet-eyed girl, who seemed to look down on William and his friends from a gigantic height.

Both girls retired immediately after dinner. The men were left to their cigars and brandy and business. Garsuvin came to the point at once. 'We do not need to have any secrets here,' he began. 'You know, Mr. Durss-ley, what offer I have made? Very good. What do you say?'

'We've talked it over,' said Ramsbottom, who was now a little drunk, but no more cheerful than he had been, 'and we agree it's not good enough. Fifty per cent and we'll tell you all we know – and you can take it from me, Mr. Garsuvin, we know a lot.'

'Fifty per cent! It is ridiculous.'

'Of course it's ridiculous,' cried the younger Ivybridge contemptuously. 'You're trying to bluff us, and you can't do it.'

The Commander looked at him wearily, opened his mouth to say something, thought better of it, shook his head, and relapsed into his deck chair.

'What's ridiculous about it?' demanded Ramsbottom. 'It's our island by rights. We were on it first. And we know exactly what's there and what it's worth, and you don't – and perhaps, if we don't tell you, you never will know.'

Garsuvin merely smiled. The younger Commander Ivybridge raised his splendid public eyebrows. The two Chileans smoked meditatively. From somewhere in the night, either from the yacht's fo'castle or from the cruiser, there came the subdued wail of an accordion.

Ramsbottom wiped his forehead. 'Ah'll tell you what we'll do, and it's rock bottom. We'll take forty per cent. Now then – forty per cent, and we tell you all we know.

And don't forget it's cost us a pretty penny finding it all out.'

Garsuvin smiled again. 'My offer is as before, and either you accept it now or I take it away. Now – you may have your ten per cent. If you refuse – you get nothing. You know your position here, gentlemen. You have no rights in this island. You cannot even visit it again without my permission. I do not want your help. My offer of ten per cent is a kind act. Even though Mr. Durss-ley would not acknowledge my partnership with his uncle, I am a little sorry for you all. You have come a long way for nothing. So I make this offer. Refuse it and you get nothing.'

Ramsbottom glanced at his two friends. The expression on his large face announced very plainly that in his opinion all this was bluff. They agreed with him. So he guffawed a little and then wagged his head. 'Oh no, you don't, Mr. Garsuvin. Oh no, you don't.'

'You refuse my offer?'

'Of course we do. We weren't born yesterday.'

'Very good. There is no offer any more. Now you get nothing, my friend.'

'We'll see about that. What do you think you're going to get?'

'What you came for,' said the younger Commander Ivybridge.

'Happen so, but you've got to find out yet what we came for, and that may take a bit of time. In fact, it might take a lot o' time. What do *you* say, chaps?' And Mr. Ramsbottom tried to laugh heartily, but was not very successful.

'You delude yourself,' said Garsuvin, in a voice without expression. 'We know now what you find here. It is the ore for radium.'

This was shattering. The bottom dropped out of their

bluff. 'Well, Ah'll be damned!' cried Ramsbottom, staring first at his friends and then at Garsuvin.

'How do you know it is?' demanded William.

'You took with you to the *Maibo* there, among other things, Mr. Durss-ley, a little instrument. My good friend, the captain here, was curious and brought it to me to-night, when he came to dinner. I was curious, too. But as I told you, we have a man of science with us, and he knew the little instrument. We have the name in English too. What is it? Ah yes – an electroscope. That is it. An electroscope – for testing uranium ores. What is this name?' He turned to the mineralogist, and they talked rapidly in Spanish for a minute or two. 'Yes, we have that name too. Pitchblende. That is what you have found here. I can guess the whole story now. Your uncle found this curious stuff. He took away a piece. He came to England and had it tested. He told you of it before he died, and then you had it tested and came here. You thought you would test it here too, for yourself. You have done so.'

'Here,' roared Ramsbottom, 'Ah call that a bit o' sharp practice – my God, Ah do!'

'I must say,' said the Commander, speaking with an effort, 'I can't congratulate you on your methods. First, you find the island by making use of a wrongly addressed letter, then you find what's on it by ransacking somebody else's haversack. That's not playing the game at all. It's just being a dirty cheat.'

'You forget, my friend, that I was cheated – as you call it – first, by the action of Mr. Durss-ley here, and more badly cheated than you have been. And even then, you tried the bluff. It was as I said, I made the offer of a little share out of kindness.'

'Oh yes,' said Ramsbottom roughly, 'we know all about that. You've said that before.'

Garsuvin's heavy drooping eyelids were lifted a trifle higher than usual, and the result was a sudden flash from his curious dark eyes. 'Then I do not say it again. Now you get nothing. You can go. You have finished with this island. You can forget about it. It is all finished.'

'All right,' said William bitterly. 'Don't rub it in, Garsuvin.'

'If you want my opinion,' said the younger Ivybridge pompously, 'it's entirely your own fault, Dursley.'

This goaded William into what was, for him, an astonishing piece of rudeness. He glared contemptuously at that grand public personage. 'Oh, go to hell!' he shouted at him.

Garsuvin held up a hand. Then he turned to the captain of the cruiser and plunged into Spanish. They talked for two or three minutes, and all William could gather from it was that Garsuvin was proposing something to which the captain was agreeing. 'We have turned away your schooner,' Garsuvin said to them, 'so we must take you away. After we have surveyed the island, this ship returns to Valparaiso, where we make our arrangements. You do not want to go there?'

They did not want to go there. They did not want to go anywhere in Garsuvin's yacht.

'The *Maibo* goes from here to Easter Island,' Garsuvin continued, 'before she returns to Valparaiso. The captain here will take you to Easter Island. If you wish to return to Tahiti—'

'We do,' said William.

'Then you will have to wait on Easter Island until there is a schooner going to Papeete. Sooner or later, there is always a schooner going to Papeete. The *Maibo* sails in the morning for Easter Island. You will go with her, eh?'

They glanced at one another and then nodded. William felt as miserable as the other two looked.

'Then you can to go the *Maibo* with the captain to-night,' Garsuvin continued. 'And that will be soon, he tells me.'

Ramsbottom was not altogether subdued, and now he pointed a fat forefinger at Garsuvin and cried: 'Here, just a minute, before you settle what we're going to do for the rest of our lives. You say you've got a concession here and the island's practically in your pocket and all that, but how do we know you're telling the truth? How do we know you've got any more right to this island – from Chile or anywhere else – than we have?'

'That cruiser ought to tell you something,' replied the younger Ivybridge severely.

'Happen so, but it doesn't tell me enough. And anyhow, Ah'm not talking to you. There's a good many things Ah could say to you, if Ah was talking to you, but Ah'm not.'

'You would like to have proof of the concession?' Garsuvin enquired, with a faint note of contempt in his voice that was maddening to William. 'That is soon done. Though you do not read Spanish, I think.'

It was no use. The document that Garsuvin produced, though they could not understand it in detail, was obviously an official confirmation of his claim to develop the resources of the island in any way he pleased, and it clearly gave him a monopoly. It only emphasised their defeat and loss. They had failed miserably. They had sought and found Faraway, had touched it, only to discover that it crumpled into dust and dream stuff. In this world, there was no Faraway Island any more.

'But let me tell you this,' said the Commander to his namesake, when they were ready to go. Shaky but indomitable, he faced the other's formidable bulk. 'Let me tell

you this, Commander. You may have cleared us out of the
way, but you haven't finished yet. No, I don't simply mean
that you'll have a job of work getting that stuff out of the
island. You will, of course. But I don't mean that.' He
waited a moment, and it seemed horribly difficult for him
to talk, as if all his mechanism of speech was rapidly
rusting and corroding. 'I mean that no good will come
of all this for you, Commander,' he continued harshly.
'You've broken too many rules. You've tried a short cut
and the back door. It doesn't work. It never works. You've
let something down, and you're going to be let down
yourself before you've finished. I *know*. I can't tell you
how I know, but I *do* know. Come on, you fellows. Give
me a hand, Dursley.'

The launch was waiting for them.

'Good-bye, Mr. Durss-ley,' said Garsuvin in his usual
melancholy tone. 'Sometime, no doubt, we meet again.
Then I will tell you all our adventures here.'

William made an effort. 'I shall be glad to hear them.
Good-bye.'

When they were crossing in the launch and the cruiser
was already towering above them like a lighted wall of
steel, the Commander brought out a poor cracked little
chuckle. 'You know, you fellows, it's ended badly and
we're out of luck, but there's always some compensation.
All my life – or ever since I first heard of it when I was a
boy – I've wanted to visit Easter Island. Those mysterious
statues have always fascinated me. I've read every book
on the place that's ever been written. And now, quite by
accident, it seems I'm going there.'

'Well, you can have it for me,' said Ramsbottom wearily.
'All Ah want to do now is to get back home. Damn their
Easter Islands. Ah've seen enough sights. Ah want to go
home.'

'So do I,' said William, and not idly either, for as he spoke he was visited by a desperate feeling of nostalgia. He ached to be away from all this remoteness, to return to the solid and beautiful reality of England and Buntingham. Sick at heart, he looked over the dark water, and there saw a great starless and blacker patch of night that gradually assumed a vague shape; and that, he concluded, must be the island. He stared hard at it and was finally rewarded by catching in it a feeble glint or two, a few points of rock in the starlight.

CHAPTER XI

EASTER ISLAND: THEY ALL GO HOME

1

'WELL,' SAID Ramsbottom, blowing hard, 'Ah thought Ah disliked them schooners, but – my word! – Ah love 'em compared with what Ah think about this damned cruiser. Another week o' this and there'd be nothing left of me.'

'Thank God we haven't another week,' cried William. 'We ought to sight Easter Island to-morrow morning. We may be on the island by this time to-morrow.'

'Let's hope so. Any sort of land will do me, after this. Ah doubt if the mind of man ever devised anything else as uncomfortable as this rotten old piece of ironmongery. She does everything she oughtn't to. She rolls and pitches if you only show her a bit of a wave. You can't walk about, and if you stand still she sends you bumping up against something or somebody. It's always either far too hot or too cold, and either you can't get a mouthful of air or your head's blown off. Ah'll admit these chaps aren't so bad as Ah thought they would be—'

'They've been quite decent really,' said William. 'Even the little fat one, who seems to be so anti-English, has come round this last day or two.'

'Ah know, Ah know. They're all right. But all the same Ah wish this old corrugated iron mouse-trap and cheese-toaster o' theirs was far enough. Nobody gets me on a cruiser again, and Ah don't care who it belongs to. It may be a free ride we're getting, but Ah'd pay a lot o' money for it to stop this minute.'

'Sea's getting up again,' said William, staring at it. He seemed now to have spent half his life staring at the sea.

'Don't talk to me about the sea. Ah don't care whether it's getting up or getting down. If it's *drying* up, you can tell me, 'cos Ah'm ready to take some interest in it then, but not before. Ah'm sick to death of the sight of it. Ah'd like to set off this minute and go on a train across America or Siberia, just to see as much land as it's possible to see. And if you ever catch me on a seaside promenade again as long as Ah live, you've my permission now to boot me off it. Ah'm fair sick o' the *sound* of it, aren't you?'

'I am. How long have we spent at sea altogether?'

'Well, to begin with, me and the Commander had six weeks right off, getting to Tahiti. Then there was that first schooner trip – oh well, you can reckon it up yourself if it amuses you. Ah'd rather think about something else – farming or something of that sort.'

'Or looking for pitchblende.' And William grinned sardonically.

'Looking for hell fire!' Ramsbottom snorted. 'You shut up about pitchblende, lad. The less said about that stoof the better. If you don't, Ah'll be sending you in a nice little bill of expenses for the Commander and me for this wild-goose job o' yours.'

William was indignant. 'Well, I've told you before—'

But Ramsbottom would not let him continue. 'Yes, you've told me before and Ah don't want you to tell me again. That's all right, lad. Ah was only pulling your leg a bit. A chap's got to let steam off somehow, after all this lot. But look here,' and he looked hard at William with enormous solemn eyes, 'about this Easter Island job. What are we going to do? You'll never persuade me the Commander's fit to land on a little island like that.'

'I know that. He ought to be taken to Valparaiso. There isn't a doctor on Easter Island, nothing of that sort, and the mere business of getting ashore is going to make him much worse. What's his temperature now?'

'Ah don't know, but it's still high. He was asleep when Ah looked in earlier on, and Ah thought he looked poorly. But Ah can't do anything with him. He's got it into his head that we'd be best off landing on Easter Island and waiting for a schooner back to Tahiti, as we fixed up originally—'

'Of course we would,' said William. 'But that doesn't matter now. And anyhow we might have to wait a long time for a schooner for Tahiti. And then again, if it's for our sake he insists on getting off at Easter Island, we could split up and he could stay on the cruiser for Valparaiso.'

'He could. But Ah don't fancy that, do you? Ah mean to say, we couldn't let the old lad go off on his own now in the state he's in.'

'I agree,' said William hastily.

'But another thing is, you see, he's dead set on seeing this Easter Island, has been all his life. That's making him obstinate – and, mind you, you'll go a long way before you'll meet anybody more pig-headed than the Commander. Once his mind's made up, there's no shifting him. He's a right lad o' the bulldog breed. Let's have a peep at him.'

They went below. Fortunately for them the ship's company of the *Maibo* was far below full strength, and the captain, influenced by the Commander's rank rather than by their acquaintance with him at Garsuvin's table, had been able to allot them officers' quarters. The Commander had a cabin to himself, and the other two shared a neighbouring cabin. They had not been comfortable, because the *Maibo* was not designed for comfort, being cramped, stuffy, and a wretched roller, but they had had what comfort was going and could not complain of their treatment. But for William and Ramsbottom, woefully disappointed at their loss of Faraway and worried about the Commander, it had been a miserable voyage. They had only one consolation – they were on their way home, even though it looked like being a roundabout and tedious way. As for the Commander, he was undoubtedly a sick man, with a weight of years he was suddenly called upon to support and very little strength with which to support it. Twice his temperature had risen rapidly to a dangerous height, and he had been delirious.

They tip-toed into his cabin and stared at him, lying there dozing. He had always been lean, but now he looked painfully thin. These last few days had brought about an evil transformation in his face, pulling in his cheeks, giving him nut-cracker jaws, now covered with grey bristles, and a dry yellow skin. But his eyes were brighter than they had ever been, an astonishing ice-blue. He opened them now, and looked at his friends for a moment or two in silence.

Ramsbottom cleared his throat. 'Well, how d'you feel now, Commander?'

The Commander frowned, and gave a little impatient shake, as if to brush away the unwelcome topic. 'I'm all right,' he said, a trifle rustily. 'Don't you fellows worry about me. Touch of fever, that's all, after that bang I got the other day. Damn it! – don't stand there looking like a pair of hospital visitors. Let's see – where are we now?'

'They say we'll be at Easter Island to-morrow sometime,' replied William.

'Good. Bit of luck that – for me. I've told you fellows,

I think, how I've always wanted to visit Easter Island. Funny thing is – did I tell you this? – when I was in the old *Incorrigible*, over twenty years ago, she was under orders to call at Easter and did do finally, but just after I'd left her. I was pulled out of her at Fiji. Mad as blazes, too. Thought I'd lost my last chance of ever seeing Easter. And now here we are. Odd bit of luck, this. Haven't had many.'

The other two gave each other meaning glances. William nodded to Ramsbottom, who, after some hesitation, said: 'Look here, Commander, we've been a wondering about this job. D'you think you're fit to land on this island?'

'Fit to land! What the devil do you mean, Ramsbottom? Of course I'm fit to land. Give me a day or two and a look at a chart and I'd take this ship as near to the bar there as she's ever likely to go. Don't say that's saying much, because, from what I can see, they're handling her like a lot of stockbroking yachtsmen. I'll be up in the morning, bright and early. I'd get up to-day only I feel a bit cheap and there's nothing to get up for.'

'I'm sure the captain would take us with him to Valparaiso, you know,' said William.

'Valparaiso? Ridiculous. We don't want to go to Valparaiso. We've got to get back to Tahiti, to pick up the rest of our kit. Besides, I wouldn't miss Easter Island for the world. Do me good, too – if that's what's worrying you. Healthy place. Winds blowing from all quarters, over two thousand miles of sea in every direction. Pick me up in no time. Not that I need it.'

Ramsbottom grunted. William made no sound, but must have looked dubious.

'What the devil's the matter with you fellows?' cried the Commander in a weak fury. 'Standing there like a couple of undertakers or washerwomen! I understand how you feel about the island and the pitchblende. Feel the same myself. No reason, though, why you shouldn't behave like sensible men. Got to take a beating and forget it.'

'That's not it at all,' protested Ramsbottom.

'Then what is it? Can't be anything else. Ever since we came aboard here, you've been acting like a pair of seasick curates.'

'Nonsense,' said William, with an entire absence of tact. 'We've been worried about you, that's all.'

'Worried about me! Very nice of you, I dare say, but there'd be more sense in it if I was worried about you two, the way you stand about and groan. No need to worry about me. I'll be up to-morrow, in plenty of time to land.' He glared at them for a moment, then closed his eyes, and his whole figure seemed to shrink. His hands, heavily veined and leathery, made a few rather spasmodic movements over the surface of the grey blanket. Then he opened his eyes again and spoke in a small tired voice. 'Sorry, you fellows. Seem to be losing my temper. Bit short of sleep, I think. Don't mind me.'

They returned to the deck, dubious and heavy-hearted, and gloomily regarded the flying spray and the interminable rollers. Somewhere there were places that had never known this salt breath, this pattern of foam, this shuddering and hissing and thundering, but now they seemed as distant and incredible as heaven.

2

His two friends protested again, the doctor protested in a mixture of Spanish, French and English, the captain protested in a grave Castilian torrent, but nevertheless the Commander joined them on deck next morning, yellow, shaky, a little bent, with a blanket round his shoulders. They were dropping anchor off Easter Island, which looked like a rather larger, greener and less precipitous version of Faraway. But at first they could not see very much, for the morning was wet and misty. There was a heavy grey sea running. They seemed to have found their way out of the tropics at last, for there was not even a hint of them in this bleached and sullen scene. They might have been landing, on a warmish morning, in the Hebrides. It was not long, however, before the sun struggled through and showed them signs of life ashore. The entire population of the island seemed to be hurrying down to the beach. Some of the men were on horses, which appeared rather odd. The coloured cotton dresses of the girls were noticeable, almost gay. Nothing else of any interest was to be seen. It might be the most mysterious place in the world, but at that hour, from the deck of the *Maibo*, it simply looked a very dull and inhospitable island.

The sea was breaking gigantically against the black basalt rocks, and frequently the whole population assembled on the beach disappeared from view behind great hissing screens of spray. The island gave the impression of being on very bad terms with the elements; the wind came screaming and tearing at it from every quarter; and the sea, boiling in fury, charged at its dark ramparts on every side. There was nothing idyllic about this part of the world. William and his friends – and, indeed, nearly everybody else in the *Maibo* – now watched a shore boat, carrying a large Chilean flag, that spent several exciting minutes trying to negotiate the bar. More than once this boat thrust her nose high in the air, only to fall back and then vanish behind a great green wave. At last she succeeded in shooting over, but there was one moment when she seemed to be vertical, on end. It looked as if landing on Easter Island would prove, that morning, to be an awkward and dangerous business. William and Ramsbottom gave this water-chute adventure many dubious glances, and even the Commander whistled softly once or twice. When the boat came alongside the cruiser, William and the others saw that her crew, who were all excited, were for the most part dressed in odd pieces of other people's uniforms, and gave the impression that they were really taking part in a comic water carnival. They had brought with them, and thoroughly drenched, the governor of the island, a faded middle-aged man who almost made a rabbit scramble and bolt into the cruiser. The crew were all Polynesians, but smaller and uglier than most of the men from the South Sea islands proper. They seemed, however, a lively lot of boys, with a passion for breaking into enormous guffaws.

It was on this boat, an hour or so later, that William and his two companions went ashore. The sea had gone down a little, but nevertheless it was a terrifying little voyage. It was bad enough getting the Commander into the boat, and if he had not been used to descending into boats from warships, it is certain that he never would have found a place in the boat, for he was very shaky indeed. But there was much worse to come. If the sea had looked unpleasantly rough from the deck of the cruiser, from the much lower level of the shore-going boat it looked mountainous and extremely menacing. The four oars were double-manned, but they had hardly got going before one oar slipped out of the rowlocks. All the crew shouted at one another, and the steersman, standing high up in the stern, using an oar to guide her, nearly burst his thick chest to make himself heard. William had not felt so terrified for years. He crouched there, helpless. The nearer they got to the bar the worse it looked. The crests of the great waves towered high above them, and every moment it seemed as if one of them would fill the boat in its stride and then toss them on to the rocks. William shut his eyes, and then immediately the boat dropped and was violently shaken, so that he had to clutch the seat hard. After that he kept his eyes open. '*Tranquillado*' the boatmen shouted to one another. The boat shot up and up, then came down, with a huge wave thundering over it, half filling it and drenching them all. But they were over the bar and within a few more minutes were alongside the crowded little jetty. Wet, gasping, and profoundly thankful, William set his foot on safe, steady, solid land. Ramsbottom looked quite green. The Commander looked grim, but very worn.

Fortunately for them, as they knew beforehand, all the trade of the island was in the hands of an Anglo-Chilean company, which raised stock there, and the representative of this company, the manager for the island, was an Englishman, Purvis, who had been there years and years. A few minutes after landing they had introduced themselves to him and were explaining the situation they were in, with the assistance of the governor, who had been told something about them by the captain of the *Maibo*. Fortunately, too, Mr. Purvis proved to be an hospitable and friendly soul. He was a middle-aged rather horsey-looking man, with a very brown wrinkled face and curiously pale remote eyes that had a two-thousand-miles-from-anywhere look about them. He seemed to be quietly glad to see them. He expressed no surprise, made no fuss, and William gathered the impression that he had lived too long away from everywhere to be capable of surprise or fuss. He was ready to accept anything. No sooner had he accepted them than Ramsbottom, with a warning glance at William, took Purvis on one side, obviously to say something about the Commander. William took the hint and was able, by asking a foolish question about the famous statues, to keep the Commander away from the other two.

Purvis then led the way to his bungalow, after ordering two of the natives to follow with his visitors' belongings. It was a rough-and-ready sort of place, with a home-made look about it, but reasonably comfortable and far more substantial than the bungalows they had visited on the tropical islands. Once there, while their host was talking to the Commander, Ramsbottom marched William outside, where the wind, which they were soon to know so well, was roaring away. It was the windiest island William had ever known.

'Ah had a talk with this chap,' Ramsbottom announced, 'and Ah told him about Commander. But he'd spotted it himself. He said right off that Commander looked a pretty sick man and ought to be in bed this minute. But he's fixing all that up for us. Luckily there's an empty bungalow just near – it's for an assistant who hasn't turned up on the island yet – and we can have that. He wouldn't take anything for that, but Ah made him agree to charge us for our food and suchlike – just whatever he thinks it costs. Up to a little time back, it seems, there was only one boat a year came here, and so they had to order a long time ahead and they used to run badly short, but now it's a bit better.'

'That's all right,' said William. 'But how long will we be staying here?'

'Well, that's the point. He doesn't know, he says. But he's got an idea there ought to be a schooner coming from Tahiti – he had the name, and Ah think it was the *Moetua*, or something like that – within these next two or three months.'

'Two or three months!' William could not help making it a cry of dismay.

'Yes, two or three months. And, as he says, we're lucky it's only that. One time it might have been nine or ten months. Well, there it is. We seem to be fixed up after a fashion, and Ah must say, if Ah've to be two or three months waiting to get a move on home, Ah'm glad Ah'm doing it on land. Ah can't say Ah'm struck on this island, from what Ah've seen of it so far, but it's solid land and there's room to move about on it. And another thing, lad. We oughtn't to do so bad, from what this chap says. You see, they raise sheep here, and we ought to get a bit of good mutton. Ay, you can laugh, but there's a lot to be said for a place where you can get a bit of good mutton. It's something to look forward to, and it's about all we've got just now – that and seeing the poor old Commander pick up again. This Purvis says he ought to go to bed and be well wrapped up, and then be dosed hard with quinine.'

The Commander was already lying down and falling into a doze when they went indoors again. Purvis thought it better not to disturb him for the time being. After a meal that included mutton and a tot of whisky, to the delight of Ramsbottom, Purvis, who had some business with the cruiser, left them alone for a few hours, but when he returned he announced that their bungalow was ready for them and that he had found a native couple who would look after them. Apparently the Easter Islanders were an easy-going, rather feckless race, but this couple, he promised them, would do what was to be done. They now proposed moving, and the Commander, suddenly waking up unexpectedly, as he had a trick of doing, declared that he would get up at once and go with them. All three of them begged him to stay where he was, but he insisted on dragging himself up, only to collapse again almost at once. So there was nothing to be done but to leave him with Purvis all night, while William and Ramsbottom moved into their own bungalow. This was very rough and contained only the barest necessities, camp beds, a table, three or four crude chairs, and a few empty boxes. The night was cool, windy, and the hue of dull vulcanite; it seemed much larger and more mysterious than all the nights William had known of late. Tired though he was, he was a long time getting off to sleep. He thought about the Commander. Then he thought about the island's fantastic crop of huge stone images, only a few miles away, with this very same wind blowing over their massive and haughty features. And then the Commander again. Then the images. The Commander. Images. . . .

3

This was their third morning on Easter Island. The Commander was with them now, having recovered sufficiently to move himself from Purvis's bungalow. This second day he had been up and had sat outside for a time. But his temperature, though not as high as it had been the first night, refused to come down, and every night took a violent jump. Purvis had lent them a clinical thermometer. The Commander disliked having his temperature taken, but they were firm with him. On this third morning it had not come down at all, and was just over 104. They would not allow the Commander to get up. He was fretful and occasionally showed traces of delirium. Purvis had given them some quinine and aspirin and plenty of sound advice, and could do no more. The cruiser had sailed away, taking with her the only doctor there was for several thousand miles.

'Dursley, have you seen any of the statues yet?' asked the Commander.

'No, not yet.'

'Well, why not?' The Commander sounded quite peevish.

'Haven't had time. You've got to go across country to find them. Purvis says the only way to do it is on horseback.'

'Haven't been on a horse for I don't know how many years,' said the Commander. 'But the minute this temperature comes down and I feel at all fit, I shall ask Purvis to rig me out. Must see those statues – and the burial platforms too – as soon as possible. Can't understand you fellows not being interested.'

'But we are. I always have been.'

'Well, you don't behave as if you were. Why don't you go to-day? Go now, then tell me all about it afterwards.'

William glanced at Ramsbottom, who came to the rescue at once. 'Can't do that, Commander. There isn't a decent sort of horse free just now for Dursley. And as for me, Ah've never been on a horse and Ah don't intend to start now, specially where there's so many stones as there is here. Now don't you worry about that, Commander, you and Dursley will have plenty of time to see as many statues as you want. You'll be both sick to death of 'em before we get off this island.'

With a sudden effort the Commander raised himself a little. 'These statues are the most – most mysterious objects left in this world, Ramsbottom. We think we know a lot – but' – and he chuckled in a rusty fashion – 'but they've got us beaten. What are they doing here? Who carved them? Hundreds of them – enormous things.

There are two outside the entrance to the British Museum – or used to be. And the platforms – all made out of great heavy rock. Most have needed thousands – tens of thousands – of men to build those platforms. And all those people couldn't live on this island. Nothing for them to live on. Barren place. I've read all about it. I like these mysteries. We think we're clever, but we don't know much. No, we don't know much.' His voice sank to a whisper. He sank down again and it looked as if he was too tired to go on talking.

'Ay, well, we'll talk about all that later on,' said Ramsbottom in a quite soothing tone. 'What about having a bit of sleep now?'

The Commander opened his eyes and glared at him. 'Sleep? What the devil do I want with sleep at this time of day? Don't be an old woman, Ramsbottom. We were talking about this island, weren't we? Just give me a sip of water, will you, old man, please? What's it like? I suppose you've seen something of it, haven't you, even if you haven't seen the statues? You've not been sticking about here all the time. Here am I – been on Easter Island three or four days – and haven't had a proper look at the place yet. Ridiculous!'

'I was walking round yesterday,' said William. 'There isn't much to see – not round here, anyhow. All the shore's very rocky, with a lot of lava beds running out. And inland it's pretty desolate, you know. Bunch-grass and any amount of rock and some craters, I think. Hardly any trees to be seen, and not many birds. Very cheerless.'

'That's it,' said Ramsbottom. 'From what Ah've seen of it – and that's not much – it's a bit like the top of the Pennines without the heather and ling. Proper wild sheep country. It's Faraway's cousin that's been tamed a bit. And if you ask me, it's the same bag o' tricks. It's an old mountain top; that's what it is. And that explains your statues and platforms and suchlike work. There was a lot o' low land – happen a thousand or two miles of it all round here – good fertile land with coconuts and all the rest of it – just like the islands – and this was simply the big mountain. Then one day – wallop! – it went under.'

'Something in that, Ramsbottom. I've had that theory too. Though I'm not sure the oceanographers would support you.'

'They can please themselves, but that's my idea. After all, you never know what's going to happen. One day, there might be another bust-up, and then England might go under, and people go sailing up to Snowdon and Scafell Pike.'

'But how – but how – just a minute – I've forgotten what I was going to say – something important. Stupid!' The Commander exclaimed peevishly at himself. He was a bad patient, because he resented any weakness and fought so hard against it that he tended to weaken himself. He would not give himself up quietly to being ill. Now they watched him anxiously, hoping that he would stop trying to talk.

He looked from one to the other, and carefully moistened his lips. 'I can't have you fellows sitting about here all day,' he said finally, 'just staring at me like that. Get out and explore the place. I'll be all right. Tell that woman – there is a native woman about somewhere, isn't there? – I thought I saw one yesterday – tell that woman to bring some more water. I get so devilish thirsty. Must be something in the air.'

They gave him another sip of water and then withdrew, pretending they were going for a walk. It was not good for him if they stayed, because he would insist upon talking. But they only went outside the bungalow. It was a day of watery sunshine and great gusts of wind. William stared about him, fascinated by the odd landscape, which was not at all like any of the South Sea islands, but like a piece of English hill country, downland, suddenly turned into something remote and slightly sinister. They sat down on a flat rock and talked quietly.

'He's not so well this morning, is he?' said William.

'He's anything but well, lad.' And Ramsbottom's enormous underlip drooped, so that he looked like a colossal baby who was about to cry. He fixed his spectacles more firmly on his nose. 'He's anything but well. Ah don't like the look of him at all this morning.'

William kept silent for a minute, looking into hazy space. 'But he ought to pull through, don't you think?'

Ramsbottom shook his head. 'Ah'm beginning to doubt it. Ah hate to say so, but Ah'm beginning to doubt it. Mind you, Ah think it depends now on himself, on his own resistance. Ah don't think all the doctors in Harley Street could do much for him now, so you needn't worry your head over that part of it. You see, he's got a lot o' will-power, the Commander has, and in a way that's keeping him going. But it looks to me as if any minute he might have a bad collapse – and then it's going to be touch-and-go.'

A few minutes afterwards Purvis came cantering up on a big bay horse with a high Mexican saddle on it. He called the island man he had sent them – his name was Ulwano, and he was astonishingly clothed in a Chilean officer's white cap, a naval uniform coat complete with badges of rank and decorations, and ancient riding breeches from Charles Baker of London – gave the man some instructions and his horse, and joined them.

'Well, how's our friend this morning?' asked Purvis.

They told him. He looked grave, and said he would just have a peep at him, without disturbing him. This he did, and returned to report that the Commander was dozing. 'I think you're right about him. He looks worse to-day. And there's nothing more we can do, I'm afraid. He never ought to have landed, of course, but that can't be helped now.'

'What bothers me,' said Ramsbottom sadly, 'is that he wouldn't have left the ship, Ah fancy, if this hadn't been Easter Island and he hadn't been so dead keen on having a look at the statues. He's been wanting to come here all his life, you see, Mr. Purvis. So we couldn't stop him. And now he's here and it's as likely as not that the poor old lad will never set eyes on your statues. That'll be a grim piece of – what's it? – irony for you, won't it?'

'Tough luck,' said Purvis, who was not an imaginative man apparently and did not trouble his mind with the ironies of chance in this life. 'Still, we mustn't give up hope. And if there's anything I can do, tell me what it is.'

They said they would, and thanked him.

Purvis filled a pipe and then smoked in silence for a minute or two. 'By the way, anything exciting happening at home?' he asked finally, with a casual air that was obviously not at all affected.

The last news they had was a good many weeks old, and even then it was only the news that found its way to Tahiti by wireless. Moreover, they could not remember anything of outstanding interest. They were for ever thinking and talking about home now, but it was of the land itself and its intimate life that they thought and spoke and not of that gossip about politicians, rich men, film actresses and murderers, which passes as news. They told Purvis all that they remembered.

'It's queer, you know,' said William, 'but I imagined,

Mr. Purvis, that the very first thing you'd say to us would be to ask about the news from home. I remember now being surprised that you never mentioned it. Being completely cut off like this, I thought you'd be dying for news.'

'I've been here too long for that,' Purvis replied carefully. He had the slow deliberate manner of a person who has spent a great deal of time alone. 'When I first came out I used to be very anxious to get all the news, and weeks and weeks before the annual boat was due, I used to work myself up into a tremendous state of excitement. And then somehow I got out of it. In fact, the last few years I haven't even been pleased to see a ship here. I've even been glad to see the last of them – seemed to be disturbing, somehow. That doesn't mean I'm not glad to have you fellows here. That's all right. I am. But I don't feel lonely here. Of course I know everybody on the island – though that doesn't mean much. But you gradually make your own life, and I wouldn't change mine. I had a long leave a few years ago, and went home, and after I'd been in London a few weeks I couldn't stand it. Now there I did feel lonely. It was all strange to me. When I'd bought various things I wanted and talked to one or two people I used to know, I was through. I was glad to come back.'

Ramsbottom stared at him in blank astonishment. 'Ah seem to have been wasting a lot o' pity on you, Mr. Purvis. Ah've been looking on you as a chap that was properly marooned – clean left out of it. What do you find to do with yourself, year in and year out?'

'Oh, there's plenty to do here. I'm always busy. But then I'm practically running my own show here, and that makes a difference. It's quite a responsibility, and I like the work. And after all, I'm free from a lot of worries. I used to pity all the poor devils I saw at home. They look worried to death.'

'They are – a lot of 'em,' said Ramsbottom grimly. 'But Ah shan't be – when Ah get back – if Ah do get back.'

Puris laughed. 'Oh, you'll get back all right. Why shouldn't you?'

'Well, when Ah do, you won't catch me worrying myself to death. If they tax me eighteen shillings in the pound and knock my business to hell, Ah'm going to manage to enjoy myself quietly on what's left. Ah shall be at home, and that'll be the great thing.'

'That's what I feel,' said William.

'It seems to me,' Ramsbottom continued, 'from what Ah've seen since we've been on this job, that there's two sorts o' men – there's men who can't enjoy life at all unless they get away from home, and the further the better; and there's men who might like to travel a bit just for a change, but who must be at home, with their feet planted on their own soil, to get anything out o' life. And Ah'm one o' the second lot, and so's Dursley here. We've found that much out, haven't we? It's taken us a good bit o' time and a good bit o' money to find it out. Still, now we know.'

'I wonder if we do, though,' said William. 'I hope so, but I must admit I'm not sure. There seems to be an awful mirage element about life now. Every place is wonderful when you're not there, and the minute you are there it just dwindles into something rather ordinary and some other place begins to look wonderful. It's a trick of the imagination, of course, but I don't see why one should go on being humbugged by it.'

'Well, I'm not,' said Purvis, smiling, 'though I might have been when I was in my teens.'

'Then it's high time I grew out of my teens,' said William.

'There's one chap that's not like that.' And Ramsbottom jerked a fat thumb over his shoulder. 'You can say what you like about the old Commander, but he's not troubled in that way. There's a chap that makes the best of whatever place he's in – just settles down to make the solid best of it – and Ah know what Ah'm talking about, for by this time Ah've been in all sorts of places with him. Ah'm not saying for a minute but what he doesn't like some places better than others—'

'Be a fool if he didn't,' said Purvis.

'Quite so. But put him anywhere and he'll get something out of it. You see, he's a chap with downright convictions, the Commander is. He always knows what his duty is and he always goes and does it, and it all comes as natural to him as breathing. Many a time – and you must have felt the same, Dursley – Ah really haven't known whether to laugh at him or envy him. And Ah wish Ah could say the same now. It's upsetting seeing him like that.'

'Yes, bad luck for all of you.' Purvis rose and stretched himself. 'Well, I'll look in to-night.'

By night the Commander's temperature was higher than ever and he was delirious. William and Ramsbottom decided to take turns through the night sitting up with him, although there was little they could do. Ramsbottom took the first half and then William relieved him at two in the morning. The bare little room was a place of grotesque shadows, for it had only the light of one tiny oil lamp, which was resting on a box and only about eighteen inches from the ground. To William, struggling out of sleep, it was like a room in a bad dream. For a few minutes there was hardly any meaning in it all; he had simply wandered into this lamplight and shadows, this tossing and muttering; and he had to tell himself slowly exactly what it all meant. Ramsbottom had whispered that the Commander was, if anything, a trifle worse and quite delirious, and that all he had done was to sponge his face from time to time and keep him covered. William, plucked out of a deep sleep and finding himself neither in yesterday nor to-day, could not rid himself of the feeling that it was all quite unreal. He might have been a ghost watching a ghost. Even the mosquito bites – and the place was a plague of mosquitoes at night – could not quite bring him to his ordinary senses. The delirium of the Commander, who tossed and muttered continually and sometimes spoke at length, almost seemed the natural accompaniment to such a scene.

For the time being, the Commander had finished with Easter Island and the present. He gave orders again in ships that had been scrap-iron these twenty years. He saluted dream admirals and castigated phantom hosts of midshipmen. He ran ashore at Portsmouth and reported for duty at Shanghai. He went fishing for trout near Lugmouth and had some bitter trouble with his rod. He would leap from middle-age back to boyhood in a phrase or two. Once or twice William caught his own name, and then he felt very ghostly indeed. He was very sleepy, but he stayed awake and just before daybreak he sank into one of the worst fits of depression he ever remembered having. He felt then that he had completely failed, that his life was over just when he thought it was about to begin, that he was as lonely as death and must remain like that for ever, that shame, disappointment, fear, and suffering were the only realities. But he wrenched himself out of this sickly self-pity by concentrating upon the fevered man who was lying there, whose consciousness was beating about like a lost bird in the house of his memories. A good deal of the sweetness and simplicity of the Commander's character made themselves queerly evident in his delirious ramblings, and now that he was not really there, but in some mad jumble of time and space of his own, William saw him more clearly than he had ever done before. Then William for a time forgot his own vaporous woes. He wanted to seize the Commander's hands and drag him back into their common life again. He discovered depths of affection for him that he had not even guessed at before now. But there was so little he could do. He stared, helpless, baffled, at the flushed and wasted face, which seemed to be gradually growing unfamiliar.

All that next day the Commander's condition was more or less the same, and he was never fully conscious. With some assistance from Purvis, who was very kind, they did what they could for him, but they knew now that the mysterious battle that was raging in the sick man's blood-stream would be won or lost without any reference to what they could do. At one time his temperature was just over 105, but towards night it fell. It continued falling throughout the night, and in the morning, which broke with a heavy downpour of rain, it was still dropping. He seemed to have a few hours of natural easy sleep, and when he awoke he was fully conscious. He was also very quiet, remote, terribly tired.

'Well, you're a lot better this morning, Commander,' said Ramsbottom, who was very yellow himself and had great purple pouches under his eyes.

Very slowly, the Commander shook his head. 'No, I don't think so. I'm afraid not.'

'Oh, nonsense. Ah can see you're a lot better. Isn't he, Dursley?'

His eyes travelled slowly from Ramsbottom to William and then back again. 'Must have been a nuisance to you fellows. Sorry about that.'

Eagerly they assured him that he had not been a nuisance.

'What's that noise?' he asked.

'Rain. It's coming down in torrents. Whole island's blotted out.'

The Commander nodded and went on nodding quite a time, as if he found some secret satisfaction in the thought that it was raining so hard. Then, after breathing quickly, he spoke again, very quietly, so that they had to go closer to catch what he said. 'Seen the statues yet, Dursley?' he asked.

'No, not yet,' William replied, making a great effort to appear quite casual. 'I'll wait for you, Commander. We'll see them together.'

A queer lop-sided grin made its appearance on the Commander's face. 'Don't wait for me. You may have to wait a long time – a long, long time.'

Nobody spoke again for a minute or so, and it seemed a silent desolate age in that little room with the rain drumming away at it and a cold light flickering in through the single small window. William tried to say something – anything – just to break the evil spell, but he couldn't.

'Well,' cried Ramsbottom at last, with a forced boisterousness that sounded horribly false. 'What about—'

The Commander only made the tiniest gesture, but it was enough. Ramsbottom stopped. The Commander opened his mouth and then, it seemed, gradually, uncertainly, found his voice again. 'One of you fellows,' he began. 'There's a Prayer Book somewhere in my kit – I've carried it all over the place – I know it's there. One of you fellows get it for me, will you, and put it here. Later on I'll read it. Time I read it again. Not now, but later on. Too dark now and I'm a bit too tired. Think I'll sleep.'

'That's right,' said Ramsbottom, 'you have a sleep. You'll feel better when you wake up and then you can have a grand read. And if you don't fancy reading yourself, we'll read it for you – do us good, especially Dursley here.'

'Very good fellow, Ramsbottom. Both of you very good fellows.' It came in a drowsy whisper.

He slept until the middle of the afternoon, and it so happened that both of them were there when he wakened. They saw his eyes open, saw his head come forward and his mouth move a little, and were about to speak to him when his head dropped back in a queer mechanical fashion and his hands clutched the blanket. But they could hardly believe that he was dead.

4

They said good-bye to the Commander in a little burying ground, high on a grassy slope, where the great sea winds were for ever blowing and the thunder and spray of the Pacific never left the air. But it was impossible to believe that there were only two of them now and not three. They were always expecting the Commander to come round the corner. After the first few days of sharp grief, during which they eased their hearts by talking to one another about their dead friend, this puzzling loss did not bring William and Ramsbottom closer together, but tended more and more to separate them. They usually spent the evenings together, but then Purvis would be with them, and the three of them would play cards, leaning forward in the narrow yellow circle of lamplight and idly throwing greasy kings and queens on to the red-chequered table-cloth. But the days found them going their separate ways. Ramsbottom seemed to have aged a good deal and to have lost a lot of his gusto. His great body sagged; his face was pouchy; and he spent much of his time dozing in the bungalow. It was fortunate for him that there was not much liquor to be had on the island; otherwise he might have soaked himself in it. As it was, he drank far more than his share. Once or twice, William remembered, with a shock of dismay, the shining, bustling, beaming figure that he had first met in the hotel at Lugmouth, so far removed from this frowzy Ramsbottom who lolled about the bungalow. It was as if the Commander had kept him in check and braced him, and now that the Commander had gone, he did not care, simply let himself go.

William was energetic and enterprising enough. Purvis found a quiet horse for him, and after a few cautious and fairly successful experiments with it, using the unfamiliar high Mexican saddle, William turned horseman and thus was able to explore the island. Day after day, if the weather was reasonably fine, he went out, sometimes with Purvis on his rounds, but more frequently, especially during the later weeks, by himself. But though he saw everything there was to see, ate well and slept well, was pestered by flies during the day and bitten by mosquitoes at night, yet through all these seven weeks William seemed to be living in a vague dream. Of all the chapters of his Pacific adventure, the one that afterwards appeared the strangest, the most unreal, was this period of waiting on Easter Island for the schooner for Tahiti. He might have spent the whole time slightly drugged. Long afterwards, when the remotest and most fantastic of the low islands or the Marquesas still shone brightly, clearly, in his memory, there would be times when he could hardly believe that he had ever passed those weeks on Easter Island; he would hesitate to talk about them, as if he might be successfully accused of inventing the experience. It was very odd, of course, this roaming about on horseback on this unvisited and mysterious island; but that was not the reason that he found it all so dream-like; it was something in himself; he was not fully alive, was half-numbed inside, a man for ever moving through mists of his own creation.

Day after day, sometimes in clear sunlight, sometimes under a lowering sky, with the wind blustering all round him, he would ride out towards the ring of burial platforms on the South and East coasts or the sculptors' workshop on Rano Raraku, with its queer avenue of fallen statues. The statues themselves, which turned up all over the island, but were most plentiful on the slope of Rano Raraku, became familiar companions, though they never lose their air of remote mystery. They all had the same flat-backed heads, the same bold noses, short upper lips and long chins, but differed from one another as members of a family differ. He spent hours dreamily answering their defiant dark stare. Sometimes they would fade into merely so much weathered stone, would hardly seem more significant than so many rocks above the trembling grass. But at other times they would come gigantically to life, and then it was like staring at giants buried up to their necks in the hillside, and it seemed as if at any moment they might shake their vast shoulders, scatter the earth about them, and arise in their dark majesty and wrath. The whole island changed like that. One day it would appear to him as it always appeared to Ramsbottom, as a windy, desolate, high place of bunch grass and volcanic rock, almost treeless and waterless, a region without a single grace of landscape or seascape, two thousand weary miles from anywhere. Another day it would take on gigantic airs of mystery and austere beauty. Generations of forgotten men, tens and tens of thousands of them, architects and sculptors and labourers, had planned and sweated on these heights, turning them into one colossal memorial of the dead. And now nobody knew who they were, where they had come from, how they had lived. There was to have been ring after ring of burial platforms, great paved dancing-grounds, and long avenues of images up which the funeral processions would pass to the higher platforms. The plan was there, and half the work was done. It had been stopped, quite suddenly, as if with one stroke of the sword. There had been a catastrophe like the end of a world, and sometimes it seemed as if sinister rumours of it still hung in the wind, and then the island was a terrifying place, in which the mind of man shrank to a pin-point of quivering consciousness.

Most of the time, however, he moved about in a cloudy dream of sea and wind, grass and rocky hillsides. He had adventures. There was the bad fall he had on one of the crumbling burial platforms above La Pérouse Bay. There was the unpleasant scrambling he let himself in for on the afternoon when he went to explore the crater lake of Rano Kao, at the southern extremity of the island. A melancholy sheet of water it was, too, this crater lake, matted with reeds, thick, slimy, of a lunar remoteness. and the mere possibility of falling into it horrified him. But these adventures only broke the spell for an hour or two. One part of him seemed to have hibernated. He neither accepted this period of waiting nor protested against it. He merely kept on living through it. He did not count the days nor try to hurry them away, but simply let them trickle past him. Only during the last few days he was there – though he did not know for certain that they would be his last few days, for the schooner had no exact date fixed for her arrival – did he find this curious spiritual lethargy breaking down, to give way to an intense desire, a sudden hunger and thirst of the soul, to be away from all this, to be back home again, pulling his business together, settling into the life of Buntingham again, perhaps marrying and having children. At these moments he felt that all this journeying up and down the Pacific had been a miserable waste of time, with something corrupt at the heart of it. This was not his place, nor was this rôle of gaping spectator his. Life, he felt, would not begin again for him until he arrived back in England again, whether Margery Jackson were with him or not. As for Terry, she was like Faraway, a mirage that had faded. And now he had done with mirages. He had grown up at last. No more would he wait, like an idle dreamy boy, for magic to happen. He did not even want enchantment now; all he asked was to be allowed to return to where the raw but rich material of a good life waited for him to build with it. He actually arrived at this metaphor of building, only to reject and shrink from it. There had been a great deal of building once on Easter Island.

But as he cantered back to the bungalow one afternoon, he caught sight of a waving figure. It was Ramsbottom, and a reformed Ramsbottom, a fine bouncing, roaring, beaming Ramsbottom. 'She's here,' he was bellowing.

William dismounted. 'Not the schooner?'

'Yes, the schooner. Came in early this afternoon. The *Moetua*, and a nice new hundred-ton schooner. Ah've seen the captain already, and a nice chap, too. Captain Sully. And all fixed up. We're off to-morrow, lad.'

'Good!'

'Good? Ah should think it is good. Now that schooner's come, Ah feel a different chap. This place was fairly getting me down, Ah can tell you. Ah didn't fancy it right from the start, and then when the poor old Commander died, that just finished me. Ah began to feel Ah'd never get away from here; it just seemed so far from anywhere. Nay – damn it! – if Ah'd been Robinson Crusoe, Ah couldn't have felt better when Ah saw that schooner. Captain's having dinner with Purvis and us to-night. Ah feel like keeping him in sight every minute till Ah'm on that schooner.'

William was astonished at the change in him. It was the old Ramsbottom all over again. He never stopped talking. He superintended all the preparations for dinner and quickly enlisted the sympathy of the islanders concerned, which was not difficult because the Easter Islander is born with a solid appreciation of a feast. He succeeded in persuading Purvis to sell him two bottles of champagne out of a solitary case that Purvis had imported for use on special occasions. He swept the other three into his own mood, and very soon was on uproarious chaffing terms with Captain Sully, a large jovial Frenchman with a slight strain of good Polynesian blood in him. There was one short interval, however, when Ramsbottom lost his hilarity. It came at the end of dinner.

'Now you chaps,' he said, after filling their glasses, 'there's only one health Ah'd like drunk to-night, before we leave this island – and that's a toast to the memory of the Commander, who came with us but stops here.'

Captain Sully raised his bushy brows. '*Comment?*'

Purvis quickly explained, and immediately the captain looked sympathetic. They drank the toast in silence.

'I didn't see much of him, of course,' said Purvis. 'But he seemed to me a very good chap.'

'He was one o' the best, the Commander was,' said Ramsbottom solemnly. 'Ah laughed at him many a time – and Ah wish to God he was here so Ah could laugh at him again – for what with being brought up in the Navy and spending nearly all his life there, you see, and being a strictish sort o' chap anyhow and a bit simple, he was an old-fashioned sort – wouldn't do this and that and the other – and sometimes, if you didn't happen to be amused, he could get on your nerves a bit. But all the same when you got down to it, he was worth ten o' most of the new-fashioned sort. You knew where you were with him. Straight as a die, and as nice and kind and simple as a kid, though he'd seen a lot in his time. There's not many of his sort left, Ah can tell you. What do you say, Dursley?'

'I agree,' said William, rather sadly. 'The Commander's type, I suppose, must be vanishing pretty rapidly now. Soon it'll be as extinct as those people who carved the statues here. Perhaps it's not a bad thing the Commander's buried here, even though he was so passionately devoted to England and this is so far away. I mean by that – well, he and these people might have got on awfully well together. I don't know, of course. How should I? It's just a foolish idea. I'm not expressing myself very well either. I think I'd better shut up.'

'A good chap,' said Purvis, nodding his head slowly. Then he turned to the captain. 'Are you calling at Pitcairn this time, because if you are there's a little job you could do for me?'

They sailed the next day on the *Moetua*, which looked like a small ark, for she was carrying on deck four cows, half a dozen pigs, and twenty sheep. She was bound for Pitcairn Island, Mangareva in the Gambiers, and Tahiti. The wind was blowing hard and in the right quarter, aft, and the big following seas lifted up the *Moetua* and hurled her on her way. Easter Island disappeared behind the shifting green mounds and the flying foam.

5

'It's almost like coming home seeing this place again,' said Ramsbottom, staring across the lagoon at Papeete's two red toy steeples.

'Isn't it?' William narrowed his eyes to try and take in every detail of the water-front. 'And it's not so long, not quite seven months, since I thought it all terribly strange. How long have we been away from Tahiti? About four months, isn't it?'

'That's all,' said Ramsbottom. 'But long enough to change our little bag o' tricks. No Faraway, no pitch-blende, and the Commander gone.'

'What are you going to do now?'

'Ah'm going home and when Ah get there, Ah'm staying there. And Ah'm going home the quickest way, too – whichever that is – even if it costs a bit more. A think Ah'll go back the way you came, up to San Francisco, then across America. That should be as quick as any, and you see more for your money, Ah fancy. Isn't that your programme, too?'

'That depends.'

'Depends on what?'

William looked at him rather defiantly. 'I think it probably depends on Margery Jackson.'

Ramsbottom pursed his thick rubbery lips. 'Ah see – thinking o' matrimony. You're what Ah should call an adventurous sort o' chap, you are, never satisfied. Just when you've a chance of a quiet going on, you want to get married. Never mind, Ah think you've picked a good one. It's not fixed up, is it?'

'No, not quite. As a matter of fact, it's not fixed up at all.'

'But it soon will be, eh? But you're going back to attend to your business, aren't you?'

'Of course I am. If we do decide to get married, we shall clear out as soon as possible. She wants to go home, too.'

'That's right, she does, Ah remember now. She's had enough o' growing coconuts, catering for lodgers in bathing-suits, and trying to run a house with a brown beauty chorus o' guitar players, and you can't blame her. Well, she's as nice a young woman as I know. But - if it isn't an awkward question – what about that other? You know, our late partner, Miss Terry Riley.'

He did know. 'Well – what about her?'

'By the way, you'll have to write and tell her what happened on this job, won't you? She's entitled to know.'

'Yes, I've thought about that.'

'But that's not what Ah meant when Ah said "What about her?" However, Ah think Ah'd better shut up. She was just a bit o' fun, eh? Well, a chap's got to have a bit o' fun in his time, and it struck me, first time Ah set eyes on you – you remember, at Lugmouth – that you were a chap that had been missing his bit o' fun.'

William did not reply. He was gazing down into the passing lagoon, losing himself among the gold blobs of sunlight there and the emerald depths. He refused to think about Terry. If he kept on refusing, very soon there would be no Terry to think about. Ramsbottom probably imagining that he had said too much already, said no more. The schooner glided up to its anchorage, where a little crowd was assembling. It was early afternoon, and the whole island was gold-dusted with a hazy but rich sunlight.

'It's summer now,' said Ramsbottom. 'No, it's not – it's winter down here. But Ah can't see any difference. Looks just the same.'

'Almost the same,' replied William. 'The flamboyants – you remember, those brilliant orange-red trees – are gone. We were lucky to get here just in time to see them in full flame.'

'We were, were we? Well, Ah'm glad you told me. Ah don't want to miss any bits o' luck we've had, because Ah know plenty about the other sort. Well, who's here, to give us a welcome?' he continued, examining the waiting crowd. 'Do you see any of our old drinking pals?'

'I don't. And I don't particularly want to.'

'Ah'll tell you who Ah do want to see. D'you remember that Nature chap Ah told you about – that chap that lived near Hockaday's place and had such a big nose and was a Russian or something – well, Ah must pop down there and try to find him again. Ah want to see if he can work his Maggie Armitage trick again. Ah must have another go at that before Ah leave; that is, if there is such a chap and Ah didn't dream him. Ah'll tell you one thing, lad – we're badly in need of a new rig-out and a good hair-cut. This steward's made a nasty job of us. Catch 'em clean clothes. Catch 'em hair-cut, savvy? Ah'll bet nobody recognises us. We'll be arrested for a couple o' beachcombers.'

Once again there returned to William's nostrils that rich confused smell which he remembered so well from his first landing, and now he was reminded of that first landing and felt rather sick at heart. But this feeling was only momentary; the pleasant excitement of going ashore at last drove it away. He came to a sudden decision. He would go to Margery just as he was, looking a brown, tattered, mosquito-bitten South Seas waif. To arrive all spruce and smiling was wrong. The adventure of the islands should end in her sight and not in a tailor's shop or the barber's just off the water-front. He told Ramsbottom what he was going to do, found a car to drive him out to her place, and was fortunate to discover her at home, resting on the verandah. When he made his appearance, there was one curious moment at first when she stared at him blankly, but it was only a moment.

'Hello, Margery!'

'William!' And she jumped up and ran with outstretched arms across the few yards of space that separated them, a different being now, radiant and tender. Saying no more, they clung together, happy. This was a real home-coming. Why, she was with his wife even now.

Then they sat down and looked at one another with eager, almost greedy eyes. 'I was going to say,' she exclaimed, smiling through a faint brightness of tears, 'why didn't you let me know you were coming, and then I saw how silly that was. You couldn't, of course. It was stupid of me – wasn't it? – not to recognise you the very moment you came, but I was half asleep and you look different, you know.'

'I know. Very disreputable.'

'No, it's not that, though you are rather ragged, aren't you? But that's not what I mean. You're much thinner and a lot browner, to begin with, and then you've got a different look. I can't explain – not now, anyhow. Now tell me everything that's happened. If you knew how I've thought and worried about you! But never mind that now. Tell me.'

'Well—' and he hesitated – 'it's a long story—'

'Oh, I don't want the long story now. You can tell me that afterwards, can't you? Just tell me about the island.

Did you find it? And did you find the what's-it, you
know—'

'The pitchblende? Yes, we did. We found both the
island and the pitchblende, but we also found that Chile
had claimed the island and that some people who arrived
on a yacht while we were there had got a concession from
the Chilean Government. It was a complete wash-out. I'll
tell you the details later. But we were arrested first and
taken aboard a Chilean cruiser, and then afterwards this
cruiser took us to Easter Island. And the Commander
died just after we got to Easter Island.'

'William! The Commander!'

He told her briefly what happened. She and the Commander had always liked one another, and the news dis-
tressed her.

'So you see,' he concluded cheerlessly, 'it's all turned
out badly. We lost the Commander, who would never have
come out here at all if it hadn't been for me—'

'Yes, but he wanted to come. He loved it all. He told
me so himself. It's silly to blame yourself. You couldn't
help it.'

'Perhaps not, but there it is. He's gone. And the island
and the pitchblende are a wash-out, and we've all spent
our time and money for nothing. Ramsbottom's been
pretty decent about it, on the whole, but I can't help
feeling guilty. And now I can't afford to play about any
longer. I must get back home and attend to my business.
I'm going to send a cable to my foreman in the morning
to learn how things are going there.'

'When are you going?'

'I'd like to go by the very first boat.'

'There's the boat from San Francisco coming in next
week, but I suppose it would be quicker for you to go
back the other way, across America.'

'Margery,' he cried, taking both her hands, 'come with me. Let's get married and go home together.'

'William!' She was alight. 'Do you mean it?'

'Yes, of course I do.'

'Do you really want to marry me?'

'Yes.'

'But, William – I must say this – do you love me?'

'Yes.'

'Then we will, because I love you, too – have done – oh! – right from the beginning, even before you were ill. There!'

Later, he said to her: 'But what about your place here? And what are we going to do? I really would like to get away as soon as possible, even now.'

'But so would I. I want to go this very minute. Listen, we'll catch that boat next week. If you don't mind, I'd like to go back to Wellington – there are one or two things I ought to see to there – and, listen, William – let's get married there, shall we, in Wellington? Then we can sail home from there – a lovely trip. Oh yes – let's do that.'

'All right. But what about this place?'

'Oh, I can sell it. I've had one or two offers already. I'll go and sell it to-morrow. Oh! – it's going to be a terribly mad rush – but I shall love it. Absolutely mad. Oh, William – I'm so excited, aren't you?'

'Yes.' But was he? 'I ought to warn you, though, Margery. You may find it rather dull at home – duller than you think – and I shall have to work hard now, and I haven't much money or anything, you know.'

'Don't be silly. Really, that's the only thoroughly stupid thing I've ever heard you say – really it is. What do I care? And it won't be dull – it'll be lovely. I know. I've thought a lot about it while you've been away – all the things I'd like to do. No, it'll never be dull for me, William, but it might be dull for you sometimes. And I'm *not* being silly. I'm not very clever or amusing or anything like that, and once we're home you may feel different about me. Though I don't think you will,' she added, hopefully, touchingly.

He gave her assurances by the score. All doubts removed, she began planning at a pace that left William dizzy; they would have to do this, that and the other, and they had only so many days to do them in; and he listened and nodded and smiled, not condescending but hardly burning with her fine flame of eagerness, happy chiefly in the thought of how much happiness he had just created.

Two days later, Ramsbottom suggested he should go with them. 'If Ah'm going to be in the way, just say so right off. Ah'm not? Well, all right, that'll suit me fine. Ah'll see you safely married and take a look at New Zealand—'

'And we'll give you plenty of good stuff in Wellington,' cried Margery.

'Let's hope so.' He looked severe. 'Ah might as well tell you now that though Ah'm all for Empire trade and all that, there's a lot of this Colonial produce could be easily improved. Ask me sometime and Ah'll tell you what's wrong. And – by jingo! – Ah never thought o' that. Do you know – if Ah go to New Zealand and then sail from there home, by way of India, Suez Canal, and so on, Ah'll have been right round the world. That's something, isn't it? Ah tell you, there's some chaps in Manchester are going to be a bit surprised when I get home. What do you say, William?'

'What's that? Sorry – I was thinking about something else.'

'So Ah see. What's that you've got there – a cable?'

'Yes,' and William held it out. 'It's from my foreman at the malting-house. I cabled him the other day, and this is his reply. It's time I was back at work.' And he returned to his thoughts, a different William now, not their man at all, but one of the Dursleys, a Suffolk maltster. But they took him with them when they sailed, on the following Thursday, for Wellington.

CHAPTER XII

ONE TUESDAY EVENING

IT WAS Tuesday evening, and so William's friend, Green-law, from the Buntingham Grammar School, was there, and already he had said: 'Let us play at the pieces.' But now there were three of them sitting in the study, for William's wife, Margery, was there. Upstairs, fathoms deep in soft rosy sleep, was yet a fourth, John Dursley, aged eighteen months. Moreover, down here in the study there were signs of a fifth, which had as yet no visible appearance, only a possible choice of names and a power, which it exercised, of disturbing the routine of its parents' lives. These parents were rather plumper and paler than they had been on their arrival here, over two years ago. William had lost a little of his hair, but still looked much younger than his years. Margery had a more decided matronly look about her; a settled woman who knew her own mind. Greenlaw was merely bushier and smokier than ever. The study had been reformed. It was still cosy, but no longer such a higgledy-piggledy room. Most of the cases of moths, the smelly old albums, the letter files, the skewered receipts, and all the geological specimens had disappeared. Their places had largely been taken by Polynesian odds and ends and numerous photographs of South Seas life. There were schooners and islands on the wall. There was also a much enlarged snapshot of

Commander Ivybridge. The two old leather arm-chairs had resigned in favour of two short, stout, chintzy fellows. there were two shaded electric lights instead of the old incandescent gasburners. But the place was as snug as ever; the chess was there still, and so were the whisky and tobacco; and wind and rain still troubled the ivy outside.

William and Greenlaw were in the middle of their first – and probably their last – game of the evening. Mrs. William, who was sitting on the other side of the fireplace, sewing away at some miniature garments, approved of these evenings of chess so long as Greenlaw, a single man, a poor sleeper, and a born stopper-up, did not keep her husband out of his bed too long with this grave and foolish game. It was her opinion that William needed all the sleep he could get even now, when he was no longer working so hard as he had done when he first came back. For more than a year, he had slaved at the business, to pull it out of the mess in which he had found it on his return. Once or twice he had showed signs of collapse, and she had had to be firm with him. Now the business was fairly prosperous again, a sound little concern, and one of the best in Buntingham. Both William and his wife were considered in Buntingham to be sound little concerns, too. If they were all to continue in this pleasant solid tradition, it was important that William should not sit up half the night, smoking too much, merely to satisfy Greenlaw's passion for this long and useless business of moving pieces across a board. Margery did not understand the game, and smilingly refused to listen to any explanation of its solemn absurdities, but the glances she directed from time to time at the board were placid enough, though touched perhaps with an indulgent condescension, as if she were watching two children at their play. She was hoping, however, that the game would not last too long, and felt relieved every time she noticed that a man or two had disappeared from the board.

To William the game looked like dragging out, which would be all to Greenlaw's advantage. Given a little whisky, tobacco, a good fire, and a chess-board on which only a rook and a bishop or two were left to fight, and Greenlaw asked no more of life; he was secure in a cosy mathematical heaven. William still preferred a brilliant *coup*, a dashing early mate, and already, this evening, he had sacrificed a knight and two pawns for such a *coup*, and all in vain. What a stubborn old devil Greenlaw was! William frowned at the board. He heard a distant rapping, then a ring, but ignored them. It was his move, and the position was tricky.

'That's the front door,' said his wife, putting down her sewing. 'And I've just remembered. Both Annie and cook are out. I'd better go.'

There was another ring. 'What's that?' said William, looking up and coming rapidly out of his dream of embattled kings. 'Is it the front door? All right, I'll go. No, don't you bother, my dear. I'll go. Excuse me a minute, Greenlaw.'

Greenlaw waved a hand and settled into his chair. He could afford to be tolerant of interruptions, for he was in a strong position. Very soon, William's Queen would find herself in trouble.

It was a black squally sort of night in early spring. William looked out at it and found there a vague fellow in a chauffeur's uniform.

'Is this Mr. Dursley's house – Ivy Lodge?'

'It is. And I'm Mr. Dursley.'

'Mr. William Dursley, is it, sir?'

'Yes,' said William, rather impatiently. 'What do you want?'

'Beg your pardon, sir, but Miss Riley sent me to enquire. She's sitting in the car there.'

'Miss Riley?'

'Yes, sir. Miss Riley, an American lady—'

Terry! William gaped at the man. 'But why is she sitting there?' he asked idiotically. He had to say something.

'Well, sir, she didn't say anything about coming in,' the man replied, and then he retreated a few steps. William found himself following him down the walk, as if the man were pulling him with an invisible cord. He heard his door close with a bang behind him.

'Here we are, sir. Miss Riley.'

Yes, in the little lighted saloon, like a lovely queen in the tiniest of blue drawing-rooms, sat Terry. She had not changed at all. She was just Terry. Perfect.

'Bill, it's really you.'

'But, Terry – what are you doing here?'

'That's easy. I got over with Avvy Paxton to do a picture. She got a big contract with one of your studios and got me roped in, too. I've just spent a long weekend down in Norfolk with some people I met on the boat, and now I'm on my way back to London. And don't think I own this automobile, because I don't – it's Avvy's and hired at that. Now it's your turn, Bill.'

'You got my letter?'

'I surely did. And didn't I tell you about that island? I knew it. And I was just as pleased being proved right as if you'd sent me a hundred thousand dollars. But, Bill, I hated to read that about the poor old Commander. I don't think he liked me – always a touch of frost in the good old-fashioned courtesy, I thought – but I liked him a whole lot, and he'd got the bluest eyes I ever saw in a man. I just can't tell you how sorry I was. And how's the big fat man with the spectacles – what was his name – Ramsbottom?'

'Oh, Ramsbottom's all right. He lives in Southport now – but then, you don't know where Southport is, do you? I saw him about six months ago. He's been here to stay once or twice. He came home with us, you know.'

'With *us*? You did get married then, Bill? That nice little Englishwoman? I got married too, Bill, in Hollywood, and I'm being divorced this very minute – for intellectual cruelty or something like that. Yes, it was a bad break, Bill. Let's not talk about it. What about you? Happy?'

'Yes – I think so,' he stammered, hardly knowing what he was saying.

'Any children yet?'

'One – a boy. And another one soon, we hope.'

'That's fine.'

They were standing by the door of the car. It was a bleak night and there was rain in the wind. William was cold and damp, but he did not notice it. All he noticed was a certain faint sweetness in the air, a wandering breath of spring. And Terry.

'Well, Bill,' and she made a little movement, as if she were about to step into the car, 'you hadn't forgotten me?'

'No, I hadn't forgotten you, Terry,' he replied gravely.

'I don't know whether to be glad or sorry. But you see – I haven't forgotten you. Ivy Lodge, Buntingham, Suffolk – I've remembered it all. And it's been grand seeing you again, Bill. Not a day older and quite handsome. I've got to be going.'

'But, Terry – don't go,' he entreated. 'You mustn't go.'

'I must. And I can give you a hundred good reasons why I've got to go this minute, and one of them is that I've to be at work in the studio early to-morrow morning.

We needn't bother about the other reasons.' She smiled at him. Then she placed her hands lightly on his shoulders and kissed him. Before he could cry out or stir after that she had jumped into the car and closed the door behind her.

He stood at the gate until the car was only a moving light in the distance. He returned to the house in a dream, a stifling dream, through which his heart went thumping, thumping. The study seemed very stuffy, and his wife and Greenlaw stared, it appeared to him, rather stupidly.

'Why, William, you're wet,' she cried reproachfully. 'You've been standing outside.'

He nodded. He was not ready to say anything yet.

'Who was it?'

He knew then that he could not tell them. It would be hopeless trying to tell them. Such as it was, it was his affair, and he could not have them giving it queer looks and mauling it about. There was nothing for it but to lie. What he would say would be mere fibbing so far as Greenlaw, who did not really count, was concerned, but it was very different with Margery. The lie to her went deeper than the verbal falsehood. He was hiding Terry away from her. These thoughts went racing through while he flicked a few rain-drops off his coat.

'Some people in a car. They were asking the way to Ipswich, and I was trying to show them.'

'Can't imagine how they got up here,' Greenlaw grunted.

'Neither can I,' said Margery. 'They must have been stupid. I can't think why you took all that trouble for them, William. Standing outside in the rain!'

He made no reply to this. No sooner had he sat down again than he felt a prisoner in that room. Life was going on somewhere else, not there. It was going on down the London Road with Terry. There, with Terry radiant in the heart of it, was enchantment. He could have cried her name out aloud, to break the spell of this dull stuffy room. Looking up, his eye was caught by the masts of a schooner and by silhouetted palms like dark stars, and at once all the photographs there came to life terribly, and he found himself overwhelmed by a great tide of longing for the Pacific and the islands, the distant blue magic of the South Seas. His wife and Greenlaw sat there like a pair of lumpish warders. He looked at them and hated them. Then he looked at them again; at his wife, whose wide clear glance met his, and who smiled, probably because the baffled expression he wore was rather droll; and at his old friend, sitting back there like a benignant and scholarly walrus; and then he hated himself.

'Your move, William.'

He stared stupidly at the pieces. He knew they were in some significant array, but for the moment he was too bewildered, baffled, annoyed with the world and himself to discover exactly what it was.